**"If you apologize again, I'll slug you." Zora glared at Lucky.**

He laughed, an unexpected rumble that rolled right into her heart. "That's my Zora." A bout of hard breathing reawakened the hope he might finally kiss her, but instead he sucked in a gulp of air and held it. "Okay. Better."

"Better than what?"

He ignored the question. "Since I inveigled you into working today, let me buy you lunch to celebrate."

"You're on." The heat in her body hadn't exactly dissipated, but it had faded into her normal pregnancy-enhanced high temperature. As for Lucky, clearly he didn't, couldn't and never would accept Andrew's babies as his own.

As common sense reasserted itself, Zora was suddenly glad nothing had happened. Going any further would have been yet another in a long line of mistakes she'd made with men. Gathering her possessions, she waited until Lucky locked up, and they sauntered out together. Friends again, nothing more.

Which was ob

# The Twin Rescue

*USA TODAY* BESTSELLING AUTHOR
## JACQUELINE DIAMOND

*NEW YORK TIMES* BESTSELLING AUTHOR
## CHRISTINE RIMMER

**Previously published as *The Baby Bonanza*
and *The Nanny's Double Trouble***

Recycling programs
for this product may
not exist in your area.

ISBN-13: 978-1-335-08136-0

The Twin Rescue
Copyright © 2019 by Harlequin Books S.A.

The publisher acknowledges the copyright holders of the individual works as follows:

The Baby Bonanza
Copyright © 2015 by Jackie Hyman

The Nanny's Double Trouble
Copyright © 2018 by Christine Rimmer

This edition published by arrangement with Harlequin Books S.A.

For questions and comments about the quality of this book, please contact us at CustomerService@Harlequin.com.

Printed in U.S.A.

www.Harlequin.com

# CONTENTS

Medical themes play a prominent role in many of **Jacqueline Diamond**'s one hundred published novels, including her Safe Harbor Medical miniseries for Harlequin. A former Associated Press reporter and TV columnist, Jackie lives in Orange County, California, where she's active in Romance Writers of America. You can sign up for her free newsletter at jacquelinediamond.com and say hello to Jackie on her Facebook page, Jacqueline Diamond Author. On Twitter, she's @jacquediamond.

### Books by Jacqueline Diamond

### Harlequin American Romance

#### *Safe Harbor Medical*

*Officer Daddy*
*Falling for the Nanny*
*The Surgeon's Surprise Twins*
*The Detective's Accidental Baby*
*The Baby Dilemma*
*The M.D.'s Secret Daughter*
*The Baby Jackpot*
*His Baby Dream*
*The Surprise Holiday Dad*
*A Baby for the Doctor*
*The Surprise Triplets*
*The Baby Bonanza*
*The Doctor's Accidental Family*

Visit the Author Profile page at Harlequin.com for more titles.

# The Baby Bonanza

## JACQUELINE DIAMOND

# Chapter 1

It was the first time Zora could recall agreeing with Lucky Mendez about anything. Although their truce surely wouldn't last long, she appreciated his good judgment this once.

"No way are you letting that creep move into our house," the male nurse told their landlady and housemate, Karen Wiggins. With his striking dark hair, muscular build and flamboyant tattoos, Lucky made an odd contrast to the pink streamers festooning their den.

"Everybody hates Laird Maclaine," Zora added as she arranged baby shower prizes on a side table. Being seven months pregnant with twins, she had to avoid any strenuous activity. In fact, as one of the shower's honorees—along with two of their former housemates—she could have dodged setup duty, but she refused to take the easy way out.

Ever.

"He's the only one who responded to the notice I posted on the bulletin board." Atop a step stool, Karen tied a bunch of balloons to a hook. In shades of pink and purple, each balloon proclaimed: Baby!

"We have a vacant room and the rent's almost due," she continued. "It's either Laird, or I post on the internet and we fend off the loonies. Unless you guys can produce another candidate, fast."

Lucky hadn't finished castigating the topic of the conversation. "One drink and Laird's telling raunchy jokes. Two drinks and he's leering at any lady who walks by." His lip curled. "Three drinks and we call the police."

"For a staff psychologist, he doesn't have a clue about how decent people act," Zora threw in.

"I don't care for him, either, but there are bills to pay." Karen, a financial counselor at Safe Harbor Medical Center, where they all worked, had inherited the five-bedroom home from her mother the previous December. Forced to take out a loan to repair the run-down property, she'd advertised for roommates. The arrangement had worked well despite the diverse personalities who'd signed on.

So far, three of the women had become pregnant, but the other two had married and moved out, unlike Zora. There was little chance she would marry the father of her babies, because he was already married. He was also her ex-husband, with whom she'd foolishly and, just before finalizing their divorce, trustingly had sex in the belief that her on-again, off-again high school sweetheart still loved her.

Zora rested her palm on her bulge, feeling the babies kick. How ironic that she'd gotten pregnant by accident at the worst possible time, after she and Andrew had tried for more than a year to conceive. They'd been on the point of seeking fertility treatments when she'd discovered he was cheating on her.

"We have plenty of other colleagues," Lucky persisted. "You guys are in a better position to meet them than me, since my office is out in the boonies." Lucky worked in the medical office building adjacent to the hospital.

"I've tried, but… Oh, yuck!" Karen broke off as a breeze through the rear screen door carried a fetid whiff of decomposing vegetation and fish from the estuary behind the property.

Zora nearly gagged, too. Karen praised the marsh ad nauseum because it provided critical habitat for plants and small animals, as well as for California's migratory birds. However, despite the cooling weather at the end of September, it stank. "Who left the door open?"

"I must have forgotten to close it after I swept the patio." Lucky shut the glass slider with a thump. "How about renting to that receptionist in your office?"

"She declined." Descending from the stool, Karen stood back to assess the position of the balloons. "She prefers to save money by living with her parents. Speaking of money, if we don't find anyone by next month, I'll have to divide the room rent among you guys and Rod."

Their fourth and newest housemate, anesthesiologist Rod Vintner, had gone to pick up the party cake. He'd also gone, in Zora's opinion, to avoid anything approaching hard labor, although he *had* promised to clean up afterward.

"We could use the spare room as a nursery." Lucky cast a meaningful gaze at Zora's large belly. "If someone would inform her ex-husband that he's about to be a father and owes child support, she could afford the extra space."

"Don't start on her," Karen warned, saving Zora the trouble. "Go set up the chairs in the living room."

"Yes, ma'am." With a salute, Lucky strolled off. Zora tried to ignore the muscles rippling beneath his T-shirt and the tight fit of his jeans. The man was a self-righteous pain in the neck, no matter how good he looked.

Surprisingly, he hadn't brought home any dates since they'd moved into the house last February. Or none that she'd observed, Zora amended. Since Lucky occupied the downstairs suite, he could easily slip someone in late and out early without the others noticing. Men did things like that.

"You can stop staring at his butt now," Karen said dryly.

"I wasn't!"

"You can lie to anyone else, including yourself, but spare me." The older woman—forty-two to Zora's twenty-nine—tightened the ponytail holder around her hair, which she'd dyed black this month. "Was that the kitchen timer?"

"I didn't hear anything." Zora adjusted a gift-wrapped box with a slot for envelopes. The front read: Nanny Fund. They planned to share the services of a specialist nanny among the three new moms and their collective total of six infants. Well, they *did* work at a hospital noted for its fertility treatments, although only one of the pregnancies had high-tech origins.

The timer buzzed. "There!" Karen said with satisfaction. "I knew it would sound any second."

"You must be psychic." Zora waddled behind her

past a table displaying shower-themed paper plates and napkins.

"I have a well-developed sense of when food is done. Call it experience." In the kitchen, Karen snatched pot holders from a hook and opened the oven, filling the air with the scents of orange and lemon, almonds and balsamic vinegar.

Karen set the tins of Mediterranean muffins on the stove to cool. "I'd better start on the finger sandwiches. Only two hours before the guests are due, and I have to dress." She tied an apron over her blouse and long, casual skirt.

"I'll finish the vegetables." From the refrigerator, Zora removed the containers of celery, carrots and jicama that she'd cut up earlier, along with sour cream to mix for the dip and peanut butter to fill some of the celery sticks. "Would you get the olives and an onion soup packet from the pantry? I'm too big to squeeze in there."

"Gladly." Karen angled her slender shape around the narrow bend that led to the storage area. "Just black olives, or green ones, too?"

"Both." Zora lowered herself onto a chair, grateful she could still reach the table around her abdomen. A railing underneath allowed her to prop up her swollen ankles, but nothing alleviated the strain on her lower back. It ached more each day.

She hid her discomforts, determined to continue working as long as possible. Being an ultrasound tech meant standing on her feet all day and angling her midsection so she could scan the patients, but she was saving her paid maternity leave for after the twins' birth. Two months left—if they didn't arrive early.

After retrieving the requested items, Karen spread

out her sandwich fixings on the counter. Through the kitchen's far door, Zora heard the scrape of folding chairs being opened and placed around the front room. She respected Lucky's work ethic; he always pitched in with an upbeat attitude. If he could only master the art of minding his own business, he'd be...well, tolerable.

Footsteps thudded on the carpet, announcing Lucky's return. His short, military-style haircut emphasized the strong planes of his face, which reflected his Hispanic heritage. "Where are the chair covers hidden? Someone else stored them after Anya and Jack's wedding."

"Upstairs in the linen closet," Karen said.

"Can I ride the stair lift or is that only for mommies?" Lucky teased. Both women narrowed their eyes at him, and he lifted his hands in a yielding gesture. "Just asking."

"Go play somewhere else," Zora muttered.

"Alone? That's no fun." With a rakish grin, he dodged out.

"You two should swap rooms so you could be downstairs," Karen observed from the counter. "Let him ride the stair lift if it gives him a thrill."

"I can't afford the extra rent." Lucky's large room commanded a correspondingly larger price. While Zora didn't care about having a personal patio exit, she did envy him the private bath. Karen had one, too, upstairs in the master suite, while Zora shared a bathroom with Rod and Melissa. Or, rather, with Rod and whoever moved into the room Melissa had vacated when she'd remarried her ex-husband.

*Some people have all the luck.* A sigh escaped Zora. Too late, she tried to cover with a cough.

"A pickle chip for your thoughts," Karen said.

"No, thanks." Zora popped a black olive into her mouth.

"You really are entitled to support," Karen observed. "I wonder whether you'd have faced your ex by now if Lucky weren't such a nag."

"He has nothing to do with it."

"You're stubborn," was the reply. "Seriously, Zora, how long can you keep this secret? I'm amazed Andrew's mother hasn't spilled the beans."

"Betsy doesn't know." Zora's former mother-in-law was the nursing supervisor at the hospital. The kind-hearted lady had suffered through the loss of two beloved daughters-in-law, thanks to her son's faithlessness.

Zora wondered whether Betsy was being more cautious about bonding with Andrew's third wife, a Hong Kong native he'd met on a business trip while he was married to Zora. Unexpectedly, tears blurred her vision. *How could he cheat on me? And then, just when I was ready to let him go, trick me into believing he still loved me?*

"Betsy sees you in the cafeteria every day," Karen reminded her.

"She's aware that I'm pregnant," Zora agreed. "But she has no idea who the father is."

Karen stuck a hank of black hair behind her ear. "She isn't stupid."

"But I doubt she believes Andrew is capable of...of being such a grade-A jerk." Damn those tears stinging her eyes again. "Aside from my closest friends, most people accept my explanation that I made a mistake after my divorce. I let them assume I picked up a guy in a bar."

"And that's better than admitting you slept with Andrew?"

"It's better than admitting I'm a complete chump."

More footsteps, and Lucky reappeared. "They aren't there. Let's skip the seat covers."

"I refuse to have guests in my house sitting on ugly folding chairs," Karen said.

The man tilted his head skeptically. "What's the big deal? People have been sitting on folding chairs without covers since the dawn of time."

"No, they haven't." Hastily, Zora shielded the relish tray from his attempt to grab a carrot. "Hands off!"

"Evidence found in caves throughout northern Europe indicates that Neanderthals shunned folding chair covers as a sign of weakness," Lucky said. "And why so stingy with the veggies?"

"I'm still arranging these. Go eat a corn chip." Zora indicated a bag set out to be transferred into a large bowl.

"I'm a vegetarian."

"Corn is a vegetable."

"Corn chips do not occur in nature," he responded. "Just one carrot. Pretty please."

She flipped it toward him. He caught it in midair.

"Try the closet in my bathroom for the covers," Karen suggested to Lucky. "Top shelf."

"I have permission to enter the inner sanctum?" he asked.

"It expires in sixty seconds."

"Okay, okay." He paused. "Before I run off, there's one little thing I should mention about today's guest list."

Zora released an impatient breath. "What?"

"I invited Betsy."

"You didn't!" Keeping her ex-mother-in-law in the dark at work was one thing, but around here the babies' paternity was no secret.

Karen turned toward Lucky, knife in hand. "Tell me you're joking."

He grimaced. "Sorry. Spur-of-the-moment thing. But your motto *is* the more the merrier, and besides, Betsy's a widow. If she's interested in renting a room, that would solve all our problems." With a carroty crunch, off he went.

"Unbelievable," Karen said.

If she hadn't been so huge, Zora might have given chase. She could easily have strangled Lucky at that moment. But then they'd have to find *two* new housemates.

"I'd say the cat's about to claw its way out of the bag," Karen observed. "Might as well seize the bull by the horns, or is that too many animal metaphors?"

"Considering the size of the rat we live with, I guess not," Zora growled.

Karen smiled. "Speaking of rats, if you'd rather not confront Andrew-the-rodent yourself, don't forget you can hire Edmond to do it." Edmond Everhart, their former roommate, Melissa's husband, had been Zora's divorce attorney.

"That'll only create more trouble." Zora scraped the onion dip from the mixing bowl into a container on the relish tray. "Andrew'll put me through the wringer."

"If that's your only reason for not telling him about the babies, I'd rate its validity at about a three on a scale of ten." Karen trimmed the crust from a sandwich.

Zora dropped the spoon into the mixing bowl with a

clunk. "He's the only man I ever loved. I want to give him the benefit of the doubt."

"Zora, what benefit of what doubt?" Karen retorted. "He dumped you in high school, married someone else, then cheated on *her* with you after he ran into you at your class reunion. Let's not forget that he then cheated on *you* with what's-her-name from Hong Kong. Why on earth would you entertain the fantastical notion that Andrew will ever transform into a loving husband and father?"

With a pang, Zora conceded that that was exactly what she *did* wish for. While her rational mind sided with Karen, the infants stirring inside her with a series of kicks and squirms obviously missed their father. So did Zora.

"It can happen," she said. "Look at Melissa and Edmond. Three years after their divorce, they fell in love again."

"They'd quarreled about having children. Neither of them cheated on the other," Karen persisted. "Andrew can't be trusted, ever."

She spoke with the ferocity of a divorcée who'd survived an abusive marriage. It had taken more than a decade for Karen to trust a man again. She and their housemate, Rod, were still easing into their relationship.

"People can change." Despite a reluctance to bring up her family, Zora wanted Karen to understand. "Did I mention I have a twin?"

"Really?" Leaning against the counter, Karen folded her arms. "Identical or fraternal?"

"Identical." Zora wasn't about to reveal the whole story, just the important part. "But we quarreled, and we aren't in touch anymore. All I know of her is what

Mom passes along." Their mother, who lived in Oregon, loved sharing news.

"Go on." After a glance at the clock, Karen resumed her food preparation.

"Nearly ten years ago, Zady ran off with a married man." Zora inhaled as deeply as she could, considering the pressure on her lungs from the pregnancy. "They live in Santa Barbara. He split with his wife and now he's devoted to Zady. They have a beautiful house and a couple of kids."

"Was there a wedding in there?" Karen asked dubiously.

"I'm sure there was, although she didn't invite me." The rift had been bitter, and there'd been no move toward reconciliation on either side. In fact, her mother said Zady had chuckled when she'd learned about Zora's divorce.

"So the guy married her, and you believe that if lightning struck your twin, it can strike you, too?" Karen murmured.

Zora's throat tightened. "Why not?"

"Because Betsy's about to arrive with her antennae on high alert. If I'm any judge, that woman's dying to be a grandmother."

"And she'll be a terrific one." The elder Mrs. Raditch did all the right grandmotherly things, such as baking and crocheting, a skill she'd taught Zora. "But…"

"You're running out of *but*s," Karen warned. "Unless you count Lucky's."

"I don't!"

"The way you guys battle, you're almost like an old married couple."

"We're *nothing* like a married couple, old or oth-

erwise." Zora could never be interested in a man with
so little class. Outside work, he flaunted his muscles
in sleeveless T-shirts and cutoffs. While she didn't object if someone had a small tattoo, his body resembled
a billboard for video games. On the right arm, a col-
orful dragon snaked and writhed, while on the left, he
displayed a buxom babe wearing skimpy armor and
wielding a sword.

Whenever she pictured Andrew, she saw him in the
suit and tie he always wore as an international business consultant. He had tousled blond hair, a laser-sharp
mind, sky-blue eyes, and when he trained his headlight
smile on her, Zora understood why some poor fools
became addicted to drugs, because the euphoria was
irresistible.

At the image, vague intentions coalesced into a firm
decision. "Andrew's the man I married. This…this *liaison* with what's-her-name is an aberration. Once the
kids are born and he holds them in his arms, what man
wouldn't love his own son and daughter?" *And their
mother.*

Even Zora's own father, a troubled man who'd
cheated on her mom, had stuck around while his kids
had grown up. Well, mostly—there'd been separations
and emotional outbursts that left painful memories. But
there'd been tender times, too, including a laughter-
filled fishing trip, and one Christmas when her father
had dressed up as Santa Claus and showered them with
gifts.

She longed for her children to experience a father
like that. With Andrew's charm, he could easily provide such unforgettable moments.

For a minute, the only sound was the chopping of a

knife against a cutting board as Karen trimmed crusts. Finally she said, "So you plan to hold it together until then, alone?"

"I have you guys, my friends." Zora struggled for a light tone. "All I have to do is stay on an even keel."

"Like a juggler tossing hand grenades on the deck of a sinking ship?" On a platter, Karen positioned sandwiches in a pyramid. "Well, it's your decision."

"Yes, and I've made it." Zora studied the relish tray through a sheen of moisture. Andrew would come around eventually. He had a good heart, despite his weak will.

"I'm happy to report that I found the chair covers and they look fine." Lucky's deep voice sounded almost in her ear, making her jump. "What do Neanderthals know, anyway?"

"Speaking of Neanderthals, how dare you sneak up on me?" she snapped. "I could go into labor."

"No, you won't." The corners of his mouth quirked.

"How would you know?"

"I'm a nurse, remember?" he said.

"Not that kind of nurse." He worked with a urologist.

"Pregnancy care is part of every nurse's basic medical training." His expression sobered. "Speaking of medicine, you're sure Cole's coming today?"

Dr. Cole Rattigan, the renowned men's fertility expert Lucky assisted, had been away this past week, speaking at a conference in New York.

"He and his wife RSVP'd," Karen assured him. "What's the big deal?"

"I can't discuss it. It concerns a patient."

"Why would you confer about a patient on your day off?" Zora asked.

"That's confidential, too." Grabbing the tray of sandwiches, Lucky whisked out of the room so fast it was a miracle the sandwich pyramid didn't topple.

"That's odd," Karen said. "I wonder what's going on."

As did Zora, but Cole, and in particular his wife, a popular nurse, were a touchy subject for her. As the first Mrs. Andrew Raditch, Stacy hadn't hidden her resentment toward Zora-the-husband-stealer, and most staffers had sided with her.

Among them, no one had been more hostile than Lucky. He'd eased up since he and Zora had started sharing this house, but in a showdown there was no question that his loyalty lay with Cole and his spouse.

Zora wished that didn't bother her. Well, she had more important things to deal with, anyway…such as facing the grandmother of her children in less than two hours.

# Chapter 2

Lucky wove between clusters of chattering people in the living room, removing soiled paper plates and cups. Although he was enjoying the party, he wished he and his housemates had kept a tighter lid on the guest list. Only half an hour into it, the place was filling up—and not all the choices had been wise.

Inviting Betsy Raditch had seemed a clever trick to prod Zora into finally accepting the help she needed. Instead, the younger woman kept dodging her ex-mother-in-law, who sneaked longing gazes at Zora's belly but maintained a respectful distance. The would-be grandmother's wistful expression sent a guilty pang through Lucky.

And he hadn't counted on Karen inviting Laird, but here he was, fawning over Zora. The psychologist's colorless eyes—okay, they were gray, but a very *light* gray—lit up whenever she so much as flinched, providing an excuse for him to offer her a chair or a drink. Was the man flirting or just trying to charm his way into the house? Either way, he had a very strange notion of what women found appealing.

When Zora winced, the guy reached out to rub her bulge. Stuck in a knot of people across the room, Lucky barely refrained from shouting, "Hands off!" To his relief, Keely Randolph, a dour older nurse Lucky had never much liked until now, smacked Laird's arm and loudly proclaimed that people shouldn't shed their germs all over pregnant women.

After scowling at her, Laird gazed around, targeted Karen and approached her with a smarmy expression. Lucky caught the words *exquisite house* and *can't wait to move in*.

Rod Vintner came to Karen's rescue, his wiry frame and short graying beard bristling with indignation. "Who's moving in where?" he growled with a ferocity that indicated he'd willingly stick one of his anesthesiology needles into Laird's veins and pump it to the max.

Satisfied that the jerk was batting zero, Lucky glanced toward the front window. He never tired of the soul-renewing view across the narrow lane and past the coastal bluffs to the cozy harbor from which the town took its name. You couldn't beat the beauty of this spot.

Yet he might have to leave. And that had nothing to do with Laird or any other roommate.

Lucky had worked hard to earn a master's degree in nursing administration, which he'd completed earlier this year. Now he sought a suitable post for his management skills, but there were no openings at Safe Harbor

Medical. Which meant he'd have to move away from the people he cared about.

They included Zora, who over the past few months had needed his protection as she struggled to deal with an unplanned pregnancy and a broken heart. They hadn't intended to grow closer; he wasn't even sure either would openly acknowledge it. Which was just as well. Because having once failed in a big way to be there for the people he loved, Lucky had vowed never, ever to take on such responsibility. Because he'd only fail again.

Still, he couldn't imagine moving away. His best hope for staying in the area would be the expansion of the men's fertility program in which he worked. Any minute now, its director, Cole Rattigan, would arrive. Most of the staff thought Cole had just been in New York to deliver a speech, but Lucky was more interested in hearing about his boss's private meeting with the designer of a new device.

It offered a slim possibility of helping one particular patient, a volatile billionaire named Vince Adams who was considering a major endowment to expand the hospital's urology program. If that happened, it might create a nursing-administration position for Lucky. Also, it would realize his doctor's dream of building a world-class program.

If not for Cole, Lucky might not be working for Safe Harbor Med at all, he reflected as he carried empty plates and cups to the kitchen. Two and a half years ago, when the newly arrived urologist had interviewed for office nurses, Lucky hadn't believed he had a chance of being hired. After his previous doctor retired, Lucky's tattoos had repeatedly knocked him out of the running for jobs. He'd been considering expensive and painful treatment to remove the evidence of his youthful foolishness.

But the tats hadn't bothered Cole. He'd asked a few questions, appeared pleased with the responses and offered the job on the spot. After that, Lucky would have battled demons if they'd threatened his doctor.

In the den, he poured himself a glass of fruit juice and noted that the sandwiches, chips and veggies were holding their own despite modest depletions. No one had cut the sheet cake yet, leaving intact the six cartoon babies, five with pink hair ribbons and one with blue.

"Aren't they adorable?" The soft voice at his elbow drew his attention to Betsy.

Lucky shifted uneasily. Despite his conviction that Zora ought to be honest with her children's grandmother, he had no intention of snitching. Still, he *had* invited the woman. "We ordered it from the Cake Castle."

She indicated the Nanny Fund box bordered by a few wrapped packages. "I didn't realize most people would be contributing money as their gift. I hope it's all right that I crocheted baby blankets."

"All right?" Lucky repeated in surprise. "The kids will treasure those keepsakes forever."

Betsy's squarish face, softened by caramel-brown hair and wire-rimmed glasses, brightened at the compliment. Why didn't Zora level with the woman? A doting grandma could provide the support a young single mother needed. Considering that Zora's own mother lived in Oregon, she'd be wise to take advantage of Betsy's yearning for grandkids.

"I'm glad to hear it," she said. "Also, much as I approve of the nanny idea, I suspect new mothers could use furnishings and toys."

"Oh, there's plenty of that." Lucky had been forced to park in the driveway for weeks due to the overflow in the garage. "Practically the entire staff has donated their baby gear. Anya and Jack got first pick, since she's already delivered, but they only have a singleton. There's plenty left."

"They're a lovely couple. So are Melissa and Edmond." Betsy indicated the long-legged blonde woman ensconced on the sofa, flanked by her doting husband and seven-year-old niece, Dawn, who lived with them. This was a rare outing for Melissa, who in her sixth month with triplets looked almost as wide as she was tall. "I'm thrilled that they remarried. They obviously belong together."

Was that a hint? Surely the woman didn't believe her son might reconcile with Zora. Aside from the fact that he had a new wife, the guy was the world's worst candidate for family man. "I'd bet in most divorces the odds of a happy reconciliation would be on par with winning the lottery."

"If that was for my benefit, don't bother," Betsy told him.

"Sorry." Lucky ducked his head. "I tend to be a mother hen to my friends. Or a father hen, if there is such a thing."

"At least you aren't a rooster like my son," she replied sharply.

"No comment."

"Wise man."

On the far side of the room, Zora circled past the staircase and halted, her eyes widening at the sight of

Lucky standing beside Betsy. Lucky nearly spread his hands in a do-you-honestly-think-I'd-tell-her? gesture, but decided against it, since Betsy didn't miss much. She must be suspicious enough already about the twins' paternity.

While he was seeking another topic of conversation, his landlady bounced into the den from the kitchen. "Who's ready for a game?" Karen called. "We have prizes." She indicated a side table where baskets displayed bath soaps and lotions, while a large stuffed panda held out a gift card to the Bear and Doll Boutique.

"What kind of game?" Dawn asked from the couch.

"I'm afraid the first one might be too hard for a child," Karen said. "It's a diaper-the-baby contest."

"I can do that," the little girl proclaimed.

"Yes, she can," Melissa confirmed. "Dawn has more experience with diapering than Edmond or me."

"I used to help our neighbor," the child said.

"Then please join in!" Karen beamed as guests from the living room crowded into the den. "Ah, more players. Great!"

Among the group was their former roommate Anya, her arms around the daughter she'd delivered a few weeks earlier. "Nobody's diapering Rachel for a game."

"Certainly not," Karen agreed.

"However, volunteers are welcome to stop by our apartment any night around two a.m.," put in Anya's husband, Dr. Jack Ryder.

Rachel gurgled. A sigh ran through the onlookers, accompanied by murmurs of "What an angel!" and "How darling!"

"I'd be happy to hold her for you," Betsy said. "You can both relax and enjoy the food."

"Thank you." Anya cheerfully shifted her daughter into the arms of the nursing supervisor.

When Zora hugged herself protectively, Lucky felt a twinge of sympathy. She'd refused to consider adoption, declaring that this might be her only chance to have children, but the sight of little Rachel must underscore the reality of what she faced.

Children required all your resources and all your strength. How did this woman with slim shoulders and defiant ginger hair expect to cope by herself?

He reminded himself not to get too involved. Lucky didn't mind changing a few diapers, but he might not be here long, unless Dr. Rattigan brought good news. Now where was the doctor?

Waving a newborn-size doll along with a package of clean diapers, Karen detailed the rules of the game. "You have to remove and replace the diaper. I'll be timing you. Fastest diaper change wins."

"That doesn't sound hard," Laird scoffed.

"Did I mention you have to do it one-handed?" Karen replied, to widespread groans. "If you drop the baby on the floor, you're automatically disqualified."

"For round two, contestants have to diaper the doll blindfolded," Rod added mischievously. A few people laughed, while Dawn's jaw set with determination. That kid would do it upside down and sideways to win, Lucky thought. With that attitude, she'd go far in life.

Then he caught the sound he'd been waiting for—the doorbell. His pulse sped up. "I'll get it."

Someone else reached the door first, however, and friends rushed to greet the Rattigans. Despite his impatience, Lucky hung back.

With her friendly manner and elfin face, Stacy had

a kind word for everyone. Her mild-mannered husband said little; Cole's reticence, Lucky knew, stemmed partly from the urologist's discomfort in social situations. It was also partly the result of having a brain so brilliant that he was probably carrying on half a dozen internal conversations with himself at any given moment.

Lucky could barely contain his eagerness to speak with the great man privately and find out if the device lived up to its promise. However, he drew the line at elbowing guests aside.

Stacy oohed over Anya's newborn and hugged Betsy, her former mother-in-law. The room quieted as the first Mrs. Andrew Raditch came face-to-face with the woman who had cheated with him before being discarded in turn. Most of the staff had cheered at Zora's misfortune, believing she was receiving her just deserts. Lucky was ashamed to admit he'd been among them. Now he wished he could spare her this awkwardness.

"Wow! Look at you." Stacy patted Zora's belly. "Have you chosen names yet?"

"Still searching," she said with a tentative smile. "For now, Tweedledee and Tweedledum."

This light exchange broke the tension. With her new marriage, Stacy had clearly moved on, and with her courtesy toward Zora, she'd brought her old nemesis in from the cold.

Silently, Lucky thanked her. Cole had chosen a worthy wife.

The game began, with guests lining up to participate. Seizing his chance, Lucky approached his boss, who spoke without prompting.

"I know you're anxious for news, Luke." Cole used Lucky's formal name. "Let's talk."

"We'll have more privacy in here." Lucky led the way into the now-empty living room.

Zora had no interest in diapering a baby. She'd be doing more than her share of that soon.

Stacy's display of friendliness left her both relieved and oddly shaky. Having been treated as a pariah by much of the hospital staff for several years, Zora still felt vulnerable as well as guilty.

Also, Stacy's question about the names reminded Zora of her idea to leave the decision until they were born. She'd figured that if Andrew had a chance to choose the names, it might help bond him with the little ones. Today, however, the prospect of what lay ahead was sinking in.

For starters, what was she planning to do, call him from the delivery room and break the news of his paternity over the phone while writhing in agony? This kind of information should be presented in person, and she ought to get it over with now. Yet being around Andrew brought out Zora's weakness for him; the ease with which he'd seduced her when she dropped by with their divorce papers proved that.

If only Lucky would stop poking at her, she'd be able to think clearly. It might be unfair to focus her anger on her housemate, but this was none of his business. And why had he, one of the party's hosts, hustled Dr. Rattigan off in such a hurry?

Hungry as usual these days, Zora munched on a peanut butter–filled celery stick from the snack table. Keely drifted alongside, following her gaze as Lucky vanished. "Nice build," the older nurse observed in her nasal voice.

Amused, Zora said, "I don't believe he's dating anyone. Interested?"

Keely snorted. "Not my type."

Zora didn't dare ask what that was.

A hint of beer breath alerted her to Laird Maclaine's approach. The psychologist must have downed a brew before arriving, because they weren't serving alcohol.

"We're discussing Mendez?" He addressed his question to Zora, ignoring Keely. "If he snags a better job with that new master's degree of his, I'd love to rent *his* room. I hear it has an en suite bathroom."

"En suite?" Keely repeated. "What a pretentious term."

Laird rolled his eyes.

"He isn't leaving." While Zora understood Lucky's desire for advancement, she couldn't imagine him abandoning his friends.

The psychologist shrugged. "Either way, this is a fantastic party house. I'm expecting to move in next weekend."

Astonished, Zora slanted an assessing gaze at the psychologist. From an objective viewpoint, Laird wasn't bad-looking, although bland compared to Lucky, and she respected him for initiating and leading patient support groups. But it would be annoying to have to run into this conceited guy every morning over breakfast and every night at dinner.

Impulsively, she addressed Keely. "We have an empty room that used to be Melissa's. Any chance you're interested?"

"It's taken, by me," Laird rapped out.

"Nothing's settled," Zora said.

"Don't you already have two men living here?" Keely inquired. "You and Karen should bring in another woman. I'd join you, but I couldn't do that to my roommate."

"You wouldn't fit in, anyway," Laird growled.

That remark didn't deserve a response. "Who's your roommate?" Zora asked Keely. "Do I know her?"

"Oh, she doesn't work at the medical complex," the nurse responded. "She's a housekeeper."

"I admire your loyalty to her."

"Anyone would do the same."

A stir across the den drew their attention. It was Dawn Everhart's turn at the game. Deftly, the little girl rolled the doll with an elbow, tugged on one diaper tab with her fingers and caught the other in her mouth, all while onlookers captured the moment with their cell phones.

"Unsanitary," Laird protested.

"But clever," Rod responded from his post beside Karen. "Besides, it's a doll."

"And she's beating the pants off everyone else's time," Edmond observed, beaming at his niece. "Literally."

Her feet having swollen to the size of melons, Zora wandered into the kitchen and sat down. Through the far door, she detected the low rumble of masculine voices in the living room.

What were Lucky and his boss discussing so intently? Had Cole made job inquiries at the conference for his nurse's sake? Although she'd instinctively dismissed Laird's comment about Lucky moving, the man couldn't be expected to waste his master's degree.

If Lucky departed, who would run out for ice cream when she had a craving? Lucky had promised to haul two bassinets and a changing table to the second floor as soon as she was ready for them. Without him around, who would cart her stuff up and down the stairs? She certainly couldn't count on Laird pitching in.

Well, she'd survive. In fact, she shouldn't be relying on Lucky so much, anyway. Zora hated to depend on others, especially someone so controlling and critical and arrogant and judgmental. She might not have the world's best taste in men, but she knew what she *didn't* like, and Lucky epitomized it. Now what were he and Dr. Rattigan talking about so intently?

No matter how hard she strained, she couldn't follow the thread of conversation from the living room. Just when she caught a couple of words, a burst of cheering from the den obliterated the rest of the doctor's comments.

Judging by the clamor, Dawn had edged out Anya's husband, Jack, by two seconds. "I can visualize the headline now—Seven-year-old Defeats Obstetrician in Diapering Contest!" roared Rod, who, as Jack's uncle, had the privilege of ragging him mercilessly. "I'm posting the pictures on the internet."

"You do that and you'll never see your great-niece again," Jack retorted. He spoiled the effect by adding, "Will he, cutie?" apparently addressing the newborn.

Zora lumbered to her feet. She was missing all the fun and worrying for nothing.

Probably.

# Chapter 3

Feeling miles from the festivities in the den, Lucky struggled to concentrate on Cole's account. He kept wishing that, if he focused hard enough, the results would be more encouraging.

"The new stent won't fix what's wrong with Vince Adams." The slightly built doctor ran a hand through his rumpled brown hair.

"Are you certain?" Lucky pressed.

Cole nodded. "It won't do anything for a patient who has that much scar tissue."

During the summer, Cole had used the latest microsurgical techniques in an unsuccessful attempt to open the billionaire's blocked sperm ducts. As the office nurse, Lucky hadn't assisted at the operation, but he'd read the follow-up report. The procedure hadn't been able to reverse the extensive damage left by a long-ago infection.

However, Vince continued to press them for options. Cole had told him about a new dissolvable, medicine-infused stent, and Vince had been excited that Cole would get an advance preview of the device. "We have the world's top urologist right here," the millionaire had trumpeted. "And I'll be the first guy he cures."

*The higher the hopes, the harder the fall.*

"Do you think his interest in Safe Harbor is entirely based on restoring his fertility?" Lucky asked.

"It's hard to say," Cole replied. "His intentions tend to shift with his emotional state."

A private equity investor, Vince Adams was powerful and rich. But wealth hadn't compensated for his inability to sire children. Over the years, he'd paid dearly for treatments without success, and others had paid dearly for his desire for fatherhood.

After several turbulent and childless marriages, Vince had wed a woman with two young daughters. Determined to adopt them, he had used his financial clout to overwhelm Portia's first husband in court.

The man he'd gleefully trounced was Lucky's housemate, Rod Vintner, who'd faced a doubly devastating loss. First, during his divorce, he'd learned that his daughters were actually the genetic offspring of his unfaithful wife's previous lover, now out of the picture. Second, Rod had been outspent and outmaneuvered fighting for joint custody.

For years, he'd been forbidden to talk or even write to his daughters, who lived a ninety-minute drive away, in San Diego. Then, earlier this year, the older girl had run away from home. The twelve-year-old had contacted Rod, who'd enlisted the aid of the girls' maternal grandmother here in Safe Harbor.

Although officially Rod was still banned, Grandma Helen had arranged for Tiffany—now thirteen—and her younger sister to visit her more often. Whenever possible, she let them meet with Rod, and, faced with Tiffany's threats to run away again, the Adamses pretended not to notice.

Vince's search for fertility, however, provided him with another avenue for keeping Rod in line. While Vince's interest in the hospital stemmed in large part from his discovery that one of the world's foremost urologists had joined the staff, it also ensured that Rod didn't dare become too much of an annoyance. An anesthesiologist would be a lot easier for the hospital to replace than a billionaire donor.

Lucky hated that the staff had to curry favor with Vince. Still, he felt compassion for a man desperate to produce a baby. The billionaire's motives might be self-serving, but his comments had made it clear that he would treasure his child. As long as parents offered a loving, secure home, it wasn't anyone else's right to pass judgment.

However, if Cole couldn't help him, it seemed likely Vince wouldn't follow through on his major donation. "Suppose he drops us," Lucky said. "Surely there are others we could approach."

"The world is full of rich people, but Safe Harbor tends to lose out to more prestigious institutions," Cole responded. "I admit, Luke, being at the conference whetted my appetite for better research facilities, more lab space and money for fellowships. In fact, I received three excellent offers to relocate."

Lucky's heart nearly skipped a beat. "You'd take another position?"

Alarm flitted across the doctor's face. "I shouldn't have said that."

Nevertheless, he *had* said it. "If you go, the program will never recover." *Neither will I. On many levels.*

At a burst of laughter from the other room, Lucky flinched. His friends had no idea that he was standing here with the ground crumbling beneath his feet.

Cole's brow furrowed. "I joined Safe Harbor with the intention of building a standout program. Although I'm no longer sure that will be possible, this is my wife's home, and mine, too. I haven't given up yet." But there was no mistaking his distress.

"Nothing else at the conference might be useful?"

"I'm afraid not. Perhaps we should suggest Mr. Adams cancel next Saturday's appointment and save himself a trip." The billionaire tended to arrive with plenty of pomp and circumstance by private plane or helicopter. On other occasions, Vince roared up the coast in a high-performance car that cost as much as many houses.

If only Lucky could find a solution, for his sake and for his doctor's. It would also be important to the medical center to achieve its goal of becoming a major player in the fertility field. Major gifts attracted additional donors; a lack of progress might, by contrast, eventually consign Safe Harbor to secondary status. And this place had been good to Lucky when he'd needed help the most.

"Don't cancel," he said. "That's a week from now. Things could change."

"I suppose you're right." Cole stretched his shoulders. "In any event, my patient deserves to hear the news from me in person."

To Lucky, it was a reprieve. He had a week to figure out the next move.

\* \* \*

Zora had never seen Lucky abandon a party before. After talking to Dr. Rattigan, he'd spent the next hour in a corner of the living room, fiddling with his phone. Searching the internet or texting people? But why?

In view of the doctor's wistful expression, it didn't take a genius to recognize that they'd suffered a blow. They must have been counting on the New York conference for some reason.

Zora tried to shrug off Lucky's absence while she and her fellow moms-to-be opened gifts. Most people had contributed money, but Betsy's gifts were special.

Zora's throat constricted as she held up the soft pink and blue blankets. Her former mother-in-law had created these precious heirlooms even without being sure of her relationship to the twins.

Zora was glad now that Lucky had invited Betsy. To learn she'd been excluded from the baby shower would have been an undeserved slap in the face.

Catching Betsy's eye, Zora said, "These mean more than I can say."

"I'm glad." Wedged among the other guests, the older woman added, "If you need anything, please call me."

"You're a sweetheart." But Zora wouldn't ask for the other woman's help, not until after the babies were born and she revealed the truth to Andrew. When she did, she hoped Betsy wouldn't resent having been kept in the dark.

Her gaze drifted to the diamond-and-emerald ring on her ex-mother-in-law's right hand. Zora had worn the family heirloom during her marriage, treasuring both its beauty and its significance. After the divorce, she'd returned it, with regret. Neither of Andrew's other wives had worn it; there'd been a special bond between Betsy and Zora that had begun in her high school days.

Now, its glitter reminded Zora of how much she'd lost. Not only her husband, but a woman who'd been as close to her as family. Well, perhaps someday she and Betsy could be close again.

She hoped her children would meet her twin sister, too. That depended on whether Zora was ever secure enough to handle Zady's inevitable gloating at her downfall. For now, distance was best. Nobody could inflict as much pain as the people nearest your heart.

After the last guest departed, the adrenaline that had powered Zora all afternoon faded. She collapsed on the living room couch while, inside her, the babies tussled.

What a blessing it would be when they were born and her body returned to normal. And what a joy to hold them and see their sweet faces.

At this point, Lucky should have arrived to offer her refreshments. She missed his coddling, even though it was often seasoned with criticism.

Instead, he bustled about collecting trash as if she weren't there. From the kitchen, Zora heard Karen opening and closing the fridge to put away food, while in the den, Rod ran the vacuum cleaner. Zora would have pitched in if she'd had the energy.

As Lucky removed the white linen covers from the folding chairs, his dark eyebrows drew together like storm clouds. The dragon protruding from beneath one sleeve appeared to be lashing its tail.

Zora broke the silence. "Won't you tell me what happened?"

He tossed a cover onto a pile of laundry. "What do you mean?"

"You've been upset since you talked to Dr. Rattigan."

Lucky snapped a chair shut. "Doesn't concern you."

Zora tried a different tack. "Laird speculated you might move out of town to take a better job. He's angling to get your suite." She deliberately baited Lucky with that reference to the obnoxious psychologist.

Lucky grimaced. "I'd rather not discuss that lowlife."

"Then let's discuss what's eating you."

"Like I said, it's none of your business."

Any second, flames were going to shoot out her ears. "Oh, yes, it is!"

"How so?" he growled, wielding a chair as if he was prepared to thrust it at her.

The guy sure was prickly. "It's obvious Cole brought bad news from the conference."

Lucky set the chair down. "I can't discuss anything involving a patient."

He was right to safeguard the man's privacy, Zora conceded. Medical personnel were required to do that, by law and by hospital policy as well as by simple decency. Still, he'd dropped a clue. Now, why would a patient's condition bother Lucky so much?

From the kitchen, Karen's voice drifted to her. "I'm looking forward to having your girls in town next Saturday. Should we invite them and Helen for lunch?"

"I doubt there'll be time," Rod replied dourly. "They're only being dropped off at their grandma's for an hour or two while Vince sees his doctor."

"Is he having problems?" Karen asked. "I don't usually wish anyone ill, but he's an exception."

"You can wish that jerk as much ill as you like." Rod's voice rose in anger. "Tiff and Amber loathe the man. He may not physically abuse them, but he's a bully, and emotional scars can be the worst kind."

As the rumble of the garbage disposal cut off further eavesdropping, Zora put two and two together. Everyone knew—because the billionaire had discussed it openly—that Dr. Rattigan was treating him. And the men's program counted on his support.

"It's Vince Adams," she said. "No, don't answer. I realize you can't confirm it."

Lucky stacked the chairs to one side. "Are you still mad at me for inviting Betsy? Is that why you're harassing me?"

Zora tried to hug her knees, but her bulge was in the way. "I'm glad you invited her."

"So we're good?" His fierce brown eyes raked over her.

"No. What if you leave?" she burst out, surprised by her rush of emotion. "We're having enough trouble finding one roommate, let alone two. We'll *have* to take Laird."

A knot in her chest warned that she was less concerned about Laird than she was about Lucky staying until the babies were born. Until Andrew hopefully came to his senses and fell in love with his children. *Until hell freezes over.* No, but if hell did freeze over, she'd counted on Lucky to be there with a warming blanket.

As a friend, of course. He'd been just as helpful to Anya—maybe more so—when they'd moved into this house. It was in his nature.

Lucky stopped fiddling around. "You shouldn't upset yourself. It might shoot up your blood pressure."

"Then talk to me."

He plopped his butt on the arm of the couch. "About what?"

"You've been delving into your phone all afternoon, trying to find a solution, right? But if Dr. Rattigan can't fix Vince—I mean, Patient X—neither can you."

"So?" Lucky folded his arms. They were muscular arms, and he folded them across a broad, powerful chest. Too bad the movement also flexed the shapely legs of a cartoon woman, which rather spoiled the effect for Zora.

"We have to figure out another way to keep the Adamses involved with Safe Harbor," she blurted.

"We?" Lucky was addicted to monosyllables today.

She'd surprised herself by saying that. But didn't she owe Lucky a favor, considering how much support he'd given her?

"Yes, *we*," Zora retorted, and, to cut off any argument, she added, "Some people have a ridiculously hard time accepting help, to quote a person I know."

That produced a tight smile. "What do you imagine you, or we, can do regarding this alleged situation?"

"I have an idea." Fortunately, a possibility had hit her. "I'll share it on one condition." She might as well benefit from this.

"Which is?"

"You stop nagging me about my personal choices, however stupid you may consider them."

Lucky didn't answer. Then, abruptly, he burst out laughing. "Sometimes I actually like you."

"Why?" she asked suspiciously.

"Because you're a tough little cookie. If only you would apply that quality to he-who-shall-remain-nameless."

"That's breaking the rules," Zora retorted. "No nagging and no smart-aleck remarks, either. Well?"

"You're draining all the fun out of our relationship." Lucky raised his hands in mock surrender. "I agree. Now, what's the suggestion?"

The sight of him leaning close, intent on her, sent a thrill across her nervous system. Must be the maternal hormones running amok. "Remember when Edmond gave that speech about trends in family law?"

Melissa's husband served as a consultant for staff and patients on the legal aspects of fertility issues.

"Sure." Another one-syllable response.

"Afterward, Vince approached him for advice." Zora had heard the story from Melissa. Quickly, she added, "It was in a public place. No attorney-client privilege."

"Advice about what?"

"About persuading Mrs. Adams to agree to in vitro." If Vince produced even a small amount of sperm, it could be extracted and injected into an egg, bypassing the need to fix his blocked ducts. "She refuses to undergo in vitro, however."

"He can afford to hire a surrogate," Lucky pointed out.

"He objects to bringing in a stranger while his wife is presumably still fertile." Although Zora detested Portia for Rod's sake, she understood why a woman approaching forty wouldn't be eager to undergo a process involving hormone shots as well as uncomfortable procedures to harvest her eggs and implant the embryos. There were also potential health risks from a pregnancy complicated by multiple babies.

"What does this have to do with us?" Lucky asked.

"Talking to Edmond renewed Vince's enthusiasm

for Safe Harbor." According to Melissa, the hospital administrator had phoned later to congratulate Edmond on saving the day.

"Renewed his enthusiasm how?" Lucky persisted. "His wife still hasn't agreed, as far as I know."

"I'm not sure, but judging by what Rod says about him, he enjoys power trips," Zora observed. "He hates to lose. If we figure out how he can win in this situation, it might keep him engaged with Safe Harbor."

"Any suggestions?"

"Ask Edmond what *he* advised."

Lucky considered this in silence. At close range, Zora noticed an end-of-day dark beard shadowing his rough cheeks. Although she preferred men with a smooth, sophisticated look, she had to admit there was something appealing about Lucky's male hormones proclaiming themselves loud and clear.

What was wrong with her? At this stage of pregnancy, she ought to have zero interest in sex. Or men. Or sexy men. Or... *Stop that.*

"Any idea which days Edmond's at the hospital?" Lucky asked.

"Afraid not."

In the adjacent dining room, Karen rose after stowing a tray in the sideboard. "Monday mornings and Thursday afternoons. Why the interest in Edmond?"

"It's private," Zora and Lucky said simultaneously.

Descending the few steps to the living room, their landlady gathered the pile of chair covers. "That's unusual, you guys being on the same page."

They both returned her gaze wordlessly until she sighed and departed. Zora chuckled. That had been fun.

Lucky held out his hand. As her fingers brushed his,

a quiver of pleasure ran through her. On her feet, she lingered close to him for a moment, enjoying the citrus smell of his cologne underscored by masculine phero-mones. Then in the recesses of her mind, she remem-bered something he often said: *it's Andrew who should be helping you, not me.*

Even without speaking, he projected criticism. Glow-ering, and ignoring Lucky's puzzled reaction, Zora headed for the stair lift.

# Chapter 4

On Monday mornings while Cole performed surgeries at the hospital, Lucky replenished supplies, scheduled follow-up appointments with patients and prepared for office procedures in the afternoon.

He'd hoped to slip out to talk to Edmond, but the attorney was fully booked and could only spare a few minutes at lunch. It would have to do. But the morning turned out to be busier than expected, due to a special request from the fertility program director, Dr. Owen Tartikoff. A new urologist, a specialist in men's reconstructive surgery, would soon be joining the staff and Dr. Tartikoff needed someone to review the applications for his office nurse. Due to Lucky's administrative degree, Cole had recommended him.

Pleased at the responsibility, Lucky sifted through digital résumés to select the best candidates. The final choice would be left to the new physician, since the relationship between a doctor and his nurse was crucial. The right person eased the doctor's job, increased efficiency and decreased errors.

The wrong person could cause all sorts of unwanted drama. Hospital lore included a by-now-legendary clash between Keely Randolph and Dr. Tartikoff shortly after his arrival a few years ago. There'd been a spectacular scene when the abrasive Dr. T had dressed her down for an error and she'd blown up, calling him arrogant and egotistical before stalking out.

In view of her long history at Safe Harbor, she'd received a second chance with another obstetrician, Paige Brennan. Miraculously, the chemistry between them had proved stable rather than explosive. Keely spoke of her doctor in glowing terms, which in Lucky's view was how a nurse should behave.

He smiled, remembering how Keely had stood up for Zora at the party, staving off Laird's attempt to touch her. While his attentions hadn't necessarily been sexual, Lucky wouldn't put it past the man.

An image of Zora filled his mind as he recalled her unexpected offer to aid in his quest to expand the men's program. Her teasing grin was irresistible, and who would have imagined a mother-to-be could radiate such sexy vibes? True, she'd been cute before she got pregnant, but Lucky had been too caught up in resenting her for Stacy's and Cole's sakes to take more than a passing notice.

Not that there was any risk of a romance developing between him and Zora. He would never fall for anyone who led such a messy life, and he didn't appear to be her type, either. Judging by Andrew, she went for slick and manipulative, hardly adjectives that applied to a tattooed guy from a rough part of LA.

A guy who'd committed his share of mistakes and was determined not to repeat them, especially if a wife and children were at stake. If he were ever so blessed, Lucky vowed to be sure his family's circumstances were as close to perfect as humanly possible. He'd give them a financial buffer. A protective circle of love, commitment and security. If he couldn't be sure he could provide those things, he'd rather not risk marrying at all.

Lucky focused on the résumés on the computer screen. There were a number of nurses eager to work in such a prestigious environment with regular hours and benefits. He struggled to view them through the perspective of an employer instead of as a fellow nurse who'd spent a year on his own job search. More than ever, he appreciated Cole's willingness to bring him on board.

Clicking open a new résumé, Lucky frowned in confusion. Was this a joke? Someone had inserted a slightly altered photo of Zora. Her face was narrower, but he'd recognize her anywhere.

Only the name on the file was Zady Moore. *Zady, huh?* He read on, prepared for humorous remarks, but the data seemed straightforward. This so-called Zady had grown up near Safe Harbor, just like Zora. Same age, too. In fact, same birth date.

She claimed to have a nursing degree and to work for a urologist in Santa Barbara, a couple of hours' drive north of here. Switching to the internet, Lucky confirmed that there was indeed a Zady Moore listed in connection with that urologist's office. If this was a hoax, someone had gone to great lengths.

The name Moore struck him as familiar. Oh, right. He'd seen mail addressed to Zora Moore Raditch.

Could Zora have a twin she'd never told him about? Or did she have a cousin with an eerily similar appearance and the same birth date?

The alarm on his watch shrilled, a reminder of his meeting with Edmond. Lucky set aside the résumé with several others marked for further consideration.

From the fourth floor, he took the stairs to the medical building lobby and strode out past the pharmacy into the late September sunshine. A salty breeze wafted from the ocean a mile to the south, while seagulls wheeled overhead.

Next door, the six-story hospital rose in front of him, a lovely sight with its curved wings. Remodeled half a dozen years earlier to specialize in fertility and maternity services, it had established a national reputation by hiring distinguished doctors such as Cole and Dr. T, and by adding state-of-the-art laboratories, surgical suites and equipment. As a result, the side-by-side buildings were bursting at the seams with staff and patients.

Lucky glanced across the circular drive at the vacant dental building that had been mired in bankruptcy proceedings. Once the bankruptcy judge allowed a sale, it would be snapped up fast. The corporation that owned Safe Harbor Medical Center had expressed interest in buying it, but had balked at the high price.

When Vince Adams had expressed interest in funding the growth of the men's program, he'd seemed a gift from fate. Since then, Vince had demonstrated mood swings and a knack for throwing everyone off balance, but his donation remained the hospital's best chance of acquiring the building and boosting the men's fertility program to the next level.

Lucky entered the hospital via the staff door. Instantly, his senses registered tempting aromas from the cafeteria. Also nearby, the chatter of childish voices drifted from the day care center, to which he presumed Zora would soon be entrusting her babies.

As he shoved open the door to the stairs—Lucky seized any chance at exercise—he wondered how long he could go without nagging her. *Somebody* had to advocate for those kids, who deserved their father's financial support even if he was incapable of acting like a real dad.

What about this Zady character? If she was a family member, Zora could sure use the help.

On the fifth floor, Lucky passed the executive offices and entered a smaller suite. The receptionist had apparently gone to lunch, and an inner door stood ajar. The placard read, Edmond Everhart, Family Law Consultant.

Lucky listened in case a client remained inside. Hearing no one, he rapped on the frame.

"Come in." From behind the desk, Edmond rose to greet him. In his early thirties, like Lucky, and also about five-ten, the guy was impeccably dressed in a suit and tie. Only his rumpled brown hair revealed that he'd had a busy morning. All the same, there was nothing glib or calculating about him.

After shaking hands and taking a seat, Lucky went straight to the point. "I understand Vince Adams was souring on Safe Harbor until he talked to you. You spoke with him in public, so I presume client confidentiality doesn't apply."

"That's true." Leaning back, the attorney removed his glasses, plucked a microfiber cloth from the drawer and polished the lenses.

"I'm curious how you won him over, because—" Lucky couldn't go into detail, since it involved Vince's treatment "—just in case he changes his mind again. What upset him in the first place?"

"He felt disrespected because the whole hospital is aware that he has fertility issues," Edmond said.

"A fact that he's publicized with his own...statements." Lucky had nearly said *big mouth*.

"Be that as it may, he believed people looked down on him because he can't father children."

"How'd you reassure him?"

"I shared a few personal details that put us on a par." After a hesitation, Edmond continued, "I explained that I'd had a vasectomy and later regretted it." His wife, Melissa, was carrying embryos donated by another couple. "I also asked his advice as a stepfather about parenting my niece while her mom's in prison. I'm not sure why, but the conversation eased his mind."

"My guess is that he felt you respected him," Lucky mused. "Did he bring up anything else?"

Edmond reflected. "Yes. He's frustrated with his wife's refusal to consider in vitro. She wasn't present, so I have no idea how she views the matter."

Lucky recalled Zora's comments. "And he rejects hiring a surrogate?" The hospital maintained a roster of screened candidates.

"That's right."

Wheels spun in Lucky's head. "If we persuaded Mrs. Adams to change her mind, that ought to solve the problem."

"It might," Edmond said. "But is it wise to try to manipulate a woman into having a child she might not want?"

"I believe she's worried more about the medical risk than about having another child." At a previous office visit, a successfully treated patient had arrived to show Cole his newborn son. In the waiting room, Portia Adams had reached out to touch the baby's cheek and studied the child wistfully. Catching Lucky's eye, she'd murmured something about missing those days now that her girls were growing up.

"Perhaps there's a compromise position that might satisfy them both," Edmond said. "What if his wife provided the eggs but didn't carry the pregnancy?"

Lucky hadn't thought about separating the two aspects of in vitro. "It's worth a try."

"Good," Edmond said. "Any other questions?"

"Yes, although it's unrelated." While Lucky had promised not to pressure Zora, he hadn't promised not to encourage others to do so. "Zora hasn't broken the news to her ex about the twins. You're her attorney. How about pointing out that the man has legal obligations?"

The attorney laced his fingers atop the desk. "I assure you, I already have."

"You may have to get in her face, so she can't brush you off."

Edmond tilted his head. "May I share something with you that I've discovered about relationships?"

"Sure." Lucky admired how much Edmond had grown and changed while reconciling with Melissa. "Lay it on me."

"It's important to respect her choices," Edmond said.

"Even if you disagree with them?"

"Especially if you disagree with them." Thoughtfully, the lawyer added, "And especially when she's the person who has to deal with the consequences."

"But Zora keeps repeating the same boneheaded mistakes," Lucky protested.

"I suspect she understands her ex-husband better than either of us," Edmond said. "Legally, she'll have to inform him about the babies once they're born, but until then, she might have reason to be cautious."

Lucky only knew Andrew by reputation. "I suppose it's hard to predict how a guy will react to that kind of news."

"Exactly."

The circumstances might not be perfect, but this was a situation of Andrew's own making. Any decent guy would accept responsibility. However, the man had proven repeatedly that he didn't care about honor *or* decency. "Thanks for the words of wisdom."

"You're welcome."

"Oh, one more thing," Lucky said as they both rose. "Does Zora have a sister named Zady?"

"I believe that's her twin," Edmond said.

"Thanks." A twin. Damn! By applying for the job, Zady had put Lucky in a delicate position. He felt as if he ought to alert Zora, but her sister's application was confidential.

He set off for the cafeteria, anxious to arrive before Zora finished eating so he could get her opinion about his discussion with Edmond. As for her mysterious twin, he'd better leave that hot potato alone.

Being around perfect people filled Zora with a sense of inadequacy. It was balanced by a fervent desire to figure out how they did it.

Take her obstetrician. Six feet tall with dramatic red hair and green eyes, Paige Brennan was a doctor, mother to an eighteen-month-old daughter and wife of the head of a detective agency. Everyone admired and adored her, including her nurse, Keely, who could barely stand most people.

Busy as she was, Dr. Brennan had fit in Zora's exam during her lunch break. The woman was a step from sainthood.

As she sat on the examining table, Zora doubted she could ever develop such an air of confidence. As for inspiring others, she'd settle for earning their good-natured tolerance.

"Surely you have *some* questions," the doctor said after listening to the babies' heartbeats and reviewing Zora's weight gain and test results. They were fine considering her stage of pregnancy. "You never mention any problems."

"Am I supposed to?" Zora had been raised to consider complaining a sign of weakness.

"Frankly, yes." The tall woman draped her frame over a stool. "At thirty-two weeks with a multiple pregnancy, you must be having trouble sleeping, and your ankles are swollen. As I've suggested before, you should be on bed rest."

"I can't afford it," Zora said. "I don't have a husband to wait on me."

"What about the rest of your family?" the doctor asked.

"My mom and stepfather live in Oregon." She'd rather not have either of them around. And there was no sense bringing up her twin, perfect Zady with her ideal husband and kids, whom their mother never failed to mention when she talked with Zora.

The doctor's forehead creased. "Is your mom flying down for the birth?"

"Not if I have anything to say about it." Her mother would expect to be catered to, regardless of the circumstances. She'd be no help with a baby. At home, Mom waited on Zora's surly, demanding stepfather, but her attitude toward her daughters—toward Zora, at least—was just the opposite.

Dr. Brennan regarded her with concern. "Have you chosen a labor partner?" At every visit, she'd recommended Zora sign up for a birthing class.

"I won't need one for a C-section." Although twins didn't always have to be delivered surgically, Zora preferred to play it safe.

"If that's what you want, okay." The physician nodded. "But remember that what we call bed rest doesn't necessarily require staying in bed. You can relax at home and perform routine tasks as you feel capable."

"I feel capable of working." To forestall further objections, Zora added, "And providing ultrasounds doesn't harm the babies. It's not like X-rays or mammograms."

"But it does require standing on your feet all day. And for safety's sake, you should stop driving." Paige raised her eyebrows commandingly.

Zora *was* having trouble reaching the pedals in her car. "I could ride to work with my housemates." Rod, whose car frequently broke down, cadged rides from others, so why shouldn't she?

Keely chose that moment to step in from the hall. "I can drive her."

"Excuse me?" Paige blinked at the unexpected comment.

"If I rent a room in their house, Zora can ride with me." The nurse mustered a faint smile.

"I thought you had a roommate," Zora said.

"So did I. Can we talk at lunch?"

"Sure."

The obstetrician cleared her throat. "Keely, would you provide Zora with an after-visit summary and schedule an appointment for her in two weeks?"

"Yes, Doctor."

The doctor typed a note into the computer. "Zora, call me if you have any problems, such as spotting or contractions, even if they don't hurt. Okay?"

"Will do." Zora accepted the nurse's assistance in rising from the table.

Once she was dressed, she tucked the printed summary into her purse and walked to the elevator with Keely. With her neck thrust forward, the woman's aggressive stance reinforced the impression of her as a difficult personality. Zora hoped she hadn't erred by suggesting Keely move in with them.

"What's the situation with your roommate?" she asked as they descended. The office was only one flight up, but in Zora's condition, that might as well be ten stories.

"She's in Iowa taking care of her mother," Keely said. "She only planned to stay a week but that's changed. Last night she emailed and asked me to ship all her stuff to her."

"That was short notice. Your rent must be due next week." It was the first of the month.

"That's right. I'm glad you mentioned the vacancy."

"Everything's subject to Karen's approval," Zora warned.

"I'll stop by her office later."

It sounded like a done deal. At least Keely would be an improvement on Laird.

In the cafeteria, the blend of voices and aromas filled Zora with eagerness to share this new development with Lucky. Where was he? Her gaze swept past the food serving bays and across the crowded room.

She spotted him sharing a table with a thin and most unwelcome companion: Laird. The psychologist was talking a mile a minute, oblivious to Lucky's irritated expression.

Zora would rather not discuss Keely in front of the competition. "Hold on," she said, turning.

Too late. Keely was stomping right over to the table. Judging by the set of her shoulders, she didn't plan to be subtle, either.

# Chapter 5

Lucky had often heard the flow of gossip referred to as a grapevine, but in a hospital, a more appropriate comparison would be the circulatory system, with its arteries and veins. And its heart, the pump through which all rumors flowed, was the cafeteria.

As a rule, he enjoyed the hum of conversations, among which his ears caught intriguing snatches of news—about hirings and firings, love affairs and broken hearts. Once in a while the drama expanded to include the doctors.

Until today, however, Lucky hadn't understood the embarrassment of landing in the middle of a scene that drew all eyes. It started when Keely announced, without preamble, "I lost my roommate. I've decided to move into your house!"

People peered toward them. The story of Karen's

home, its assorted occupants and the resulting pregnancies and marriages had already set many a tongue wagging.

Laird choked, although Lucky couldn't figure out on what. The psychologist hadn't stopped yammering long enough to eat anything. Instead, he'd plopped his butt into a chair at Lucky's table and begun citing his plans for throwing parties.

He'd also proclaimed that his huge TV screen would transform their outdated living room into game central. Not that Lucky would mind, but the guy apparently didn't consider it necessary to solicit *Karen's* opinion.

"Like hell you're moving in!" Laird finally blurted in a voice that rose to a squeal. "Whatever gave you that idea?"

"I cleared it with Zora." Keely indicated that redhaired person, who gazed warily from the hot food line before ducking out of sight.

Lucky nearly bellowed, "Get over here!" but more heads were swiveling. Not his doctor, mercifully. Through the glass doors, he spotted Dr. Rattigan out of earshot on the patio.

"It's a party house!" Laird, his usually pale face reddening with anger, didn't appear to care who heard him roar. "You're the last person in Safe Harbor anyone would invite to a party."

Silence fell save for the clink of tableware and glasses. The chatter of a man talking on a cell phone sounded abnormally loud, and then that too ceased.

"Let's skip the insults, shall we?" Lucky deliberately employed a soft tone in the hope the others would follow suit.

The effort fell flat. "Oh, really?" Keely boomed. "I

was invited to the baby shower, in case you forgot. As for you, Laird, you can take your grabby hands and go live in a brothel."

Lucky wouldn't show cowardice by retreating from the scene. But he could remove himself from the line of fire on the pretext of assisting the pregnant lady.

"Excuse me." Springing up, he narrowly restrained the temptation to break into a run.

Behind him, Laird snarled something about Keely being jealous because nobody made passes at her. Whatever the nurse responded, Lucky shut it out.

"Let me help with that," he told Zora, who had set down her tray as she paid for her lunch. He seized the tray without waiting for permission.

She stepped away from the register. "People are staring."

"Can you blame them?" Lucky halted as a tableful of volunteers arose, blocking their path. Grateful for the delay, he smiled encouragingly at an elderly lady, a gift shop regular who creaked to her feet at glacial speed. To Zora, he asked, "How'd you hook up with Keely?"

"She glommed on to me at Dr. Brennan's office," she explained.

"You had to see the doctor? You aren't having problems, are you?"

"Routine checkup."

"You sure?" He searched her face for signs of pain. She had a bad habit of toughing things out, but she looked well enough today.

What a sweet face, he thought, with a full mouth and a youthful sprinkling of freckles. Standing this close to Zora was having a weird effect on him. In light of their new pact, he wasn't sure how to respond to her. It had been easier when he could drop a comment about Andrew into any conversation and receive a predictably angry retort.

"Did you promise Keely she could move in?" That ought to stir a response.

"Yes, but I warned her Karen has the final say." Biting her lip, Zora peered toward Keely and Laird, who were continuing to insult each other. They'd lowered their voices a notch, but at this stage it only meant other diners leaned forward in their seats to hear them. One orderly went so far as to cup his hands around his ears. "She'd be a zillion percent better than Laird," Zora said.

"For once—twice, actually—we agree on something. Let's not make it a habit."

"Certainly not," Zora replied. "Life would get boring."

"I'm sure we'll find plenty to squabble about." Lucky dodged away as the elderly volunteer snapped her cane to the floor inches from his foot. "Hey!"

She ambled out, not hearing him. Another volunteer responded with a quiet, "Sorry."

"Excellent reaction time," Zora observed.

"Thanks."

They resumed their journey toward the table, where Laird and Keely stood with arms folded, as if whoever was victorious in their staring contest would win the privilege of moving into the house. Around them, conversations slowly resumed.

"Isn't Keely eating lunch?" Lucky murmured. "She didn't stop to pick up anything."

"Look on the bright side," Zora said. "They can't have a food fight."

"I'd enjoy a food fight," he teased.

"Of course you would."

"I didn't say I'd participate." He lowered her tray onto the table beside his. "Guys, how about easing off?"

"Not till we settle this," Keely said.

"We can't do that without…" He broke off at the approach of their landlady, who projected authority despite being no taller than Zora. Maybe it was this month's black hair or the distinctive long skirts she favored, but more likely it was the quelling expression she wore. "Hey, Karen," he ventured.

Her frosty gaze swept the four of them. "Have a seat, everyone, and stop creating a spectacle."

They obeyed. "Now, what is this about?" Raising a hand to stop a barrage of words, Karen said, "Starting with Keely."

As the nurse explained about her roommate departing on short notice, Lucky watched Zora tuck into her food and thought about her twin. How could there be a carbon copy of her anywhere in the world? Surely no one had the same fiery temperament, or the same gift for frustrating the hell out of him while appealing to his masculine instincts. And why was Zady seeking to work near her sister, when the two appeared to be estranged?

Still, twins were supposed to have a special bond, in contrast to Lucky and his older brother. He didn't even know where Matthew lived now or whether he was still serving in the navy, and he didn't care.

Best friends during their teens, they hadn't spoken in sixteen years. Their last fight, after their parents' deaths, had been too bitter for either of them to forgive. Lucky deeply regretted his mistakes, but that didn't give his brother the right to make vicious, unfair accusations and repeat them to other family members. As a result,

Lucky had distanced himself not only from Matthew but also from his aunts, uncles and cousins.

When Keely paused for breath, Laird jumped in. He insisted he had a prior claim and that the household needed him to liven things up.

"I wasn't aware we were dull," Karen snapped. "Frankly, after the behavior I just witnessed, I'd drop you both from consideration, but for financial reasons, I need someone to move in next weekend."

Laird lifted his chin. "Considering my position as staff psychologist, I outrank this woman."

Didn't the jerk realize he'd insulted Lucky, who was an RN on a par with Keely? And Karen herself held the middle-level post of financial counselor.

"This isn't a promotional position," she said. "No offense, Laird, but I think having a nurse across the hall from a pregnant woman would be the most sensible choice. However, I won't approve anyone without the consent of my other renters. Lucky? Zora?"

Nobody wished to become Laird's enemy. Nevertheless, Lucky tilted his head toward Keely, as did Zora. Turning, Karen pinpointed Rod. The anesthesiologist, who was sitting with his nephew and several other doctors, mouthed, "Kee-lee."

If Lucky imagined they'd fallen below everyone else's radar, a rustle of movement proved otherwise as people shifted to observe Rod, then moved their attention back to his table.

"I'm sorry," Karen told the psychologist. "The group agrees with my rationale."

Laird scrambled to his feet. "I hope you'll keep me in mind if there's another opening. Keely might not fit in as well as you assume."

"You're the one who doesn't fit in," the nurse sneered.

"You'll regret this." Noticing everyone's reaction to this threat, Laird added, "I mean, it wouldn't surprise me if they threw you out in a few months."

He stalked off, leaving his dirty dishes. Nostrils flaring, Keely watched him go before excusing herself to buy food.

"Alone at last," Lucky teased after Karen, too, departed.

Zora swallowed a mouthful of milk and wasted no time changing the subject. "Did you talk to Edmond?"

He sketched what he'd learned about Vince and Portia Adams. "My plan is to encourage her to donate eggs and him to hire a gestational surrogate."

"Splitting the difference? Excellent," Zora said. "I suspect you're right about Portia's maternal instincts. During Tiffany's last visit, she mentioned that her mom's developed a fascination with her friends' babies."

"Any suggestions how to nudge her further in that direction?"

"Talk to Rod," she advised.

First she'd recommended he consult Edmond, now Rod. "Why?"

"He used to be married to Portia. If anyone can comprehend how her mind works, it's him." Having polished off her entrée, Zora tackled her custard.

He should have thought of that, Lucky mused. But a marriage that had ended bitterly half a dozen years ago hardly qualified the anesthesiologist as an expert. "You're a mom, or soon will be. Put me into her perspective about this pregnancy business."

"She's a fashion plate who I'm sure injects stuff into her wrinkles and suctions her flab," Zora said. "It's partly ego but I also think she feels she has to compete for her husband's affection. How's she going to fend off gold diggers ten years younger when she has a big round pregnant body?"

"But donating eggs might be okay?"

"Better, although those hormone shots and the mood swings aren't fun," Zora said.

Lucky sighed. "Well, thanks for bouncing ideas around with me."

"Glad to do it." Abruptly, Zora set down her fork. "Something just hit me."

If it would help bring the Adamses together, he was eager to hear it. "Yes?"

"I—" She broke off as a ringtone sounded and she took out her phone. "This is Zora."

Lucky could happily have smashed the device for interrupting them. "Don't lose that thought!"

Frowning, Zora answered. "Yes? Now? Okay. I'll be right there." She clicked off. "It's radiology."

How frustrating. "Before you go, tell me what occurred to you."

"No time. We can discuss it tonight." Hands on the table, Zora hoisted herself upright. "Will you dispose of my dishes? I'd hate to be a slob like Laird."

"Of course," he said. "But—"

"It's a patient of Dr. Tartikoff's," she explained. "The tech went home sick, and he's waiting with her."

Nobody wished to cross the imperious head of the fertility program. "I understand."

"Thanks, Lucky," she said. "I can always count on you."

It was on the tip of his tongue to note that she ought to be able to rely on the father of her children, but he'd promised to lay off that subject. And Lucky found it rather gratifying that he and no one else was the person she counted on.

\* \* \*

Talking to Lucky was more fun now that he no longer poked at her sore spot, Zora reflected as she lumbered along the sidewalk to the medical office building. And even though she hadn't planned it, she'd rather enjoyed needling him by withholding information.

On the third floor, she entered Dr. T's medical suite and headed for the room set up for the ultrasound. Nurse Ned Norwalk, a surfer type with a deep tan, appeared around a corner. "You?" he demanded.

"Me, what?" Zora asked. Although she and Ned moved in different circles, she'd never had any problems with him.

"There wasn't any other tech available?" He obviously didn't expect an answer. "Never mind. Fair warning—Dr. T hasn't eaten lunch."

Great—he'd be crankier than ever. "I'll tiptoe around. Where's the patient's chart?"

"The doctor has it. The patient has a mass on her right ovary. You'll be doing a transvaginal ultrasound."

"Okay." Sonograms to examine ovarian cysts—fluid-filled pockets in or on the surface of an ovary—as well as other growths were commonplace. While most cysts vanished on their own, some caused pain, and there was the scary possibility that an ovarian growth could be cancerous. The best view of the ovaries was obtained by inserting a probe into the patient's vagina. "Is she pregnant?"

"No. But—you're sure there wasn't anyone else available?"

"If you doubt me, call radiology."

"Never mind."

Zora had often assisted Dr. T's patients. She didn't understand why Ned was making a big deal of this, but she didn't intend to question him and keep the great physician waiting.

Ned opened the door and retreated. Near the small ultrasound machine paced a scowling Dr. Owen Tartikoff. Even his russet hair seemed to be sizzling with impatience. "Finally," he growled.

"Sorry for the delay. The scheduled tech went home sick." Zora's gaze shifted to the dark-haired woman lying on the examining table, her lower half covered with a paper sheet.

When almond-shaped brown eyes met hers with a jolt, Zora struggled to catch her breath. The patient was Lin Lee Raditch, Andrew's third wife.

Although they'd never been introduced, she'd seen the woman with him around town, and judging by the other woman's reaction, Lin recognized Zora, as well. That explained Ned's attitude. Either the scheduler hadn't noticed that they shared a last name, or had no other options.

"Is there a problem?" The doctor's cross tone slapped at her. He didn't seem aware of their connection.

Zora darted a glance at Lin. The patient had the right to object to an inappropriate care provider. And for the sake of her own emotional state, Zora wasn't sure she ought to go through with this.

Lin's lips pressed tightly. Was she reluctant to offend the celebrated doctor? Then Zora noticed tears glittering in the patient's eyes. *She's frightened.*

In that instant, Lin transformed from the jezebel for whom Andrew had abandoned Zora into a scared woman who might face a terrifying diagnosis.

"This won't hurt," she assured the patient, and went to work.

## *Chapter 6*

"These appear to be fluid-filled cysts," Dr. Tartikoff told the patient as Zora finished her scan. "However, before recommending a treatment plan, I'll have the radiologist review the images."

"It isn't cancer?" Lin's body had gone nearly rigid, although Zora had encouraged her to relax during the procedure.

"I doubt it." The obstetrician continued studying the screen. "If these were solid, or partially solid, I'd be more concerned."

The patient swallowed, evidently still worried. "Will you have to remove my ovaries?"

"It may be possible to perform a cystectomy, excising only the largest cyst." Dr. T patted Lin's shoulder reassuringly. "Or we might remove one ovary, leaving the other in place."

"I can still have children?" Lin's slightly accented voice trembled.

"Yes, but first let's deal with the discomfort you've been suffering."

"Thank you, Doctor." She regarded him gratefully.

How ironic, Zora thought, that Andrew's wife was concerned about being able to bear his children, while Zora herself stood there with his babies thumping inside her. Nevertheless, her heart went out to the anxious young woman.

Did life have to be so complicated? It would be easier if Zora could simply blame Andrew's faithlessness on his new wife. Instead, she related to Lin's pain. Carrying twins was hard, but being unable to bear children would be worse.

"The radiologist's report should reach me within a few days. I'll review it immediately," Dr. T advised. "Please set up an appointment for next week. Your husband should accompany you."

Lin's smile vanished. "He travels and is very busy."

"You're his wife. There's nothing more important than your health." In his intensity, Zora heard the conviction of a man devoted to his wife and children. "Would you like me to explain the situation to him?"

"No, no, Doctor, that isn't necessary." Lin sounded anxious.

"You're sure?"

When she again declined, Dr. T excused himself and left.

"I'll be out of here in a minute so you can dress," Zora said. She shifted the equipment cart away from the examining table.

Lin touched her arm. "Thank you for being gentle."

Astonished, Zora wondered what the woman had expected. "You're welcome."

"I am wondering…" She indicated Zora's expanded midsection.

Was she asking about the father? Zora pretended not to pick up the hint. "Twins," she said. "Due in late November."

"You are fortunate to be fertile." The patient sat up. "I am desperate for children to bind my husband to me and prove my family is wrong."

"Wrong about what?" Zora asked.

"They believe I married a man who will treat me badly." She sniffled. "And they're angry that I moved to another country after they sacrificed to send me to college. My mother will not talk to me on the phone."

On the verge of inquiring why Lin was sharing this with her of all people, Zora realized how isolated the woman was. "That must be difficult." She handed over a tissue.

Lin wiped her eyes. "Pardon me, but also, I wonder why you are pregnant when you did not want children."

A weird sense of déjà vu swept over Zora. During her marriage, Andrew had claimed his first wife had refused to have kids. Only later had she learned that the opposite was true: Stacy had longed for children but delayed pregnancy at Andrew's request.

Same lies, same manipulations. Pain knifed inside Zora. *Lucky's right. I must be the most gullible person on earth.*

"What is wrong?" Gathering the paper covering her, Lin eased off the table. "The babies are hurting you?"

This show of compassion undid her. Suddenly Zora couldn't hold her secret inside for another instant.

"Andrew lied to you. These are his children, except he doesn't know that yet."

Lin stood frozen with her bare feet on the linoleum. "That is impossible. He had a vasectomy. You insisted on it."

"No, I didn't. When…?" Zora gave a start at a tap on the door.

Ned Norwalk entered, holding a sheet of paper. "How's everything in here?" The nurse halted at the sight of them obviously engaged in a discussion. "Are you okay, Mrs. Raditch?"

"I'm fine," both women said.

"The current Mrs. Raditch."

They glared at him.

He blinked, registering the unexpected collusion, and, to his credit, decided to respect their privacy. "I'll be at the nurses' station if anyone wants me."

After Ned beat a strategic retreat, Zora refocused on her companion. "If Andrew had a vasectomy, it wasn't at my request. And these *are* his children."

"You are wrong," Lin insisted. "He showed me the scar."

Zora preferred not to think about the location of that scar or the intimate circumstances under which he'd displayed it. "When was that?"

The other woman, a few inches shorter than her, considered briefly before saying, "Eight months ago, while we were engaged. Before you became pregnant, if you are in the seventh month."

Could he have faked the scar? Then a better explanation occurred to Zora.

"After a vasectomy, a man's sperm count doesn't immediately drop to zero. It can take a month or more before the sperm is completely gone." She absorbed a lot of medical information in her work. "We were still married—barely. He must have been fertile, because I haven't slept with anyone else."

Lin steadied herself on the edge of the examining table. "These babies, they really are his?"

"I'm afraid so. It all makes more sense now. No wonder he didn't insist on contraception—he'd had a vasectomy." Zora had assumed that, at some level, Andrew had wished to father a baby with her. Instead, he'd believed he was safe.

Lin hugged herself and shivered. "You will take away my husband."

That was precisely what Zora had fantasized. Now, witnessing the other woman's distress, she faced the fact that Andrew had coldheartedly plucked Lin from her family and country, then lied to her and manipulated her. He'd also played on Zora's love for him, using and discarding her yet again. Why? For ego's sake?

The man had no heart and could never be trusted. Zora was truly alone in this pregnancy. Except for Lucky. And her other friends, of course.

To her astonishment, the primary emotion pumping through her was relief. She didn't have to pretend any more. She could tell the truth, to herself most of all.

"I don't want him back," Zora said.

The dark-haired woman studied her in confusion. "But you carry his babies."

*The man isn't capable of loving anyone except himself.* A burden lifted from her shoulders, filling her with unaccustomed lightness despite the weight in her womb. "You can keep him with my blessing."

A couple of quick steps and Lin flung her arms

around Zora. "You are my sister in spirit. I shall try to be strong like you."

Zora hesitated only a second before returning the hug. When she and Andrew broke up, she'd been utterly friendless. That experience intensified her empathy with this woman whose world was collapsing. "What will you do?"

Lin breathed deeply before replying, "I will think hard."

"If you need a divorce attorney, I recommend Edmond Everhart," Zora said. "He's a consultant on staff at the hospital."

"That is good advice," Lin said.

"Best of luck."

As Zora exited, she ignored a questioning look from Ned in the hall. Struggling to sort through what she'd learned, she wished she didn't have to endure Lucky's comments when he heard about this encounter.

And yet, she felt liberated. "Sorry, babies," Zora whispered. "We're all better off without your dad."

Then fear quivered through her. How could she raise these kids without a father? Her own might have been flawed, but she'd always sensed that he loved her and Zady.

Unlike her dad, Andrew lacked the capacity to care about others. Zora had to accept that and move on, no matter how badly it hurt.

She hoped she wouldn't have to put up with any I-told-you-so taunts tonight from Lucky, who would no doubt hear about this entire scene via the gossip mill. With her heart aching and her mood unsettled, she was in no mood to tolerate his sniping.

With everyone eager to chat about Keely's pending arrival, Lucky and his three housemates gathered at the dining room table earlier than usual on Monday night. While they ate, they relived the scene in the cafeteria and speculated about Laird's not-so-veiled threat.

Would he try to intimidate Keely to keep her from joining them? Did he honestly believe they'd accept him if he did?

Karen related that Keely had paid a deposit and arranged to move in Saturday afternoon. Her only question had been whether the nearness to the estuary caused illness among the residents. Karen had assured her that, despite the smell, they all stayed remarkably healthy.

Questions and comments flew, but the usually talkative Zora didn't join in, Lucky noted. Instead, she downed her soup and salad while avoiding his gaze. Was she annoyed at him?

Perhaps she'd found out about her twin applying for a job. After reviewing the remaining résumés, he'd confirmed that Zady's qualifications merited a spot among the top half dozen contenders and had scheduled her for an interview next week, when the new urologist would be visiting. But if that was the problem, why wasn't Zora interrogating him?

During a lull in the conversation, she slanted a glare at him. He'd done nothing to deserve that, Lucky was almost certain. "What?" he demanded.

"What do you mean, what?"

"I mean, why are you scowling at me? I haven't done anything." *Recently.*

"You will," she muttered.

"Suit yourself." Lucky let the subject drop. If he'd offended Zora, it was her responsibility to be frank about it.

Rod and Karen finished eating and carried their

dishes into the kitchen. As Zora started to rise, Lucky recalled her hasty departure from lunch and the idea she'd mentioned. "Hold on a sec."

She grimaced. "We might as well get this over with."

"Get what over with?"

Still not meeting his gaze, she said, "I refuse to make it easier for you."

He was growing more confused by the minute. She'd been friendly at lunch, and Lucky had been too busy during the afternoon to ruffle anyone's feathers. To compensate for his absence at the convention, Dr. Rattigan had squeezed in so many patients that Lucky had skipped his coffee break and stayed at the office late.

"Is this about your—" He nearly said *sister*, but caught himself. Besides, there was another thing he'd been waiting to discuss. "Idea about the Adamses?" he finished.

"What idea about the Adamses?"

"In the cafeteria, you said something hit you, and then you took off to see a patient," Lucky reminded her.

"Did I?" Zora rested her chin in her palm. Pregnancy had darkened her cute freckles and rounded her cheeks. Her hair had thickened and taken on a shine, as well.

"Please don't tell me you forgot the idea."

She frowned so hard that Lucky feared she'd get a headache. Then she brightened. "I remember!"

"Shoot."

"Portia has mixed feelings about pregnancy because she fears it will turn Vince away from her, but she might change her mind if she realizes it could save her marriage," Zora said.

"Why is she so afraid of losing him?" Lucky countered. "In a divorce, she could take her husband to the cleaners."

"There's always the possibility that she loves the guy. Besides, from what I've read, Vince's previous two wives didn't fare very well," she replied.

Lucky recalled news reports about the man's insistence on prenuptial agreements. Nevertheless, the women had been left financially comfortable by ordinary standards. "A few million apiece might not be much compared to his billions, but it ain't too shabby."

"It's not only the money." Rod joined the conversation from the kitchen entrance. "Portia loves having a ringside seat at New York Fashion Week, being invited to A-list parties and hobnobbing with celebrities. A couple of million dollars doesn't do that. Being married to Vince Adams does."

Lucky supposed Rod knew her better than any of them. "Wouldn't having a baby interfere with all that partying?"

"Not when you can afford live-in nannies," he growled.

"You can be a devoted mom and still hire a nanny," Zora said. "Don't forget, she has lots of free time during the day, since she doesn't work."

"Portia will do whatever she believes is in her best interest, and to hell with anyone else," Rod snarled, and ducked out of sight.

While Lucky had a less jaundiced view of Mrs. Adams than Rod, he did agree that she'd fight to save her marriage. "Interesting point," he told Zora. "It's worth bearing in mind."

Silence descended, aside from random noises in the

kitchen. Zora poked at the remaining bits of lettuce on her salad plate. "Stop torturing me."

He might as well take the bull by the horns, Lucky decided. "Is this about your sister?"

"My sister?" Her blank expression indicated he'd missed the mark.

He had to cover his mistake, fast. "I heard you have a twin sister."

"From who?"

He couldn't cite the job application and he'd rather avoid implicating Edmond, who'd merely confirmed what Lucky had already stumbled across. "Informed sources."

"She's none of your business," Zora snapped. "We aren't in touch. Stop changing the subject."

Rod stuck his head through the door again. "Oh, seriously, Lucky, quit acting coy. Everyone's dying to find out what happened between the two Mrs. Raditches."

*That* was what had gone down today? And he hadn't heard a word.

Lucky threw up his hands. "I skip my coffee break for one afternoon and miss the gossip of the century. You went mano a mano with the new Mrs. Raditch?"

"She's a patient. I can't discuss..." To his dismay, Zora's face crumpled, and tears rolled down her cheeks.

Lucky scooted over and put his arms around her, enjoying the warmth of her pregnancy-enhanced body. "You discovered she's no more a demon than you are, and Andrew's an even bigger rat than you realized. Am I close?"

"I feel bad for her." Zora scrubbed her cheek with the back of her hand. "Her family rejected her when she married him. She's alone in a foreign country. And he lied about me, like he lied about Stacy. As if we're interchangeable."

To Lucky, there was nothing interchangeable about Zora and any other woman on the planet, including her twin. That was irrelevant, however. "You're crying for her sake?"

"And because what I learned means he'll never love these babies. Before today, I believed that deep down, he wanted them." Her gray eyes darkened with sorrow. "Ever since I've been steeling myself for you to say, *I told you so*. Go ahead and get it over with."

Cradling her against him, Lucky said, "Okay. I told you so."

A painful whack in the ankle sent him jolting backward, nearly overturning his chair. "Ow! How'd you do that from this angle?" Releasing her, he rubbed the spot where she'd kicked him.

"Public opinion agrees that you deserved it," noted Rod, who'd resumed snooping from the doorway.

"Beat it," Zora ordered him.

"Me?" Rod feigned innocence.

"This is between me and this pain in the neck," she retorted.

"Pain in the ankle," Lucky corrected.

From behind Rod, a feminine hand gripped his shirt collar and tugged him out of sight. Lucky wafted a mental thanks in Karen's direction.

"If my shin is black-and-blue tomorrow, I'll sue for assault." He moved to a chair at a safer distance.

"Felled by a pregnant midget?" Zora wisecracked. "What a wimp."

Footsteps moved through the den and around to the

front. The stairs creaked as their housemates ascended, leaving them in privacy.

Once Lucky heard Karen's door close upstairs, he felt safe to ask, "What's your next move?"

Zora stretched her legs under the table. "I talked to Edmond. He says Andrew has to pay half of the uninsured costs for my pregnancy and half the child-care expenses."

"You'll let the attorney deal with him?" That seemed wise.

Zora nodded. "I'm still not sure how I'd react to Andrew in the flesh."

"More importantly, how would he react to *you*?" Lucky's hands formed fists at the idea of the man bullying Zora.

"I hate being weak." She dabbed her eyes with her napkin.

"There's nothing weak about using good judgment," he said. "You don't have to prove how tough you are."

"That's not what I mean." She indicated her enlarged abdomen. "When I'm alone with Andrew, he slips past my defenses. Here's the living proof."

"You can seize control if you're determined." Surely she could resist the man after everything he'd put her through. "Zora, you're strength personified with everyone else."

"Am I?" She gazed into space. "My dad used to swing between being a jerk and being the most loving father in the world. No matter how hard I resolved to stay angry, I couldn't."

"Did he drink?" In Lucky's observation, alcoholism was often associated with that sort of behavior.

"Yes, sometimes." Zora inhaled deeply. "I used to

long for a family I could rely on, where people were actually happy. That's still my dream, I guess."

It was Lucky's, too, he reflected with a lump in his throat. Money had been tight for his family when he'd been young, and his parents had struggled to keep their store profitable. There'd always been love, but there'd been stress and long work hours, too.

While nothing could excuse the way Lucky had let them down, the pressure to help support the family had been difficult for him to handle as an immature teen. Before he risked establishing a family of his own, he'd make sure their finances were on a secure footing and find a wife who shared his values. Those included careful planning, postponing having kids and communicating honestly.

"What happened to your dad?" Lucky knew Zora's mom was a widow, but had never heard any details.

"When I was twenty-two, they had a big fight and he moved out." She paused, and then the words spilled out. "Mom claimed he'd cheated on her, which to me was such a betrayal of the whole family that I refused to speak to him. A few months later, he dropped dead of a heart attack. We never said goodbye."

"I'm sorry." What a burden of guilt that must place on her. "It wasn't your fault."

"If you love somebody, shouldn't you keep trying to rescue the relationship?"

"But past a certain point, you're only enabling him." Lucky eased farther away in case she tried kicking him again.

Instead, Zora lurched to her feet. "Well, I'm done enabling Andrew. Edmond can handle him from now on."

"I agree in principle." Reaching over, Lucky collected her dishes and piled them with his. "You can't avoid him forever, though."

"I can try." A pounding on the front door sent Zora's hand flying to her throat. "Oh, my gosh, you don't suppose that's him, do you?"

The thuds grew louder. "Stay there. I'll get it." After depositing the dishes in the kitchen, Lucky went to answer.

On the porch, hand raised for renewed hammering, stood a man of about thirty, a tailored suit jacket failing to disguise his pudgy gut. Blond hair, blue eyes, sneering expression. "Andrew Raditch?" Lucky guessed.

"Where is she?" The man stomped in. Had Lucky not dodged him, they'd have collided. "I insist on talking to my wife."

"Which wife would that be?" Finally, here was the man who'd created endless trouble—and, Lucky conceded, a measure of entertainment—over the past few months. Andrew was shorter than he'd imagined, and not nearly handsome enough to explain his appeal to women.

"Don't mess with me, mister." Feet planted in the entry, Andrew bellowed, "Zora, where the hell are you?"

How could this rude oaf be the son of Betsy Raditch? But then, he had alcohol on his breath.

From around the corner of the staircase, Zora regarded her ex-husband coolly. "What's your problem, Andrew?"

"What did you say to Lin?" the man demanded. "She admitted to my face that she talked to you."

As if that were a crime, Lucky thought.

"So?" Still half in the living room as if prepared to dodge away, Zora watched him guardedly.

"She packed a bag and walked out on me," Andrew said. "She was crying. Did you enjoy hurting her?"

"I'm not the one who hurt her." Zora remained admirably calm, in Lucky's opinion.

"You must have filled her head with lies!" Andrew smacked his hand against the wall.

"You accuse *me* of lying?" Zora stood her ground. "You should study the definition of truth. It seems to be an alien concept to you."

"Cut the crap." Andrew prowled toward her. "You call Lin right now and apologize."

"For what?"

"For whatever you…" As Zora stepped into full view, big belly and all, Andrew's jaw worked without producing another sound.

Lucky enjoyed the man's shock. Finally, Andrew had discovered he was going to be a father.

# Chapter 7

To Zora, Andrew seemed different tonight. Was it the extra height of the ceiling that dwarfed him or the contrast between him and Lucky? Andrew's muscles from playing high school football were running to fat—in contrast to Lucky's well-toned build—and his once-thick blond hair had begun receding at the temples.

As for his blustering manner, usually it yielded to calculated charm as soon as he saw that he'd intimidated her. Tonight, though, with Lucky on hand and the memory of the afternoon's anguished scene still raw, she remained in control of her emotions. No intimidation, and hence no charm to obscure his true reaction.

For a revealing moment, she watched Andrew's expression shift from disbelief to anger to disdain as he weighed his response to her pregnancy. Before today, while Zora had recognized the self-serving motives that rippled below the man's slick surface, she'd soon been sucked under by his charisma. Tonight, the curl of his lip and the flare of his nostrils might have belonged to a stranger. A stranger she disliked.

"Now I understand what you dropped on Lin." With a wave of his arm, he indicated—and dismissed—her pregnancy. "You persuaded her it was mine, didn't you? I can't imagine how you fooled her. She knows I had a vasectomy."

Behind him, Zora caught Lucky's startled blink. Funny how keenly she registered her housemate's responses, and how grateful she was for his protective stance.

"Your doctor did warn you that a vasectomy doesn't instantly render you sterile, I presume," she said.

"It takes a few weeks," her ex responded confidently. "I gave it a month."

He'd calculated the timing, or so he believed. "I have two words for you," Zora told Andrew. "Paternity test."

"You went out and slept with someone else," he sneered. "No doubt right after I signed the divorce papers."

"Did your doctor confirm that your sperm count had dropped to zero?" Lucky asked. In response to Andrew's who-the-hell-are-you? scowl, he added, "I work in a urologist's office. It takes ten to twenty ejaculations to completely clear the sperm."

Andrew paled. "The baby *can't* be mine."

"Babies, plural," Zora corrected.

"Beg pardon?"

"I'm carrying twins," she said. "And in California, a paternity test isn't necessary for you to owe child support. According to my attorney, if the parents are married, by law the husband is automatically the father. And we *were* still married that night."

At the memory, pain threatened her detachment. She'd dropped by Andrew's apartment to urge him to sign the divorce papers after weeks of him playing games. Instead, he'd sworn that he regretted cheating on her, declared that she was his true love and drawn her into his bed. A few nights later, while she nursed the hope that he planned to cast off his fiancée and stay with her, he'd dropped the signed divorce papers on her porch and fled.

"You waited, what, seven months to inform me?" His other tactics having failed, Andrew assumed the mantle of outrage. "Any man would doubt these children are his. I refuse to pay for what isn't mine."

"If you insist, I'll arrange for a test." Might as well seal the deal.

That didn't appear to be the answer he'd expected. "You'd risk your babies' safety by sticking a needle in there?"

"You're out-of-date, man," Lucky announced. "It doesn't take an invasive test to establish paternity anymore. They can extract the baby's DNA from the mother's blood with ninety-nine-point-nine percent accuracy."

Andrew grimaced. "Fine. Whatever."

Zora seized on his apparent consent. "The test's expensive and insurance won't cover it. Since you're insisting on it, you can pay."

He shifted on the balls of his feet. "Half."

She supposed arguing the point would be futile. Instead, she added, "Okay, but legally you also owe half of my other maternity-related expenses." Oh, drat, her voice was trembling. Did the man feel absolutely nothing after learning that he'd fathered two children-to-be? He hadn't asked their genders, or Zora's due date, or whether she'd selected names.

Names. She'd planned to let him choose those in the absurd belief that doing so would strengthen his connection to the twins. After tonight, though, Zora resolved that he'd have nothing to do with selecting the names if she could help it.

"Let's run that test before you start counting my money," Andrew snarled. He turned abruptly, side-stepped Lucky and stalked out of the house.

Zora struggled to catch her breath. Since learning of her pregnancy, she'd imagined this scene repeatedly, in a thousand variations. Anger and awe, apology and acceptance—she'd credited Andrew with those feelings. Well, he'd shown the anger. Aside from that, however, the only other thing he'd displayed was utter indifference to his own kids.

"High five or knuckle bump?" Grinning, Lucky raised his hand for her response.

She burst into sobs.

"What's wrong?" The man looked flummoxed. "Zora, you were magnificent. You stood up to every trick he threw at you. Didn't you hear me silently cheering you?"

She struggled for control. "How could I hear something silent?"

"It was written all over my face." His dark eyes glowed. "Tonight, I witnessed a miraculous transformation. Right here in our living room, you became a kick-ass superhero."

His praise felt wonderful. It also filled her with wariness, because she didn't deserve it. "I forced him to agree to a blood test, that's all."

"And hit him up for half your expenses."

"He hasn't paid yet."

"Zora!" Lucky gripped her gently under her arms. "I'd swing you around to celebrate, only I doubt the twins would appreciate it."

"You're right." The duo were squirming. At this stage, she'd read, their auditory functions had developed enough for them to hear the argument. How sad that on their first exposure to their father's voice, it had been filled with rage.

Already, the babies might be forming lifelong impressions of masculine and feminine behavior. She hoped that Lucky's gentler tones offset Andrew's harshness. "He didn't ask a single question about his children. Maybe it hasn't sunk in yet."

"And maybe he's a self-centered prick. If I accidentally fathered babies, I'd be determined to give them the best," Lucky assured her.

"You'd take care of their mother, wouldn't you? You'd never let her down." Zora caught her breath, unsure why his answer mattered so much.

"I certainly wouldn't whine and try to weasel out of my obligations," Lucky responded. "But I'm doing everything in my power to avoid running that kind of risk. I won't be ready for a family till I pay off my education loans and save a down payment for a house. My kids deserve a happy childhood with two parents who're mature enough to provide them with stability."

Zora's spirits plummeted. During the confrontation with Andrew, she'd drawn strength from Lucky's nearness, from having a man care about her without making demands. Well, of course he didn't make demands, because he didn't want anything from her, as he'd just indicated. He wanted the perfect wife, the perfect family, and she was far from perfect.

*Why can't he love me, messy life and all?*

What was wrong with her? She didn't love Lucky. Or if she did, it was the casual, friendship kind of love. He wasn't her type. Too rough around the edges and too judgmental. Still, the way he'd stood by her these past months had been more than kind. It had been... fatherly. And maybe more.

He was still holding her. Still gazing at her fondly. "I wish my children had a father like you," Zora blurted.

Lucky stared down at her for a moment. Then he released her. "I appreciate the compliment, but these are Andrew's kids."

She was on the verge of pointing out the obvious, that her ex-husband didn't want them, when it struck her what Lucky really meant—that he couldn't or wouldn't be their father, either.

The discovery chilled Zora. How naive she'd been, to believe even for an instant that Lucky could fill the void in her heart. How utterly unrealistic. *Typical of me, I guess.*

"I'd better lie down," she said.

"I didn't mean to upset you," he responded. "I only meant..."

Zora waved away the explanation. "Don't bother. I'm a total idiot when it comes to relationships."

"Did I miss something?" Lucky asked.

How adorably clueless he was. "I'm tired. It's been a long day."

"It's only eight thirty."

Zora struggled to ignore his worried gaze. "That's late, for a pregnant woman." A pregnant woman whose last lingering illusions had been shattered.

Until tonight, her bond to Andrew—imaginary though it had been—had shielded her from any other man like a brick wall. Now, vulnerable and hurt, she seemed to be stumbling over a bunch of loose bricks. "Good night."

"If you're sure."

"I am." Zora hurried away, although she wasn't sure about anything. Okay, about the no-more-Andrew part, yes. But as for Lucky, somewhere along the line, love had mushroomed in the dark. What defense did she have against her best friend?

In her bedroom, she dropped onto the floral bedspread, grabbed a dainty pink pillow and began punching the stuffing out of it.


Too bad standing up to her loathsome ex-husband had exhausted Zora when she ought to be celebrating, Lucky thought. And how typical that Andrew hadn't bothered to consider how his actions might affect a woman coping with a multiple pregnancy.

What a joy to witness Zora bravely tackling that creep. How frustrating it had been these past months, watching such a smart, feisty woman repeatedly yielding to foolish delusions.

Yet, unfortunately, she might still forgive the jerk. If Lucky had learned anything about Zora, it was that her emotions regarding her ex-husband seesawed like crazy. Once the babies were born, if Andrew showed any paternal instincts at all, her resistance would probably crumble.

That remark about wishing her kids had a dad like Lucky…for a split second, he'd wished the same thing. Then he'd faced reality. To her, the twins would always belong to Andrew.

Lucky sighed and clicked on the lamp in his bedroom, which was spacious enough for his video games and exercise equipment. During the day, when he opened the curtains, the sliding glass doors revealed a splendid view of the gray-and-green wetlands with their ever-changing tableau of wildlife. Tonight, by contrast, the lamp—on a ceramic base enlivened by a turquoise-and-black geometric pattern—bathed the room in a cozy radiance.

When he'd moved in here, Lucky had purchased several Hispanic-inspired accents, including the rainbow-striped serape draped across a chair as well as a ceramic Aztec calendar plaque that hung on the wall, its buff background covered with red-and-black designs. Although his family was three generations removed from its Mexican-Indian roots, Lucky valued his connection to ancient traditions. He'd worked hard to master Spanish both because of his heritage and to assist patients.

Overhead, the floor creaked, a reminder that Karen and Rod were awake. Lucky tried not to speculate about what they might be doing in Karen's suite. Whatever it was, he appreciated that they'd remained out of sight during the verbal fireworks with Andrew.

If only Zora had more energy, Lucky would have enjoyed sharing a late snack with her, teasing her across the table. It had been fun earlier tonight, figuring out how to persuade Vince to stay involved with Safe Harbor.

How sharp of Zora to note that Portia would do whatever was necessary to preserve her marriage. Especially since, in Lucky's observation, the woman's longing for a baby might tip the scales in favor of undergoing fertility treatments.

Whatever happened at Saturday's appointment, his involvement, if any, had to be discreet. Unhappily, he acknowledged that all this head scratching and cogitating might be for naught. It was possible that, upon receiving Cole's bad news, Vince would simply haul his wife out of there and bid Safe Harbor adios.

It would help to have a second set of eyes and ears. Zora had proven perceptive, and if she were around…

Why not? In addition to working weekdays, Zora filled in occasional evenings and weekends. Cole hadn't scheduled a full roster of patients for Saturday morning. Lucky could identify a few men due for ultrasounds who might be glad to move up their appointments. He'd request that Zora be assigned.

Satisfied with that plan, he changed into exercise clothes and switched on his elliptical machine.

While growing up, Zora had never had a close girl-friend. Her twin, who should have been her dearest pal, had become a rival because their mother had constantly pitted them against each other with criticism and shifting favoritism. By high school, Zora had transferred that competition to other girls as well, a view reinforced by Andrew's flirtations while they were dating.

Then she'd started working at Safe Harbor and, during the lowest period of her life, met Anya. She'd never understood why bubbly, popular Anya had defied the staff's general hostility to Zora and invited her to share an apartment, but she'd been deeply appreciative.

Sharing confidences and movie nights with a friend had been a revelation. A year later, after their rent increased and they moved into Karen's house, they'd continued to be best friends. Zora had been the first to learn that Anya was carrying Jack's baby, and it had been Anya who accompanied Zora to buy a pregnancy kit and discover her own impending motherhood.

Anya's marriage a few months ago, followed by the birth of her daughter, meant that Jack and little Rachel came first. Lonely again, Zora had drifted into Lucky's company, despite his irritating attempts to run her life. But now that her feelings toward him had changed, being around him was dangerous.

Zora needed a friend. And although Keely was far from the warm, cuddly type, she had a kind side. Late Tuesday afternoon, when Zora stopped into Dr. Brennan's office to inquire about paternity testing, the nurse immediately arranged for the doctor to order the lab test. She requested Andrew's email address and promised to send him the information, as well.

"The results take eight working days after you both provide blood." The older woman refastened the pink barrette in her hair. "Say, are you driving home with Karen today? I saw you arrive together. In case she has to stay late, I'd be glad to take you."

A hint of anxiety in the nurse's expression, as if the response really mattered, touched Zora. Not only did she need a friend, but Keely did, too. Also, Karen had texted that she'd be delayed about an hour and hoped Zora didn't mind waiting. The alternative—calling on Lucky—went against Zora's resolve to steer clear of him.

Dr. Brennan's warning about safety had resonated

with her on the drive home yesterday, when she'd found that she could no longer reach the pedals without her baby bulge pressing against the steering wheel.

Thank goodness her housemates had volunteered to pick up the slack, and now Keely was joining in. "Actually, I *could* use a ride, if it's not too much trouble."

The lines in Keely's face softened. "Let's do it!" They arranged to meet in the medical building lobby in fifteen minutes, after Keely got off work. Zora had finished her shift an hour earlier.

At the lab, she had blood drawn. Thank goodness for the newer technique, which extracted fetal DNA from her blood plasma and compared it to the father's DNA. All the same, she'd be willing to bet that Andrew would complain about it. Too bad he didn't have to endure the doctor's poking, the morning sickness, the sleepless nights and the labor pains.

As she rose to leave with a small bandage on her arm, Zora supposed that women from the dawn of time had resented men for escaping the painful consequences of pregnancy. She wouldn't resent Lucky, who took care of her, though. But as he'd pointed out, these weren't his babies.

Recalling that she ought to alert Karen to the change in plans, Zora sent the other woman a text. When she reached the meeting place, Keely was already there, pacing. "Am I late?" Zora asked.

"No. I wasn't sure you'd be here."

"Why not?" Stupid question. Keely's low self-esteem spoke for itself. "I mean, you're doing me a favor. Of course I'm here."

"I'm parked in the main garage," the nurse said. "Is that too far? I could pull around."

"The exercise is good for me. And it's not far." As they set out at a slow pace, Zora asked, "Are you ready for the move this weekend? Did your landlord hassle you about the short notice?"

"Not after I explained the circumstances with my roommate." Keely brushed a speck of dust off her navy uniform. "And told him it was my birthday."

"It's your birthday?" Zora wondered about her new friend's age. It seemed rude to ask, though.

"Last Sunday."

"You should have mentioned it earlier! We'd have celebrated."

"Why?" Keely's eyebrows drew into a dark, straight line. "Turning fifty isn't anything to cheer about."

Well, she'd answered *that* question. "Every birthday is precious," Zora said as they passed a flower bed crowded with red, white and purple petunias. "Considering the alternative."

"What alternative?"

"Dying young."

Keely snorted, which appeared to be her manner of laughing. "Never thought of that." Halting at the garage's elevator, she pressed the button. "I can't afford to get old and sick, without a family to lean on." She punched the button again, although it was already lit.

"Fifty isn't old," Zora ventured.

"My mom was fifty when she had to go on disability." Keely's forehead creased. "I moved in with her after Dad died. She was forever consulting one doctor or another. Aches and pains, high blood pressure, swollen ankles. They ordered her to exercise and quit drinking. She insisted the booze was medicinal and that it hurt to move around."

"To move around at all?" Zora asked. "What did she do, spend the whole day on the couch?"

"Pretty much. I did the shopping and cleaning, while working full-time."

No wonder the nurse had a grumpy attitude. "Is she living?"

A shudder ran through Keely. "I'd rather not talk about it."

"I didn't mean to pry."

The elevator arrived and they rode up in silence. Had she offended Keely? Zora wondered. The woman had a reputation for being touchy.

At last the nurse spoke again. "I take it back. It's better for you to hear the truth."

"About what?"

They exited onto the third level. "About what happened to my mom," Keely answered. "I got arrested and lost my last job because of it."

That sounded shocking. Zora struggled to contain her reaction as they strolled between rows of vehicles. Behind them, an SUV pulled out cautiously. Ahead, a woman beeped open her sedan. Although there was a faint smell of exhaust, the garage's open-air design dissipated the fumes.

"What happened?" Quickly, Zora added, "Obviously, the police made a mistake." *Or did we agree to share our house with an ax murderer?*

"One morning Mom claimed she sensed a heart attack coming on." Keely's voice echoed off the hard surfaces around them. "She was constantly saying such things and complaining to the neighbors about how I neglected her. I'd missed too much work already, running Mom to doctors for no reason. I told her to call nine-one-one if her symptoms worsened."

"Oh, dear." Having grown up with a mother who insisted on being the center of attention at any cost, Zora empathized.

Keely's eyes glittered with tears. "After work, I found her stone cold in her favorite chair. A neighbor told the police I'd been abusing her."

"You must have been devastated." If Zora had ignored her mother's complaints and then she'd ended up passing away, she'd be overwhelmed by guilt.

"The clinic fired me as soon as they heard I'd been arrested." Keely paused at a bend in the row. "There I was, out on bail, handling my mother's funeral arrangements and terrified of being sent to prison."

"That's horrible." Zora's heart went out to the woman. "What did you do?"

The nurse sucked in a long breath before continuing. "Mom's doctors explained to the investigators that I was always bringing her in for one symptom or another. The district attorney decided not to prosecute."

"What about your job? Surely they offered to hire you back."

"I wouldn't work for those doctors again. They were cruel and unfair." Lifting her chin, Keely resumed walking. "I got a job at Safe Harbor. It was a community hospital in those days, before the remodeling. If the top brass now had any idea I'd been arrested for elder abuse, I doubt they'd put up with me."

"But the DA cleared you," Zora responded.

"Dr. Tartikoff hates me. If it weren't for Dr. Brennan..." Keely broke off. "Oh, no!"

She was staring at a boxy brown sedan with bumper stickers that read, Ask Your Doctor—Not Your TV Commercial, Cancer Cures Smoking, and Get Off Your Phone and Drive. The car also sported four flat tires.

"That's yours?"

Keely nodded grimly.

Four flat tires couldn't be a coincidence, Zora thought. "This is vandalism. We should call the police."

Keely shifted for a closer inspection. "They aren't slashed." Her jaw tightened. "Somebody let the air out. It's a nasty prank kids used to do to me in high school."

Keely had been bullied as a teenager, and someone was bullying her again. That aroused Zora's fury, along with her sympathy. "We should at least tell security."

"I'll call the auto club. They'll handle it." Keely swung toward her. "Please don't hold it against me that you have to wait."

"I wouldn't hold it against *you*!" Zora protested. "You're the victim here."

"I appreciate that."

Near the curve where they'd stood talking a moment ago, a motor started and a blue hybrid with a bike rack on top pulled out. It occurred to Zora that the perpetrator of this so-called prank might have lingered to observe—and enjoy—the consequences. "Do you recognize that car?"

"Afraid not."

In the dim light, Zora could see only enough of the driver to be fairly sure it was a man. Then, as the car drove off, she noticed that Keely wasn't the only staff member to display bumper stickers.

The one on the hybrid read, Psychologists Do It on the Couch.

# Chapter 8

"Thanks for calling me," Lucky told Keely after parking his car across from hers in the garage. She'd phoned to alert him to what had happened and asked if he could drive Zora home.

Reclining in Keely's rear seat with the door open, Zora eyed him askance. "You're both very kind, but I'm not a fragile doll."

Not a doll, but more fragile than she was willing to admit, Lucky thought, assessing her swollen calves and the weariness in her gaze. He was tempted to stroke a damp strand of hair from her temple, but her stubborn expression warned him against fussing over her.

"The auto club could take half an hour," Keely responded tartly to Zora. "Meanwhile you're breathing auto fumes. It's bad for the baby."

"She doesn't always exercise the best judgment," Lucky agreed.

"I'm right here! Please refrain from talking about me in the third person," Zora snapped.

Ignoring the complaint, he continued addressing Keely. "I notified security. A guard should be here soon to take a report."

Keely shrugged. "Fine. I have nothing else to do till the auto club arrives, but we can't prove Laird did this."

"Motive plus bumper sticker equals Laird," Lucky replied.

"*We* know that," Zora said. "But who else will believe a psychologist would stoop to such juvenile tricks over being bumped from a room rental?"

"Anyone who heard him squabbling with Keely in the cafeteria." Realizing that his comment might seem insulting, Lucky added, "No offense. I meant that he was the one squabbling."

Keely waved off the apology. "Don't bother softpedaling, Lucky. I'm tough. I butted heads with Dr. Tartikoff and survived, in case you forgot."

"How could anyone forget?" he teased. "You're a hero."

"Heroine," Zora corrected.

"You planning to argue with everything I say?" Lucky didn't mind, though, as long as she was safe. No sooner had he clicked off the call than frightening scenarios had rampaged through his head. What if the vandal had tampered with Keely's brakes and they'd crashed? "Keely, as a precaution, have the auto club tow your car to Phil's Garage to check the brakes and engine. I think they're open till seven."

"And spend my hard-earned money for nothing?" She shook her head. "I doubt the louse would go that far."

"I recommend playing it safe, but it's your decision." Reaching out, Lucky helped Zora rise.

He was glad he'd replaced his old low-slung coupe with a practical black sedan he could drive for years. And which didn't force a pregnant woman to pretzel herself into the front seat.

"All set?" He leaned inside to adjust Zora's seat belt.

A slap on the wrist knocked his arm away. "No touching the merchandise!"

"The seat belts can be tricky." He didn't attempt to assist again, however.

As a rule, Lucky preferred mild-mannered women, but Zora's peppery manner had its pluses. Never boring, for one thing. Also, no stored-up complaints to be unleashed later. One ex-girlfriend had unloaded on him out of the blue, calling him an arrogant muscle head before breaking off their relationship. Until that evening, Lucky had believed they were doing fine.

Zora didn't hesitate to lob insults at him on the spot. In fact, *arrogant muscle head* was mild by comparison to some of her descriptive phrases. But at least he knew what she thought of him.

Yet despite her feisty spirit, she had a knack for landing in scrapes that begged for a rescue. If he had to move elsewhere for a job, who would show up on a moment's notice? *Somebody* had to take care of her.

As he navigated the curving ramp, Lucky glanced at the resolute mommy-to-be beside him. The full lips, the curving line of her lashes—spicy and sweet, like hot chocolate with a dash of cayenne pepper.

It occurred to him that he hadn't yet updated her on the latest twist to his plan. "Did you hear from the radiology scheduler about working Saturday morning?"

"No. Will I?"

He explained that he'd requested her. "You'll be nearby when the Adamses are here."

"To do what?" Zora demanded. "I doubt I'll get anywhere near them."

"I'd like your insight." Belatedly, he asked, "Do you mind?"

"I suppose not, but next time, ask me first." She flinched as, ahead, a car shot back into the aisle, blocking their path.

Lucky tapped the brake. "I saw it."

"Of course you did."

"You doubt me?"

"Always."

He chuckled. "About the Adamses, you might observe something I miss."

"Seriously?" When they emerged from the garage, lingering daylight glinted off the coppery highlights in her hair. "I thought you considered me a borderline drooling idiot."

"That's a wild exaggeration," he said.

"Which part—the drooling or the idiot?"

"The borderline."

She laughed. "I should have figured."

Heading south on Safe Harbor Boulevard, they crested a coastal bluff. Before them spread the shimmering harbor and adjacent stretch of sand. The arrival of October's cooler weather meant less traffic and smaller beach crowds, a situation Lucky relished.

Growing up, he'd been accustomed to his family's flat, landlocked neighborhood in LA. But after living in Safe Harbor, he'd never be satisfied being far from the expanse of the ocean.

Zora lowered her window. "That sea air smells wonderful."

"Better than exhaust?"

"Thank you for picking me up, if that was a hint." She stretched her shoulders. At this stage of her pregnancy, she ought to have regular massages to ease her discomforts. Lucky nearly volunteered, but the notion of running his hands over her body struck him as dangerously intimate, especially since she was sexy as hell.

"I'll drive you to and from work the rest of the week." He swung left onto Pacific Coast Highway. "Karen can alternate with me, but your hours are more in line with mine. Next week, after Keely moves in, I'll coordinate my schedule with her."

"You sure are bossy," Zora joked.

"Save your grousing for the Sunday meet-up." The residents of Casa Wiggins, as they referred to Karen's house, assembled once a week to review plans and problems.

"Keely will be there, which means I'll have an ally," she said.

"I'm used to you and Anya ganging up on me," Lucky replied calmly. "I can handle it."

"Handle it? You enjoy having women around even if they aren't bowled over by your tats," Zora said.

"That's true. Women share ideas and support each other more than most men do." Living in Casa Wiggins had taught him the value of friendships with the opposite sex. He'd grown up in a predominantly male household, with a strong-minded father and brother. His mom had been quiet by comparison, with a steady, low-key temperament. Lucky wished he'd had a chance to know her as an adult, but he'd lost her, a painful memory he'd rather not dwell on. "So, have you set up the paternity test?"

"None of your business."

He grinned. It felt normal to bicker with Zora. And he was glad she'd agreed to be at Dr. Rattigan's office on Saturday. Whether or not her input proved helpful, he was glad she'd be there.

Throughout her shift on Saturday morning, Zora stayed attuned to the activities in the rest of the office. Usually she only paid attention to her patients, but today she noted Lucky's familiar footsteps, registered the steady tone of his voice, and picked up the fact that Vince Adams was late. Very late.

Perhaps he and his wife had abandoned the possibility of a pregnancy under any circumstances, or decided to use a surrogate in San Diego. All of Lucky's planning could be for nothing.

He might have to leave. How would she handle that?

The sight of him at the garage on Tuesday had been far more welcome than Zora had expected. Since then, riding beside him to and from work, she'd been keenly aware of his powerful thigh close to hers and his muscular arms controlling the steering wheel. Fortunately, their habit of verbally poking at each other made it easy to hide her reactions.

Today, they'd arrived together but then separated to attend to their duties. The schedule kept Zora busy with a series of male patients.

During Zora's training, performing scrotal ultrasounds had required considerable getting used to. She had to adjust the patient's penis and scrotum, apply gel and move the paddle to obtain varied views.

During the procedure, the man often stared at the ceiling, responding to her requests as if commanded by a robot. Others cracked jokes to cover their embarrassment during the twenty-to thirty-minute procedure. Occasionally, she encountered a man whose sexual innuendos crept toward harassment. Her crisply professional manner and request for a nurse to observe had always sufficed to dampen the patient's ardor.

Zora preferred it when the wife accompanied her husband, which was the case with her fourth patient of the morning. A thin fellow in his late fifties, he gripped his wife's hand as Dr. Rattigan checked him before departing.

During the sonogram, a booming voice from the hall alerted Zora that Vince had arrived. Why did he trumpet every word? The man behaved as if everyone else, except a select few such as Cole, was not only invisible but also deaf.

Then a door closed and silence fell. Ominous silence. Scary silence.

Suddenly Lucky's faith in her powers of observation seemed ridiculously misplaced. His future and the expansion of the men's fertility program at Safe Harbor might be crashing and burning, and unable to see or hear what was happening, Zora had nothing to contribute. If only she could do *something*.

"How does it look to you?" The patient's question broke into her thoughts.

Instead of dwelling on the obvious fact that she wasn't a doctor, Zora tried diplomacy. "Dr. Rattigan will review the results with you personally. He takes great care with his patients."

"Yes, but…" The man broke off as his wife patted his shoulder. "I can't help worrying."

"We're almost finished," she told him. "Am I hurting you?" The procedure was painless unless the man was especially sensitive. However, asking the question ought to distract him from further inquiries.

"No, no. Thank you."

While she did observe some anomalies in the man's images, Zora wasn't qualified to interpret what they meant. Entering the medical field, she'd dreamed of helping others rather than simply clocking in to a routine job each day. And often, she *did* help them. She hoped that whatever was wrong with this patient could be put right.

The early loss of both her grandparents had inspired her interest in health care. She cherished memories of her mother's parents, who'd adored her and Zady. Unfortunately, they'd smoked, avoided exercise and ignored symptoms of heart and lung disease until it was too late for lifesaving treatments.

Zora didn't hold an exalted position like a surgeon, but she was part of a team that improved people's lives. She wouldn't trade her career for anything.

Once she'd finished the exam, she gently wiped off the conductive gel. "You can resume normal activities immediately."

"I think a leisurely lunch at Salads and More is in order," the wife said. "Don't you, honey?"

"How about Waffle Heaven?"

Their gazes locked. "Papa Giovanni's?" she countered.

"Done," he said.

Zora envied their easy rapport. How wonderful to

have a spouse with whom you communicated in short-hand and who stood by you through life's ups and downs. The way Lucky did with her…but that was temporary.

"You may get dressed," she told the patient. "I'll be out of here in a minute."

"No hurry."

As she bent to retrieve a cord, her babies squirmed. Did they sense she was hungry? Pushing the cart out of the room, Zora smiled at the idea that her growling stomach had awakened them.

In the hall, she nearly ran into a bulldog of a man. His powerful frame corded with tension, Vince Adams scowled at the elegant woman beside him. Model thin, Portia Adams wore a svelte pink suit and to-die-for designer shoes. She struck Zora as determined and apprehensive.

Apparently the couple had finished their meeting with the doctor. Most patients avoided private discussions in the hallways, but not these two.

"You call that a compromise?" Vince demanded of his spouse. "I've told you I won't tolerate a surrogate! No stranger will be carrying my children. That's what I have a wife for."

In Portia's smooth face, only her eyes betrayed her fury. "I agreed to hormone injections and egg retrieval," she said in a low voice. "And I want a baby, well, almost as much as you do. But at my age, to take on a possible multiple pregnancy…" She shook her head and let the sentence drift off.

Spotting Zora, the billionaire maintained his glare for an instant before his expression softened. "Excuse me," Zora said, and eased the cart to the side to clear a path.

Instead of picking up the hint to exit, Vince bathed her in a smile. "What a beautiful sight you are, miss. Frankly, I find a pregnant woman's body irresistible."

"Thanks." Zora gritted her teeth, eager to escape.

Vince advanced toward her. "Your husband must be thrilled."

His wife glowered. Her twisting mouth conveyed resentment, but there was also a trace of fear in her eyes. Was she really that afraid of losing her husband?

"I don't…" Zora cleared her throat.

"She isn't married. She lives in that house with Rod," Portia snapped. She and Vince had attended Anya and Jack's wedding there when their daughters—Jack's cousins—had served as flower girls.

"You're not married?" Touching his thumb to Zora's chin, Vince tipped her face up. "The men around here must be blind."

*Okay, that's enough taunting of your wife.* She stepped back. "I'll remove this cart so you can get past."

"You do that," Portia snarled.

Before Zora could squirm farther away, however, Vince laid a meaty hand on her abdomen. "Boy or girl?"

"One of each." She wished she dared smack his arm.

To her dismay, he caressed her bulge with relish. Enjoying his wife's discomfort, or Zora's? Or both? "They're active little rascals, aren't they?"

Behind him, Lucky appeared. Mercifully, the interruption allowed Zora to break free and dodge behind the ultrasound equipment.

Unfazed, Vince addressed his wife. "Well, honey?"

The threat was unmistakable. If Portia didn't yield to his demands, he'd find a woman who would.

A long breath shuddered out of the socialite. "You

don't care about the risk to me? Never mind, I already know the answer."

"You're exaggerating the dangers," her husband retorted. "You're only thirty-nine. Lots of women in their forties have babies."

Lucky intervened politely. "There is an increased risk, Mrs. Adams, but if there are no underlying health issues, it ought to be manageable with careful monitoring. You should discuss that with your doctor."

Her nose wrinkled. "What does a man know? He doesn't have to carry a baby."

Lucky didn't miss a beat. "We have excellent female obstetricians on staff."

Portia gripped her purse. "Do any of them perform in vitro?"

"Several," he said.

Vince faced Zora again. "Who's your doctor, honey?"

"Paige Brennan," she said.

"Dr. Brennan often works with in vitro patients," Lucky added. "You'd find her sympathetic, Mrs. Adams. She underwent fertility treatment herself in order to have her daughter."

That was none of their business, Zora thought. However, Dr. Brennan *had* spoken publicly about that aspect of her medical history.

"And she's married?" This appeared important to Portia. Did she think her husband so lecherous that he'd chase her obstetrician? Of course, he *had* just groped an ultrasound tech.

"Quite happily," Lucky assured her.

Portia gave a reluctant shrug. "I suppose she's acceptable."

Triumphantly, Vince draped an arm over his wife's

shoulders. "Well done. Why don't we stay an extra day and attend that charity event you mentioned? I'll buy you a new outfit at South Coast Plaza."

"Not that I'll fit into it for long," his wife muttered, but quickly rallied. "Thank you. I suppose this might work out okay. A baby really will be a lot of fun."

To Lucky, her husband said, "Set up an appointment with Dr. Brennan. My wife can send you her schedule."

"Glad to." Judging by the light in Lucky's eyes, he was barely keeping a lid on his excitement.

While he escorted the wealthy couple to the front, Zora stowed the cart in its closet. On her return, she found Lucky performing a victory dance around the nurses' station. Fortunately for his reputation, there was no one else present.

He beamed at her. "I have no idea how you persuaded them, but you were brilliant."

"I didn't do anything." *Except let him grope my baby bump.* However, Zora supposed that Vince's behavior fell within what many might view as acceptable limits. A lot of people assumed—wrongly—that it was okay to touch a pregnant woman's belly.

"Too bad it's illegal to shoot off fireworks in a doctor's office." With a whoop, Lucky caught her. "We did it!"

Zora's discomfort evaporated. Close to him, she felt safe and sheltered. How easily she could forget everything and everyone, except… "Isn't Dr. Rattigan around?"

"He had to perform emergency surgery." Lucky rubbed his cheek over her hair. "He left right after talking to the Adamses."

"An emergency in urology?" Unlike obstetrics, the specialty rarely dealt with life-or-death situations.

"A patient suffered injuries in a car crash." Lucky mentioned a nearby hospital that handled trauma patients. "The lead surgeon called Dr. Rattigan to assist. Would you stop fidgeting and let me hug you?"

"That's nearly impossible in my shape." But Zora yielded happily as he wedged her against him. How strong he was, yet he held her with a tenderness that almost overwhelmed her.

Zora became acutely aware of his quick breathing. The discovery that she excited him spurred her passion. She floated in the heady scent of his citrus cologne, her nerve endings coming alive.

When Lucky's mouth brushed Zora's, her lips parted. The flick of his tongue sent rivulets of desire streaming through her, and an answering moan burst from him.

She grabbed his shoulders and lightly rubbed her breasts over his hard chest. The sensations flaring through her were almost painfully intense. Lucky angled her tighter, his hands closing over her derriere.

The urge to bring him inside her, to merge with him, proved irresistible. "Let's find a place to be alone," she began, and then, shifting position, he stumbled.

"Oh, hell!" Lucky caught his balance against the counter, anchoring her against his hip. "Are you all right?"

"Delirious," she murmured.

Drawing in a ragged breath, he studied her in confusion. "We shouldn't be doing this."

"You're right. It's a terrible idea." Clinging to him, Zora didn't mean a word of it. "But as long as we've gone this far…"

"I never expected to get carried away." His thoughts seemed to turn inward. "What's wrong with me?"

"Wrong?" Zora bristled.

"I never lose control this way," Lucky said. "Considering your condition and our situations, I apologize."

"For what?" Oh, why was she torturing herself by prolonging this conversation? Zora wondered. She'd acted impulsively, and clearly Lucky didn't like the way he'd reacted. What a control freak! "Never mind. Forget the whole thing."

"That's a good idea." He sounded as if he was struggling for composure. "That wasn't how a gentleman behaves."

"If you apologize again, I'll slug you."

He laughed, an unexpected rumble that rolled right into her heart. "That's my Zora." A bout of hard breathing reawakened her hope, but he sucked in a lungful of air and held it. "Okay. Better."

"Than what?"

He ignored the question. "Since I inveigled you into working today, let me buy you lunch to celebrate."

Was that his interpretation of what they'd been doing—celebrating? Slapping him would have been totally satisfying. Still, she was starving. Why reject a good meal? "Where did you have in mind?"

"There's a new vegetarian Chinese restaurant I've been meaning to check out."

Zora loved Chinese food. "Do they serve anything besides tofu?"

"Kung pao mushrooms, according to the online menu. Deep fried, with a tangy sauce. And more, I'm sure."

"You're on." The heat in her body hadn't exactly dissipated, but it had faded to her normal pregnancy-enhanced high temperature. As for Lucky, he'd evidently banished whatever desire he'd experienced.

*I guess I'm nowhere near close enough to perfection to suit him.*

As common sense reasserted itself, Zora recalled his previous comment about her babies. Never mind Lucky's withdrawal from her—he didn't, couldn't and never would accept these babies as his own.

She was glad they'd stopped. Going any further would have been yet another in a long line of mistakes she'd made with men.

Gathering her possessions, she waited until Lucky locked up, and they sauntered out together. Friends again, nothing more.

Which was obviously how they both preferred it.

# Chapter 9

Lucky enjoyed the Sunday meet-ups at Casa Wiggins. He'd learned from his parents, who'd run a small business, that organization was the key to controlling your destiny. In the eight months since the household had formed, the gatherings had enabled the group to stay on track through changes in occupants and in individual situations.

This afternoon, despite his awareness that the future was more of a meandering path with speed bumps than a superhighway, he felt optimistic about his plans. Thanks to whatever diplomacy Zora had exercised toward the Adamses yesterday, all systems appeared to be a go.

Relaxing in his favorite armchair in the den, he sipped white grape juice from a glass. As usual, Rod and Karen had chosen the couch, with their sock-covered feet propped on the worn coffee table. Zora preferred the straight chair, which was easier for a pregnant woman to get in and out of. That left newcomer Keely, who clomped down the staircase to join them.

"Am I late?" she asked. "I had trouble finding the laundry room."

"It's the narrow door next to the garage," Zora said.

"I thought that was a closet."

"Everybody assumes that," Karen assured her. "Don't hesitate to ask where things are."

"You're running laundry already?" Rod fingered his short, graying beard. "You just moved in."

Karen nudged him. "Not our business, dear."

"It's a harmless question."

"I'm a strong believer in hygiene." Crossing the den, Keely lowered her sturdy frame onto the remaining armchair. "How often do we clean and who does what? With a pregnant woman on the premises, we must be vigilant about germs."

*Don't tell me she's a germophobe.* Lucky rolled his eyes, then caught Zora's stern gaze and subsided.

"We have a rotating schedule. I'll give you a copy," Karen promised. "Feel free to swap chores with anyone who's willing."

"Surely Zora doesn't have to handle chemicals or do heavy work." Keely slid to the edge of her seat, no doubt having discovered that otherwise she sank into the depths of the chair. Lucky decided to ask Karen about replacing the cushion. They maintained a household fund for that sort of thing.

"We have a great system," Rod said. "We chain pregnant women to a wheel in the basement so they generate electrical power."

Keely's jaw dropped.

Zora, who was seated closest to her, murmured, "There is no basement. I handle dusting and other light chores."

Their newest housemate nodded. "I forgot that Dr. Vintner is famous for joking."

"Dr. Vintner? Anytime you see me with my shoes off, you can call me by my first name." Rod wiggled his sock-clad toes on the coffee table.

Karen presented a few more house rules, such as putting snack plates and cups in the dishwasher rather than accumulating them in the sink. "And no sticking them in the oven because you're in a hurry," she tossed in Zora's direction.

"Anya and I only did that once," she replied cheerfully. "It's not our fault someone turned on the oven without checking if there was anything inside."

"Oh, dear." Keely clutched her hands together. "What if I do things wrong?"

"We'll toss you out," Rod replied.

"Where would I go?" To Lucky's astonishment, Keely regarded Rod in dismay. The woman needed to develop a sense of humor.

Zora reached over to pat the newcomer's hand. "You'll get used to our silliness. Are you still upset about what happened on Tuesday? That must have thrown you off balance."

The older nurse's head bobbed. What had happened on Tuesday? Lucky had to search his memory before he dredged it up. "You mean that nasty prank with your tires? What's the connection?"

"She was bullied in school," Zora said fiercely. "I understand what it's like to be an outsider. Keely, nobody will bully you in this house. If they do, we'll toss *them* out."

"You bet," Karen affirmed.

"I'll cheer while Lucky does the physical tossing," Rod said.

"No problem." Lucky was pleased when Keely responded with a smile.

What a spirited defense Zora had mounted, he thought. As for that outsider business, he bore a share of the responsibility for being tough on Zora. When she first arrived at the house, he'd considered her a heartless predator who'd hurt Stacy. Gradually, he'd forgiven her, and since she'd stood up to Andrew, he'd come to respect her. As for her empathy toward Keely, that demonstrated her kind heart.

The doorbell rang. "I'll get it." With unaccustomed speed, Rod hurried to the door. Lucky heard low voices and then caught a heavenly whiff of garlic, tomato sauce and cheese.

Rod returned toting three large pizzas. "My treat. This will be my atonement for cracking jokes at Keely's expense."

"Three pizzas?" the nurse replied in astonishment. "That's too much for five people."

"Don't you like leftovers?" Lucky asked.

"And it *is* Sunday," Karen said. "People might drop by."

"I'll set out the paper plates and stuff." Rod was definitely acting out of character today—for a reason, as Lucky knew.

To distract Keely, and also because he cared about the answer, Lucky said, "I've been wondering about the timetable for the in vitro process. It's not a situation Dr. Rattigan and I usually deal with. We have a patient who might be affected."

"I'm happy to answer, but are we finished discussing house rules?" The dark-haired woman glanced from him to Zora to Karen.

"Yes, unless you have more questions," Karen said. "Don't let Lucky rush you."

"I'm fine. Is everyone interested in hearing about in vitro?"

"I am," Zora said. She, too, was probably wondering how long it might take before Portia and Vince saw results.

Keely launched into a spiel that she must have heard Dr. Brennan deliver to patients a hundred times. "Depending on the phase of the woman's cycle when you begin, the whole process can take about a month."

"Fantastic." Noting her puzzled reaction, Lucky quickly added, "Go on."

With increasing confidence, she complied.

Zora listened attentively, though that was partly for Keely's sake—the other woman obviously craved reassurance that she belonged here. The subject matter was familiar to her, but she wanted a clearer picture of how things might progress for the Adamses.

The first stage, Keely noted, was the administration of medication to stimulate the ovaries, almond-size glands that flanked the uterus. Normally, only one or two eggs matured each month, but drugs could produce the simultaneous maturing of multiple eggs. This improved the chances of harvesting and fertilizing enough viable eggs.

Keely was explaining step two, harvesting, when the doorbell rang again. From the table at the farthest part of the den, Rod plummeted toward the front door. No one attempted to rise; if they had, he'd have bowled them over.

A creak of the door, and excited, girlish voices filled the air.

"Daddy!"

"Grandma Helen, give Daddy the cake before you drop it."

"I'm not that decrepit," responded the dry voice of their grandmother.

"I'll get it." Lucky, who'd ordered the cake, went to join the new arrivals.

Until yesterday, the plan had been for the Adamses to return to San Diego that same day. However, Portia had been lobbying to stay over at a hotel so she and Vince could attend an exclusive charity concert and reception tonight, and in his expansive mood, he'd agreed. Helen Pepper had promptly called her former son-in-law to inform Rod that she and the girls could join the household for dinner tonight.

As long as they were having guests, Lucky had decided this was a good chance to show their new roommate what a great group she'd joined. Zora couldn't wait to see her reaction to the cake honoring Keely's birthday.

"I smell pizza!" cried thirteen-year-old Tiffany Adams, her red braids bouncing on her shoulders. "Ooh, where are my manners? Hi, everybody. Zora, you're *huge!*"

"The twins have grown since August." Last summer, Rod's daughters had visited often, since their parents had rented a beach house nearby while Vince underwent surgery.

Eleven-year-old Amber followed shyly. "Have you picked names?" she asked Zora.

"Not yet."

"Gee, they brought dessert." Grinning, Lucky carried in a castle-shaped pink box bearing the logo of the Cake Castle. "Is somebody having a birthday?" No one responded. "Or did someone have a birthday last weekend?" he asked with feigned innocence.

Keely shook her head. "You don't mean me, do you?"

"Hmm. Let's check."

As Lucky passed Zora, she studied his physique appreciatively. His tattoos and muscular build used to remind her of her stepfather, a foul-mouthed ex-gangbanger. Now, she knew that Lucky was nothing like that loser. In fact, as yesterday's encounter had proved, she found him tantalizingly attractive.

Last night, she'd lain awake, her brain defiantly replaying the incident. What if he hadn't stumbled? How far would they have gone? At this stage of pregnancy, making love wasn't wise. Just as importantly, if he'd repeated his insistence afterward on holding out for Ms. Perfect, she'd never have forgiven him.

It was fortunate for Zora's sanity and their friendship that they'd stopped. If only her dreams would quit defying her common sense. But then, where a man was concerned, this was familiar territory.

Carefully, Lucky opened the box to reveal the cake. "It says, 'Happy 50th Birthday, Kelly.' Doggone it! I spelled 'Keely' for them twice!"

The amazement on Keely's face touched Zora's heart. "It's for me?" She approached the table and stared at the icing inscription. "But being fifty isn't worth celebrating. I'm over the hill."

"You consider fifty old?" The girls' grandmother patted Keely's shoulder with an arthritic hand. "My fifties were my best years. Still, I don't mind growing older, not when it means watching these darling girls grow up."

When Zora reached fifty, she reflected, she'd have twenty-year-old twins. For a second, she visualized them with dark hair and smooth olive skin, like Lucky. But of course, they'd either have her reddish hair or Andrew's blond coloring.

Amber joined the small group around the cake. "It's beautiful. I want a rainbow on my next birthday cake, too."

Tiffany took out her cell phone. "I'll snap a picture so we don't forget."

"Hang on, honey." Rod caught his daughter's wrist. "You said Vince snoops through your stuff, right?"

"Oh, rats." The girl scowled. "He'll demand the details of who it was for and where we saw it."

"He's mean." Amber's frown mirrored her sister's.

Keely looked puzzled. "I don't understand."

"I'll explain while we eat," Rod said.

Over pizza, they filled in the story of how Vince had wrested his stepdaughters from the man who'd raised them and attempted to banish Rod from their lives.

"Surely the Adamses must suspect that they visit Dr. Vintner." Keely had chosen a tight spot at the table's corner, declining the place of honor toward which the others had tried to direct her.

"They sort of know but pretend they don't," Amber said. "I'm sure Mom has an idea."

"It's like a game," Tiffany put in.

"Despite the satisfaction of flipping them the bird, we shouldn't be forced to sneak around." Rod spoke from the head of the table, the seat Keely had bypassed. "I spent my life's savings fighting that man in court."

"If you run into Mr. or Mrs. Adams, please don't mention that you met their daughters," Karen told Keely.

The nurse swallowed a bite of food. "I won't. I promise."

Lucky met Zora's gaze. They were both thinking the same thing, she gathered: that it was fortunate Karen had issued the warning before Portia became Paige Brennan's patient. Keely would be running into her often.

"The girls might be in town more often now that my daughter's trying for another baby," Helen observed.

"Mom and Vince plan to rent a beach cottage again, closer to the medical center," Tiffany filled in.

"What about your education?" Rod asked. "You'll have to switch schools."

"I don't mind," Amber answered. "The kids at my school are snotty."

"Besides, private schools bend over backward to accommodate you if your parents give a big donation." Tiffany's cynical attitude bothered Zora until the girl said, "Oh, yeah, and Mom and Vince promised a gift to the animal shelter here, because it's our pet project."

"Pet project?" Rod waggled an eyebrow.

"Tiffany made a pun!" Amber giggled.

"And you volunteer there, Dad," his older daughter said. "It'll be cool for Vince to be funding *your* favorite charity without realizing it."

Zora wondered how Vince would treat his future genetic child or children. And how would he behave toward his stepdaughters? Perhaps he'd mellow out. She doubted it, though.

After wiping her hands on a napkin, Zora rested them on her bulge. Thinking about daddies reminded her that Andrew had had his blood drawn on Wednesday. The results might arrive by the end of the week, not that she had any doubts about them.

"Let's cut the cake." Tiffany jumped up to clear the table.

They'd polished off the better part of two pizzas, with leftovers to stock the fridge. Karen, with her usual efficiency, would jot on the cardboard box the number of slices allocated to each resident. Despite occasional carping in the early days—accustomed to living with other guys, Lucky had pushed for the first-come-first-served approach—they'd found that this method maintained the peace.

Karen produced birthday candles, which Lucky lit using a strand of spaghetti in lieu of the fireplace torch they'd misplaced. Then they sang, lustily if raggedly, a round of "Happy Birthday."

Keely stood with hands clasped and eyes sparkling. As they finished amid cheers, she sniffed. "I can't believe you guys did this."

"You're part of the family now," Karen said.

"Hurray for Keely!" added Tiffany, who hadn't had a clue to the woman's identity until today.

Amber sidled up to the newcomer and took her hand. "Being fifty sounds good. I bet nobody bosses you around."

Too choked up to speak, Keely nodded.

Rod did the honors, at Karen's request. "This is as close as I get to performing surgery," the anesthesiologist said as he divided the cake. "Keely, which piece do you prefer?"

"Take the one with the rainbow roses on it," Amber advised.

The nurse bestowed a quavering smile on the youngster. "If you recommend it."

"I do."

Across from her, Zora watched Lucky beam at the cozy tableau. He was deriving as much joy from the situation as if they'd thrown *him* a surprise birthday party. What a natural father he'd make.

Whenever he found the perfect time and the perfect woman.

That week, Keely, Karen and Lucky alternated providing rides for Zora. Since Rod's unreliable car was in the shop, he tagged along, too. That led to hilariously nonsensical discussions, and kept Zora from feeling that she was imposing too heavily on her friends.

On Friday, the radiology scheduler assigned her to the same-day surgery unit on the fourth floor of the hospital. Busy with clients, Zora only glanced at her phone in rare free moments in case of urgent voice messages or texts. There was one asking her to call Keely, which she presumed meant a change in whoever was driving home from work.

During her break that afternoon, Zora headed for the fourth-floor staff lounge, eager to put her feet up and answer messages. Waddling around a corner, she nearly collided with her ex-mother-in-law. Her hand shot out to the wall for support.

"Sorry." Betsy braced as if preparing to catch her. "Are you okay?"

"Sure." Zora removed her hand. "I, uh, don't usually see you here." The nursing supervisor's office was on the fifth floor, although Betsy's duties might take her anywhere in the building.

"I was looking for you." The older woman walked with her toward the lounge. "Radiology said you were on this floor today. Can we talk?"

Zora occasionally chatted with Betsy about crocheting or mutual acquaintances when they ran into each other, but the older woman didn't usually single her out this way. "Is there a problem?"

"Hold on." Opening the lounge door, Betsy scanned the interior. It was empty, Zora saw. The vending machines and kitchenette appeared in pristine condition, no doubt tidied since lunch. "Good. We're alone."

Why was that good?

Zora settled on a couch. Without asking, the older woman brought her a cup of herbal tea from a machine. "You ought to stay hydrated," Betsy said from an adjacent chair. "In fact, you should be on maternity leave."

"I'm saving as much of my time as possible for after the twins are born." Zora hoped she could hold out another few weeks.

"You don't have to go through this alone." Betsy's green eyes, augmented by her spectacles, zeroed in on her. "I wish you'd felt comfortable confiding in me, although I understand your reluctance."

"Andrew told you that he's the father?" He must have received the lab results of the paternity test today.

"Yes, he did." Worry lines deepened in Betsy's square face. "That's why I wanted to talk with you. I believe you ought to hear his plans."

He was up to something already? With a sinking sensation, Zora conceded that she should have expected this. She sighed. "Hit me with it."

# *Chapter 10*

Trying not to panic while Betsy gathered her thoughts, Zora stretched out along the couch. As usual, she'd been floating on what Lucky had once termed the river of denial. She hadn't bothered to consult her attorney to prepare for Andrew's stratagems, such as ducking child support payments. She'd let matters drift, while he'd apparently prepared a trap.

Betsy spread her hands in dismay. "There's no way to soften this. He might sue for custody."

"What?" Zora would have bolted to her feet except that she was long past the ability to bolt anywhere. "How ridiculous! He doesn't want the kids." More objections tumbled through her mind. "And since Lin walked out, who does he think would care for them on the wildly improbable chance that he won the court battle?"

"Me," her ex-mother-in-law said. "He asked me

to raise the babies. I guess he assumed I'd leap at the chance, because he knows how much I would love grandchildren."

Zora stared at her, stunned. Never in her most bizarre dreams could she have concocted such a scheme. Finally she found her voice. "You told him no, right?"

"Without a moment's hesitation."

"Can you please explain what he was thinking?"

Betsy rolled her eyes. Zora didn't recall ever seeing her ex-mother-in-law do that before. "I long ago gave up on understanding my son. Sadly, he takes after his father. In case you don't remember Rory very well, my ex is a total narcissist."

"He seemed distant." As a teenager, Zora didn't recall exchanging more than superficial greetings with Andrew's father. When she and her old flame reconnected ten years later, his parents had divorced.

Rory hadn't attended their wedding, a lovely ceremony followed by a reception she'd rather forget. Zora's mother had drunk too much, waxed maudlin about her baby girl, then vomited on the buffet table.

"I asked Andrew why the hell—excuse me, heck— he'd sue for custody," Betsy said. "He claimed you'd tricked him into fathering kids just so you could hit him up for support, and he doesn't plan to let you win. His words, not mine."

The man had incredible nerve. "He lied to me about reconciling so he could seduce me. That's how I got pregnant." Embarrassment heated Zora's cheeks. "I was naive. The fact that he didn't bother with protection struck me as a sign that he was serious, because we'd been trying to have kids. I had no idea until later that he'd had a vasectomy and believed he was sterile."

Then she realized what she'd revealed. "I'm sorry to drop that on you."

"Oh, my son already did," Betsy said wryly. "He was almost gleeful as he informed me these are the only grandchildren I'll ever have. He failed to grasp that I can be their grandmother without depriving them of their mom."

Betsy was running a risk by bringing Zora the truth—she might offend her son and she had no guarantee Zora would grant her access to the kids. "Of course you're their grandmother. I'd love for you to be part of my children's lives, and mine, too."

The other woman glowed with relief. "I've always felt as if you were my daughter."

"Me, too." In high school, Zora had often relied on Betsy for comfort and advice, since she couldn't trust her own mom. A rush of happiness ran through her, to be on intimate terms with Betsy again.

"I doubt any court in California would hand my son sole custody," Betsy added. "If you need me to testify about how unfit he is, just say the word."

Zora swallowed hard. "You're a saint."

"Oh, I have my faults." With a quirk of the eyebrow, the grandmother-to-be inquired, "To change the subject, I've been wondering—have you picked names?"

Suddenly, Zora had an answer. Half of one, anyway. "The girl will be Elizabeth."

Betsy's eyes widened. "For me?"

"Absolutely." Also, Zora liked that name.

"Count on me as your number one babysitter." The nursing supervisor appeared about to explode with joy. "Do me a favor, would you?"

"Sure. What?"

"Don't name the boy Andrew." Quickly, Betsy added, "Not to deprive my son. It's because being a junior can cause confusion."

"Understood." The reason scarcely mattered; Zora wouldn't name her little boy Andrew for a million dollars. Well, maybe a million. And then she'd use a nickname.

Outside in the hall, she heard light footsteps approaching. In midafternoon, there hadn't been much traffic in this wing. Same-day surgeries were conducted early enough for patients to recover by late afternoon, and most were still recuperating at this hour.

Zora glanced at her watch. "Sounds like we're about to have company, and I'm due to see a patient."

"If you need help arranging for leave, let me know."

"Thanks, but…"

The door opened and a woman peered in, reddish-brown hair rioting around her head. "Excuse me. I'm supposed to be interviewing with Dr. Davis on the fourth floor but I can't find his…"

Utter and total silence fell over the lounge. Because the face looking back at Zora was her own.

For Lucky, Friday afternoons could be crammed with last-minute patients or, like today, extremely light. Cole had accepted several extra surgeries and ordered him to reschedule office appointments.

Since Keely had to work late, Lucky was happy to switch their arrangement and drive Zora home, but she wasn't answering her phone. Not unusual—she might be with patients. After determining that she'd been assigned to the same-day surgery unit, he decided to grab a snack at the cafeteria and stop by the fourth floor to try to catch her in a free moment.

Emerging from the stairs, he had a moment of disorientation when he spotted her down the hall. Why was Zora wearing street clothes, and— Wait a minute— what had happened to her pregnancy?

Then he remembered that Dr. Davis was in town to interview nurse candidates and find a place to live. He'd be joining the staff at the beginning of November, a few weeks from now. Zady, one of the nurses slated for an interview, must have been confused about which fourth floor was involved—she'd gone to the hospital instead of the office next door.

"Miss Moore?" Lucky didn't like to shout, but she failed to hear him. Instead, with no nurses' station in sight, she headed for the next best thing, the staff lounge.

After opening the door, she stood frozen, her shoulders rigid. A warning bell rang in Lucky's head.

Standing behind the slender figure with hair a shade lighter than Zora's, he peered inside. Sure enough, staring at Zady with her mouth open was the shocked face of his housemate.

From the recesses of his suddenly sluggish brain, Lucky dredged up the words, "I can explain." But before they reached his vocal cords, a third woman spoke from the side.

"What a pleasure to run into you, Zady." Betsy Raditch, he realized, must have met Zora's twin when the girls were teens.

While she and Zady exchanged greetings, Lucky tried wafting apologetic vibes in Zora's direction, but she ignored him. It hadn't occurred to him the sisters might come face-to-face today. In the event that Zady landed the job, he'd assumed there'd be plenty of time for him to break the news once it was no longer a matter of confidence.

He wondered what issues had separated the sisters. If someone unexpectedly threw him together with his brother, there'd be hell to pay. But their split had occurred under unusually traumatic circumstances.

He snapped to attention, hearing Zady say she was in search of Dr. Davis's office. "That's on the fourth floor of the building next door," he said.

"Dr. Davis?" Betsy's forehead wrinkled. "Oh, the new urologist. I heard you were vetting the nurse candidates, Lucky."

Two pairs of large gray eyes fixed on him. "You must be Mr. Mendez," Zady said.

Zora mouthed the formal name—*Mr. Mendez?*—and grimaced.

He'd have to wait until later to provide the details of his involvement. "I'll escort you," he told Zady, adding for Zora's benefit, "I'm driving you home today. Keely has to stay late."

"Fine," she growled. Since he'd brought her in this morning, she knew where he'd parked his car.

The twins regarded each other hesitantly. "I don't understand why—" Zady began.

"What're you doing—" Zora started.

They paused, radiating mistrust. But something else too, Lucky thought. Hope, perhaps?

"You ladies should talk," Betsy said. "But right now, I gather there are people waiting. Do you have each other's phone numbers?"

Both heads shook. While they input the numbers in their mobiles, Zady said, "I'm staying at the Harbor

Suites. Let's meet when you finish work." She provided her room number.

"I don't mind driving you over there," Lucky put in, although he didn't expect to receive any thanks.

"Okay." To her twin, Zora said, "Good luck with the interview, I guess."

"Yeah, thanks. I guess."

Lucky accompanied Zady to the elevator. In answer to her query, he said he was one of Zora's housemates, which seemed to puzzle her even more.

She had a lot of questions, including why Zora was renting a room in a house instead of living with her husband. Lucky told her he'd leave that for her sister to answer.

How strange that Zady didn't know her twin was divorced. But then, he had no idea whether his brother was married or had kids, or what Matthew had been doing these past sixteen years. The only cousin with whom Lucky kept in touch diplomatically avoided the subject.

Occasionally, Lucky had considered searching online to scope out Matthew's status, but that risked arousing old fury and resentment. Better to let sleeping dogs lie. He'd fought hard to regain his equilibrium after his brother lined up the rest of the family against him. Now that he'd found a second home among friends, why revisit the past?

Unlike Lucky, these sisters had a mother with whom Zora was in contact, and Zady probably was, too. Why hadn't she passed along vital information such as Zora's marital status?

Lucky expected to learn more in due time. Although he might catch a scolding from Zora during the drive, it would be worth it.

\* \* \*

After Zady departed, Zora struggled with a wave of bewilderment and regret. Had it really been nine years since they'd fought? Her outrage had long ago dissipated. But according to Mom, Zady did nothing but boast about her happy marriage and loving children while dropping snide remarks about Zora. Yet if Zady was content, why did she want to leave Santa Barbara? And why apply for a job at the medical center where Zora worked?

Betsy broke the silence. "I know you two are estranged, but I've never heard why. Granted, it's none of my business. Still, I noticed during high school that whenever I saw the two of you laughing and having fun together, the next thing I heard, you were fighting. I hope you've outgrown that."

Zady used to play nasty tricks on Zora, after which she not only feigned innocence but leveled accusations at *her*. It would be childish to dredge that up, however. "A lot of siblings fight."

"I can't speak from experience. My brother was much older, more like an uncle, and I only had one child." Betsy arose. "You have a patient scheduled?"

"Oh, that's right!" She'd forgotten to watch the clock.

"I hope you'll talk to your attorney about Andrew," Betsy added.

"I will." After a quick hug, Zora departed, her mind buzzing with the latest developments.

Good thing she'd have Lucky to review them with after work. Right after she read him the riot act.

On the second level of the garage, Zora approached the familiar black sedan where Lucky was comfortably ensconced, apparently listening to music. On the sloped ramp, she paused to observe him.

With his dark coloring and dramatic cheekbones, Lucky had drawn her attention as soon as he'd started working at Safe Harbor, about a year after she had. While she'd considered him handsome, he wasn't her type, and she'd been married to Andrew.

Later, when Cole fell in love with Stacy, loyalty to his doctor—although Cole had never indicated any animosity toward Zora—had turned Lucky into her fiercest critic. She'd refused to let him scare her out of moving into Karen's house, however, and over the past months, he'd changed.

When he'd reviewed the nurses' applications for Dr. Davis, why had he chosen her twin as a finalist—to create trouble? Surely he hadn't eliminated more qualified applicants for Zady's sake, though. Perhaps she simply deserved to be considered.

"Oh, good, I caught you." Rod's voice yanked her from her reflections. "My transmission's on the fritz again. Blast that car. I'm definitely trading it in."

"Hi, Rod." He must have received Lucky's permission to join them—how else would he know the car's location? Zora mused as they strolled side by side to the car. "We have a stop en route," she informed the anesthesiologist. "My sister and I are having a, well, touchy reunion."

"Fine with me." He opened the rear door for her. Inside, the blare of country music cut off. "I'd offer to sit in the back but it's safer for you to be there."

"Thanks." Zora hefted her body inside.

"I'll drop you at the Harbor Suites," Lucky said from

the front. The one-bedroom suites rented by the day or week. "I'll pick you up again after I take Rod home."

"That's a lot of driving," Zora said.

"It's ten minutes in each direction." Rod closed her door and hopped into the front, adjusting his fedora to avoid it bumping the roof.

Lucky put the car into reverse. Although tempted to ask why he'd approved her sister as a potential colleague, Zora wasn't keen on reviewing the whole business in front of Rod.

Fortunately, he was preoccupied with the latest developments concerning his daughters. Helen had reported that the girls were starting at their new school next week, and that Vince had insisted both of them play soccer, which Tiffany hated.

When the youngster begged to study dance instead, her stepfather had said he was tired of her complaints. He planned to send her to boarding school in Switzerland when she entered high school the following autumn.

"Her mother doesn't bother to defend her," Rod said angrily. "If the girls are too much trouble to have around, they should let me raise them."

"Not much chance of that, is there?" Lucky observed.

"I wish there were. Karen would welcome them. They can have my room." Rod and Karen had begun spending nights together in her master suite.

Vince would never let go of anything he considered his, Zora reflected. The thought of the billionaire sent a shiver through her. The memory of him groping her abdomen repulsed her. Well, he'd accomplished his goal of arousing his wife's jealousy, and hopefully that was the end of that.

They pulled into the parking lot in front of the Harbor Suites. Among the vehicles, she spotted license plates from neighboring states: Arizona, Oregon, Utah, Nevada. Patients undergoing fertility treatments often rented rooms here.

Lucky halted in front of the office. "You want me to stay? If you're worried, I will."

What a sweet offer. "I'll be fine."

"If we hear screaming, we'll turn around," Rod joked.

After Zora got out, Lucky lowered his window. "I'll pick up food on my way back."

Why was he acting so nice? In self-defense, Zora supposed. "Chinese would be good. Or Italian."

"Okay."

Despite her brave words, dread filled Zora as the car drove off. Years of silence between her and Zady loomed in front of her like an abyss.

Still, she was curious about her sister's situation, she conceded as she followed a sidewalk between the one-story buildings. And if Zady ended up at Safe Harbor, they'd have to reach an accord sooner or later.

Halfway across the grassy courtyard, past a few squatty palm trees, Zora spotted the room number Zady had given her earlier. Taking a deep breath, she knocked on her sister's door.

# *Chapter 11*

Inside, footsteps rushed across the carpet. Zora's pulse sped up as the door opened and she stared into a face at the same height as hers, a face that mirrored hers, from the freckles to the wary expression.

A memory sprang up. For their senior prom, they'd accidentally bought the same dress and, after a horrified moment, they'd dissolved into laughter. Rather than quibble about who should return the gown, they'd coordinated the rest of their outfits, as well. Their classmates had assumed they'd deliberately picked matching dresses and shoes, while they'd confounded their mother. It had been rare fun.

"Hi." Zady moved aside, admitting her to an austere living room furnished with a nondescript sofa and reproductions of seascapes on the walls.

Zora noted a can of soup in the kitchenette next to

the microwave. If that was her sister's idea of dinner, Zady was either on a diet or short of money. Well, according to their mother, her sister had three children, enough to strain any budget.

"Let's get one thing straight." Zady's words sounded rehearsed.

"What's that?"

"If Dr. Davis offers the job, I'm accepting it."

It hadn't occurred to Zora to suggest otherwise. "That's fine. I won't beat around the bush, either."

"Okay." Hands clenched, Zady waited by the couch.

Ignoring the sofa, Zora chose a hard chair. "Regardless of what Mom may have claimed, here are the facts. Right before Andrew and I finalized our divorce, I slept with him because I believed he still loved me. Then he married his new girlfriend. Now I'm pregnant with twins, which I plan to keep."

Zady dropped onto the couch, eyes wide. "You're divorced? Mom said your husband dotes on you. Takes you on luxury cruises, showers you with jewelry—I'll admit, it didn't sound like the Andrew I remember from high school, but—you're carrying twins? Are they identical?"

"No. A boy and a girl."

"That's good. Maybe they won't hate each other."

The remark brought an unexpected pang. "Do you hate me?" Zora asked.

"No, I assumed…" Zady broke off.

Although Zora was dying to learn more about her sister's feelings, first things first. "Why did you apply to Safe Harbor? What about your husband and kids—are they moving here?"

"Dwayne and I never married." Zady kicked off her

low-heeled pumps. "And I don't have kids, unless you count his three obnoxious children who treat me as their personal maid."

The world was shifting on its axis. "Are you still living with him?"

"No." Her twin didn't look up, apparently fascinated by her stocking-clad feet. "He's like Dad, forever cheating."

"So is Andrew!"

"And I was too stubborn and proud to admit it until he forced my hand."

"Me, too."

They regarded each other across the coffee table. Zora could almost have laughed, except the situation was pathetic.

"You didn't finish your story," Zady said. "Since Mom obviously lied about everything, I'd like to hear the truth. She said Andrew sought you out during his first marriage because he'd never stopped loving you. Is that right?"

"No. We bumped into each other at our high school reunion. Wish you'd been there."

"Are you kidding? I was too embarrassed about my situation with Dwayne. Go on."

Zora poured out the tale of how Andrew had dumped Stacy, then cheated on Zora. "In high school, you told me he sneaked around with other girls," she recalled. "I'm sorry I accused you of being jealous."

"And I'm sorry I didn't listen when you warned me that Dwayne was a jerk."

"I guess I did." With all that had happened since, Zora had forgotten that she'd tried to steer her sister away from him. She'd had more sense about Zady's choices than her own.

"You were right not to trust him." Zady waved her hands in a gesture Zora recognized, because she did it herself when agitated. "Not only didn't he marry me, Dwayne refused to have kids. He stuck me with his unholy brood during their vacations, claiming I should learn to love my 'stepchildren.' He used the free time to play around. I closed my eyes to it, until his new girlfriend got pregnant."

"How did he react to that?"

"Oh, he's excited about being a proud papa again." Bitterness laced Zady's voice. "I wouldn't count on it lasting, if I were her."

"Andrew didn't refuse to have children with me," Zora said. "We were trying for a pregnancy before he met, well, *her.* I stopped taking birth control pills during our last year together, but nothing happened until after we separated."

"Hmm…that timing is weird." Zady frowned.

"I agree, but it's not as if he tricked me while we were married. I'd have noticed if he was wearing a condom."

"If I've learned anything, it's that a manipulative jerk will do stuff you'd never dream of."

"Maybe, but I can't imagine how…" Zora stopped. "Oh, Lord, you're right. I may have just figured it out."

"What?" Her sister leaned forward.

Zora smacked herself in the forehead. "After I stopped taking the birth control pills, he claimed he threw them out. I was touched. But what if he crushed them into my food?"

"For an entire year?"

"There was a three-month supply in the drawer."

He'd become solicitous about her diet, preparing breakfast to be sure she ate properly for their future children. "As my husband, he'd have had no problem refilling the prescription."

"But a year's a long time." Zady appeared both disgusted and fascinated.

"He went out of town on occasion," Zora conceded. "But we weren't having sex during his absences, either. And I marked our wall calendar with what I assumed were my most fertile days. I was frustrated when he always claimed to be exhausted after he got back from a trip right when we should have been making love. I should have suspected something."

"What a lot of trouble. He could have sneaked off and had a vasectomy without telling you," Zady said. "The scar's usually very small."

Zora threw up her hands—just as her sister had done moments earlier, she realized. "Why be straightforward when you can be manipulative? Andrew enjoyed playing games and tricking people. Or I could be wrong about this."

"I'm sure it must be illegal to dose a person with prescription medication without her consent," Zady added.

"That wouldn't bother Andrew." Nothing could be proven now, Zora supposed, even though the scenario explained a lot about Andrew's behavior. "Well, eventually he did have a vasectomy, but he assumed his sperm count was zero after a month. Now he's attempting to punish me for demanding child support."

"How?"

She described the plot to sue for custody and persuade his mother to raise the kids. "Betsy gave me all the details earlier today."

"That's what you were discussing in the lounge?" Zady slapped the coffee table. "How could we have fallen for such jerks? Why didn't we tell them to go to hell a whole lot sooner?"

"Gullibility. Love," Zora assessed. "And pride. Mom kept bragging about how perfect your life was."

"I cried on her shoulder practically every week. And she regaled me with stories of how happy you were." Zady blushed. "I couldn't give up on Dwayne because I refused to let you win."

"I felt the same way." Zora winced at how easily they'd been maneuvered. "How long do you think she's been lying to us?"

"Since we were born?"

Zora recalled Betsy's observation. "You're right. Whenever we had fun together, you could count on something happening to mess it up."

"Such as you borrowing my new sweater and ruining it." That incident had triggered their final blowup while they were in college. The squabble over a minor transgression had deteriorated into cross accusations and name calling. Soon afterward, Zady had left town with Dwayne.

"I didn't touch your sweater," Zora said. Had their mother really stooped that low? Obviously, yes. "You didn't borrow my earrings and lose one, either, did you?"

"No." Zady buried her face in her hands, then peeked between her fingers. "How sick, that she was jealous of her own children being close."

"Mom destroyed your sweater and my earrings so we'd fight." Zora struggled to grasp how cruel that had been.

"She always had to be the center of attention," Zady noted.

"That's why we were sitting ducks for Andrew and Dwayne," Zady said. "We grew up being manipulated."

"Imagine how she'll react when she learns we're on good terms again." Zady blew out a long breath. "She'll do anything to split us up."

"Let's not tell her." As she spoke, Zora could almost hear Lucky coaching her in the background, urging her to avoid her old traps by changing her behavior.

"How can we avoid it?"

"If we confront her, she'll start scheming," Zora pointed out. "We should say as little as possible to her."

A smile lit Zady's face. "That'll drive her crazy."

"Exactly."

"But if I land the job at Safe Harbor, she'll realize we must be talking," Zady said.

"We can say we only see each other around the building. End of story."

"She'll interrogate her old friends who live here."

"If she has any, they won't know anything." Zora's only contact from her mother's generation was Betsy, who was too smart to play those games.

"Wow." Zady regarded her in admiration. "That's both simple and diabolical."

"Let's function as a team. Full disclosure about everything."

"Done!"

Across the coffee table, they high-fived each other. For nearly ten years, Zora had been missing part of herself. "I'm only sorry it took us this long to come together. I'm glad my kids will have an aunt."

"Me, too." Zady regarded Zora's bulge wistfully.

"How will you raise them alone? If I'm living here, I'll pitch in, but I'll be working all day, too."

"There's day care at the hospital. And I have friends." Zora would be lost without her supportive household. "They've already raised money for a part-time nanny." Her phone buzzed with a text. Glancing down, she saw Lucky's message. "And there's my ride, waiting out front."

"Is that Mr. Mendez?" Longing shaded Zady's expression. "He's very kind. And he admires you, I can tell."

This was interesting news. "Did he say so?"

Her sister shook her head. "Not specifically. It's the way he looks at you, and how he avoided revealing too much about your situation while he walked me to the office building. He was protecting you."

"As a friend." Yet what if it meant more? Was it possible Lucky was falling in love with her, too? But he'd never abandon his ideal scenario, let alone agree to raise Andrew's children. "I shouldn't keep him waiting."

"Of course not."

Rising, Zady held out her hand to boost Zora. Then they flung their arms around each other.

"We're back," Zady crowed. "Twins forever!"

No more allowing others to separate them. "I hope, hope, hope you get the job."

"Me, too."

Amazement filled Zora as she eased out of the suite and along the path. How wonderful it would be to have family in town, especially the person who ought to be closest to her.

She couldn't wait to share their conversation with Lucky.

\* \* \*

As the October darkness gathered, Lucky drummed his fingers on the steering wheel. He had no idea what to expect from Zora—complaints? Fury? But his tension also derived from another matter.

Rod's complaints on the drive home had reminded him that Vince and Portia were barreling ahead on their pregnancy project. Once his wife had yielded, the billionaire hadn't wasted a moment. Since his treatment needed to be coordinated with hers, Lucky was able to follow their efforts.

After reviewing Portia's up-to-date medical records and confirming that she was in excellent health, Dr. Brennan had started her on medication to adjust her cycle. Once her eggs ripened, Dr. Rattigan would remove sperm from Vince's testes. Then her eggs would be harvested and injected with her husband's sperm.

Despite the most advanced treatments available, there were no guarantees. The average pregnancy rate per cycle was in the 20 to 35 percent range, but Portia's age lowered her chances. It was likely to take more than one cycle for the implantation to be successful.

But the men's program had to win Vince's support sooner than that. Cole had informed Lucky yesterday that the bankruptcy court was expected to approve the vacant dental building going on sale by mid-November. Several doctors' groups had expressed interest in the space.

Without that building, expansion of Lucky's program would be difficult. No comparable facility with offices and labs existed in Safe Harbor. As for constructing a new one, the logistics of acquiring land and receiving government approvals made that option prohibitive.

So if Vince delayed too long, Lucky might have to choose between using the degree he'd worked so hard for and leaving his friends. Friends who, as he'd become keenly aware, filled the lonely places in his soul.

The creak of the car door jerked Lucky from his reverie. Zora swung onto the seat beside him. "Have you met Dr. Davis? Is he a nice guy? Do you think he'll hire Zady?"

She sounded excited rather than angry, thankfully. "You're in favor of her landing the job?" Lucky switched on the ignition.

"Yes!" She drew the seat belt across her body. "It would be fantastic to have my sister here. My kids could grow up with their aunt, and besides, we belong together."

Things had gone well, then. Lucky smiled. "I was afraid you'd take my head off."

"For keeping her interview a secret?" Zora issued a growly noise. "You deserve it! But no."

"Her application was private." Moot point, now that Zady had revealed the facts to her sister. "I only met Dr. Davis briefly, but I like him. As for who he'll choose, the other candidates are also excellent. Tell me, what did you and Zady discuss?"

"Everything! It's incredible." Any concern that she'd keep Lucky in the dark vanished as she described Zady's selfish boyfriend and the similarities in their romantic experiences. The revelation about Andrew's possible abuse of her birth control pills was outrageous, but, unfortunately, in character for the louse.

Navigating along Coast Highway toward their house, Lucky maintained a leisurely speed to prolong the conversation. Beside him, Zora radiated an almost sexual intensity. The curve of her cheek invited his hand to stroke it, but he gripped the wheel tightly.

It wasn't safe to get distracted while driving. And once he touched her, he might not be able to stop there. He'd recognized his susceptibility to her that day in the office, when they'd nearly gone too far.

If it were only a question of the two of them, maybe... but he refused to risk giving his whole heart to a family that he couldn't be sure he could provide for. And what if Andrew decided he wanted to be a father to the twins? How he could be sure he'd never let Zora or the children down when, ultimately, control could be snatched out of his hands?

He'd made a workable plan for the future, one he could live with and sustain, and right now that plan did not allow for a wife and kids. No matter how he felt about Zora, ultimately he'd have to move past it.

"I understand better now why we fell for Mom's crap." She adjusted the seat belt, which tended to creep up on her abdomen. "Our mother pulled stunts to pit us against each other, and we bought it. She's been lying to us for years, convincing each of us that we were in competition."

She'd never told him that before, only that her mother was an alcoholic and her stepfather a bully. Lucky hadn't pressed for details, partly because he and Zora hadn't been close until recently, and partly because he resented it when people probed his own past. "I had no idea she was fomenting trouble for you."

"Neither did I. It's because of her that Zady and I had our last big blowup." She outlined how their mother had destroyed their property and tricked them into blaming each other. "It was cruel. We've lost nearly a decade.

Our mother must be a— Who was that Greek guy that fell in love with his own reflection?"

"Narcissus."

"That's it! She's a narcissist."

"You should cut her off," Lucky said. "It's what she deserves."

"We're putting up a united front," Zora responded. "Keeping her at arm's length will drive her nuts."

"Don't play games." Zora's assertiveness was new and likely fragile. She could easily be sucked back into self-defeating behavioral patterns if she continued to speak to her mother. "You should have nothing further to do with her."

In the faint light as they passed a streetlamp, he saw frown lines pucker her forehead. "She's our mother."

"To feed her ego, she groomed you to be patsies," he retorted. "Don't let Zady persuade you to stay involved with your mother. It's great that you've reconnected with your twin, but not if she's a bad influence."

"My sister isn't a bad influence!" Zora's shoulders stiffened. "And how we handle our mother is none of your business."

"It is if you spiral back into codependency," he said. "Because I have to live with you."

She appeared about to argue, but curiosity won. "What's codependency?"

"Codependents try to save loved ones from the consequences of their own actions because of a misguided sense of loyalty." After reading about the subject in a class on substance abusers and their families, Lucky had been astonished at how often he spotted the behavior in acquaintances and patients. "They feel guilty and trapped and blame themselves for the other person's faults, as you did with Andrew. You're a raging codependent, Zora."

"Now you're claiming I have a mental defect?"

"I'm helping you keep your life on track." To him, it seemed obvious.

"Wow, and I thought you'd changed." Far from heeding his warning, she was working up a head of steam. "Mr. Judgmental."

"It's for your own good." Lucky winced at the banality of his words. "That may be a cliché but in this instance, it's true."

"You expect me to abandon my mother and my sister because that's what you did with your brother when he crossed you."

Anger flared. Her situation didn't remotely compare to Lucky's. "You have no idea what separated Matthew and me."

"I know you're estranged from your entire family," Zora snapped. "He offended you, so Mr. High and Mighty Luke Mendez rejected him and everyone who stood by him."

"I had very valid reasons."

"What reasons?"

"He said vicious things no one could forgive, and obviously he doesn't regret it, since he never apologized."

"What did he say that was so terrible?"

"I have no intention of repeating it." Although Lucky had been only eighteen, his older brother's cruel words remained seared into his brain. *It's your fault our parents are dead, and you cheated me of my inheritance. You should be in prison.*

Matthew had repeated the lies to their aunts and uncles, who had barred Lucky from family gatherings.

After several attempts to reason with them, he'd decided to cut himself off from them entirely.

True, he'd messed up, badly. He'd never forgive himself for the mistakes that had hurt their parents. But he hadn't caused their deaths and he would never, ever cheat anyone.

"Maybe he's changed," Zora suggested.

"I've led a fulfilling life without my brother's destructive influence," Lucky replied tautly. "You should do the same with your mother."

"I'm not you." As they entered the driveway, Zora said, "Thank heaven."

"I agree."

"You do?"

"If you were like me, you'd be the first pregnant man in history."

She didn't laugh. Too bad. Lucky had been aiming to lighten the mood.

He supposed she believed that his promise not to nag her over Andrew also applied to the rest of her behavior. But to him, she'd come so far in the last couple of weeks, he didn't want to see her lose her newfound confidence and self-esteem.

If he'd annoyed her, it was worth it.

# Chapter 12

Angered by Lucky's arrogance, Zora avoided him over the weekend. She kept busy exchanging photos and messages with Zady, and went grocery shopping with Keely, although the nurse's insistence that she buy organic foods ran up the bill.

It was more than Lucky's haughty attitude that disturbed her, she realized after a second night of troubled sleep. In her dreams, her angry father raged at her, Zady and their mom. After his sudden death from a heart attack when she was twenty-two, Zora had pushed those ugly memories aside, preferring to dwell on her father's kinder, more loving moments. But the discovery of this rigid, unforgiving side of Lucky's nature had reawakened them.

Not that she hadn't expected this, at some level. After all, he insisted on the perfect family situation, including, presumably, a wife who arrived without baggage. No messy old relationships, and no children.

Yet, foolishly, she'd allowed herself to count on Lucky, to venture close to loving him, as if he might find it in his heart to change.

*Why do I keep falling for the wrong guy?*

If she entered another intimate relationship, Zora vowed to do it with her eyes open. Until then, once she discovered a man's fatal flaw, she'd distance herself from him, no matter how much her heart ached. And Lucky's fatal flaw was his intolerance for other people's flaws.

On Monday, she consulted Edmond regarding child support. He promised to file for half of Zora's unreimbursed medical and other maternity expenses.

"Once the babies are born, their father will be entitled to visitation and possibly shared custody," Edmond advised from behind the desk in his fifth-floor office. "That doesn't necessarily mean he gets physical custody half the time, but he will have an equal say in decisions about their care."

Much as she would hate sharing the children with their unworthy father, Zora supposed that she could hardly refuse contact. "He can't take them away from me, though, can he?"

"That would be extremely unusual," Edmond assured her. "He would have to prove that being around you endangers the children, such as if you were using drugs."

"I'd have to prove that for him, too, to block shared custody?"

"That's right." He adjusted his glasses. "In a case like this, it's tempting to try to cut him out. However, the courts have ruled that it's in a child's best interest for him or her to have a relationship with both parents."

Privately, Zora doubted it. However, she understood that laws and legal rulings had to apply to a wide range of cases.

When Lucky drove her home that evening, she suppressed the instinct to spill out what she'd learned from Edmond. She hadn't shared Betsy's confidence about Andrew's latest ploy, either.

*He's judgmental and pitiless.* The words played through her mind on a repeating loop, warning her to maintain a distance.

So when the silence weighed too heavily, she broached the merits of organic foods, a topic that interested him. Lucky explained that he was vegetarian more for health reasons than for philosophical ones, although sparing animals' lives was a bonus. The man didn't appear to notice that she was withholding any information of a personal nature.

On Tuesday morning, Zora was assigned to perform sonograms at Dr. Brennan's office. Her obstetrician urged her to stay off her feet as much as possible, and Keely brought enough cups of tea to double her already frequent trips to the restroom.

While every patient was important and required her focus, Zora sensed an undercurrent of excitement building among the staff in the late morning. The reason became clear when she wheeled her cart into an exam room where Portia Adams lay on the table. Her auburn hair highlighted with chestnut and gold strands, she wore a hot-pink hospital gown that she must have brought with her. The only other person present was the doctor.

Lips pressed into a thin line, Portia watched Zora with a flare of the nostrils. Was the woman still jealous? *How sad,* Zora thought as she readied her equipment.

She was thankful for Dr. Brennan's narrative during the sonogram. "Everything's right on target." Seated on a stool, the doctor crossed her long legs. "We may be ready to harvest your eggs by the end of next week. Are you experiencing mood swings?"

"No more than usual," Portia said tartly. "How soon will my pregnancy start to show? I'm on the committee of a Christmas charity ball for the animal shelter and I must be sure my dress will fit."

Dr. Brennan blinked. She must have heard a lot of odd questions, Zora mused as she removed the probe, but this one evidently caught her by surprise.

"If you become pregnant on the first try, you'd still only be a few months along by Christmas," she said. "Maternity clothes probably won't be necessary. However, for comfort, I recommend a loose-fitting style."

"That's what I meant," Portia said. "I just want to buy the right style."

When Keely entered the room, Zora started to wheel her equipment out. As she opened the door, she heard the nurse say to Dr. Brennan, "Mr. Adams has arrived. Shall I send him in?"

"Wait till I straighten my gown," Portia responded. "How's my hair?"

It was too late for her to retreat, Zora realized as the door closed behind her, leaving her alone in the hallway. And there he was, his large frame nearly filling the corridor and forcing her to halt.

"Well, well." Despite the expensive cologne and expertly cut hair, Vince had a sleazy air. "If it isn't the lady with the earth-goddess body."

"Your wife's waiting for you, Mr. Adams." Zora peered past him, hoping to spot another staff member. No such luck.

"Has anybody told you lately how sexy you are?" The man's low voice might not carry into the closed examining room, but Zora wished it would. Then surely Dr. Brennan or Keely would respond.

"Thank you." She rattled the cart. "Excuse me."

Vince's expression hardened. "I'm an important man around here. You should consider the advantages of keeping me happy."

What nerve! "That's hardly appropriate for a woman in my condition." *Or any woman in any condition.*

"There are other ways of pleasing a man," he muttered close to her ear.

Zora's stomach churned. "I have a patient waiting." Not true, but she didn't care. And neither, she gathered from Vince's unmoving stance, did he.

Mercifully, noises from inside the examining room finally penetrated his awareness. From his pocket, he produced a business card and scribbled a phone number on the reverse. "My cell." He stepped aside. "Call me."

Zora stuck the card in her pocket and hurried away. As she stored her equipment, her hands were trembling.

What was she going to do? The only way to be sure of avoiding the man in the future was to complain about his disgusting behavior. Sexual harassment violated hospital policy, but it was his word against hers.

No, not entirely. She'd attended a talk by the hospital's staff attorney, Tony Franco, highlighting the seriousness with which such claims were regarded.

But if the hospital hassled Vince, that ended any chance of a donation. His wife could transfer to a doctor in San Diego. Was it worth it? The man hadn't tried to *force* Zora to do anything against her will. He'd merely been unpleasant.

Still shaky, she headed for the elevators. In her pocket, she imagined the card covered with slime. Best to discard it immediately. Except, what if she needed to prove that he'd propositioned her? Zora resolved to let her emotions settle before reaching a decision.

After washing her hands—it was impractical to take a shower, despite the icky emotional residue left by her encounter—she went to the cafeteria. In her present mood, she'd rather avoid Lucky, and was glad to see no sign of him. Instead, she spotted Betsy at a table with Lin. The third Mrs. Raditch must have had her follow-up appointment with Dr. T this morning.

With her tray of food, Zora joined them. At nearby tables, heads swiveled and voices murmured. Didn't these people have anything more substantial on their minds?

Betsy pulled out a chair. "I'm glad you're here."

"Me, too, Grandma," Zora said lightly. "Lin, how are you?"

"Dr. Tartikoff found nothing suspicious," the young woman replied.

"That's wonderful." Zora hesitated to raise another sensitive topic. Lin's next comment spared her that.

"I have talked to the attorney you recommended." Lin placed her dirty tableware neatly atop her empty plate. "He suggests an annulment on the grounds that Andrew defrauded me."

"By pretending to be a human being?" Embarrassed

at her bluntness, Zora glanced apologetically at Betsy. "Sorry."

"No offense taken." Her ex-mother-in-law's mouth quirked.

"He lied about the vasectomy," Lin answered. "He claimed he had it during your marriage and promised to reverse it for me."

"Instead, he had the vasectomy *after* you got engaged." Which meant he didn't intend to reverse it, in Zora's opinion.

"Mr. Everhart called me after he contacted Andrew's attorney. It appears he will agree to the annulment," Lin said. "It will be as if the marriage never occurred."

How strange that, a month ago, this was what Zora had dreamed of, she mused as she ate. No more third wife. Instead, her sympathies now lay with Lin. "Will you stay in America?"

The other woman sighed. "I called my parents and they are eager for me to return."

"I wish you all the best," Betsy told her. "I hope you meet a man who deserves you."

"I doubt I will have as nice a mother-in-law," Lin said.

"How sweet." Betsy gazed at her pensively before turning to Zora. "If I may ask, what's the latest on your sister?"

Zora sketched the situation to her rapt audience. When she finished, she spotted Lucky standing with his tray, gazing around. A tremor ran through her at the reminder of the difficult choice she faced about Vince.

If she told him what Vince had done, how would he respond? Was it possible he'd think Zora had invited the other man's attention? Or, with his rigid insistence on propriety, would he pressure her to report Vince's harassment?

"You look pained," Betsy said. "Are you okay?"

"It's heartburn." Zora didn't dare reveal the truth. As nursing supervisor, Betsy would be obligated to inform the administrator.

"I must go." Lin stood, and Betsy, who'd finished her meal, did the same. "It is good to meet you again, Zora."

"Congratulations on your annulment." Zora almost regretted that Lin was returning to Hong Kong. She'd grown fond of her fellow sufferer.

How had Andrew managed to trick three intelligent women into loving him? Zora recalled Lucky describing her as a raging codependent. It must be a common condition.

He strode over, nodding to Betsy as she departed. Keely headed in their direction as well, her strong-boned face alight.

As the housemates settled, Keely spoke first. "I have great news! Mr. Adams plans to announce his donation soon."

Lucky gave a start. "He told *you*?"

"Dr. Brennan and me." The nurse transferred her dishes from the tray to the table. "He said the hospital is arranging a press conference. They're rushing the announcement because the dental building is going on sale."

Lucky slapped his thighs. "Fantastic!"

"He won't be able to jerk us around anymore," Zora burst out.

"Absolutely." Lucky's dark eyes sparkled. "Once he donates the money, we can stop worrying."

"That's right." This development reinforced Zora's

resolve to keep quiet. Losing the billionaire's support at this point would be devastating, and unnecessary. But what a relief that she only had to hold out for a little while longer.

"He and his wife were joking about whose name will go on the building," Keely added. "Just his, or both of theirs."

"I can guess which side Vince was on." It wouldn't surprise Zora if the man's monstrous ego required the hospital to paint an enormous portrait of him covering the front of the structure as well. She wondered how hard it would be to sneak out and ornament it with a large mustache, blackened tooth and eye patch.

"They can put their daughters' names on it, too, as far as I'm concerned." Lucky popped open his carton of milk. "We can call it the Everybody Who's Ever Been Named Adams Medical Building."

Zora tucked into her tapioca pudding, relishing the creamy texture and vanilla flavoring. The rest of her meal had gone down almost untasted.

Idly, she wondered why a number of other diners were sneaking glances at them. Betsy and Lin had left, and Keely hadn't spoken loudly enough for her disclosure to carry above the general chatter. Lucky's enthusiastic reaction might have drawn attention briefly, but the staring seemed to be increasing.

"What do you suppose Laird's up to?" Lucky indicated a compact male figure perched triumphantly on a chair while the listeners at his table leaned toward him attentively.

Keely stiffened. "He keeps smirking at me."

"That's the third table he's bestowed his noxious presence on." Lucky didn't miss much. "The man already took his petty revenge on you for beating him to the rental. What more does he expect to gain?"

A lull fell across the room as a group of prominent physicians—Dr. Tartikoff, Cole Rattigan and hospital administrator Mark Rayburn—entered from the patio dining area. Into the quiet, Laird's words—*her own mother*—jangled like an old-fashioned telephone. The administrator frowned at him before glancing in Keely's direction with a troubled look.

The nurse paled. "Oh, my gosh! How did Laird find out?"

"Find out what?" Lucky asked.

As Zora tracked the path of the doctors toward the exit, the answer hit her. "He must have heard Keely and me talking in the garage. He was lurking in his car to watch her discover the flat tires."

"What were you discussing?" Lucky queried.

"It's…personal." Keely closed her eyes, her face a study in anguish. Fury rose in Zora at the jerk who'd inflicted this on her.

Or could she be mistaken? "That was two weeks ago. I don't understand why Laird would wait till now to attack you."

Keely's shoulders slumped. "I do."

"Would somebody please enlighten me?" Lucky said, clearly growing frustrated.

"I'll start at the beginning." Keely described her mother's death and the false allegation of elder abuse made against her that she'd eventually been able to disprove. "On Monday, Dr. Brennan asked if I was involved in any legal proceedings. I told her I wasn't. She apologized for jumping to a conclusion."

"I don't follow." What did Dr. Brennan have to do with Keely *or* Laird?

"Neither did I, but it worried me," Keely admitted. "When I pressed her, she said her husband had asked if I was still her nurse. That's all, but it reminded me that he's a private detective."

"Laird must have hired him to dig into your background." Unbelievable. To go that far, the psychologist had to be deadly serious about driving Keely away.

"I'm sure the detective informed him that the charges had been dropped." Lucky scowled in Laird's direction.

"People already dislike me." Keely shuddered. "Did you notice Dr. Rayburn's expression? Laird must have gone to him."

"You haven't done anything wrong," Lucky insisted.

"When the old community hospital was sold, we all went through a rehiring process and background check." Keely's thick eyebrows formed an almost straight line. "They asked if we'd ever been charged with a crime. I put down 'No.'"

"Well, you weren't," Zora protested.

"But I was arrested," the older nurse said. "Some people assume that's the same thing."

"Let's call an emergency house meeting tonight," Zora said. "We'll help you deal with this. Okay?"

Keely nodded. Lucky tilted his head in agreement, but in view of his judgmental tendencies, Zora was prepared to stand up to him tonight. She might not be able to take on Vince Adams, but Lucky Mendez was another story.

# Chapter 13

Due to schedules and commitments, it was nine o'clock before the household assembled in the den. Lucky had filled in Karen and Rod, who were ready for action.

"I'll chip in for an attorney." As usual, Rod shared the couch with Karen. "Legal costs can grind you under. That might be part of Laird's agenda."

Lucky assumed the anesthesiologist's view was colored by his own experience with the legal system.

In her chair beside Zora, Keely twisted her hands. "Do I *have* to get a lawyer?"

"It might be premature. Has anyone from Human Resources spoken to you about this?" Karen asked.

Keely's straight dark hair slashed the air as she shook her head.

"Edmond offers a free consultation." Lucky studied Zora's reaction, and was disappointed that she gave no sign of how she felt. He'd been hoping to learn that she'd met with Edmond herself to set the wheels rolling against Andrew.

How frustrating that she'd barely spoken to him since their disagreement on Friday. When Lucky had urged her to shut out her mother and, if necessary, her sister, he'd never expected her to shut *him* out instead. He had to admit, he might have gone overboard where her sister was concerned. Although he didn't entirely trust Zady's influence, she meant a lot to Zora. And family was precious—unless they performed a demolition act on your happiness.

But he hadn't had a chance to soften his position in the face of Zora's stonewalling. Talk about driving a person crazy.

*Talk to me.* Not this instant, of course, but he wished she'd stop avoiding his gaze.

This afternoon, he'd confirmed that the hospital had scheduled press conference for a week from Thursday to announce a major donation. Lucky should have been exultant, but his emotions refused to cooperate because he couldn't share his happiness with Zora. After all, expanding the program would allow him to stay in Safe Harbor. It angered him that she seemed willing to forgive Andrew almost anything, and him nothing.

However, they had a more immediate matter on the floor. Lucky seized the initiative. "We should advise Dr. Rayburn about Laird's behavior. Don't forget he let the air out of Keely's tires—"

"We can't prove that," Zora interrupted.

"You saw his car at the scene." Lucky had checked, and her description, including the bumper sticker, fit

Laird's vehicle. "He also hired a private detective to snoop into a staff member's background for revenge."

"We can't prove that, either," Rod observed. "And if there was a hospital policy forbidding nosiness, we'd all be out of a job."

Keely hunkered down, arms crossed protectively. Zora scooted her chair closer to Keely's as an indication of solidarity.

"Laird's an embarrassment to the hospital." Lucky had developed a disgust for the man since witnessing his drunken, lecherous behavior more than a year earlier during Elvis Presley night at the Suncrest Saloon. "I'm willing to march into Dr. Rayburn's office and demand he put a stop to this bullying. Who's with me?"

Zora laid a hand on her bulge, which was rippling beneath her maternity top. "Before we start painting protest signs, let's hear Keely's opinion."

"Fine." From his easy chair, Lucky fixed his attention on the older nurse.

She cleared her throat. "I'd like to run this by Dr. Brennan."

"Tomorrow?" Lucky urged.

"She's busy on Thursdays," Keely said. "She has surgeries scheduled."

"She can spare five minutes." The doctor had already showed concern for her nurse when she mentioned her husband's question, hadn't she? "Get her on your side."

"I don't want to drag her into my personal business."

"Don't let Laird intimidate you." With adrenaline pumping through his system, Lucky felt the urge to jump to his feet and pace.

"Oh, quit pressuring her," Zora snapped. "Keely has a right to handle this however she chooses."

"You mean through avoidance?"

Karen raised her hands. "Peace, everybody. As Zora said, this is Keely's decision. We're the backup team."

"Yeah, okay." How had this conversation become an argument between him and Zora, anyway?

Keely released a breath. "I'll talk to my doctor tomorrow."

"Good for you," Zora said.

How come she didn't give Lucky any credit? He'd pushed Keely to do exactly that.

"Are we finished?" Rod asked. Everyone nodded. "Before we break up, you'll all be pleased to hear that I plan to replace my broken-down junkmobile. Any suggestions?"

"A hybrid," Zora said. "You'll save a fortune on gas."

"Consult the online ratings," Keely contributed.

"I'm considering a sports car," Rod added. "Possibly red."

"Watch out. The cops will ticket you every time you edge a few miles over the speed limit." Lucky had heard that from officers who'd chatted with him during his stint as an ambulance driver.

"I should drive a gray SUV instead?" Rod demanded. *"Boring."*

"Buy a car that seats five or six," Karen recommended. "So you can transport the girls and their friends."

"If only."

"Speaking of guests, that brings us to the topic of Thanksgiving," their landlady said, deftly seizing control of the discussion. "How about cooking our dinner a day or two after the holiday? There'll be more chance your daughters can join us."

They speculated on how next week's announcement might affect Vince and Portia's holiday plans but weren't able to reach a conclusion. As for the dinner, scheduling it on a Saturday was fine with Lucky. He usually volunteered to serve food at a homeless shelter on the holiday.

Amid yawns—they were an early-rising bunch—the meeting dispersed. Aware that Zora customarily drank a glass of milk before bed, Lucky watched for his chance and slipped into the kitchen when she was alone.

He noted her cute freckled nose, red hair that frizzed by day's end and legs propped up on a nearby chair. Choosing a chair around the corner of the small table, he reached for her nearest foot.

"Hey!" Zora attempted a glare that bore a strong resemblance to a squint.

"Tired?" Lucky drew his thumb along her instep.

"It's been a busy day." She patted her belly for emphasis.

She should go on maternity leave before she collapsed and delivered in a hall. However, Lucky was trying to reconnect with her, not irritate her. "How're things with Betsy and the third Mrs. Raditch?" he ventured.

"Fine."

He gritted his teeth. As he lifted her other foot and massaged it, her body relaxed. Progress! "Any word from your sister about the job?"

"No." She sank lower in her chair, eyelids drooping.

As Lucky stroked her feet, he noted they were puffy. It must be agony for her to stand all day. *None of your business.* Great—he didn't have to speak any longer; her responses sprang up automatically in his thoughts.

"It must be interesting, working in a different department each day," he said.

"Oh, there are a lot of repeats," she murmured, and fell silent.

"Doggone it!" Oops, he hadn't meant to speak out loud.

Her eyes flew open and her muscles tightened. "What's your problem?"

"You never talk to me anymore." Had he really said that? He sounded like an old married woman. *Or man. Don't be sexist.*

"Why should I? So you can critique my behavior and complain about how stupid I am?" she demanded.

"Of course not." Resentment flared at this unfair description of his statements. "I'd merely advise and counsel you."

"Same difference." Her feet vanished from his hands. Lucky felt like the prince, caught on his knees, rejected by Cinderella.

"What happened to our truce?" He realized he'd entered dangerous territory, since their pact had required him to refrain from criticizing her. But their agreement had been specifically about Andrew. It was unreasonable of her to extend that to a blanket ban on all helpful comments.

"Don't pretend we're teammates," Zora grumped. "We agreed to collaborate to secure the Adamses' donation, and apparently we succeeded."

"There's still a week to go." Lucky was grasping at straws. But surely they could resume their camaraderie.

"I promise not to screw things up before then. Satisfied?" An unfamiliar tightness transformed her into a woman he scarcely recognized, older and more guarded.

This was what he'd been trying to prevent by steering Zora past her poor choices. Before he could assess what it meant or frame another question, the tension vanished and she was once again his peppery little friend.

"I'm off to bed." She handed him her empty glass. "Do something useful. Put this in the dishwasher."

"Not the oven?"

"Whatever." Thrusting her feet into her slippers, she padded off.

Well, at least she'd addressed him directly, Lucky mused as he carried the glass to its destination. He'd count that as a victory.

How fortunate that Lucky had the male clueless gene, Zora reflected tartly while she prepared for bed. He'd mentioned nothing was certain for another week, and at the prospect of facing another week in which she might be exposed to Vince's obnoxious behavior, she'd suffered a wave of revulsion. She'd schooled her features quickly, though, and was fairly sure Lucky hadn't noticed.

She was unclear about the precise mechanism of the donation, but she assumed the billionaire would hand over a check or sign a document when he announced his gift. After that, she doubted he'd withdraw it merely because an ultrasound tech refused to service his needs.

Wrenching her mind away from the whole awful situation, Zora climbed into bed for the night. Mercifully, maternal hormones zapped her into an instant deep sleep.

Over the next few days, the housemates did everything in their power to counter the spread of the rumors about Keely. They told others the true circumstances, including that the charges had been dropped. They pointed to examples of the older woman's kindness, which were often overlooked due to her downbeat personality. They also cited Laird's unscrupulous motives, although by now he must realize they'd never let him move into their house.

It was an uphill battle. Gossip spread madly and either distorted Laird's account even further, or else he embellished it himself. According to one version that reached Zora, Keely had gotten off murder charges on a technicality. By another, she'd been suspected in the deaths of several elderly patients. Many workers, having consulted Laird about their personal problems in the past, were inclined to trust him implicitly.

Keely declined to mount a defense. "I should have stayed home with my mom that day," she told Zora. "I deserve my share of blame."

"Stop acting like a codependent," Zora replied, and, for clarification, displayed the definition on her cell phone. Keely just shrugged.

As they'd expected, Dr. Brennan supported her nurse. Although a few of her patients who were staffers at the medical center claimed to feel uncomfortable around Keely due to her history, no one requested a change of doctors.

But rather than fading, the opposition was growing. In the corridors, people avoided Keely. Zora had been ostracized to an extent for stealing Stacy's husband, but it had never sunk to this level.

Human Resources had contacted Keely and reviewed her history, but there'd been no attempt to fire her. Nevertheless, on Thursday she informed her housemates that she was tired of being a pariah and planned to search for another job. Shoulders hunched, she brushed off their objections.

"She feels guilty," Karen observed after Keely left the room. "The hardest person to forgive is yourself."

"That's ridiculous," Lucky growled. "The past is the past and we should leave it there."

Zora didn't bother to point out that he ought to leave his quarrel with his brother in the past. She was too worried about Keely to waste her energy bickering.

On Friday at lunch, a lab technician deliberately bumped Keely as she walked to their table. Fortunately, Keely kept a tight grip on her tray. Her stoic air didn't fool Zora, though. She knew her friend was close to tears.

"Don't you dare leave without eating," she told the nurse, and walked beside her to their seats. Karen, Rod and Lucky closed ranks with them.

Once they were settled, Zora dared to hope they could eat in peace. Then a tall woman of about fifty, with short brown hair and weathered skin, stalked over and stood over Keely, scowling until the chatter quieted.

"What's on your mind, Orla?" Rod demanded.

The name prodded Zora's memory. Orla Baker was a circulating nurse, which explained how Rod knew her—circulating nurses set up the operating room and checked the stock of instruments and disposable items, which they refreshed during the procedure. They played a key role in protecting patients from mistakes by verifying their identities and reviewing the site and nature of the operation with the surgeon.

"It's disgusting that she left her mother to die." She spat out the words as if it had been *her* mother who'd perished. "The DA may not have charged her, but what kind of person does that? She should be ashamed."

In the stillness, Zora spotted Laird leaning against a wall, arms folded and a smile playing around his mouth. If she'd had a rubber band, she'd have shot it at him to wipe the smirk off his face.

Rising, Lucky pointed at the psychologist. "Orla, *you* should be ashamed for allowing that man to manipulate you into bullying her. He's trying to drive her away because of petty resentment."

Zora had never admired anyone more in her life. Awkwardly, she rose, too. "Laird Maclaine played a mean prank on Keely by letting the air out of her tires. What is this, high school?" Her voice rang out with a touch of shrillness. "He also hired a detective to dig up dirt that he then distorted for his smear campaign. How can any decent person be a party to that?"

Karen sprang up. "Keely may not be slick and persuasive, but she has a kind heart and I'm with her one hundred percent."

Rod stood beside her. "That goes double for me, Orla."

The circulating nurse wavered. "My mother has Alzheimer's. I understand the stresses involved, but there's no excuse for abandoning her mother."

Keely sat silent, unwilling to speak on her own behalf. Zora feared others would take that as an indication of guilt.

Across the cafeteria, a six-foot-tall woman with a commanding air uncoiled. All attention fixed on Dr. Paige Brennan, whose eyes flashed with anger.

"This situation has been discussed at the highest levels and the case is closed," she declared. "If anyone continues creating a hostile work environment for my nurse, I will ensure that disciplinary measures are taken against them. And that is the last I or any of us had better hear about this."

The other obstetricians at her table burst into applause. With a spurt of amusement, Zora registered that the loudest clapping came from Dr. Tartikoff. Apparently he'd forgiven Keely for their long-ago dispute, or else he had zero tolerance for bullying.

Orla spoke directly to Keely. "I apologize. I shouldn't have listened to gossip."

"Have a seat." Karen waved her over. "I'm sorry about your mom, Orla. How're you holding up?"

After a brief hesitation, the circulating nurse sank into a chair. "Some days are better than others."

As the conversation flowed, Zora noted that Dr. Brennan's declaration had restored the color to Keely's face. Orla's apology appeared to have helped, too.

But best of all was watching Laird slink from the cafeteria. Paige Brennan's scorching setdown must have impressed on him that his campaign against Keely had not only failed, it had also damaged his own reputation with the top staff.

A wise person would take a long, hard look in the mirror. She didn't credit Laird with wisdom, however.

That night, Casa Wiggins celebrated the victory with meatless burgers and fizzy apple juice. There was no more talk of Keely changing jobs.

Still, it was too soon to let all her anxiety go. In less than a week, the future of the men's program would be secure, Zora hoped, and prayed silently for nothing to go wrong.

# Chapter 14

"I produced fifteen eggs?" From the examining table, Portia stared in dismay at Dr. Brennan. "You must be kidding!"

"That's an excellent number to ripen," the doctor assured her as Zora carefully adjusted the position of her ultrasound wand. "We'll select those in the best condition, fertilize them and choose the healthiest embryos to implant. If we have more than three, we can freeze the rest for later."

"Three? Surely two is plenty!" Portia's fingers curled, as if she longed for someone to hold her hand. Vince, who'd positioned himself in front of the ultrasound monitor, didn't appear to notice.

He'd barely glanced at Zora, either. She'd been disturbed on discovering she'd been assigned to Portia, but the scheduler had insisted.

"I'd prefer four," Vince announced. His wife gasped. Zora might not like her, but she empathized with the woman.

"That would violate hospital policy," Dr. Brennan said. "Portia, if you don't want more than two, we'll respect your wishes."

After a tense pause, the patient said, "Three will be fine."

"You're sure?"

Vince blew out an impatient breath.

Tautly, Portia said, "Yes."

Dr. Brennan jotted a note in the computer. To Zora, the doctor appeared concerned, but didn't press the point. "Now that the eggs are mature, timing is crucial. As I explained, you'll need an injection of HCG—human chorionic gonadotropin—to prepare for ovulation. Harvesting should take place thirty-six hours later."

As Zora finished her work, she half listened to the details. Normally, the patient's husband, after being shown how to give the shots, would have injected her with hormones for the past week or so, and would administer HCG at ten o'clock tonight. Instead, the Adamses had hired a visiting nurse.

"We'll set the egg retrieval for Wednesday morning," Dr. Brennan continued. "Mr. Adams, we'll coordinate with Dr. Rattigan to be sure he collects your sperm before then."

"I can attend the egg harvesting, I presume." The billionaire shifted from one foot to the other as if cramped by the confines of the examining room.

"Absolutely," the doctor said.

"We'll use the same sonographer, as per my instructions?"

Zora's stomach tightened. Today's assignment hadn't been by chance. Did the billionaire simply enjoy throwing his weight around or was there more to it?

Dr. Brennan looked startled. "The egg retrieval is a specialized procedure. We'll have a team in place."

"It's good luck to have a pregnant woman nearby. Maternal hormones and all that." Vince gestured toward Zora. "The process has gone smoothly so far with her present, hasn't it, Doctor?"

If Portia had had a death ray, Zora didn't doubt she'd have used it. *On me.*

"That's true." Dr. Brennan smiled. "However, I'm not sure we can credit Zora's maternal hormones." Without further comment about the sonographer request, she provided them directions to the hospital's retrieval room on the second floor, where the procedure would take place. "Don't eat or drink anything after midnight Tuesday, Mrs. Adams, and be sure to arrive an hour early."

"I'll be asleep for it, I hope," Portia grumbled as she sat up, finally receiving her husband's hand in assistance.

"You'll be sedated, and in recovery for two to three hours afterward," the doctor said. "We'll let you know later the same day how many eggs were retrieved. They'll be examined by an embryologist, and by Thursday we'll inform you of how many we were able to fertilize."

Thursday was the day of the press conference. Of course, the embryos wouldn't be implanted into Portia's womb for a few more days to give them time to grow in the lab. Was Vince also going to demand that Zora be present for the implantation?

He wasn't likely to succeed; as Dr. Brennan had indicated, the fertility team worked with its own techs. However, to be sure of preventing any further contact with the man, Zora could schedule her maternity leave. She had to admit that, with her ankles swollen and her abdomen sore, she was overdue.

When Keely entered the room, Zora rolled out her cart. Her knees weak with relief at having weathered the encounter with Vince, she headed around a corner toward the storage closet.

She'd just stowed the equipment when heavy male footsteps jolted her pulse into high gear. Turning, she spotted Vince Adams at a bend in the hall.

This late in the afternoon, there was no one else in view. Before she could exit, the heavyset man blocked her escape.

"What're you doing?" Zora demanded.

"You should have called me." He reached for the nearest door and shoved it open to reveal an empty examining room. "Let's talk inside."

"I'm fine right here." The words emerged breathlessly. "This is a private conversation."

"Forget it." Zora tried to dodge past, lost her balance and stumbled. He caught her arm as if to assist, but instead pulled her into the room.

"Listen, I'm donating twenty million dollars to this hospital. And I'll spend money on you, too, if you make it worth my while." This close, she caught the scent of alcohol on his breath. Zora knew all too well what effect that had on the wrong kind of man.

"Leave me alone." She pressed her palms against his chest, but that only seemed to amuse him.

"Be nice to me, honey," he slurred.

She flashed on stories she'd heard about Vince's past:

that he'd gotten his start through gang connections in a rough part of Phoenix and that a former business rival had disappeared under mysterious circumstances. Yet she'd never imagined he'd dare to assault her.

The door flew open. There stood Keely, aghast. "What is this?"

Vince glanced over his shoulder. "If you know what's good for you, Nurse, you'll keep your mouth shut."

Instead, Keely commanded, "Get your hands off her!"

"Shut up, you…"

While he was distracted, Zora grabbed a pair of scissors from a drawer. "Let go of me!"

Startled, the hulking man released her. "Neither of you says a word to anyone or you're both out of a job."

Angry breathing filled the room. No one spoke, and finally, he left. Heart pounding, Zora clutched the scissors, ready to fight if he returned.

"Are you all right?" Keely asked.

The adrenaline seeping out of her, Zora set the instrument on the counter. "Thank goodness you showed up." How far would that monster have gone?

"Has he done anything like this before?"

It was on the tip of her tongue to deny it. *Keep the secret, don't cause problems.* But Zora had kept his secret once, and this was where it had led. "Yes, although it wasn't this bad."

"We have to report him."

Despite her outrage, Zora hesitated. "If we raise a fuss, there goes the donation. Think what that will do to the hospital, and to Lucky."

"Men like Vince Adams depend on their victims keeping silent," Keely growled. "That's how they get away with it."

"I don't want to involve the police." Zora had no idea how this situation would appear to an officer.

"You might have to," Keely said. "But you can start with Dr. Rayburn if you prefer. I'll come with you."

How brave of her, and what a great friend. Tearfully, Zora nodded. "Okay."

"First, let's settle your nerves," the nurse advised. "How about tea and peanut-butter crackers?"

"Thanks."

Twenty minutes later, after a snack in the lounge, Zora could speak without trembling. Her brain still skipped from objection to objection, however. What if her complaint smashed Lucky's dreams? What if the administrators believed she'd encouraged Vince? But she had to do this, for other potential victims as much as for herself.

It was nearly five o'clock when they reached the hospital's fifth floor. What if Dr. Rayburn had left for the day? If Zora had to wait until tomorrow, she wouldn't be able to sleep.

As they approached the executive suite, she heard movement inside. Then the last two people on earth she'd expected to see emerged into the corridor.

Vince and Portia Adams. He regarded Zora with a superior smirk. His wife gave a start, her face pale.

With the sensation of falling into an abyss, Zora realized that her tormenter had performed an end run around her. Whatever story he'd concocted, it would make her sound like a liar—and possibly end her career.

Lucky knew something was wrong when Keely texted that she'd drive Zora home instead of him. Why the last-minute change? Keely had added that she was calling a house meeting as soon as everyone arrived.

When he tried to call Zora, her phone went to voice mail. Was she in labor? But if she was, why would Keely be bringing her home?

Perhaps Laird had pulled another stunt and the women wanted to talk about it in private. Or maybe Dr. Brennan had discovered something worrisome about Zora's pregnancy.

Adrenaline pounded through Lucky's system. If Zora was in danger, he should be there to protect her.

In the garage, he cruised up along the ramp in search of Keely's car. With most of the staff gone and few outpatients or visitors on hand, he should have been able to spot it, but no luck.

Cursing himself for wasting time, Lucky headed home. He had to fight the tendency to stomp on the gas pedal.

Why was he reacting so strongly? It was silly and useless. But he kept imagining Zora's emotions in turmoil and longing to reassure her.

At the house, he was glad when he spotted Keely's car in the driveway. Just ahead of him, Karen pulled into the remaining open spot, with Rod beside her.

Lucky parked at the curb and broke into a lope. "What gives?" he asked when he came within earshot.

"No idea." Karen straightened her blazer. "I haven't heard any gossip from our receptionist." That young woman, Caroline Carter, reputedly had the keenest radar in the hospital.

Rod's fedora shadowed his face as the three of them followed the walkway. "I haven't picked up anything in the doctors' lounge, either."

Inside, Lucky barreled into the den, grateful that neither Karen nor Rod objected when he bypassed them. He felt a spurt of relief when he saw Zora in her usual chair, sipping a cup of juice. Keely paced nearby, unable to contain her restlessness.

*Just like me.* "Are you okay?" Lucky demanded.

Zora didn't answer.

"Sit down." No sign of Keely's customary reticence. "Everyone."

He took his favorite chair, while Karen and Rod slid onto the couch, not bothering to remove their shoes or hats or jackets. "Don't keep us in suspense," Rod said.

"This afternoon, I walked in on Vince Adams assaulting Zora." Disgust emphasized the deep lines in Keely's face.

"He did what?" Lucky sprang up, prepared to find the man and pummel him. "Were you hurt? You should go to the police."

"Let us finish, please." When he subsided, Keely described the scene she'd interrupted in an examining room. Thank goodness she'd arrived when she had, although Lucky would have paid a fair amount of money to watch Zora stab that jerk with scissors.

But before they could take the matter to Dr. Rayburn, Vince had beaten them to the punch, claiming Zora had tried to extort money by threatening to accuse him of harassing her.

"Mark can't believe that," Karen protested when Keely paused for breath. "It's ridiculous."

"Still, I'm glad to have Keely as a witness." Zora's voice trembled. "And I showed Dr. Rayburn the business card Vince gave me with his private number scrawled on the back. He pressed it on me the last time he cornered me."

"He's done this before?" The revelation sickened Lucky. "Why didn't you report it?"

"It didn't go this far," she told him. "And I was worried it might have an impact on the men's program."

"The program isn't your responsibility," Karen said.

"But I care about—about the rest of the staff," Zora replied.

"You were protecting me?" Lucky would never allow her to put her safety at risk. "I didn't ask you to do that."

"You were happy enough when Portia agreed to in vitro," Zora shot back. "He all but said he'd leave her for some 'earth mother,' as he described me, if she didn't agree to in vitro instead of insisting on surrogacy."

Stunned, Lucky recalled the scene outside Dr. Rattigan's examining room. He'd never known the details of how Portia had made her decision. And all this while, she'd kept Vince's mistreatment a secret?

Once, long ago, Lucky had vowed never again to let down anyone he loved the way he'd let down his parents. Yet now he had. Worse, by scheduling Zora to work that first morning because he valued her insight, he'd put her in harm's way.

Wordlessly, he listened as the conversation moved on around him. In the administrator's office, Mark had been accompanied by attorney Tony Franco. They'd assured Zora that her job was safe and that she had every right to contact the police.

"Great idea." Lucky would love to see Vince hauled off in handcuffs.

"As if I'd have any chance against a billionaire and his legal team," Zora said miserably.

"We have honest cops in Safe Harbor," Karen responded. "Tony Franco's brother is a police detective."

"Vince will just repeat his claim that I tried to extort money from him," Zora said. "How can I prove I didn't? And if he sues me for slander, I can't afford to fight."

It was unfair that his wealth enabled a man like Vince to crush people, as he'd already done with Rod. If only Lucky had been the one to discover that scene today, he'd have taught the bastard a lesson on the spot.

And probably lost his job, not to mention being locked up for assault. But it would have felt good to smash his fists into the man's oily face.

"Dr. Rayburn seemed worried about the emotional and physical effects on Zora," Keely put in. "He offered her an extra two months of paid maternity leave, not in lieu of anything else, just for health reasons."

"He suggested I go on leave immediately while he sorts this out," Zora added. "I refuse to slink away as if I did anything wrong, but I am going to start my leave on Monday, because I already had that in mind."

"Extra paid leave—that's a positive thing, anyway," Karen said.

"How does Dr. Rayburn intend to sort this out?" Lucky persisted. Zora had been attacked at work, and other staffers could be at risk, too. If only Vince weren't so rich, and the hospital staff so eager for his donation.

*Including me.* It revolted Lucky to think of how hard he'd worked to keep Vince involved with Safe Harbor.

"Dr. Rayburn said there are complicating issues." Having practically worn a path in the carpet with her pacing, Keely plopped into an armchair.

"Like what? Vince's money?" Rod grumbled.

"He and Portia are patients, so disrupting their care

would be unethical if no wrongdoing is proved." Zora clasped her hands atop her baby bump. "It's a crucial week for them."

"The hospital should cancel that damn press conference." No matter what the donation meant for Lucky or his doctor, he'd never sacrifice an innocent person's well-being. Especially Zora's.

"Dr. Rayburn has to discuss it with the hospital corporation," Keely said. "They'll make the final decision. Except he was very clear that he will not allow any repercussions against Zora or me."

"Dr. Brennan would be up in arms if he did, I'm sure," Karen said.

"Along with the rest of the medical staff," Rod added. "No one would believe Vince's story."

Zora set her empty cup on the table. "Keely and I aren't exactly the most popular members of the staff."

"You've seen what our household can do," Lucky reminded her. "If you need us, we're here."

Both women nodded. "Oh, we aren't supposed to discuss this," Zora added. "Please don't tell anyone else."

Despite an eagerness to rally the troops behind Zora, Lucky supposed he had to respect her decision. "All right." *For now.*

"How about dinner?" Karen got to her feet. "I'll bet the mommy-to-be is starving."

Rod stood also. "My cooking skills may be notoriously bad, but Jack taught me how to cook angel-hair pasta with wine and onions. It doesn't take long. And the alcohol in the wine evaporates."

"I'll fix a salad," Lucky volunteered.

The dinner went well, but he continued to be frustrated for the rest of the evening. He should be the person Zora turned to, but instead she remained glued to Keely's side. Lucky tried in vain to catch her alone so he could massage her tense little shoulders. Or fetch her ice cream—why didn't she send him on errands anymore?

How ironic that he'd criticized her for leading a messy life. Now she'd landed in her biggest crisis yet, and the person most to blame—after Vince, of course—was Lucky himself.

Yet again, he'd been responsible for causing pain to someone he cared about. And yet again, there didn't seem to be any way to make up for his mistakes.

## *Chapter 15*

Catching sweet, sympathetic glances from Lucky all evening, Zora yearned to fly to him. Temporary though the respite might be, she longed to curl up in his arms and enjoy the illusion of safety.

But it *was* an illusion. She understood Lucky too well. Their relationship could only progress to a certain point before he'd slam the door on her. She and her babies would never fit his requirements for a perfect family.

How ironic that, while she failed to measure up to Lucky's standards, his influence had helped her shake free of her old codependent habits. She'd told off Andrew, stood up to Vince Adams and marched into Dr. Rayburn's office when her instincts screamed at her to flee.

It had been terrifying to confront two such powerful men in the meeting. Dr. Rayburn had towered over her dauntingly when they'd shaken hands. As for Tony Franco, beneath his reserved manner lurked a brain capable of raising who-knew-what legal complications against which an ordinary mortal was defenseless.

Zora had been grateful that Keely was there, and for the strength that she was beginning to realize had been within her all along. She'd managed not to break down in tears when the administrator repeated the lie Vince had told them. She'd stuck doggedly to the facts, painful as they were. There'd been two previous incidents, and she had the business card to prove it. Not much evidence, but it helped, as did Keely's testimony.

Tossing and turning in bed that night, she searched without success for a solution. If the Adamses canceled their planned donation, the whole hospital would suffer and Lucky might have to go elsewhere to build his career. But if the grant went forward, how could Zora stay? The vengeful billionaire would find a way to destroy her.

In the morning, she received a message from her sister: Got the job! Start in 3 weeks!

Under other circumstances, that would have been fantastic news. Now, Zora worried that if Vince saw her identical twin, he'd target Zady, too.

She arrived at the medical center on Tuesday with her senses on high alert. As the day progressed, no one mentioned Vince's accusations, but the news spread about Zora starting maternity leave on Monday. The hospital's public relations director, Jennifer Serra Martin, presented Zora with a pair of adorable teddy bears that played lullabies. Dr. T's nurse, Ned Norwalk, slipped Zora a gift card to Kitchens, Cooks and Linens.

"I'm not sure whether you're short of pots and pans, but you can always use more knives." He whisked off before she could ask what he meant. Had that been a veiled reference to her scissors wielding?

By Tuesday's end, the press conference hadn't been canceled, nor, apparently, had the next day's egg retrieval. And she learned that Vince had undergone the procedure to collect his sperm. The only change Zora observed was that the billionaire was now accompanied everywhere by a male patient care coordinator, supposedly to ensure his comfort.

*And to protect me and the other women on staff?*

On Wednesday morning, Zora was again assigned to Dr. Brennan's patients. No danger of running into the Adamses, whose egg retrieval was taking place in the hospital. Dr. Brennan, Zora discovered, had arranged for Dr. Zack Sargent to perform the procedure on the grounds that he performed more of them.

The moment she spotted Zora, Dr. Brennan zeroed in on her. "I'm sorry that you were assaulted."

"I'm fine."

"It was an unforgivable act, and I'm furious that it took place on my watch," the tall woman said. "If you need me to go to bat for you, just say the word."

Zora thanked her, pleased to have another person on her side.

At lunch, aware of prying ears, Zora and her housemates were careful not to discuss what was foremost on everyone's minds. She had almost finished eating when a call came from Dr. Rayburn's assistant, asking Zora to meet with him.

"I'll go with you," Keely announced.

"You have patients," Lucky reminded her.

"You can't let them down," Zora echoed. Despite her words, Zora shivered to think of what lay ahead. What if the corporation insisted on firing her? What if… Her brain wouldn't stretch further than that.

"Dr. Rattigan's in surgery for another hour, so I'll go with you." Lucky piled her dishes onto his tray. "No arguments."

"I didn't plan to raise any."

On the elevator ride to the fifth floor, Zora held Lucky's hand. Tension rippled across the muscles in his neck and arms, with the ironic effect that the dragon protruding from beneath his navy blue sleeve appeared to be winking at her.

"I hope I don't break down." She released her grip as they stepped into the empty hallway. "I've always been terrified that someday everything would fall apart and I'd be alone."

He touched her shoulder gently. "You aren't alone."

Zora blinked back tears. Impulsively, she asked, "What's *your* biggest fear?"

"Failing the people I love," Lucky said without hesitation. "And I'm not about to do that again."

Did he include her among the people he loved? Zora cautioned herself against leaping to conclusions. She had a bad habit of hearing only what she wished to hear.

"Don't go out on a limb for my sake," she told him.

"My integrity isn't for sale," Lucky answered. "Cole's isn't, either. He has opportunities elsewhere, although before he leaves Safe Harbor, I'm sure he'll consider the impact on Stacy."

"Oh, great." Zora hadn't considered how wide the fallout might be from the loss of Vince's donation. "As if I haven't done Stacy enough harm already."

"You did her a favor, taking Andrew away," Lucky returned. "I should have realized that sooner."

In the administrative suite, the assistant regarded Lucky in surprise. "I'm here for moral support," he said.

"Hold on." She picked up her phone.

From one of several inner rooms, Tony Franco appeared, his rust-brown hair rumpled as if he'd been running his fingers through it. After introducing himself to Lucky, he shook hands with them both. "Dr. Rayburn and I would like to speak to Mrs. Raditch alone."

"Without her lawyer?" Lucky demanded.

Tony gave a start. "If she wishes…"

"Lucky, that isn't necessary." How could she afford it? Also, since Edmond worked as a consultant for the hospital, he had a conflict of interest. Where would she find another lawyer on short notice?

"Then I'm sitting in," Lucky responded firmly. "I'll keep quiet, I promise."

To Zora's surprise, the attorney acquiesced. "Very well."

Tony's expression remained opaque. Did they learn how to do that in law school? she wondered, and pictured a classroom full of law students training their features to remain flat.

When they entered Dr. Rayburn's office, the administrator rose to shake their hands, and it was obvious he hadn't mastered the same art. In his face, she read unease, a touch of surprise at Lucky's presence and regret.

*Oh, damn.*

True to his statement, Lucky took a seat in a corner of the large office. Dr. Rayburn, whom she'd expected to retreat behind the desk, instead positioned himself in a chair beside hers. "I'll get straight to the point. The corporation insists we accept the Adamses' sponsorship of the men's program and move forward with tomorrow's press conference."

Zora swallowed. She hadn't seriously expected the hospital to reject millions of dollars simply to spare the feelings of one ultrasound tech, had she?

"They would have preferred that I not talk to you directly about this, but that's bull," he continued.

"Mark," the attorney warned.

"Hey, Tony, you're the guy who recommends our doctors apologize to patients when they've made a mistake." Dr. Rayburn's thick eyebrows rose in emphasis. "Isn't it your opinion that honesty and contrition cut the risk of lawsuits?"

"Mark!" Tony said more forcefully. The reference to lawsuits must have set off alarm bells in the man's head.

Dr. Rayburn returned his attention to Zora. "I disagree with this decision, but I've done all I can. I've negotiated for you to receive six months of paid parental leave." Normally, staffers received two months. "Afterward, you can resume your job if you wish, with a guarantee that you won't be assigned to attend to either of the Adamses."

Relief warred with an awareness of how touchy the situation would be, in numerous respects. "What about my sister?"

"Your sister?" Dr. Rayburn asked blankly.

"My identical twin sister is joining the staff." *Please don't let this mess things up for Zady.* "She'll be assisting the new urologist, Dr. Davis."

The administrator regarded the attorney, who fielded the question. "That's tricky, since Mr. Adams is a patient in the men's program. However, we can take precautions so she won't be put at risk."

*But what about other women who might be subjected to Vince?* Then Zora remembered the patient care coordinator shadowing the billionaire. Apparently, safeguards were already in place. "Okay."

"To bring you up to date, the corporate vice president will be flying in for tomorrow's events," Dr. Rayburn said. "There'll be a gala reception beforehand at the yacht club. The press conference will be at 5:00 p.m. in the auditorium. The staff is invited."

"I plan to skip it." Zora had no interest in watching the billionaire gloat.

"That's your choice." Dr. Rayburn still sounded dissatisfied. "You've undergone a traumatic experience. The hospital will be happy to provide sessions with a therapist."

With Laird? Zora's fists clenched. "No, thanks."

"We can arrange outside counseling with a woman." Tony must have noticed her reaction.

"I don't think that will be necessary. But I'll let you know if I change my mind." Despite her anxiety, Zora hadn't suffered nightmares about the incident. Still, she respected the value of professional help. If she'd received it during her divorce, she might not have clung to her foolish delusions for so long.

Neither she nor Lucky had any more questions, and the meeting ended. She still disliked the situation, but not enough to consider leaving Safe Harbor.

In the hall, Lucky kept pace with her. "Are you okay? I'm glad you mentioned Zady. I was wondering whether to bring her up, but you beat me to it."

"I appreciate the backup," she said. "Having someone who was in my corner there was important."

How had she failed for so long to realize what a strong, kind man he was? Of course, his previous antagonism toward her might have had something to do with that, Zora reflected.

And now? Circumstances had thrown them onto the same team, their loyalties more or less aligned. But was she really destined to remain nothing more than friends with him?

Now that she'd summoned the courage to confront her problems, maybe she ought to call Lucky to task for ignoring how much they meant to each other. But standing up for herself at work was one thing. Relationships were an entirely different matter. Where men were concerned, Zora still didn't trust her instincts.

That afternoon, the gossip mill at the hospital focused on possible developments at tomorrow's press conference, and she heard no mention of Vince's misconduct. On the drive home, Lucky agreed with Zora's observations.

"Dr. Rattigan doesn't seem to have any idea what happened between you and that jerk or that there was any question about accepting the donation," he told her as they headed south. "He was singing to himself in French this afternoon, which means he's excited."

"Why in French?" Zora asked.

"His father's French," Lucky said. "They aren't close, but Cole has an affinity for the language."

"At least he's happy." She sighed. "And this means he and Stacy won't have to consider moving." *Nor you, either.*

"I only wish the circumstances were different."

Stopped at a red light, Lucky drummed his hands on the wheel. "When I threw myself into winning Vince's support for the program, I had no idea he'd harm someone I care about."

"Even me?" Zora teased.

"Especially you!" But his next words disappointed her. "Or anyone." The light changed and he tapped the gas pedal. "If the men's program does expand and I land a management post, I'll stand by my nurses. That man better leave them alone."

"After he donates the money, surely he won't continue meddling." Zora assumed that was the case. "If he and Portia have children, there'll be no reason for further treatment."

"I suspect he'll find a way to keep us dancing on his strings." Lucky's jaw tightened.

Reluctantly, Zora agreed. Then she decided not to worry about matters beyond her control. For once, her practice in denial stood her in good stead.

A lot of stomping shook the two-story house that night. Rod stomped to and from the kitchen, complaining about the upbeat conversations he'd overheard in the operating room. "Everyone thinks Vince's generosity is fantastic. Don't they realize they're bringing in a monster?"

Lucky did his share of stomping as he carted a pair of cribs upstairs and assembled them in Zora's oversize closet-turned-nursery, which had a small window. To accommodate her displaced clothes, he also hauled a rack to the second-floor alcove.

While he was happy to help, he mused that Andrew ought to be chipping in so the new mom could afford the larger downstairs suite. Fond as Lucky was of his quarters, he would willingly swap.

Did Zora plan to let her ex continue to ignore his financial obligations? Surely she didn't maintain the fantasy that he'd return to her after the babies' birth. Yet in spite of everything, she might.

Lucky feared that in her mind, the twins would always be Andrew's babies. And with his current marriage dissolving, the man might decide to toy with her emotions again, just to feed his ego. Until he found another wide-eyed young woman to fall for his manipulations, and broke Zora's heart all over again.

Lucky went downstairs for a snack. "You going to the press conference tomorrow?" he asked Rod, who'd taken the next-to-last slice of apple pie left over from dinner.

"You bet. I never miss a chance to see my girls." The slender man tugged at his short beard, which, like his hair, was going gray. Rod was only in his early forties, but stress from his long custody battle might have played a role in giving him more gray hairs. "I'm sure he'll require Tiff and Amber to show up, since it's scheduled after school hours."

"I'm not sure I should attend," Lucky admitted. "My opinion of Vince might show on my face."

"I doubt he'll care," Rod said.

In the den, a phone rang. Lucky heard Karen answer. "Edmond? What…?" Then her tone grew urgent. "Of course. I'll meet you at the hospital. No problem!"

Lucky's brain leaped to the likeliest conclusion: Melissa was having her triplets. In their haste to talk to Karen, he and Rod collided in the doorway. "Sorry!"

"Ow, damn it!" Rod snapped. "I mean, I'm sorry, too."

"Anyone need medical attention?" Karen inquired

dryly. "No? Great. Rod, want to ride with me to pick up Dawn? She's spending the night with us." Karen occasionally babysat the seven-year-old, who always proved good company.

"Sure." Rod plucked his fedora from a coat rack. "Melissa's in labor?"

"Her water broke. She's at thirty weeks, earlier than they were hoping for but not bad for a multiple birth. They're assembling a team."

"I'll notify Zora and Keely." There were others who should be informed, too, Lucky thought. "Also Anya and Jack. Should I make up one of the couches for Dawn?"

"She can sleep with me," Karen assured him.

Rod sighed. "Guess I'm alone in my bed tonight."

She punched his arm. "Discretion!"

He grinned.

"Please tell Melissa and Edmond I'm rooting for them," Lucky said. Despite the skill of the hospital's doctors and nurses, the birth of triplets would pose a challenge.

"I will." Karen headed out with Rod behind her.

If all went well, this would be a joyous event, Lucky reflected on his way upstairs to spread the news. What a timely reminder of the miracles wrought at Safe Harbor.

Although his gut churned at the prospect of tomorrow's press conference, the donation would enable the staff to perform even more miracles. Too bad the price tag included putting up with a preening, triumphant Vince Adams. At Zora's expense.

# Chapter 16

"We had a devil of a time agreeing on names for three girls," Edmond remarked to Zora at midday as they viewed the triplets in the intermediate care nursery.

Weighing over three pounds and with mature lungs, little Simone, Jamie and Lily were in excellent shape. Nevertheless, they had to be observed for signs of infection or other potential problems.

Wrapped in pink and attached to monitors, the trio were adorable. Zora's arms ached to reach through the viewing window and hold them. A tiny yawn from one—was that Jamie?—was almost too cute to be real.

"I still don't have a name for my son." Zora rested her hand on her by-now enormous bulge. "My daughter's name will be Elizabeth."

"After her grandmother?" The attorney knew Betsy, of course.

She nodded. "I read that the first Queen Elizabeth was named after *her* grandmother."

"Here's a bit of trivia—both her grandmothers were called Elizabeth." Edmond adjusted his glasses.

"I'm impressed that you know that."

"History fascinates me. Melissa and I used to travel and tour historic sites as often as we could." He gazed dreamily at the babies. "Someday we'll take the kids abroad."

"I'm envious." Since there was no one else nearby, Zora added, "Any further word from my charming ex?"

"His attorney indicated he'll comply with the law," Edmond said. "I did forward your list of expenses, but I've heard nothing since."

"Thanks, and I'm sorry to bring this up when you must be exhausted." Zora had spoken without thinking.

"I took a nap this morning." The new father grinned. "I went home and crashed after dropping Dawn at school." The excited seven-year-old had visited the hospital early to meet her new cousins, after spending the night with Karen.

"You've adjusted well to fatherhood." As Melissa's former housemate, Zora recalled that her friend's marriage had broken up over Edmond's refusal to have children.

"I'm grateful for the second chance. I had no idea what I was missing." Joy shone from his face.

A lot of events had changed Edmond, from accepting custody of his niece after his sister went to prison for robbery to the discovery that Melissa had "adopted" three embryos. Parenting Dawn had awakened Edmond's suppressed instincts, and his renewed love for his once and future wife had filled in the rest.

Once, Zora had believed Andrew might undergo a similar change of heart. Witnessing his cruelty to Lin had erased the last of her delusions, however. That, and being around Lucky. He demonstrated how a man ought to behave, in contrast to her father, her stepfather and her ex-husband.

A touch of heartburn roused Zora with a reminder that she ought to eat. "I'm going to the cafeteria," she told Edmond. "Please assure Melissa I'll visit her later."

"I'll do that," he said. "And soon she'll be visiting you in the maternity ward, too."

"That's true, isn't it?" When Lucky installed the cribs last night, it had emphasized to Zora that soon her babies would emerge into the world. Despite an eagerness to lighten her physical load, she wasn't sure she was ready to cope. But then, what single mother *was* ready to cope with twins?

On the ground floor, receptionist Caroline Carter waved her to a halt. "I have something for you. Can you hang on a minute?"

"Sure."

The young woman darted into her nearby office, returning with a children's book. "Sorry it's not wrapped, but I wanted to catch you before your leave starts."

"How beautiful!" Zora traced a finger over the stunning cover photograph of a butterfly. The book described how to study nature in your backyard, a topic she found especially relevant in view of the fact that her home was located next to an estuary.

"Nurse Harper Gladstone took the photos," Caroline said. "And her husband wrote the text."

Harper, a widow with a young daughter, had married a biology teacher. "It's perfect. Thank you."

"Enjoy your lunch. Oh!" With a confidential air, Caroline leaned closer, her brown eyes alight with her favorite subject: gossip. "Did you hear that Vince Adams assaulted a woman?"

Zora couldn't breathe. Apparently, the news had spread. Yet Caroline didn't seem to realize she was addressing the target of that assault. "Who told you that?"

"Laird," the receptionist said.

Since he had an office near Dr. Rayburn's, he must have caught wind of the confidential discussions. What a creep to shoot his mouth off! "He isn't always truthful." That was the best Zora could do.

"Yes, but he usually has reliable sources." Caroline shrugged. "Do you suppose it will spoil the press conference?"

"The less we talk about it, the better." Zora hoped the other woman would heed her warning.

"You're right." Caroline wrinkled her nose. "I keep swearing I'm going to stop spreading rumors. It's addictive, though."

"Thanks for the book. I'm sure the twins and I will enjoy it." On that note, Zora beelined for the cafeteria.

If word of what Vince had done reached the media, how would that affect the billionaire's donation? And if her name became attached to the rumor, there was no predicting what the reporters would say. The notion of the press camping out on Karen's lawn horrified her. Whiffs of swamp gas might discourage them, but she doubted it.

Zora decided not to mention the story to her friends. As she'd said to Caroline, the more discreet they were, the less risk the press conference would be disrupted.

The staff, reporters and VIPs filled the auditorium, leaving Lucky and a scattering of press to line the edges. Standing in the back above the steeply raked rows, he studied the scene uneasily.

Seated on the stage with the administrator, the public relations director, the corporate vice president and the Adamses, Cole appeared relaxed and cheerful. He evidently didn't notice what Lucky considered warning signs that something was going to go wrong.

Vince's ruddy complexion was flushed and, judging by his gait when mounting the steps, he'd imbibed more than he should have at the reception. While he sprawled on his chair with his legs apart, Portia's shoulders were painfully stiff beneath her ivory suit jacket. Her gaze traveled frequently to her daughters, who fidgeted in the front row beside their grandmother.

Around Lucky, more members of the press squeezed in, with cameras bearing the logos of LA news teams and a couple of national networks. He hadn't seen this much media since Cole presented a speech on men's declining sperm rates, sparking a furor that had blown the matter wildly out of proportion. Surely Dr. Rattigan's involvement couldn't account for this much interest, but what did?

Next to him, a reporter murmured to a photographer, "Wonder if Adams can keep his hands to himself on stage? That PR lady's awfully pretty."

"And he's well oiled," the other man responded. "Hey, it's a slow news day. We can always hope."

Anxiety churned in Lucky's stomach. What had these guys heard? He was grateful that Keely had driven Zora home earlier, sparing her any immediate fallout.

On the stage, Jennifer Martin took the microphone. After a brief greeting, she introduced Medical Center Management Vice President Chandra Yashimoto.

The dark-haired executive, whose striking black-and-white suit rivaled Portia's for elegance, glided to center stage. With a practiced smile, she sketched the history of the medical center's transformation from a community hospital to a national center for fertility and maternity care.

When she cited the importance of Dr. Cole Rattigan, Lucky braced for an audience reaction. If reporters planned to revive their silly stories terming him Dr. Baby Crisis, they'd start lobbing questions now. But no one reacted.

They seemed to be waiting. For what?

Ms. Yashimoto didn't call on Dr. Rayburn, whose furrowed brow reflected a less than enthusiastic attitude, nor did she ask Cole to speak. Instead, she cut to the announcement: Safe Harbor was poised to become an international center for the treatment of and research into men's fertility, thanks to a twenty-million-dollar gift from San Diego financier Vincent Adams and his wife, both of whom were—according to Chandra—well-known philanthropists.

Lights flashed and lenses clicked as Vince strode to the front and shook hands with the vice president. A staff photographer captured the moment, but to Lucky it seemed that others snapped only perfunctory shots.

"Thank you, Chandra." Vince beamed, in his element as the center of attention. "This program means more to me than merely putting my name on a building. It means leaving a legacy of children, mine and other men's, that will last until the end of time."

"There's modesty for you," the nearby reporter observed in a low tone.

"This week, my wife and I moved forward in our quest to expand our family," Vince continued. "My wife prefers that I not go into detail, but thanks to Dr. Rattigan, we expect to have a blessed event of our own by next year."

Portia's eyes narrowed. No doubt she'd asked him to keep that private, too, especially since they hadn't implanted the embryos yet.

The reporter murmured, "I wonder if she'll be the only woman popping out his offspring."

Was the man referring to Zora? Lucky wouldn't put it past the more irresponsible members of the press to imply that her pregnancy was the result of a liaison with Vince. Never mind facts or her DNA test—they'd drag her name through the mud.

When Vince paused for breath, a man in a central row scrambled to his feet. "Mr. Adams, this morning your former personal assistant Geneva Gabriel filed a five-million-dollar lawsuit against you in San Diego Superior Court, alleging sexual assault. We understand the district attorney is investigating. Care to comment?"

That explained the reporters' snide exchanges! Lucky experienced a spurt of relief, then immediately regretted it. He was sorry that Ms. Gabriel had suffered, too.

"She's just out for my money." Vince spluttered with fury. "I fired that witch because she's stupid and incompetent."

Chandra Yashimoto stood frozen. Cole's face registered his confusion, while Lucky could have sworn Mark Rayburn was barely suppressing a smile.

Jennifer rose to the occasion, literally. Crossing the stage to seize the microphone again, she said, "I'm sure Mr. Adams will have his attorney respond to your questions. My assistant is handing out a press release with the details of Mr. and Mrs. Adams' generous gift. Thank you for joining us."

After a few inaudible words to Vince, she steered him and Portia toward a side door. Shaking with anger, the billionaire gestured at the front row, summoning his daughters. Tiffany might have stood her ground, but when Amber raced up the steps, the older girl followed.

Cole and the others left the stage via a second exit. Unable to reach them as the crowd filled the aisles, Lucky shuffled out with the rest of the audience.

In the corridor, he passed Laird, who'd shanghaied a couple of puzzled reporters. "I'm embarrassed to be associated with a hospital that would accept money from a man like Vince Adams," the man announced. "That's why I'm handing in my notice and joining a private practice in Newport Beach. My name is Laird Maclaine."

A listener thrust out a small mic. "Are you a doctor in the men's fertility program?"

"I'm the staff psychologist."

"You're the staff opportunist," Lucky called, and dodged away. He wove through the milling assemblage, in case his doctor had been hemmed in by the press. He'd learned from experience that a show of muscle could prove handy.

Rounding a corner, he spotted a small group bunched near the staff entrance—the Adamses and the public relations director. All Lucky could see of the man blocking their escape was his fedora.

"You're in no condition to drive." Rod's voice was shrill with emotion. "The girls stay here."

"Get out of my way, Vintner." The bigger man towered over his opponent.

"Rod, you're making things worse." That was Portia, hovering beside her daughters. Jennifer, the only non-family member of the group, regarded the scene with uncertainty.

Where was Mark? The administrator, a former football player, was a physical match for Vince, but he must be occupied whisking Cole and Chandra out of harm's way.

"You're drunk," Rod persisted. "I'll take the girls to their grandmother." They'd left Helen behind in their rush, Lucky saw.

"Out of our way!" Vince shoved Rod, hard. The girls gasped as the smaller man staggered and fell against the wall. When blood spurted from his nose, Vince raised his fists in a victory gesture.

Rage surged in Lucky at the man's brutality. His fury mounted when the billionaire clamped onto Amber's wrist. "Let's go."

His younger daughter wriggled fruitlessly. "We're not supposed to get in a car with a drunk driver."

"Shut up." Vince yanked the girl toward the exit.

"Leave her alone!" Tiffany screamed.

As their stepfather wrenched open the door, Lucky barreled forward. The others parted, leaving him a clear shot at the distracted billionaire, who half turned to gape at him.

Lucky's kick hit its target: Vince's knee. With a cry of pain, the big man released Amber and stumbled out into the parking area reserved for administrators.

"Let's get out of here." Tiffany gestured to her sister. "Dad needs a doctor." Clearly, she meant Rod.

"Never mind him. You're both coming with us," their mother snapped.

"No." Tiffany slid an arm around the dazed Rod, who had a tissue pressed to his nose. "Thank you, Lucky."

"My pleasure."

Portia flinched as, outside, her husband bellowed for her. "He's too impaired to drive," Lucky warned, following her through the door. "Please stop him before he injures someone."

She glared. "Mind your own business."

"Where are the girls?" Vince roared, standing between his high-performance sports coupe and Dr. Rayburn's sedan.

"They're staying," Lucky retorted.

"I'll have you fired for this," the billionaire snarled.

"You planning to push me around, too?" Lucky demanded. "Or do you only attack people smaller than you?"

He could see Vince weighing the urge to punch him out. The man might have tried, but a shift of position put too much weight on his injured knee and he stumbled and then produced a deep groan. Regaining his balance with a hand on the sedan, the man snarled at his wife, "In the car. Now!"

"Let her drive," Lucky said. "For both your sakes."

"Shut up, you punk."

Mouth pressed into a thin line, Portia slid into the passenger seat while Vince got behind the wheel. How sad that she'd thrown in her lot with her husband, willing to sacrifice her safety to maintain her wealth and status. Worse, she'd been ready to risk her daughters' safety, too.

A hand on Lucky's arm alerted him to Jennifer's presence. Holding her phone in the other hand, she said, "Thanks for intervening. I arranged with Mark to make sure Rod gets medical treatment and the girls stay with their grandmother."

"Watch out!"

They beat a quick retreat as the sports car shot in reverse. After scraping the bumper of another car, Vince twisted the wheel, hit the gas and zoomed forward. He and Portia disappeared around the building.

"I'm calling the cops." Lucky took out his cell. "That's a hit-and-run. Also, he shouldn't be driving in his condition."

"Good." Jennifer straightened her spine. "I'd better corral the press. I don't want them harassing the staff."

Lucky thought of Laird. "Nor do we want the staff taking advantage of this mess."

Despite a puzzled glance, she didn't request an explanation. Duty was calling, and she hurried inside.

He dialed 911 and explained the situation to the dispatcher. Although Lucky hadn't observed which direction Vince took, the Adamses' beach cottage lay south of here. The most direct route would be along Pacific Coast Highway.

The dispatcher thanked him and said she'd alert patrol officers to be on the lookout. One would stop by to take a report about the hit-and-run, as well.

Bathed in October sunlight, Lucky eased his breathing. He'd never imagined such a devastating outcome of today's announcement. There was nothing anyone could have done to prevent this, he supposed. The lawsuit filing had changed everything.

Damn Vince and his arrogance. But at least the girls were safe. As for Rod's injury, the man had every right to report the assault and to sue for damages. However, he'd learned a hard lesson about the difficulties of fighting Vince in court.

Checking his phone, Lucky saw he'd missed a call from Zora. He returned it, and after two rings, her excited voice said, "Lucky! Keely's driving me to the hospital."

"Why?"

"I'm in labor!" she said happily.

"Everything's okay?"

"Yes—the pains aren't bad yet," she said. "I called ahead and they're setting up a C-section. Honestly, I was surprised what a relief it is. And the day after Melissa! Must be fate."

He gave a low chuckle. "Well, if that doesn't put the cap on an already over-the-top day."

"What happened?" She must not have been following the news. He presumed that radio reporters were already describing the brouhaha on the air.

"Vince's former assistant is suing him for sexual assault," Lucky told her. "He stalked out in a huff. Guess you're not the only one he's victimized."

"I hope she nails him to the wall."

"Five million dollars' worth of wall," he agreed.

"Yay for her." Then Zora gasped, "Watch out!"

"What…?"

The call went dead.

Inside Lucky, fear tightened into a knot. Had there been an accident? Surely not, yet…

The shortest route from Karen's house to the hospital was via Pacific Coast Highway—directly in Vince's path. His heart nearly stopped.

*Don't be ridiculous.*

On his phone, Lucky pressed Zora's number. He listened, struggling for calm, as it rang and rang, then went to voice mail.

He heard a siren in the distance. Then another. They sounded as if they were heading for Coast Highway.

Lucky began to pray.

# Chapter 17

The sports car appeared out of nowhere, weaving madly across lanes, and only Keely's swift veer to the right prevented a crash. Overcorrecting, the other car swerved, hit the curb and went airborne.

With a horrifying crunch, it landed on its roof. Shaken, Zora realized that she'd recognized the occupants as they sped past: Vince and Portia.

A siren shrilled almost instantly. Within seconds, a patrol cruiser and a fire truck swarmed in, followed by paramedics. An officer stopped behind Keely's brown sedan, which was parked on the right shoulder.

The police had been watching for Vince's car, he explained while examining Keely's license. After asking whether the two women were injured—neither was—he prepared to take their statements.

Zora cried out as another pain gripped her. "She's in labor," Keely explained.

"I'll call for another ambulance."

"We're only two miles from the hospital. It'll be faster if I drive," Keely said. "Don't worry. I'm a nurse."

After radioing the dispatcher, the officer offered to follow them in case they required aid, and they accepted. As they drove, Zora and Keely listened to a news station's account of billionaire Vince Adams facing a harassment lawsuit. There was no mention of the crash yet.

As the initial shock wore off, Zora recalled Vince's puffy face behind the windshield and Portia's terrified expression. How weird that the Adamses had nearly hit them. Since she hadn't observed any reporters in pursuit, Vince had no one but his arrogance to blame for his speeding.

However, he was probably in no condition to blame anyone. And what about Portia?

Zora regarded Keely, who'd remained stoic throughout the incident. "That was awful. Do you suppose they're...?"

"Badly injured or worse, unless they had their seat belts fastened." Swinging onto Hospital Way ahead of the cruiser, the nurse said, "I don't believe there was anyone else in the car."

*The girls.* How could Zora have forgotten them? "I sure hope not."

They stopped at the maternity entrance. Staffers rushed out with a gurney to assist them.

Keely checked a message on her phone. "Dr. Brennan's on site. She'll do the surgery."

"Fantastic." That was reassuring.

"They have the pediatricians prepping, too." There'd be one for each twin, the doctor had said earlier.

"Okay." After the near miss on the road, Zora had no strength left. Fortunately, she could simply lie back and entrust her care to the experts.

Her thoughts returned to the Adamses. Vince might be a repulsive man, but she'd never wished him dead. And certainly not Portia. How badly were they hurt? How would this affect their daughters?

As Zora was transferred onto the gurney, Lucky raced to her, breathing hard. "Is she okay? Zora?"

"I'm fine. Sorry I left you dangling." In the heat of the moment, she'd forgotten their interrupted conversation. Later, she'd been vaguely aware of her cell ringing, but had been too overwrought to answer.

He stared down, desperately drinking in the sight of her. She'd never seen him so shaken.

"The Adamses nearly hit us." Zora stroked his arm, yearning to take away his tormented expression. "Keely steered out of their path."

"What about Vince and Portia?"

"We saw their car flip over," Keely said, joining them after conferring with the officer. "Beyond that, I have no idea."

Lucky swept the older nurse into a hug. "Bless you!"

"I didn't sneeze," she said tartly.

"You kept a cool head, from what I hear," Lucky responded.

Keely extricated herself from the hug. "Anyone else would have done the same."

"Not necessarily." Lucky turned to Zora. "How's my sweetheart?"

"Still trembling." Lying on the gurney, Zora was glad when he took her hand, his strength flowing into her.

She wished *he* was the babies' father. Then he could stay with her, comfort her and share her joy.

An orderly moved the gurney forward, toward the entrance. "I'll stay with her after I answer a few questions for the police," Keely told Lucky.

"So will I."

"If you wish, but how is Dr. Rattigan handling all this?" the older woman asked.

"I have no idea."

Reminded that their plans for the future might have been crushed today, Zora felt a twinge of concern. "You should check on him."

"I'll text you when she goes into surgery," Keely volunteered. "They won't let you in, anyway."

Another spasm seized Zora. "Ow!" A curse word slipped out. How did women bear this for hours and hours? She was very glad she was having a C-section and the doctor would give her something to stop the labor.

As the contraction eased, she wished Lucky would stay. But when he excused himself to attend to his doctor, Zora merely nodded.

"Later," she whispered into the air.

Zora was safe. Yes, there were risks in surgery and childbirth, but nothing like what Lucky had feared: a head-on smashup at high speed, pieces of car scattered across the highway, horrifying injuries to the occupants.

He'd witnessed the aftermath of such tragedies as an ambulance driver and a paramedic. The fact that Safe Harbor Medical didn't have an emergency room had added to its appeal when he'd joined the staff, because he didn't have to witness the arrival of trauma patients and relive those terrible memories. But today they'd hit him full force.

*I love her*, Lucky acknowledged as the gurney vanished into admitting. It was foolish and irrational and inescapable. He had no idea when he'd fallen in love with Zora, or what to do about it.

He'd clung to his ideals of perfection since his parents' deaths. If they had a family at the ideal time and in the ideal circumstances, money problems didn't force parents to neglect their children's internal struggles and teenagers didn't have to work such long hours that they rebelled—or so he'd rationalized.

He'd been trying to control the future, to prevent a repeat of his family's tragedies. But danger could strike without warning, as it had today. How stubbornly blind he'd been to his own flaws, criticizing Zora's illusions while harboring his own.

Yet she was still having another man's babies. Even a slug like Andrew would surely visit them, and there remained a possibility—remote, but real—that she would reconcile with her ex. Lucky might love her so hard and deep that his entire soul throbbed with it, only to have her torn away from him.

He could do nothing about it while she was in surgery. Frustrated, he decided to make himself useful elsewhere.

Since people gathered in a central location in a crisis, Lucky set out for the cafeteria. En route, he passed the elevators, one of which opened to reveal a welcome pair: Karen, her expression worried, and Rod, holding a cold pack to his nose.

Lucky halted. "I hope it's not broken."

"No, fortunately," Karen said. "They X-rayed him and gave him pain pills."

"Hurts to talk," Rod muttered.

Lucky didn't doubt that. "Zora's having the twins. Keely's with her." He filled them in on the details.

"I'm so glad they're okay," Karen said.

"The girls." Rod peered down the hall. "Where are they?"

"Helen said she was going to get them something to eat. Let's try the cafeteria."

Sure enough, they spotted Tiffany and Amber huddled with their grandmother at a table. Doctors, nurses and other staffers were sprinkled around the large room. Although some were eating dinner, most appeared to be waiting for news. Cole looked tense but composed, drinking coffee alongside Dr. Tartikoff.

From the food service area, Jennifer greeted them and asked Rod how he was feeling. Her dark hair was rumpled and her mascara had smeared. Today's events must be a PR director's nightmare.

"Thank you," she said after her questions had been answered. "Now I'm sure you're eager to join your daughters."

Rod agreed, and off he went with Karen. Lucky lingered, unsure where he could help the most.

"Any word about the Adamses?" he asked.

"So far, only that the police are on the scene."

"Well, I have a little more info than that."

She listened intently to the account of Zora and Keely's close call. "Thank heaven they escaped," she said, then raised a hand for silence. "Hang on. I'm monitoring news reports." She listened on her earpiece before saying, "No updates."

"Where's the press?" Lucky had expected to find them crowding the hallways.

"They went haring off to the crash scene," she said. "The police public information officer is handling them, although I'm also receiving calls for our reaction."

"What kind of reaction?" How could anyone respond to such a complex situation?

"Our official position is that our thoughts and prayers are with their family," Jennifer said.

"That sounds right." Lucky admired the publicist more than ever.

"Keep on the alert for stray reporters, will you?" she asked. "We can't let them eavesdrop or hassle people."

"Agreed." While he respected the job of the media, this was a traumatic enough situation without the press breaching people's privacy.

"There should be a counselor on hand. For some reason, I can't reach Laird," Jennifer fretted.

"He's leaving for private practice." Lucky repeated what he'd heard the psychologist announce.

She groaned. "Great timing. I'll arrange for an outside crisis counselor."

A murmur ran through the room. Tony and Mark had just entered. The attorney strode over to the girls' table and spoke in a low voice. The group, including Rod and Karen, got up and accompanied him out.

Lucky's chest clenched. This couldn't be good.

Once the girls and their entourage had departed and Jennifer gave the all clear from the hall, Mark took a position in full view of everyone. Thanks to his height and deep baritone, he had no trouble commanding attention.

"I'm sure you've heard that Mr. and Mrs. Adams were involved in a single-car crash on Coast Highway," he said. "I've just received word from the police chief that both of them died at the scene."

Gasps and a few sobs rose from the crowd. Even Lucky, angry as he'd been at Vince, was shocked by their deaths. Yet this could have been worse, much worse. Tiff and Amber might have died, too, if he and Rod hadn't prevented the girls' parents from forcing them into the car.

Mark resumed addressing the staff. "For those of you wondering how this will affect the men's fertility program, I'm afraid we don't have an answer on that yet. Any other questions?"

There were a few, which the director fielded with complete frankness. Then a buzz of conversation broke out as staffers shared their grief with each other.

At a tap on his arm, Lucky swung around to meet Betsy Raditch's solemn gaze. "I heard Zora's having her babies," she said. "Have you talked to her?"

"Yes. Did you know she and Keely had a near miss on the road?"

"What do you mean?"

He repeated the story. The nursing supervisor clamped her hand over her mouth. "That was close!"

"She should be in surgery now," Lucky added.

"I'll tell Andrew," Betsy said. "And, Lucky, I heard what you did, keeping Rod's daughters safe. That was heroic."

"Thanks, but I don't deserve that," Lucky responded. "Heroes are people who risk their safety, like Rod. I knew I was a match for that—" in view of Vince's demise, he decided against using a harsh term "—that man."

"You and Rod both deserve credit," the nursing supervisor said. "Well, I'd better get moving. Some of my nurses are in shock, and we have a hospital to run."

"Absolutely right." If Lucky had a supervisory position like hers, he'd be eager to support his nurses, too.

Outside the cafeteria, Cole caught up with him. "We're holding a strategy session in Dr. Tartikoff's office. You should be part of it."

"I'd like that." Lucky joined his doctor and a handful of others. To be included with this prestigious group was an honor, and his future might depend on what they devised.

All the same, en route to the fifth floor, his thoughts were mostly on Zora. She'd been his collaborator this past month, as invested as he was in trying to ensure the billionaire's gift. All she'd requested was for him to stop nagging her.

She'd kept Vince's hateful harassment a secret, no doubt to prevent this type of blowup. What had she gained by it? Her position and her advancement didn't depend on the program's expansion.

*She did it for me.* From simple generosity, or because she hadn't been able to bear the prospect of Lucky leaving? Had Zora started loving him, too, perhaps without realizing it?

If Andrew reached her first, would she still fail to recognize that her heart belonged to Lucky?

Suddenly he couldn't wait to be with her. But Dr. Rattigan was counting on Lucky's input.

He steeled himself to have patience. In view of Andrew's track record, there was no reason to assume he'd show up promptly.

The distinguished group of top staffers, including several whom Owen Tartikoff had brought with him from his Boston practice, gathered around the conference table in the fertility director's office. They included Alec Denny, the director of laboratories, and Jan Garcia Sargent, head of the egg donor program.

For the next hour, they brainstormed, tossing out the names of distinguished foundations, government grant programs and Silicon Valley billionaires. Could or would any of them respond—let alone quickly enough to purchase the dental building?

Just as they were about to call it a night, the administrator entered. Dr. Rayburn's dark eyes were rimmed with red.

"Have a seat." Lucky vacated his chair, since all the others were taken.

The big man accepted the offer. "Considering you're a hero, I shouldn't, but I've had a rough day. As we all have."

Lucky decided not to bother arguing about the hero designation. No one questioned it, so apparently they'd all heard the tale.

"On such a terrible day, I'm pleased to bring good news." When Mark coughed, Lucky fetched him a glass of water from the sideboard. The administrator swallowed a few gulps before continuing. "Portia's mother, Helen Pepper, is a very kind woman. In the midst of her grief, she informed me that her daughter and son-in-law placed their estate in a living trust. They designated her as the successor trustee on behalf of the couple's children."

Lucky had assumed Vince's money would be tied up for a year or more as the estate was settled. Without a living trust, probate in California could be a lengthy, expensive and complicated process.

"She and her granddaughters intend to carry out the Adamses' wishes to donate twenty million dollars to our program." A smile broke through Mark's weariness. "And a million dollars to the Oahu Lane Animal Shelter, which appears to be a favorite of the girls."

Around the table, the others expressed relief and gratitude. "I hate to raise the question, but how soon can this happen?" Cole asked. "That building will be snapped up quickly."

"Helen plans to talk to an attorney tomorrow." Mark downed more water. "She's agreed to let Jennifer Martin and Ms. Yashimoto arrange the funeral while she looks into setting up a foundation to underwrite the men's program. She said that having her daughter and son-in-law's names on the building will be a fitting tribute."

Lucky was pleased that they'd include Portia's name. She deserved it.

The news buoyed the exhausted participants, though no one was happy about the circumstances. The impact of today's events would play out in everyone's emotions for a long time, including Lucky's.

A glance at his watch sent his heart speeding off. Several hours had passed since he'd last seen Zora. He'd received texts from Keely, indicating the C-section had gone well. By now, the new mom should be out of the recovery room, which meant he'd finally be able to visit.

After excusing himself, he hurried down to the third floor. Despite his eagerness to reach Zora, the window of the intermediate care nursery drew him irresistibly.

He spotted Melissa and Edmond's triplets—had it really been only two nights since their birth?—and a sprinkling of other newborns. Among the half dozen babies in clear isolettes, he wasn't sure which were Zora's, but if he had to bet, he'd put his money on a red-haired little girl and the blond boy beside her. Both appeared alert and healthy.

At the nurses' station, Lucky obtained Zora's room number. "Mr. Raditch is with her," a nurse advised him.

A lump stuck in Lucky's throat. He hadn't thought Andrew would arrive so fast.

Why was he here? To stake his claim? He *was* the babies' father. But it was his claim on *Zora* that worried Lucky most.

It was up to her whether she would reconcile with Andrew, but Lucky didn't intend to let her go without a fight. He'd waited too long already to realize that she was the perfect woman for him.

# Chapter 18

The first thing that occurred to Zora when her ex-husband entered was, *You're the wrong man.*

She longed for Lucky's honest, caring presence. Why hadn't she told him she wanted him to stay with her, that he was the most important person in her life? Sure, it meant taking a big emotional risk. Maybe he'd never accept her, flaws and all, but something about the way he gazed at her said otherwise. She'd taken leaps of faith, over and over, with the unworthy Andrew. Now she'd let Lucky go off without asking for what meant the most to her—keeping him close.

He must be busy, though, with the hospital in an uproar. Keely had brought news of Vince and Portia's deaths, and the two women had shared their turbulent reactions. Zora supposed the aftermath would affect her for a long while. Her heart went out to Tiffany and

Amber on the loss of their mother, but mostly she was thankful she and Keely had escaped injury.

After Keely left for dinner, Edmond had peeked in. He'd been visiting his wife and triplets, and stayed just long enough to express his best wishes and present a gorgeous bouquet that perfumed the room.

And now here was her ex-husband. "So you had the babies." Andrew hovered near the exit as if fearing a giant clamp might drop from the ceiling to hold him in place, forcing him to—what?—take responsibility? "They look, uh, cute."

That was the sum of his reaction? When Zora had cradled the babies after their delivery, their delicate scent and wonder-filled faces had instantly become engraved on her heart. Elizabeth had a tumble of reddish-brown hair and inquisitive gray eyes, while the boy was blond with bright blue eyes. As she crooned to each of them, she'd been rewarded with a gaze of pure devotion.

She'd have died for them. Their father thought they were, *uh, cute*.

Andrew shifted from one foot to the other. "Have you picked names?"

"The girl's Elizabeth."

"Like my mother."

"That's right." She waited, wondering if he had ideas about the boy's name. What a silly fantasy she'd harbored, that he would leap at the chance, yet the moment had played through her mind so often that it almost seemed real: Andrew declaring that he'd always loved the name something-or-other, or that he couldn't wait to take Elizabeth and what's-his-name to the zoo. When he didn't speak, she blurted, "I might call the boy Luke." That ought to get his attention.

"Okay." Obviously, Andrew hadn't connected the name to Lucky. Maybe he was too busy preparing his next revelation, which was: "I'm transferring to New York."

He was moving out of state? That seemed sudden. "When?"

"Next month."

"Permanently?"

"That's the idea."

Once, this news would have arrowed pain deep into Zora's gut. Now, she experienced relief tinged with sadness for this self-absorbed man. He would never do anything more important than fathering these children, yet clearly he didn't intend to play much of a role in their upbringing. As she'd suspected, his bid for custody had been merely an attempt to one-up her.

"Good luck with that." She didn't bother to point out that states enforced each other's child-support requirements. Her lawyer could take care of the details.

"Do me a favor, would you?" Andrew muttered.

Warily, she asked, "What?"

"Let my mom play with the kids once in a while. She's into this grandmother thing."

He'd been around Zora since they were teenagers, yet he believed she might exclude Betsy? "You don't know me at all," she said.

"Is that a yes?" He sounded like a sales agent impatient to conclude a deal.

Zora lifted her head from the pillow for a better view of the man who used to dominate her world. Yep, he'd definitely shrunk. "Okay," she said. "Thanks for stopping by."

Andrew regarded her with a shade of disappointment. "That's it?"

He must have expected her to plead for him to stay in Safe Harbor. After Lin's rejection, his ego was hungry to be fed. "That's it. Sayonara."

He glared at her. "Whatever," he said, and stalked out.

The air smelled suddenly fresher, and the colors of the flowers intensified. Then the best thing of all happened.

Lucky peered in. Although his face could use a splash of water and his navy blue uniform had picked up bits of lint, he was the handsomest man in the world.

The dismay on Andrew's face as he stomped down the hall thrilled Lucky. "You knocked him down to size," he told Zora admiringly as he entered her room. "You're such a tiny thing but wow, you pack a punch."

She lifted an eyebrow. "You're just figuring that out?"

Careful to avoid jostling her, Lucky sat on the edge of the bed. "Among other things. A lot of them."

Including that his image of a perfect wife and kids had been nothing more than a defense mechanism to protect against the kind of devastation that had torn his family apart. That his delusion about controlling the future was as self-defeating as anything he'd accused her of. That he didn't see how he could go through life without this delightful, maddening woman.

"Did you figure out yet that you're in love with me?" As soon as the words flew out, blood rushed to her cheeks. "Oops. I didn't mean to say that aloud."

Lucky nearly bounced off the bed in glee. "Yes, I'm in love with you. Now tell me you're in love with me, too."

"Um… I have to think about it."

"Zora!" He could barely tolerate the delay.

She folded her arms. "What other things did you figure out today, smart guy?"

"That you have the most precious children in the world." Lucky visualized the babies again. "Your twins are the red-headed girl and the blond boy, right? I couldn't read the names on the isolettes."

Her face remained adorably flushed, this time with pride rather than embarrassment, he guessed. "Elizabeth and Luke."

Lucky couldn't have heard correctly. "You're giving him my name?"

"I'm trying it on for size." Zora shifted against the pillow.

Much as Lucky cherished the idea, it wouldn't be fair to the boy. "He should have his own name," he said. "How about Orlando?"

"Like the city in Florida?"

"Like my father." He'd meant to reserve that honor for his firstborn son. Well, this little guy had taken over that spot in Lucky's heart.

"I might go for that," Zora responded. "But if you name him, you might have to claim him."

"I'm claiming both of them." Lucky smiled at the dear, freckled person studying him expectantly.

"You don't still consider them Andrew's children?"

Her question startled him. "I consider them *your* children. I meant that *you* considered them Andrew's children."

"Really?"

"I believed you might forgive him for past sins if he, shall we say, embraced the miracle of fatherhood."

Zora's nose wrinkled. "I was an idiot. I believed love

could conquer all, but it can't conquer heartlessness. Or a weak character. Or—should I go on abusing him, or is that enough?"

"For now, because I have something important to say." Lucky gathered his courage. "Let's get back to the part where I confess I'm in love with you."

Why didn't she respond in kind? But perhaps she was waiting for him to lay out the whole picture. Well, he'd better start by being cautious. Although it appeared Lucky might be able to stay in Safe Harbor, there was no guarantee he'd be hired in the new program. He might not be as hung up on financial security as before, but he couldn't ask for a commitment from Zora without pointing out that his situation was still unsettled.

"Another thing I discovered today was that I couldn't bear to leave Safe Harbor unless you go with me," he blurted. "Will you?"

"You have to go?" Her joy dimmed. "But…that means leaving our friends."

"I'll make it worth your while."

"I'd go with you in a heartbeat," Zora answered. "Except…"

"What?" His breath caught.

"My sister did that and ended up unmarried and unloved." She stared down at her hands.

"Such trust," he murmured.

She folded her arms and hunkered down.

His impatience nearly exploded. But what did he expect, reassurance before he popped the question? *Put it out there, fella. Quit stalling.*

From the zipper compartment in his wallet, Lucky produced a gold ring set with diamonds and emeralds.

Then he slid off the bed and onto one knee. "Zora, will you marry me?"

She stared at him in astonishment. "What about your perfect family?"

He pushed past the lump in his throat. "You are my perfect family. You, Elizabeth and Orlando."

"But your plans...saving for a house..."

"I nearly lost you today," he said. "That put everything into perspective. I want you today, and tomorrow, and forever. Marry me, Zora."

"Yes."

"Yes?" He couldn't quite believe she'd said it so simply and plainly. "No ifs, ands or buts?"

"Don't be silly. I love you."

"I love you, too!" Hoisting himself onto the bed again, he showered kisses on her forehead and cheeks and mouth.

Chuckling, she held up the ring. "Let me put this on."

He straightened. "Of course."

As she angled it toward her finger, her forehead creased. "Where did you... This looks familiar."

"I borrowed it from Betsy." Lucky had run into the nursing supervisor in the hall and shared his plans. When he mentioned that he wished he had a token ring to present until he had a chance to buy a new one, Betsy had removed the heirloom from her finger and loaned it to him.

"Did she mention that I wore this ring during my marriage to Andrew?" Zora asked, laughing.

"She left out that part." Lucky sighed, sorry that he'd screwed up such an important detail. "I was planning for us to choose our rings together later."

Zora studied it fondly. "It's beautiful and it means a lot to Betsy. How sweet of her to loan it to us."

"This doesn't change your answer, does it? We *are* engaged, right?"

"You bet."

Sliding his arms around Zora, he leaned down for a long, tender kiss. She smelled of babies and happiness. Lucky's heart swelled as her arms closed around him and the two of them hung there, happily suspended in a private world.

A world they would share with their little guys. A world that would be full of bumps and twists and imperfections, exactly as it ought to be.

"For the record, I came to the conclusion that we loved each other long before you did," she whispered in his ear. "It didn't occur to you until today? Slow, slow."

Lucky grinned. "Guess I am. By the way, there's an excellent chance we won't have to leave Safe Harbor." Releasing her, he explained about Helen's proposal to fund the expansion.

"That's fantastic." Zora tapped her fingers together restlessly.

"What?" he asked.

"Maybe I shouldn't bring this up now."

"Let it out," Lucky told her. "If you have reservations, now's your chance to air them."

"It's not exactly a reservation."

"What is it?" He stroked her hair. Whatever the problem was, they'd deal with it.

"Your brother," Zora said.

Lucky blinked. He hadn't been expecting *that*. "What about him?"

"Do you still reject him for whatever he did?" she said earnestly. "Are you still so rigid?"

Despite an urge to protest that he could never forgive what Matthew had done, Lucky paused to reflect. This past month, he'd learned a lot from Zora's generous nature. While her weakness for Andrew had infuriated him, she'd also befriended Lin Lee, mended fences with Zady and regained her closeness with Betsy. He could use some of her grace.

"I'd like to tell you what happened," he said.

Zora gripped his hands. "Please do."

As Lucky began, the hospital faded around him and he was once more in his parents' convenience store in LA. He could hear the street traffic and smell the salty temptation of potato chips. When he looked up, a security mirror revealed a bulging image of shelves crammed with the odds and ends of a neighborhood market.

"My brother Matthew joined the navy at eighteen," he said. "I was proud of him, but that left me to juggle attending high school and helping my folks keep the store afloat." He'd unloaded supplies, stocked shelves, carried receipts to the bank and fetched change. He'd also operated the cash register many evenings late into the night.

"It must have been hard, missing school activities," Zora said.

"Yes, and I longed for the occasional evening to hang out with my friends." Lucky felt a twinge of his old resentment. "I rebelled in small ways. Sneaking a cigarette, showing up late or leaving early. Mom used to scowl and Dad complained that I was letting down the family while my brother risked his life for his country."

"How did you feel about that?" she asked.

"Guilty, but angry, too." In retrospect, his selfishness haunted him. Still, he owed her the whole truth. "One evening, we were supposed to close at nine, but my mother insisted on staying open late because customers kept drifting in. While she worked the register, she sent me into the storage room to open boxes of supplies we'd received that day and catalog the contents. I was furious."

"Where was your father?"

"He'd put in twelve hours and gone home exhausted." Lucky's gut twisted. "If I smoked on the premises, my mom would smell it. So I sneaked out the rear door into the alley."

Strange—he'd relived that night repeatedly in nightmares, yet now he had trouble dredging up the details. *Get it over with.*

"While I was outside, a junkie entered the store and demanded cash from my mother," he said. "The store surveillance tape showed he had a bulge in his jacket, but not whether it was a gun."

"How terrifying." Zora's gaze never strayed from Lucky's face. "What happened?"

"My mom collapsed." Lucky swallowed. "Later, the coroner said she died from stress cardiomyopathy, which is a response to overwhelming fear. A huge jolt of adrenaline can cause the heart to develop ventricular fibrillation—abnormal rhythms. She literally dropped dead."

Zora shivered. "I'm sorry. But you weren't at fault."

"If I'd been inside, I might have heard the robbery, rushed in and scared the creep away," Lucky said. "Maybe before Mom succumbed."

"If he did have a gun, he'd have killed you," she countered.

"I doubt he did." Lucky refused to let himself off that easily. "Anyway, he snatched a handful of cash and ran."

"Did they catch him?"

"More or less." His jaw tightened. "He was a meth addict—a couple of days later the police found him dead of an overdose, probably with drugs he bought at my mother's expense."

"And that didn't bring her back," she observed sympathetically.

"No, it didn't." The discovery of his mother lying on the floor, the sirens, the arrival of police and paramedics had blurred into a montage of pain. Worst of all had been accompanying the police to inform his sleepy, disbelieving father.

Lucky had feared his father might collapse, too. Instead, Orlando Mendez had thrown himself into his work. "He gave his all to that store. I offered to postpone college and put in longer hours, but he refused. Instead, he hired an assistant. Nearly a year later, we discovered the assistant was embezzling from us."

"That's terrible." Zora stroked his arm.

Lucky had had trouble believing anyone could take advantage of people who were already suffering. Sadly, he and his father had learned otherwise.

"The guy fled to South America and we never recovered the money. A month after that, Dad died of an aneurysm," Lucky said grimly. "Literally, of a broken heart. I had to sell the store. There was barely enough to cover the debts and the funeral expenses."

That brought him to the bitter quarrel with Matthew. When his brother had attended their mother's funeral, he'd scarcely spoken. After their father's death, Matthew had blown up at Lucky.

"He accused me of contributing to our parents' deaths." Although the years had lessened his outrage, the memory stung. "He claimed I cheated him of his inheritance, that I'd used the profits from the sale of the store to pay for college. He even filed a theft report with the police. After they cleared me, Matthew informed our relatives I'd hidden the money and gotten away with it."

"Wow," Zora said. "That puts my quarrel with Zady in the shade."

As she spoke, guilt and regret flooded through Lucky. "If I hadn't been such an immature jerk, we might have avoided the argument. In a way, he was right. I let everyone down with my irresponsible actions the night my mother died. And I vowed that I'd never do that again to anyone I cared about, yet I let you down with Vince."

"What?" Astonishment filled Zora's face.

To his dismay, a sob shook Lucky. He never cried. He was the strong one, the tough guy. But the idea that Zora had put up with that man's groping in order to protect Lucky's career was intolerable. "I'm glad he's dead. I'm sorry about his wife, but…" His hands formed fists. "I messed up. And I had the nerve to rag on you about *your* mistakes."

"Yeah, that was the worst thing. I mean, death and destruction and being estranged from your brother hardly count compared to your nagging."

Her mischievous tone had the desired effect of banishing his self-pity. "You little goof."

Zora reached out to cup his cheek. "You're a wonderful man, Lucky. You've carried this burden for too

long. I don't think you need to forgive your brother as
much as you need to forgive yourself."

"I let everyone down. I can't undo that." Her touch
soothed him, though.

"How many people did you save as a paramedic?"
she asked. "And according to what I heard, if not for
you, Rod's daughters might have died today. You were
a kid when you sneaked out for a smoke. I don't know
if you can mend the rift with Matthew, but as for the
rest, let it go, Lucky."

Relief spread through him, a healing balm. "When
did you get so smart?"

"When I fell in love with the right man," she said.

Lucky hugged her again, careful of her surgical
wound. "You don't mind sharing a house with Karen
and Rod? We could rent an apartment."

"I'd rather stay there, if it's okay with you," she said.
"It's like having a big family."

"I agree." While it might not be possible for that
family to include his brother, Lucky intended to try.

They were starting fresh, a man and woman who'd
stumbled and screwed up plenty. Yet the future gleamed
ahead of them in rainbow colors, because together they
were stronger and wiser than separately.

They'd have a lot more fun, too.

## Chapter 19

The adobe house had neatly trimmed bushes and a red tile roof, with striped woven curtains tied back at the windows. Mounting the porch steps, Lucky rubbed his damp palms on his jeans.

In response to his inquiry, a cousin had emailed that Matthew was stationed here in Point Hueneme, a few hours' drive to the north of Safe Harbor. Lucky hadn't even been sure how to say the town's name, which he'd learned on the internet was pronounced WY-nee-mee.

When he'd phoned, Matthew had cautiously agreed to meet with him. He'd suggested meeting at his house today while his wife and school-age children were attending a birthday party.

It might have been more sensible to choose a public place, Lucky mused. What if his brother threw a punch at him?

Well, he hadn't slammed down the phone or insulted

Lucky. Although his tone had been wary, Lucky's mood was cautious, too.

Not finding a bell, he knocked, then wiped his palms on his pants again. Had Zora been this nervous when she'd prepared herself to see her sister? She must have waited like this, uncertain, anxious...

The door opened. Sixteen years had matured Matthew's olive face. He was, surprisingly, a couple of inches shorter than Lucky— *I must have grown.* Yet in every other respect, despite the passage of time, Matthew was incredibly familiar. In a rush, Lucky realized how much he'd missed the pal who'd taught him to play baseball when their dad was too busy and had advised him on which classes to choose in high school.

"Thanks for agreeing to meet me," Lucky said.

Matthew extended a strong, callused hand. They shook, and then his brother pulled him close and clapped his shoulder. "I'm glad you had the guts to make the first move."

"Damn," Lucky said. "If I start to cry, I'll be embarrassed."

"Nothing to be ashamed of." Releasing him, his brother moved aside to let him enter.

A couch and comfortable chairs, along with a bookshelf, TV and game system, filled the living room. On the wall hung a red, black and buff ceramic Aztec calendar almost identical to Lucky's. "Hey, we have the same interior decorator."

Matthew followed his gaze to the plaque. "It's like the one Grandpa and Grandma used to have."

"I'd forgotten."

"Aunt Maria and Uncle Carlos own it now. Man, I'm sorry." Matthew stood squarely balanced on both feet, his khaki T-shirt emphasizing the breadth of his chest and shoulders. "You should have been at those family gatherings all these years."

Their grandparents had died before their parents, so Lucky hadn't been denied the chance to say goodbye to them at least. As for the aunts and uncles, it had been their decision to exclude him without hearing his side. "I'm fine. Just got engaged, in fact."

"Fantastic!" Matt raised his hands to signal he had more to say. "Let me get this out. I nursed my anger at you for years, until gradually it dawned on me that I was angry about a lot of things that had nothing to do with you. At myself for not being there when our parents needed me. Also at leaving you to carry the burden. I worked such long hours that I ran off to join the navy to get away from the store."

Lucky had never suspected that his brother's motives in enlisting had included escape. Not that he blamed Matthew. "I resented working so hard, too. That's why I sneaked out for cigarettes, which was totally irresponsible. I should have been there with Mom that night."

"I wasn't there, either. Even though I'm proud to serve my country, I signed up partly for the wrong reasons." His brother shook his head. "The other day, looking at some new recruits, I noticed how young they were, and it hit me you were about that age when our parents died."

"Eighteen," Lucky recalled. "Grown-up."

Matt tilted his head. "A baby."

"So were you when you enlisted."

"That's no excuse for my behavior." A crooked smile brightened his brother's face. "Enough beating ourselves up. Can we put this in the past?"

"That's why I'm here," Lucky said.

"Tell me about this fiancée of yours," his brother said.

"I'll show you a picture." He took out his phone.

Soon they were lounging on the furniture, downing soft drinks and catching up on everything they'd missed.

"You've never been able to fix a pie crust as beautiful as mine." Playfully, Zady indicated the luscious apple pie on a side table reserved for Thanksgiving desserts. "I admit, your pecan pie looks yummy, but your crust isn't as shiny. The secret is to brush the unbaked crust with an egg mixed with a couple of tablespoons of cream."

Zora gave her sister a poke. They'd turned their old rivalry into friendly teasing since Zady had moved to town a few weeks earlier. "Insult it all you like. Lucky bought the pecan pie at the supermarket."

"You're kidding! You didn't bake your own pie?" Zady chuckled. "Mom would have a cow."

"Feel free to tell her."

"I doubt she's speaking to either of us since we informed her of your wedding after the fact."

At the reminder, Zora gazed happily down at the ring Lucky had placed there a week earlier. Although he'd offered to buy a more expensive one, she preferred this simple, classic design in gold. "I'm not sure which bothered her most, that I didn't invite her or that you served as my maid of honor."

She'd been a little saddened not to be able to include her mother. But after Mom's drunken behavior at Zora's first wedding and her cruel manipulations with Zady, Zora had stuck to her resolve to keep some distance between them. Afterward, she'd written her mother informing her of her marriage and asking for her blessing. There'd been no reply.

The wedding at the county's picturesque Old Courthouse had been modest but magical, thanks to the love flowing between the bride and groom. And they'd been surrounded by friends and family. While Betsy and Keely held the twins, Zady had served as maid of honor and Matthew as best man. Zora had immediately liked Matthew, as well as his dark-haired wife and children. They planned to hold another reunion at Christmas.

"Are you ladies squabbling?" Lucky's arm around Zora's waist restored her to the present. "You'll set a bad example for our children."

"It'll teach them to stick up for themselves," she countered, and rested her cheek on his shoulder. "Besides, Zady and I don't fight any more. Just a little sisterly competition."

"That's okay, then."

What a wonderful man she'd married, she thought, nestling against Lucky.

As for a honeymoon, that was on hold until the babies were old enough to wean and leave with others. When she and her husband took a trip, there'd be no interruptions, however cute.

"These little guys are ready for their nap." From the den, Betsy brought Orlando into the kitchen, yawning in his hand-crocheted blanket. On her finger glittered the ring that would always remind Zora of their close connection.

"Elizabeth's dozing, too." Keely cradled her precious charge.

"Much as I adore them, thank goodness they're asleep." Breast-feeding two babies consumed more energy than Zora had imagined, and she was grateful for the help. "I'm starving."

The aroma of roast turkey and stuffing had been wafting from the kitchen all afternoon. Tiffany and Amber had insisted on pitching in to help Karen cook, while Rod and Grandma Helen arranged the dining room.

"Upstairs we go," Betsy said. "Keely?"

The nurse gave a start. "Of course." Head lowered, she hurried after the older woman.

Keely had been acting distracted since the wedding. Guiltily, Zora reflected that she hadn't been paying much attention to her friend.

For a while, Keely had been upbeat, buoyed by the news of Laird's departure. As his replacement, the hospital had hired a family and child counselor named Franca Brightman, whom Edmond had recommended. Already, she was helping the Adams girls adjust to their loss.

But since the wedding, Keely had retreated into long silences. Now that Zora was on leave and no longer required rides to work, they had less chance to speak privately.

Today was hardly the occasion for a tête-à-tête, but Zora resolved to find a moment alone with Keely later. Perhaps she was suffering a posttraumatic reaction to their brush with death, or struggling to adjust to the many changes at the hospital.

With the purchase of the dental building, buzz filled the halls about the planned renovations and new staff to be hired. Exciting though it was, Zora remembered all the disruptions over the past few years as the hospital had been transformed. Perhaps that had contributed to Keely's downcast mood.

Her stomach growled as Tiffany and Amber paraded in and set hot dishes on the breakfast table, which would be used for serving. "I wish we lived here instead of at Grandma's," Amber said as she placed a casserole carefully on the tablecloth.

Tiffany glanced around. No sign of Helen. "I love Grandma, but honestly, we're underfoot in her house." Helen owned a two-bedroom cottage a few miles away.

"Especially with her arthritis," the younger girl added. "She's always cleaning up after us. I try to be neat but hey, I'm a kid."

Although newfound wealth had enabled Helen to hire a housekeeper to shop, cook and handle major cleaning, hosting a pair of active granddaughters was taking its toll, Zora had noted from the older woman's increasingly stiff movements. However, she respected that Helen chose not to buy a mansion or invest in more staff. She insisted on keeping the girls in touch with reality. In addition to sharing a bedroom, they would be transferring to public school next year.

Also, Tiff had enrolled in a dance class. Amber, who had loved to swim competitively until Vince turned every meet into a do-or-die situation, was easing into the sport again.

Partly to assist Helen, Rod had offered to relinquish his room to them and move in with Karen. The grandmother had replied firmly that she couldn't let the girls grow up in a home with a pair of unmarried adults sharing a bed.

Karen brought out a bowl of mashed potatoes, and Rod followed with a platter of sliced turkey. His daughters hurried into the kitchen to collect the salad and stuffing.

Helen joined them, along with Betsy and Keely. That was the whole group for today—Melissa, Edmond, Dawn and the triplets were dining with his parents,

while Jack, Anya and their baby had flown to Colorado
to share the holiday with her large family.

"I put the monitor by my place in the dining room,"
Keely told Zora. "That way, if the babies fuss, I can
check on them. If you don't mind."

"Mind?" Zora repeated. "You're doing me a favor!"

"No problem." Keely avoided her eyes.

Before Zora could question her friend, she felt Lucky's
hand on her spine, propelling her toward the food. "Serve
yourself first. You're a nursing mommy."

Amid a chorus of agreement, she complied. Soon they
were all seated, and after a prayer of gratitude for this
special gathering, they dug into their heaped-high plates.

What a year it had been, Zora thought as she took
in the beloved faces around the table. When a group of
friends had moved into this house last February, they'd
had no idea that by the end of November, there would
be six babies born and three marriages.

"Have you found an apartment yet, Zady?" Betsy
asked amid the chatter. Zora's sister was staying in a
small unit at the Harbor Suites.

"Nothing I really love," Zady admitted.

Keely toyed with her food. In contrast to the others,
she appeared to have little appetite for her meal.

Zora shot her a concerned glance. Keely ignored it.

"Can we have dessert?" Amber indicated the plate
she'd cleaned at top speed.

"Where are your manners?" reproved her grandmother. "Not till everyone's finished."

"How about the pumpkin bread?" Amber persisted.
"That isn't really dessert, is it, Grandma?"

"I suppose not." Seated between her granddaughters,

Helen acquiesced fondly. "Why don't you bring in the plate for everyone?"

"I'll get it." To Zora's surprise, Rod sprang up. Usually the anesthesiologist moved at a slower pace than everyone else, and he'd milked his injured nose for sympathy until the bruising faded. He whisked out of the room, and Zora heard a cabinet open and shut in the kitchen.

"What's Dad doing?" Amber asked.

"I guess we'll find out," Tiffany said.

The slightly built man returned, jauntily hoisting the plate of pumpkin bread. When he set it in front of Karen, Zora saw a miniature van displayed in the center.

"What's this?" Their landlady lifted the little vehicle to inspect it.

"It's the first part of my surprise." Rod stood next to her, bouncing with anticipation. "That's a stand-in for the van I'm buying. I'll be taking delivery of it next week. It carries eight, so we can drive the girls and their friends. Helen, I made sure it was accessible for you to get in and out of."

"That's lovely." She sounded puzzled, though, and Zora suspected they all were. Why display this in the middle of Thanksgiving dinner?

"The doors and hood open," Rod prompted.

"It would be hard to drive it otherwise." Beside Zora, Lucky smirked at the other man.

Instead of riposting as he usually would, Rod cleared his throat. "I mean the miniature. Open the hood."

With a bemused expression, their landlady tipped it open and gasped. "Oh, Rod!"

"What is it? What is it?" The girls crowded around.

Karen held up a diamond engagement ring. "My gosh."

Rod dipped, suggestive of lowering himself to one

knee, although he never quite touched the floor. "Will you make an honest man of me?"

Karen's mouth hung open. Then she gathered her wits. "Of course I will, you crazy man!" To the girls' cheers, she kissed him.

Zora could have sworn Helen's smile revealed a hint of relief. This meant the girls could move in with their father and new stepmother, while living only a few miles from their grandma.

"Congratulations." Betsy seemed as thrilled as the rest of them.

A soft sob on Zora's far side riveted her gaze to Keely. The woman appeared to be fighting tears.

"What's wrong?" Surely the nurse hadn't fallen in love with Rod. Zora had seen no sign of it.

"I don't mean to spoil the happy occasion." She sucked in air.

"Calm down and share what's bothering you," Zora urged. "Please."

Glumly, Keely answered. "You're all families now. Of course your sister should live here, too."

"Why?" Zady asked.

Keely didn't have to answer, because Zora understood. "You've been expecting us to ask you to leave?"

The older nurse nodded.

"No way," Lucky said.

"You belong here," Karen chimed in.

"She's your twin," Keely said doggedly. "It's only right."

Zora wished she'd addressed this issue long ago. It simply hadn't occurred to her. "You saved my life. The twins' lives, too."

Zady spoke up, too. "Keely, my sister and I have

been feuding for years. Yeah, we love each other and we're friends again, but share a house? We'd be at each other's throats in five seconds."

"Blood on the floor," Lucky said calmly.

"No, you wouldn't." Keely refused to be comforted. "You're a member of her family, and I'm not."

"I can fix that," Zora said. "I hereby dub you the babies' honorary aunt. You are therefore a relative. And we love you."

There was a chorus of agreement. "Including me," Rod put in. "Don't tell anybody at work."

Keely joined in the ripple of laughter that greeted this remark. "Really?"

"Really," Zora said.

"Will you help me plan my wedding?" Karen asked. "Since my mother died last year, I've been wishing I had more family."

"You have?" Keely sniffled.

Their landlady gazed dreamily around the table. "Growing up, I wished I had a houseful of brothers and sisters, and other relatives to celebrate holidays. My wish has come true. Keely, you have a home here as long as you want it."

The nurse appeared too choked up to speak.

"Can we eat dessert now?" Amber asked.

"That's the best idea I've heard all day," Lucky said. "Aside from Rod and Karen getting married, and Keely becoming an honorary aunt to our children."

Zora couldn't have agreed more.

\* \* \* \* \*

**Christine Rimmer** came to her profession the long way around. She tried everything from acting to teaching to telephone sales. Now she's finally found work that suits her perfectly. She insists she never had a problem keeping a job—she was merely gaining "life experience" for her future as a novelist. Christine lives with her family in Oregon. Visit her at christinerimmer.com.

## Books by Christine Rimmer

### Harlequin Special Edition

#### The Bravos of Valentine Bay

The Nanny's Double Trouble
Almost a Bravo
Same Time, Next Christmas

#### The Bravos of Justice Creek

Not Quite Married
The Good Girl's Second Chance
Carter Bravo's Christmas Bride
James Bravo's Shotgun Bride
Ms. Bravo and the Boss
A Bravo for Christmas
The Lawman's Convenient Bride

Garrett Bravo's Runaway Bride
Married Till Christmas

#### The Bravo Royales

Her Highness and the Bodyguard
How to Marry a Princess
Holiday Royale
The Prince's Cinderella Bride
The Earl's Pregnant Bride
A Bravo Christmas Wedding

#### Montana Mavericks: The Lonelyhearts Ranch

A Maverick to (Re)Marry

#### Montana Mavericks: The Great Family Roundup

The Maverick Fakes a Bride!

Visit the Author Profile page at Harlequin.com for more titles.

# The Nanny's
# Double Trouble

CHRISTINE RIMMER

For Marie Campbell,
friend and fellow book lover,
whose totally adorable basset hounds,
Fancy, Luke, Beau, Moses, Rachel, Clementine
and Sampson, are the inspiration for Daniel Bravo's
basset, sweet Maisey Fae.

# *Chapter 1*

When Keely Ostergard entered the upstairs playroom, she found Daniel Bravo lying on the floor. His eighteen-month-old daughter, Frannie, sat beside him, rhythmically tapping his broad chest with a giant plastic spoon.

"Boom, Da-Da," Frannie said. "Boom, boom, boom."

Meanwhile, Jake, Frannie's twin, stood at Daniel's head on plump toddler legs, little hands over his eyes in a beginner's attempt at peekaboo.

Watching them, Keely couldn't help thinking that for a man who'd never wanted children of his own, Daniel sure was a dream with them. The guy rarely smiled, yet he lavished his kids with attention and affection.

"Boo!" cried Jake, followed by a delighted toddler belly laugh that had him toppling head over heels toward his father's face. Daniel caught him easily and started to tickle him, bringing more happy chortling from Jake.

Frannie spotted Keely first. "Keewee!" She dropped her spoon, lurched to her feet and toddled across the floor with her little arms wide.

Keely scooped her up. She smelled so sweet, like vanilla and apples. "How's my girl?"

Frannie's reply was almost in English. "I goo."

Daniel sat up, Jake still in his arms. "Keely." He looked a little worried at the sight of her. She came by often to see the kids, but she'd always called first. Not this time. He asked, "Everything okay?"

"Absolutely." She kissed Frannie's plump cheek. "Sorry, I know I should have called." But if she'd called and said she would like to speak with him, he would have asked what was going on, and she didn't want to get into that until they were face-to-face. He could too easily blow her off over the phone.

Grace, Daniel's youngest sister, who had answered the door at Keely's knock, entered the playroom right then. "Keely needs to talk to you, Daniel."

"Sure—down you go, big fella." He set the giggling Jake on his feet.

"Come on, you two." Grace took Frannie from Keely and held out her hand for Jake. "Bath time." She set off, carrying Frannie and pulling Jake along, on her way to the big bathroom down the hall.

Daniel stood still in the middle of the floor, watching her. "How 'bout a drink?"

"Sounds good."

Downstairs in the kitchen, he poured them each two fingers of very old scotch, neat. Keely wasn't much of a drinker, and scotch wasn't her favorite. But she had an offer to make, and she wanted him to say yes to it. Sharing a drink first might loosen him up a little.

She raised her glass and took a small sip. It burned going down, and she tried not to shudder. "Strong stuff."

He looked at her sideways and grumbled, "Why didn't you just say you hate scotch?"

"No. Really. It's very good."

He stared at her doubtfully for a couple of awkward seconds and then, with a shrug, he looked out the window. It was after seven on a cool Friday night in March, and already dark out. Beyond the glass, garden lights glowed golden through the thickening fog. Behind her, somewhere far out in the bay, down the tree-covered hill from the front of the house, a foghorn sounded.

Keely rested her hand on the cool, smooth soapstone counter. It was a beautiful kitchen. Her cousin, Lillie, had redone it with meticulous, loving care. It had lustrous heated wood floors in a herringbone pattern, a giant farm-style sink, twinkly glass backsplashes and chef-grade appliances.

*Lillie.*

Keely's throat got tight just thinking of her. She'd died eighteen months ago, leaving behind two adorable newborn babies—and one very grim husband. For the last fifteen years or so, Daniel had hardly been what Keely would call a happy guy anyway, but since they lost Lillie, the man rarely cracked a smile.

She took another sip and inched up on the reason she'd stopped by. "So then, what will you do for childcare now?"

He shifted his gaze back to her. "What *can* I do? Guess I'll try the nanny service again."

Keely almost laughed, though it wasn't all that funny. "Will you ask for the one with the alcohol problem or the one who gets sick all the time? Or maybe the one who's in love with you?" Daniel was a Viking of a man, big and buff and really good-looking in his too-serious, borderline-broody way. It wasn't the least surprising that one of the endless string of nannies and babysitters had decided she was meant to become a second mother to his children and show him how to heal his wounded heart.

He pinched the bridge of his manly nose as though he might be getting a headache. "Something will come up." His eyes—of a rather eerie pale blue—had circles under them. Clearly, he hadn't been sleeping well lately.

Keely felt kind of guilty for teasing him. Okay, she harbored some animosity toward him for what had gone down between him and her cousin in the last months of Lillie's life. But that was private stuff, husband-and-wife stuff, stuff Lillie had shared with Keely in strictest confidence.

Daniel wasn't a bad guy. He'd just had to shoulder too much, too soon. On the plus side, he was a man you could count on—and pretty much everyone did. Keely needed to remember his good qualities whenever she felt tempted to blame him for making Lillie unhappy.

He was doing the best he could, and he did have a real problem. President and CEO of Valentine Logging, Daniel worked long hours. He needed reliable childcare for the twins. Yet the nannies came and went. And Daniel's mother-in-law, Keely's aunt Gretchen, had always been his nanny of last resort, stepping up to take care of the kids every time another caregiver bit the dust.

Then two days ago Gretchen tripped and fell—over Jake. The little boy was fine, but Gretchen had four broken bones in her right foot. At seventy and now on crutches, Keely's aunt was no longer in any condition to be chasing after little ones. Daniel needed another nanny, and he needed one now.

And that was where Keely came in.

She knocked back the rest of her scotch. It seared a bracing path down her throat as she plunked her glass on the counter. "Okay, so here's the thing..."

Daniel gazed at her almost prayerfully. "Tell me you know a real-life Mary Poppins. Someone with excellent references who can't wait to move in here and take care of my kids."

"'Can't wait' might be a little strong, and Mary Poppins I'm not. But as for references, your mother-in-law will vouch for me. In fact, Aunt Gretchen has asked me to take over with the kids for a while, and I've said yes."

Daniel's mouth went slack. "You? You're kidding."

Should she be insulted? She answered tartly, "I am completely serious. The kids know me, I love them dearly and I'm happy to step in."

He pinned her with that too-pale stare. "It's just not right."

"Of course it's right. Lillie was my sister in all the ways that matter. Jake and Frannie need me right now. I know you and I aren't best friends, but you've got to have someone you can depend on. That would be me."

"You make it sound like I've got something against you, Keely. I don't."

She didn't believe him. But how he felt about her wasn't the point. Jake and Frannie were what mattered. Yes, he could probably hire yet another nanny from the service he used. But the kids deserved consistency and someone who loved them.

"Great." She plastered on a giant smile. "Daniel, It's

going to be fine, I promise you. Better me than yet another stranger."

His brow wrinkled to match the turned-down corners of his mouth. "You're busy. You've got that gallery to run and those quilt things you make."

*Quilt things?* Seriously?

Keely was a successful fabric artist as well as the proud owner of her own gallery, Sand & Sea, down in the historic district of their small Oregon town of Valentine Bay. And whatever Daniel chose to call textile arts, he did have a point. Taking care of Jake and Frannie on top of everything else she had going on would be a challenge.

She would manage, though. Gretchen had asked her to help. No way would she let Auntie G down.

"I'm here and I'm willing," she said. "The kids need me and they know me." She raced on before he could start objecting again. "Honestly, I have a plan and it's a good one. This house has seven bedrooms and only four people live here now—including the twins."

After his parents died, Daniel and Lillie had raised his seven surviving siblings right there in the Bravo family home. All the Bravo siblings had moved out now, though. Except for Grace. A junior at Reed College in Portland, Grace still came home for school breaks and between semesters. She had the only downstairs bedroom, an add-on off the kitchen.

Keely forged on. "I can take one empty upstairs room for a bedroom and one for my temporary studio—specifically, the two rooms directly across the hall from the twins' playroom and bedroom. It's perfect. And most nights, once you're here to take over, I'll probably just go home." She had a cute little cottage two blocks from the beach, not far from her gallery. "But if you need me, I can stay over. With a studio set up here, I can work on my own projects whenever I get a spare moment or two. I have good people working at Sand & Sea, trustworthy people who will pick up the slack for me."

He leaned back against the counter, crossed his big arms over his soft flannel shirt and considered. "I don't know. I should talk to my sisters first, see how much they can pitch in."

Besides Grace, who would be leaving for Portland day-after-tomorrow, there were Aislinn, Harper and Hailey. Aislinn worked for a lawyer in town. She couldn't just take off indefinitely to watch her niece and nephew. As for Harper and Hailey, who'd been born just ten months apart, they were both seniors at U of O down in Eugene and wouldn't be back home until after their graduation at the end of the semester.

And what was it with men? Why did they automatically turn to their sisters and mothers-in-law in a childcare emergency? Daniel had three brothers living nearby. Keely *almost* hit the snark button and asked him why he didn't mention asking Matthias, Connor or Liam if they could pitch in, too?

But she had a goal here. Antagonizing Daniel would not aid her cause. "Well, of course everyone will help out, fill in when they can. But why make your sisters scramble when I'm willing to take on the main part of the job?"

"It just seems like a lot to ask."

"But, see, that's just it. You're not asking. I'm offering."

"More like insisting," he muttered.

"Oh, yes, I am." She put on a big smile, just to show

him that he couldn't annoy her no matter how hard he tried. "And I'm prepared to start taking care of Frannie and Jake right away. I'll move my stuff in tomorrow, and I'll take over with the kids on Sunday when Grace leaves to go back to school."

He scowled down at his thick wool socks with the red reinforced heels and toes. Daniel always left his work boots at the door. "There's still Gretchen to think about. If you're busy with the kids, who's going to be looking after her until she can get around without crutches again?" Keely's uncle, Cletus Snow, had died five years ago. Auntie G lived alone now.

"She's managing all right, and I will be checking in on her. And that's not all. She's called my mom."

One burnished eyebrow lifted toward his thick dark gold hair as Daniel slanted her a skeptical glance. "What's Ingrid got to do with anything?"

It was an excellent question. Ingrid Ostergard and Gretchen Snow were as different as two women could be and still share the same genes. Round and rosy Gretchen loved home, children and family. Ingrid, slim and sharp as a blade at fifty, was a rock musician who'd lived just about all her adult life out of her famous purple tour bus. Ingrid had never married. She claimed she had no idea who Keely's father was. Twenty years younger than Gretchen, Keely's mother was hardly the type to run to her big sister's rescue.

Keely said, "Mom's decided to change things up in her life. She's coming home to stay and moving in with Aunt Gretchen."

Daniel stared at her in sheer disbelief. "What about the band?"

Pomegranate Dream had had one big hit back in the

nineties. Since then, all the original members except Ingrid had dropped out and been replaced, most of them two or three times over. "My mother pretty much *is* the band. And she says she's done with touring. She's talking about opening a bar here in town, with live music on the weekends."

He just shook his head. "Your mother and Gretchen living together? How long do you think that's going to last?"

"There have been odder odd couples."

"Keely, come on. Those two never got along."

She picked up the bottle of scotch and poured them each another drink. "How 'bout we think positive?" She raised her glass. "To my new job taking care of your adorable children—and to my mom and your mother-in-law making it work."

He grabbed his glass. "I would insist on paying you the going rate." He looked as grim and grouchy as ever, but at least he'd essentially accepted her offer.

"Daniel, we're family. You don't have to—"

"Stop arguing." He narrowed those silvery eyes at her. "It's only fair."

Was it? Didn't really matter. If he had to put her on salary in order to agree to accept her help, so be it. "Go ahead then. Pay me the big bucks."

"I will." He named a figure.

"Done."

He tapped his glass to hers. "Here's to you, Keely. Thank you." He really did look relieved. "You're a lifesaver." And then something truly rare happened. Daniel Bravo almost smiled.

Well, it was more of a twitch on the left side of his mouth, really. That twitch caused a warm little tug in the center of her chest. The man needed to learn how to smile again, he really did. Yes, he'd caused Lillie pain and Keely resented him for it.

But Lillie, diagnosed with lupus back in her teens, had craved the one thing that was most dangerous for her. She'd paid for her children with her life and left her husband on his own to raise the sweet babies she just had to have.

Life wasn't fair, Keely thought. At least there should be smiles in it. There should be joy wherever a person could find it. Jake and Frannie needed a dad who could smile now and then.

"What are you looking at?" Daniel demanded, all traces of that tiny twitch of a smile long gone.

Keely realized she'd been staring at Daniel's mouth for way too long. She blinked and gave an embarrassed little cough into her hand. "Just, um, thinking that you ought to smile more often."

He made a growly sound, something midway between a scoff and a snort. "Don't start on me, Keely. You'll give me a bad feeling about this deal we just made."

It was right on the tip of her tongue to come back with something snippy. *Do not get into it with him*, she reminded herself yet again. They would be living in the same house at least some of the time, and they needed to get along. Instead of a sharp retort, she gave him a crisp nod. "Fair enough."

Claws clicking gently across the floor, Lillie's sweet basset hound, Maisey Fae, waddled in from the family room. The dog stopped at Keely's feet and gazed up at her longingly through mournful brown eyes.

"Aww. How you doin', Maisey?" She knelt to give the dog a nice scratch under her jowly chin. "Where's my sugar?" She pursed her lips, and Maisey swiped at her face with that long, pink tongue.

When Keely rose again, Daniel was holding out a house key. "I'll give you a check tomorrow to cover the first week."

"Thanks. I'll be here nice and early with my car full of clothes, equipment and art supplies."

"I can't wait," he said with zero inflection as she headed for the front door. "What time?"

"Eight," she said over her shoulder.

"I'll come over and help."

"No need." She waved without turning. "I've got this."

The next morning, as Keely was hauling her prized Bernina 1015 sewing machine out to her Subaru in the drizzling rain, Daniel pulled up at the end of her front walk in his Supercrew long-bed pickup.

He emerged from behind the wheel, his dark gold hair kind of scrambled looking, his face rough with beard scruff, wearing a heavy waffle-weave Henley, old jeans and the usual big boots.

"I told you I can handle this," she reminded him as he took the sewing machine from her.

"You're welcome. Happy to help," he said, and for a split second she imagined a spark of wry humor in those ice-blue eyes.

She remembered her manners. "Thank you—and be careful with that," she warned. "Those aren't easy to find anymore, and they cost a fortune." She swiped at the mist of raindrops on her forehead, then stood with her hands on her hips watching his every move as he set the machine carefully in the back seat of his truck.

When he shut the door again, she asked, "So Grace has the kids?"

"Yeah, they're with Grace. Let's get the rest." He headed up the walk, his long strides carrying him to the front porch of her shingled cottage in just a few steps.

She hustled to catch up. "You want some coffee? I can make some."

"I had two cups with breakfast. Let's get this done."

Half an hour later, all her equipment, including her spare Bernina—a 1008 model—a raft of art and sketching supplies and the giant pegboard loaded with industrial-sized spools of thread in just about every color known to man, was either in the rear seat of his crew cab or tucked in the long bed beneath the camper shell. He'd loaded up her two collapsible worktables, too, and the smaller table she liked to keep beside her easel. That left only her suitcase to go in the Subaru. She'd figured it would take three trips to get everything up to the Bravo house. Thanks to Daniel, they would get it done in one.

"See you back at the house." He climbed in his truck.

"Thank you. I mean that sincerely."

With a quick wave, he started the engine and drove off.

She locked up and followed him, leaving the mist-shrouded streets of town to head up Rhinehart Hill into the tall trees and then along the winding driveway that led to the beautiful old Bravo house, with its deep front porch flanked by stone pillars.

Keely stopped behind Daniel's truck in the turn-around in front of the house. She grabbed her biggest suitcase and hauled it inside and up the curving staircase to the room she planned to use for sleeping whenever she stayed over.

He emerged from the other room to meet her as she headed back down. "I'm putting your sewing stuff in the white room." He shot a thumb back over his shoulder. "You're using it for work, right?"

"How'd you guess?"

"It has better light than the other one. You want me to get the bed and dressers out of there?"

"I can use the dressers for storage, if that's all right. Are they empty?"

"I think they've got a bunch of old clothes nobody wants in them. Just clear out the drawers, and I'll take everything away."

"Thanks." *Note to self: be nicer to Daniel.* He really was a handy guy to have around when a girl needed to get stuff done. "And as for the bed, yes, please. I would like it gone."

"I'll have it out of there before dinnertime." And off he went down the stairs to bring up the next load of her stuff.

She peeked into the kids' bedroom and also the playroom before following him. Nobody there. Grace must have them downstairs somewhere.

Working together, they hauled everything up to her two rooms, bringing the big thread pegboard up last.

"You want this board mounted on the wall?" he asked.

"That would be terrific."

"I'll get to that tonight. Once we get the bed out, we can set things up pretty much like the room you were using at your place."

It was exactly what she'd hoped to do, and she got

a minor case of the warm fuzzies that he'd not only pitched in to help move her things, he'd also given real thought to making her as comfortable as possible in his house. "Totally works for me. Thanks."

With the barest nod of acknowledgment, he pulled a folded scrap of paper from his pocket—a check. "First week's pay." She took it. "I need to go on up to Warrenton," he said. Valentine Logging operated a log sorting and storage yard, deep water and barge cargo docks, and a log barking and chipping facility in nearby Warrenton at the mouth of the Columbia River. The company offices were there, too. "You planning to look in at the gallery today?"

"I am, yes. But I'll be back in the afternoon, ready to take over with the kids."

"No rush. Grace is here until tomorrow. She'll watch them today and tonight so you can get settled in."

That didn't seem fair. Grace had spent her whole week helping with the kids. "I'm fine on my own with them."

His regular frown got deeper. "Grace'll be here. In case you need her."

She considered the wisdom of arguing the point further. But his mouth was set and his eyes unwavering. Maybe not. "See you later then."

With a grunt, he turned and went down the stairs.

From the docks in Warrenton, Daniel called a handyman he trusted to haul the bed from the white room down into the basement. He'd been feeling pretty desperate yesterday when Keely showed up to save his bacon on the childcare front.

True, her offer had seemed like a bad idea at first.

He'd been afraid they wouldn't get along. In the last years of Lillie's life, as his marriage unraveled, Keely had never said a mean word to him directly. But he got the message in her disapproving glances and careful silences whenever he happened to be in the same room with her. She'd been firmly Team Lillie, no doubt about it. Still, for the twins' sake, she'd stepped up to provide the care they needed.

It was important to do everything he could to make her happy in his house. He planned to be home for dinner and then to help her get everything just the way she wanted it.

But the day came and went. By late afternoon, he still needed to go through the stack of paperwork he hadn't managed to get to during the week. After a short break to grab some takeout, he headed for the office, ending up by himself at his desk until after seven.

When he finally pulled his truck into the garage, he caught Grace, in tight jeans and full makeup, as she was coming down the stairs from the inside door. She flashed him a smile and tried to ease past him on the way to her car.

"Hold on."

"Daniel." She made his name into a serious complaint. "I have to go. I'm meeting Erin at—"

He caught her arm. "We need to talk."

"But—"

"Come on."

She let out a groan, but at least she followed him back into the house. "What? Can you please make it quick?"

"Let's talk in my study." She trudged along behind him to his home office off the foyer. Once they were both inside, he shut the door. "The kids and Keely?"

There was an eye roll. "Jake and Frannie are already in bed. Keely's upstairs, putting her stuff away, fixing up her room and her workroom. She said it was fine for me to go."

A hot spark of anger ignited in his gut. But when he got mad, Grace just got madder. He reminded himself to keep his cool. "The agreement was that you would give Keely a hand tonight, help her get comfortable, pitch in with the kids." He kept his voice level. Reasonable.

Still, Grace's eyes flashed blue fire. "The kids are in *bed*. Got it? And what agreement? You told me what to do as you were going out the door."

"Grace, I—"

"No. Uh-uh. I talked to Keely. I *asked* her if she needed me. She said go, have fun."

"Of course she would say that."

Grace looked up at the ceiling and blew out a furious breath. "You know, some people go to Cancún for their spring break. Me, though? I come home and help your mother-in-law look after your kids. And then when she trips over Jake, it's just me. Until Keely stepped up—which I totally appreciate. Keely's about the best there is. But me, I've got one night. One night of my spring break to myself. A few hours with my friends, and then I'm on my way back to school."

When she said it like that, he felt like an ogre. A litany of swear words scrolled through his brain. Playing stand-in dad to his own sisters and brothers should be more rewarding, shouldn't it? How come so much of the job just plain sucked?

*She's the last one at home*, he reminded himself. He was pretty much done with raising his siblings.

Too bad he still had a couple of decades ahead with his own kids.

"Come on, Grace. Don't exaggerate. You've spent time with your friends this week."

"Not much, I haven't."

"You went out last night, remember?"

Another giant sigh. More ceiling staring. "For like two hours."

"I want you to stick around tonight in case she needs you."

"But I promised Erin—"

He put up a hand. "You're needed here. And that's all I have to say about it."

If looks could kill, he'd be seared to a cinder. He waited for the yelling to start, dreaded the angry words about to erupt from her mouth—*I hate you, Daniel* and *Who died and made you king?* and the worst one of all, *You are not my father.*

As if he didn't know that. As if he'd *asked* for the thankless job of seeing that his brothers and sisters made it all the way to fully functioning adulthood without somehow crashing and burning in the process.

But this time, Grace surprised him. "Fine," she said way too quietly. And then, shoulders back and head high, she marched to the door, yanked it wide and went out.

He winced as she slammed it behind her. And then, even with the door shut, he could hear her boots pound the floor with each step as she tramped through the downstairs to her room off the kitchen—and slammed that door, too.

# Chapter 2

Daniel scrubbed both hands down his face. And then he stood stock-still, listening for cries from upstairs—Jake or Frannie, startled awake by Grace's slamming and stomping. He didn't breathe again for several seconds.

Finally, when he heard nothing but sweet silence, he stuck his head out the door and listened some more.

Still nothing.

By some minor miracle, Grace had failed to wake up the kids.

Daniel retreated into the study and quietly shut the door. He really ought to go straight upstairs to see how Keely was managing.

But Grace might still have angry words to hurl at him. He would check his email now, hide out for a few minutes. If Grace came flying back out of her room again loaded for bear, he didn't want to be anywhere in her path.

* * *

Keely was in her bedroom, putting her clothes in the dresser when she heard a door slam downstairs, followed by the loud tapping of boots across hardwood floors.

Grace. Had to be. Keely tucked a stack of bras into the top drawer, quietly slid it shut—and winced as another downstairs door slammed.

Apparently Daniel had come in before Grace could escape.

Keely felt a stab of guilt. Daniel had made it abundantly clear he intended for his sister to stay home tonight. If Keely had only asked Grace to stick around, the confrontation that had so obviously just occurred downstairs could have been avoided.

But come on. Grace had a right to a little fun with her friends now and then. And Keely really didn't need her tonight.

The question now: Should she leave bad enough alone and stay out of it?

Yeah, probably.

But what had just happened was partly her fault. At the very least, she could offer Grace a shoulder to cry on.

Still not sure she ought to be sticking her nose in, she tiptoed out into the hall, down the stairs, past the shut door to Daniel's study and onward to the back of the house, into the hall off the kitchen. She tapped on Grace's door.

After a minute, a teary voice called, "Go away, Daniel!"

Keely tapped again. "Grace, it's me."

Silence. Keely steeled herself to be told to get lost.

But then she heard footsteps in there. Grace opened the door with red-rimmed eyes and a nose to match.

Keely held out a tissue. "I come in peace."

Grace took the tissue and wiped her nose. "Where is he?"

"Still in his study, I think."

"Jake and Frannie?"

"Not a peep."

Grace sniffed again. "Come in." She stepped back. Keely entered and followed her to the bed where they sat down side by side.

Keely made her apology. "He told me this morning that he expected you to stay in. I should have warned you that he seemed kind of dug in about it."

"He's kind of dug in about everything." Grace stuck out her chin. "You know it's true." Keely didn't argue. Why should she? She agreed with Grace on that. "He treats me like I'm a borderline delinquent. I'm twenty-one years old, getting decent grades in school, doing a perfectly fine job of adulting, thank you so very much. I could just get up, get in my car and go."

"But you won't. Because you are sweet and helpful. You love your brother, and you want to get along with him. You know he's got way too much on his plate, and so you try your best to be patient with him."

Grace let out a reluctant snort of laughter. "Yeah, right."

"I want to make a little speech now. It will probably annoy you, but I hope you'll listen anyway."

"Go for it."

"When he was your age, he was married, working, fitting in college classes as best he could and raising you and your brothers and sisters—and probably getting zero nights out with his friends."

Into the silence that followed, Grace shot her a surprised glance. "That's it. That's the speech?"

"That's all."

Grace seemed to consider. "I know you're right. He hasn't had it easy. But he still drives me crazy. I mean, does he *have* to be such a hard-ass *all* the time?"

Keely put her hand over Grace's and gave it a pat. "I'll go talk to him."

Grace scoffed, "Like there aren't a thousand ways that could go horribly wrong."

"Trust me."

"I do. It's *him* that I'm worried about."

Daniel was still holed up in his study, reluctant to venture out and possibly have to deal with his sister again when the tap came on the door.

Grace? Doubtful. Probably Keely. He didn't really want to listen to whatever she had to say right at the moment either. Chances were she'd only come to give him a bad time about Grace.

There was another knock.

He gave in and called out, "It's open."

Keely pushed the door wide and then hesitated on the threshold. She wore what she'd had on that morning—jeans rolled at the ankles, a black-and-white-striped shirt half-tucked-in and hanging off one shoulder, with high-tops on her feet. Her hair was naturally reddish blond, but she liked to change it up. Today, it fell in fog-frizzed brown waves to her shoulders. Her big, wide-set green eyes assessed him.

He leaned back in his swivel chair and cracked his

neck to dispel some of the tension. "Go ahead. I'm listening."

She braced a shoulder in the doorway, stuck her hands in her pockets and crossed one high-top in front of the other. "I really did tell Grace I didn't need her, and I urged her to go out and have a little fun."

Women. They always knew how to gang up on a man. "All right."

She pushed off the door and straightened her shoulders. "All right, she can go—or all right, you heard what I said and I should get lost?"

He stared at his dead wife's cousin and reminded himself all over again that he was really grateful she'd come to look after his children, even if she did consider him to blame for all that had gone wrong between him and Lillie.

And maybe he *was* to blame.

When his parents had died suddenly on a second honeymoon in Thailand, he was eighteen. The most important thing then was to keep what was left of his family together. He'd stepped up to take care of his three surviving brothers and four sisters. Lillie, a year behind him in school, stepped right up with him. He and Lillie had been together—inseparable, really—for two years by then. They'd agreed to get married as soon as Lillie graduated high school.

A born nurturer just like her mother, Lillie was only too happy to take over as a second mom to his big brood of siblings. She always claimed that choosing a life with him and his ready-made family was the perfect solution for her. She could have the kids she longed for and not risk her health.

But as the years passed and his brothers and sisters

grew up and moved out, her yearning for babies of their own only got stronger. He didn't share that yearning. No way. An empty nest. That was what he'd looked forward to. He'd thought they might travel a little, get to know each other all over again...

"Daniel? You all right?" Keely was waiting for him to answer her last question.

He shook himself and put his regrets aside. "Sorry." *Grace.* He needed to smooth things over with Grace. "You're sure you don't need her?"

"Positive."

He got up. "I'll go talk to her."

Grace opened the door at his knock. "What now?"

"Grace, I'm sorry we got into it."

"It's all right," she said flatly. He got the message. It was not all right. It was anything but.

"Listen, go ahead. Go meet Erin. Enjoy your last night home."

She almost smiled. But she was still too pissed at him for that. "Thanks."

*Don't stay out too late.* He closed his mouth over the words. She was an adult after all. He had trouble sometimes remembering that. She'd been a sweet little six-year-old in pigtails with two missing front teeth when George and Marie Bravo decided they needed a romantic getaway in Thailand. They got there just in time for the tsunami that killed them. And Grace had had to grow up without them.

No, he wasn't his baby sister's father, but sometimes he felt like it. He liked it when she stayed home—and not only because she helped out with the kids. He wanted her safe, damn it, wanted all of them safe. Life was too dangerous. Anything could happen. He knew that from hard experience.

"Have a good time." He pushed the words out of his unwilling mouth.

"I will," she said obediently and then lifted her arms in a limp offer of a hug.

He gathered her close, but only for a moment. She pulled free quickly, and he left her to go offer Keely some help setting up the white room for her studio.

By a little after eleven, they had the thread pegboard hung and covered with giant spools. He'd put up some shelves for her, ones he'd found down in the basement. The shelves used to be in his brother Matthias's room way back before Matt moved out. She had two work-tables set up, one for sketching and one for her sewing machine. There was an easel in the corner and another, smaller table next to it piled with paint and brushes.

"This is looking good, Daniel. Thank you."

"What else needs doing?"

"That's it." She hid a yawn behind her hand. "We are finished."

"You sure?"

She pushed in the chair at her sewing table. "Yep."

He felt the oddest reluctance to head for his own room. After Grace left for her night out, it had been pretty much a no-pressure evening. He'd felt useful, helping Keely get the room the way she wanted it. And besides that, it was kind of good just to hang with her. Kind of companionable.

He hadn't had much of that, of companionship. Not for a long time. Not for a couple of years at least. Not since he'd found out that Lillie was pregnant.

And really, since before that, even. More like five years, since about the time Lillie started really pushing him to try for a baby of their own.

"Okay, what'd I say?" Keely asked.

"Huh? Nothing. Why?"

"You looked… I don't know. Faraway. Unhappy."

He tried for a laugh. It came out as more of a grunt. "I always look unhappy. Ask anyone who knows me."

"Now, see. I want to say that's not true. But, Daniel, it kind of is."

He had the absolutely unacceptable urge to start talking about Lillie, about how angry he still was at her after all this time, for betting on her life. And losing.

What was the matter with him? To even consider spilling his guts about Lillie to Keely, of all people? That would be a bad idea of spectacular proportions.

Wouldn't it? Why did he have this powerful feeling that Keely would understand?

Didn't matter. He just wasn't going there. No way.

And he needed to get out of there. Now.

He rubbed the back of his neck. "What can I say? Except, yeah, I'm a gloomy guy. And since you're good to go here, I'll see you in the morning."

She didn't reply for several seconds, just looked at him, kind of thoughtful and sad, both at once. A soft sigh escaped her. "All right then. Night."

"Night—come on, Maisey. Let's go." The dog, stretched out by the window, got up and followed him from the room.

With Maisey trotting along behind, he went down the stairs to let her out before bed. He walked fast, too, just in case Keely got it in her head to try to stop him, to start asking questions he saw no win in answering.

* * *

Daniel got in bed around midnight. He had trouble sleeping until a little after two, when he heard Grace come in. Relieved that she was home safe, he finally drifted off.

He woke to the sound of one of the kids crying. Maisey was already out of her dog bed and sniffing at the door. She gave a worried little whine, urging him to hurry as he yanked on track pants and a frayed Go Beavers T-shirt. When he opened the door, she pushed out ahead of him, leading the way along the hallway to the twins' bedroom.

The door stood open, dim light spilling out. Maisey went in first.

Keely was already there, Frannie in her arms. She was pacing the floor in the muted light from the little lamp on the green dresser. She turned when he entered, her hand on the back of Frannie's head, stroking gently as Frannie sobbed against her shoulder.

He felt that familiar ache his chest, the one he got when one of his own was hurting. A quick glance at Jake's crib showed him his boy was still asleep. That miracle wouldn't last long. "Let me take her," he whispered.

Keely kissed Frannie's temple. "Here's your daddy," she murmured, keeping it low, probably hoping Jake wouldn't wake up.

*Yeah. Good luck with that.*

Daniel held out his arms. With a sad little cry, Frannie twisted in Keely's hold and fell toward him. "Da-Da!" she wailed. He caught her and gathered her in. She dropped her head against his chest. "Ow. Ow, ow, ow."

Keely moved in close, the soft sleeve of her flannel

pajama top brushing his arm. He got a faint whiff of sweetness—her shampoo? Her perfume? "Ear infection?" she whispered.

He felt the back of Frannie's neck as she sobbed against his chest. "She seems kind of hot."

"I thought so, too."

"We should take her temperature."

"I'll get the thermometer."

"It's the one that says *rectal* on the case," he advised over Frannie's unhappy cries. *Rectal.* Story of his life. Rectal thermometers and never enough sleep—and did Keely know where to look? "Cabinet in the big bathroom," he added. "On the left, second shelf. Just to be sure it's sterile, clean it with alcohol and a little soap and water."

"You got it." She disappeared into the hallway. Really, she was a champ, that Keely.

About then, Jake woke up with a startled cry. "Da?"

"It's okay, big guy."

"Fa-Fa?" It was Jake's name for his sister.

"She's not feeling so good."

Jake stood up in his crib. "Fa-Fa?" he called again.

Frannie answered, "Day!" She couldn't make the *j* sound yet, and she tended to drop hard sounds at the ends of words, so the *k* got lost, too, and she called her twin Day. "Ow, ow, ow!"

"Shh." Daniel soothed her. "It's okay…" Gently, he laid his wailing daughter on the changing table. As she wiggled and whined, he took off her one-piece pajamas and her diaper. Meanwhile, Jake jumped up and down in his crib, calling out "Fa-Fa, Fa-Fa!" in frantic sympathy, followed by a bunch of nonsense words to which Frannie replied with nonsense of her own—well, maybe not nonsense to the two of them. They had their own language that only they understood.

Keely came back with the thermometer in one hand, a bottle of liquid Tylenol and a dosing syringe in the other. "We'll probably need it," she said, meaning the Tylenol. Chances were way too good she was right.

He held out his hand as Frannie continued to cry and squirm. Keely passed him the thermometer—and Jake let out a wail from his crib.

"I'll get him," she said. "Tylenol's right here." She set it on the shelf above the changing table and went to reassure Jake.

The thermometer registered 102 degrees. He put a fresh diaper on Frannie and dosed her with the Tylenol as Keely sat in the corner rocker, soothing the worried Jake.

Once he had Frannie back in her pajamas, he walked the floor with her until the Tylenol seemed to kick in. She went to sleep against his shoulder.

He kissed the top of her sweaty little head and glanced over to find Keely watching him.

She mouthed, *Sleeping?* At his nod, she nodded back, pointing at Jake, who was curled up against her, sound asleep, too.

It was only a few steps to Frannie's crib. He carried her over there and slowly, gently, laid her down. She didn't stir as he tucked the blanket in around her.

Across the room in the other crib, Keely was tucking Jake in, too. She turned off the lamp, and they tiptoed from the now-quiet room together.

"Psst. Maisey," he whispered. The dog lurched to her feet and waddled out after them. Daniel closed the door. "Whew."

Keely leaned back against the wall next to her bedroom and said hopefully, "Maybe they'll sleep the rest of the night and Frannie will be all better in the morning."

"Dreamer. And what rest of the night? It's already morning, in case you didn't notice."

"Don't go overboard looking on the bright side there, Daniel." She glanced through the open door to her room and blew out her cheeks with a weary breath. "Sadly enough, though, you're right. The clock by my bed says it's almost five. Tonight is officially over."

"Let's hope we get lucky and they both sleep till, say, eight."

"As if." She laughed, a sort of whisper-laugh to go with their low, careful whisper of a conversation. The low light from the wall sconces struck red glints in her brown hair, and she looked sweet as a farm girl, barefoot in those flannel pajamas that were printed with ladybugs.

He thought of Grace suddenly, knew a stab of annoyance that kind of soured the companionable moment between him and Keely—and there it was again, that word: *companionable*. He'd felt companionable with his dead wife's cousin twice in one night, and he didn't know whether to feel good about that or not.

"What?" Keely asked. "Just say it."

He went ahead and admitted what was bugging him. "Grace. She's got one of the baby monitors in her room, so she had to hear what was happening. But she didn't even come check to see if we needed her."

"Yeah, she did. She came in the kids' room before you. I knew she'd been out late and could use a little sleep, so I said I could handle it and sent her back to bed."

He hung his head. "Go ahead. Say it. I'm a crap brother."

Maisey chose that moment to get comfortable. She yawned hugely, stretched out on the floor and lowered her head to her paws with a soft doggy sigh.

Keely said, "You love Grace. She loves you. Ten years from now, you'll wonder what you used to fight about."

"Uh-uh. I'll remember."

"Maybe. But you'll be totally over it." Would he? He hoped so. She said, "When I was little, living with the band on my mother's purple bus, I used to dream of a real house like this one, dream of having sisters and brothers. Family is hard, Daniel. But it's worth it. And I think you know that it is."

"Yeah," he admitted. "You're right."

Family was everything. But that didn't stop him from fantasizing about totally non-family-related things. Partying till dawn, maybe. A game of poker that went on till all hours, with a keg on tap and all the guys smoking stinky cigars, telling politically incorrect jokes. A one-night stand with a gorgeous woman he'd never met before and would never see again, a woman who only wanted to use him for hot sex.

Now there was a big *as if.* He'd been with one woman in his life and was perfectly happy about that—until the past few years anyway. He just wasn't the kind of guy who went to bed with women he hardly knew. The one time he'd tried that, six months ago, he'd realized at the last possible moment that sex with a stranger just wasn't for him. His sudden change of heart had not endeared him to the lady in question.

And Keely was watching him again, a hint of a smile on her full mouth.

"I'm going to work on thinking positive," he promised her, because she did have a point about his negative attitude.

She gave a whisper-chuckle. "Anything is possible."

He clicked his tongue at Maisey and she dragged herself up on her stubby legs again. "Night, Keely." He turned for his room at the end of the hall.

"Night, Daniel," she whispered after him.

When Keely woke up it was ten after eight Sunday morning and no one was crying. She put on her vintage chenille robe over her pajamas and looked across the hall.

Both cribs were empty.

Downstairs in the kitchen, she found two smiling cherubs eating cut-up pancakes off their high chair trays and both Daniel and Grace at the breakfast table, neither one scowling.

Yes. Life was good on this beautiful, foggy-as-usual Sunday morning in Valentine Bay. She poured herself coffee.

Grace said, "I'm here till two, Keely, so if you need to run errands, go for it."

"Keewee!" crowed Jake, pounding on his tray.

Keely stepped over and kissed his gooey cheek.

"Kiss, kiss, Keewee!" Frannie pounded her tray, too, and smacked her rosebud lips.

Keely kissed her as well, and then returned to the stove where a stack of pancakes waited. She put a couple of them on a plate. "Thanks, Grace. I'll run by Sand & Sea and stop in to check on Aunt Gretchen."

\* \* \*

The gallery opened daily at eleven. Keely arrived at nine thirty. Her top clerk, Amanda, promoted temporarily to manager, joined her five minutes later. They went through the books and discussed the schedule. Sand & Sea was 3500 square feet of exhibit space on Manzanita Avenue, in the heart of Valentine Bay's downtown historic district. With a focus on Oregon artists, Keely offered contemporary work in just about every form imaginable, from painting to printmaking, sculpture to woodworking. She displayed and sold artisan jewelry, furniture, textiles and photography.

Sand & Sea also hosted receptions and special events. Every month or so, she featured an individual artist or a group of artists in a themed joint show. The first Friday in April, she would hold an opening for a new group show with several top Pacific Northwest artists working in various mediums on the theme of the ever-changing sea. Everything was on schedule for that one so far. Amanda was knowledgeable, organized and more than competent, and they had almost three weeks until the opening. Keely needed to find help with Frannie and Jake for the opening-night reception party and the few days before it. But that should be doable, one way or another.

Feeling confident that Sand & Sea wouldn't suffer while she focused on Daniel's twins, she left the gallery at eleven thirty to check in on her aunt.

Gretchen still lived in the house she'd shared with her husband, the house where she'd raised her precious only child, Lillie. Keely considered the four-bedroom craftsman-style bungalow her childhood home, too.

Yes, she'd spent most of her growing-up years living on the tour bus. But now and then, Ingrid's career would get a boost and the tour schedule would get crazy. Those were the times that Ingrid took Keely to Valentine Bay to live temporarily with Aunt Gretchen and Uncle Cletus. Keely loved when that happened. She was constantly begging her mother to let her live with the Snows full-time.

When Keely was fifteen, Ingrid finally gave in. Keely moved in with her cousin. At last, she got the settled-down life she'd always dreamed of in the seaside town she considered her true home.

Keely knocked on the green front door, but only to be considerate. She had a key and she used it, sticking her head in the door, calling, "It's just me! Don't get up!"

"I'm in the kitchen!" Gretchen called back.

Something smelled wonderful. Keely followed her nose to the back of the house. She found her aunt balanced on her good foot, one hand braced on the counter, as she pulled a tray of cookies from the oven.

Keely waited until Gretchen had set the tray on top of the stove and shut the oven door to scold, "You're not supposed to be on that foot."

"Sweetheart!" Gretchen turned and hopped toward her.

"You are impossible." Keely caught her and hugged her, breathing in the familiar, beloved scents of vanilla and melted butter. Her aunt not only always smelled delicious, she was still pretty in a comfortable, homey sort of way, with smooth, pale skin and carefully styled hair she still had professionally colored to the exact Nordic blond it used to be when she was young.

Gretchen laughed. "You know you need cookies."

Keely grabbed a chair from the table and spun it around. "Here. Sit."

"Oh, don't fuss." Gretchen held on to Keely for balance as she lowered herself into the chair.

Keely tried to look stern. "You will stay in that chair. I mean it."

Gretchen swept out a plump arm in the direction of the big mixing bowl on the counter. "I have two more cookie sheets to fill."

"Stay where you are. I'll do it." She grabbed another chair and positioned it so that Gretchen could put her foot up. "There. Want coffee?"

"Please—and where are my babies?"

"At Daniel's." Keely filled a cup and set it on the table next to Gretchen. "Grace isn't going back to Portland until this afternoon, so she's watching them."

"I miss them already."

"I'll bring them by during the week."

"You're a good girl. The best."

Keely got to work dropping spoonfuls of dough onto a cookie sheet. "Looking after Frannie and Jake is no hardship. You know how I always wanted babies." She'd been married once. A hot and charming driftwood artist, Roy Varner had come to town six years ago, before Keely opened Sand & Sea. Another local gallery had given him a show. Keely went to his opening. The attraction was instant and mutual. Roy swept her clean off her feet. They'd married within weeks of that first meeting. Roy traveled a lot to various art shows all over the west. Slowly Keely figured out that all the traveling wasn't only about selling art. When he traveled, Roy behaved like a free man in every way. Including sleeping with other women. Keely had divorced him four years ago.

"Don't you worry," said Gretchen. "You've still got plenty of time. A good man and babies will be yours."

Keely sent her aunt a fond glance over her shoulder. "Love you, Auntie G."

"Love you more."

"Heard from Mom?"

"Not since the other day."

"So we still don't know exactly when she's coming?"

"Keely, I am managing just fine—and what about you? All settled in at Daniel's?"

She considered mentioning Frannie's earache. But the little girl had seemed fully recovered this morning, so why worry Gretchen? "It's going great. And I'm all set up. I've got a bedroom across from the twins, and I'm using the room beside it as a work area—and you know, I've been thinking that we could get you some live-in help. Or you could move to Daniel's temporarily."

"I like my own house."

"But—"

"Don't start. I mean it. I've hired the boy next door to handle the yard. His sister will come in and clean when I need her. I'm having my groceries delivered. I'm used to doing things for myself, and I like my independence. Plus, in the Bravo house, all the bedrooms except Grace's are upstairs. That's not going to work with this foot."

Keely scooped up another spoonful of dough. "I'll call Mom, pin her down on when she'll be here."

"Don't you dare. I will handle this. You've got enough to do, and you know it."

"Auntie G, it's just a phone call," she said into the bowl of dough.

"Put down that spoon and look at me."

Keely dropped the spoon back in the bowl and turned to face her aunt. "Yeah?"

"Your mother *is* coming, but she'll be doing that in her own good time. That's how she rolls and don't we all know it."

Keely stifled a laugh. "How she *rolls*?"

Gretchen's blue eyes twinkled. "You know it's true. Ingrid makes her own rules and sets her own schedule. Trying to change her at this late date? Never going to happen."

Keely picked up a cooling cookie, took a bite and groaned in appreciation. "You shouldn't be up making cookies. But these are *so* good."

"I made lunch, too. It's in the fridge. Don't ruin your appetite."

"No chance of that. Not when it's your cooking—and were you on your feet to make the lunch?"

"Don't nag, sweetheart. Nagging is not attractive."

"What am I going to do with you?"

"Finish your cookie, get the rest of them in the oven—and then serve us both the amazing crab salad and crusty rolls I threw together."

Keely got back to the Bravo house at a quarter of two, and Grace left for Portland a few minutes later. As usual, Daniel had stuff to do at the office. He promised to be back by dinnertime.

She stood on the porch, one twin on either side of her, waving as Daniel headed off down the driveway. The sun had made an afternoon appearance, so for a while she took the kids out back, where there was a big wooden playset that had been there for as long as she could remember. They played in the sandbox, slid down the slide and she swung them on the toddler-friendly swings.

Back inside, she gave them a snack and took them upstairs for diaper changes and nap time. They went down like little angels, reaching for kisses, settling right in and closing their eyes.

She got a full hour in her new studio, bent over her precious Bernina before Frannie started crying. When Keely went to check on her, she had a fever again.

That night, poor little Frannie didn't sleep much. Neither did Keely or Daniel. Or Jake, for that matter. Frannie's ear hurt, and nothing seemed to make it feel better.

The next day, one of the ladies from Gretchen's church came by to watch Jake so that Keely could take Frannie to the pediatrician. Diagnosis: ear infection. Keely picked up the antibiotic and eardrop prescriptions on the way home.

Frannie had another bad night. All day Tuesday, she fussed and cried. Tuesday night, though, she only woke up crying twice.

"I think she's better," Keely whispered to Daniel when they tiptoed from the kids' room for the second time that night.

"I hope so." He had dark circles under his eyes. "We could all use a good night's sleep."

Wednesday morning, Frannie woke up smiling.

When Keely said, "I think you feel better, honey," the little angel replied, "I fine, Keewee. I goo."

And she really did seem fully recovered. After breakfast, Keely took both kids to see Gretchen, who still had no idea when Keely's mom would be showing up. But Auntie G was all smiles to get to spend an afternoon with her beloved babies. She held them on her lap and sang the nursery songs she used to sing to Keely when she was little and staying with the Snows.

On Thursday, Jake got sick.

It was some weird flu bug. There was vomiting and a lot of mucus. Keely called the pediatrician, who suggested a humidifier, cool baths, cough medicine and Tylenol for fever. No need to bring Jake in, the doctor had said, unless his fever hit 104 or he wasn't better within a week.

The next three nights were hell. Jake woke up crying and that woke Frannie. Keely and Daniel took turns looking in on them. The weekend went by somehow, not that Keely even cared what day it was. Making art with her sewing machine? Not even happening. And as for the original plan that she might go back and forth between the Bravo house and her cottage?

She never once made it home. In fact, she had to call a neighbor to water her plants.

She was exhausted, run ragged—and she found herself beginning to seriously admire Daniel. He worked all day and then stayed up with her all night to help with the kids. So what if he wasn't the happiest dad on the planet? The man was dedicated to the well-being of his children. He mopped up vomit and changed diapers with the best of them.

By late Sunday, Jake had weathered the worst of it. He coughed less frequently and the mucus factory seemed to be shutting down. The sweet little guy was definitely on the mend. Sunday night, Keely actually slept straight through. The kids didn't wake once, from bedtime until six the next morning.

Monday, Daniel woke her with a tap on her door.

"Ugh?" She blinked and yawned. "It's open."

He peeked in the door, looking almost rested for once. "Sorry to wake you."

She yawned again. "It was bound to happen sometime. What's up?"

"I'll get them up and downstairs if you'll start the breakfast."

"Deal."

She was at the stove when he came down with the little ones. She glanced over her shoulder to see him wiping Frannie's streaming nose. They stared at each other across the gorgeous expanse of the soapstone island. "Oh, no," she whispered, as though if she didn't say it too loudly, Frannie wouldn't be getting the bug Jake had just recovered from.

"No fever," Daniel said. He didn't add *yet*, but it seemed to her the unspoken word hung in the air between them.

By that afternoon, Frannie's nose ran nonstop. By dinnertime, she'd thrown up twice and a persistent cough seemed to rattle her little bones. By then, she also had a fever. It hovered at around 101.

Keely and Daniel spent another night taking turns waking up to soothe a sick baby. Really, they were getting the nighttime nursing care down to a science, as though they had radar for whose turn it was. Keely barely stirred when it was his turn, and the master bedroom door remained shut when it was hers.

Once that night, she woke when it was his turn.

"This one's mine," he mumbled when she stuck her head out into the hall.

"Unh," she replied and went back to bed.

On Wednesday, a week and a half into the endless string of illnesses the twins had been suffering, Daniel had a timber owner he had to go meet with. It was a small grove of Douglas firs ready to harvest, and Daniel would walk the grove with the landowner, explaining how Valentine Logging would maximize each tree to its full potential. The landowner wanted to meet at eight in the morning and Daniel wanted the contract, so at a quarter after seven he staggered out of the house, bleary-eyed, armed with a giant travel mug of coffee.

Keely spent the morning alone trying to keep her eye on Jake while doing what she could to ease poor Frannie's misery. She dosed the little girl with over-the-counter meds, kept the humidifier running and gave Frannie cold-water sponge baths at regular intervals.

The day never seemed to end.

Finally, at around two in the afternoon, she got both kids down for a nap. To the soft hissing of the humidifier, she tiptoed from their room with Maisey at her heels. Across the hall, both of her doors were open. She cast a despairing glance toward her studio room. *As if.*

Right now, her beloved Bernina was the last thing she wanted to cuddle up with. The bed in the other room, though...

Nothing had ever looked so beautiful.

She dragged her tired body in there and fell gratefully across the mattress as Maisey flopped down on the rug right beside her. Blessed sleep settled over her.

She dreamed of walking the foggy beach not far from her back door—with Daniel of all people. They didn't talk, just strolled along the wet sand, side by side but not touching, the waves sliding in, foaming around their bare feet.

"Keewee! Da-Da!"

"Wha—huh?" Keely shuddered, instantly wide-awake.

"Da-Da!" Frannie cried from the other room, followed by a long wail of sheer misery.

Keely shoved herself backward off the bed, raked her hair out of her eyes and hustled for the other room. Frannie was standing up in her crib, sobbing and coughing, snot running down her flushed little face.

"Oh, honey…"

"Keewee! Ow!"

Keely ran over and lifted the poor sweetheart into her arms. "Frannie. Oh, now. It's okay…" She settled her on her shoulder.

At which point, Frannie threw up. It went down Keely's back. That caused Frannie to wail all the louder.

"It's okay. It's all right," Keely promised, though clearly it was anything but. Gently, she peeled the little girl off her shoulder. "Shh. Shh. Let me…"

It was as far as she got. Frannie hurled again, this time down Keely's front. "Oh, bad!" Frannie wailed.

"No, no," Keely promised her. "It's not bad, honey. It's okay."

That was when Frannie threw up again, all over herself. She wailed even louder, "Keewee, I sowwy. I sowwy, sowwy, sowwy."

From his crib, Jake cried, "Fa-Fa? Fa-Fa, oh, no!"

"She's okay," Keely promised and wished it were true. "Jakey, she's going to be fine."

Maisey appeared in the doorway to the hall. She moaned in sympathetic doggy distress.

Keely carried Frannie to the changing table and quickly got her out of her soiled clothes. "Jakey, we'll be right back," she promised the increasingly agitated little boy as she grabbed the little girl and a clean diaper. Holding both out and away from her vomit-soaked body, she stepped over Maisey and carried baby and diaper across the hall to her room, moving straight through to her bathroom, which had a traditional tub-and-shower combination.

Shoving the shower curtain aside, Keely lowered the little girl into the tub. "Here. We'll get you all cleaned up."

"'Kay." Frannie sniffed.

Keely turned on the water. Once she had it luke-warm, she grabbed a washcloth and rinsed Frannie off.

Frannie was quiet, sniffling a little, watching her through wide eyes, as Keely dried her off and carried her—held out and dangling—to her own bed, where she put on the diaper.

"You feel better now, honey?"

Frannie solemnly nodded, eyes wide and wet. Keely scooped her up again and put her in the playpen she kept set up in the corner for any time she needed to corral the kids in her room.

"Fa-Fa? Keewee?" Jake cried from the other room.

"Coming, Jakey. Just a minute!" Keely called back.

A plush pink squeaky kitten lay waiting in the play-pen. Keely squeezed it and it meowed. Frannie took it and hugged it close.

"I'm just going to go into the bathroom to clean up. I'll be right back. Okay, honey?"

For that, she got another somber nod from Frannie. Though still flushed, her eyes red and her nose running, Frannie did seem much calmer at least.

Thank God, the vomiting bout seemed to be through.

Jake called again, "Keewee?"

"Just another minute, Jakey. I'll be there. I promise!" Peeling off her smelly shirt as she went, Keely darted for the bathroom. Standing on the bathroom rug by the tub, she wiggled free of her bra, kicked out of her shoes and shoved down both her jeans and panties at once.

"Keewee!" Jake shouted.

"Jakey, I'm right here! Just a minute!" she called, as she hopped around in a ridiculous circle, whipping off one sock and then the other. Flipping on the taps, switching the flow to the showerhead, she got in under the still-cold spray and yanked the curtain closed.

Three minutes, tops, she was in there. Jake called her name repeatedly. Once or twice, Frannie did, too. Keely got the mess off, rinsed in record time, flipped off the tap and shoved the shower curtain wide.

She'd stepped, dripping wet to the bath mat, and reached for her towel before she happened to glance through the open bathroom door to the bedroom.

Jake in his arms and Maisey at his feet, Daniel stood by the playpen staring at her with his mouth hanging open.

# Chapter 3

Keely grabbed her towel, whipped it around her, stepped to the bathroom door and shoved it shut.

Only then did she sink to the toilet seat and hit her forehead with the heel of her hand. Never in her life had she been so embarrassed. Not even the day she wore white jeans on the tour bus and got her first period. Except for her and her mom, everyone on that bus was a guy. Keely just knew all those rockers had seen her shame—and okay, on second thought, that might have been worse.

But this was plenty bad.

The look on his face. Like someone had just dropped a safe on his head.

God. Daniel had seen her naked. That was so wrong. In all the ways that really counted, she was Lillie's sister and a man ought never to see his wife's sister naked.

Seriously. Would it have killed her to shut the damn bathroom door?

But she'd thought they were alone—just her, the kids and Maisey. She'd wanted to be able to hear them while she cleaned up, just in case...

Just in case, *what*? Come to think of it, she had no idea.

*It's not the end of the world, Keely. No one will die from this. Get over yourself.*

Daniel tapped on the door. "Keely? You okay?"

"Fine! Really!" Her voice had the tinkling brightness of breaking glass. "We, uh, had a little accident."

"But...you're okay?"

*Oh, hell, no.* "Yes. I'll be out in a few minutes."

He made a nervous throat-clearing sound. "I'll just take the kids into the other room."

"Great! Be there in a few."

"Uh. Take your time."

She started to call out something frantic and cheerful. "Righto!" or "Absolutely!" But she shut her mouth hard and folded her lips between her teeth so that not one more ludicrous word could escape.

Fifteen minutes later, she found Daniel and the kids in the bedroom across the hall. He sat in the rocker, holding Frannie, who looked like a slightly flushed angel, all curled up in his arms, sucking peacefully on a baby bottle half-full of water. He'd dressed her in a cozy pair of pink pajamas.

Jake lay on the floor nearby, gumming a plastic teething pretzel, one plump arm thrown out across Maisey, who lay at his side. He took the pretzel from his mouth and gave her his most dazzling smile. "Keewee. Hi there."

"Hey, honey."

"Da-Da home."

"Oh, yes, he is."

Jake stuck the pretzel back in his mouth and chewed some more. Maisey nuzzled him, and he gave a lazy little giggle around the toy in his mouth.

The puddle of vomit on the rug was only a damp spot now, and the room smelled of the all-natural cleaner they used around the kids, a citrusy scent.

She made herself raise her gaze and look at Daniel. Those sea-glass eyes were waiting. She made herself speak. "You're home early."

"I was worried about Frannie and thought maybe you could use a break or at least another pair of hands."

She forced a smile. "Thank you. I see you cleaned up the mess already."

"Seemed like the least I could do." Gently, he stroked Frannie's fine gold hair, his rough hand big enough to cradle the whole of her little head. He pressed a kiss to her temple. "She's cooler. I think the fever might have broken."

"Wonderful."

He rocked slowly, back and forth. In his arms, Frannie looked so peaceful. Safe. Content. "I am sorry." His fine mouth twisted, and a hot flush swept up his thick neck. "For barging in on you. I should have knocked. But Jake was calling for you and for Frannie. I picked him up and he pointed at your room…"

Did they really need to talk it over?

Maybe. After all, it could be good, right? To be frank and open about it? They could clear the air, so to speak. "I left both doors open. It's not your fault. Of course you came right in." How red was her face? As red as his? *Oh, God.* "It's not a big deal, Daniel."

"You're right," he said and swallowed hard. "Not a big deal at all."

And it wasn't.

Oh, but it *was*.

For Daniel anyway.

Nothing had changed. But for every minute of the rest of that day, Lillie's cousin was suddenly very much on his mind.

Not to mention wreaking havoc lower down.

His longtime sexual abstinence had never felt so painful. Could he *be* more inappropriate? All of a sudden, he was a man obsessed. Who did that? Who *thought* like that?

He needed to stop. Stop thinking of her, fantasizing about her, imagining what it might be like if they...

No. Uh-uh. That wasn't going to happen. Ever. And it *shouldn't* happen.

She was family. She was great with the kids. He no longer felt that she judged him for the troubles between him and Lillie during the last years of her life.

They were, well, *friends* now. Weren't they? He counted on Keely, enjoyed talking to her. Liked having her around.

No way would he mess with that.

He wasn't even considering messing with that.

Uh-uh.

He needed to focus on the positive and forget the smooth white curves of her shoulders shining wet from her shower, not think about those full, tempting breasts, her dusky pink nipples puckered and tight. He needed to block out the memory of that tiny, shining rivulet of water sliding down the center of her, filling her navel, spilling over and dribbling lower, into the water-beaded landing strip of red-brown hair that did nothing to cover the ripe swell of her mound.

Yeah.

Right.

All that. He needed to damn well forget about all that.

To focus on what mattered.

Family. The kids. Not rocking the fragile boat of their lives, a boat that had finally steadied after almost capsizing with the loss of Lillie.

By that evening, Frannie seemed fully recovered. She ate a big dinner and kept it down. Both children slept straight through that night and the next night and the night after that, too.

Daniel could go to the office or out on a job in the morning and concentrate on both his bottom line and the potentially dangerous work that needed doing. His kids were safe and well with Keely. He needed her, and he was grateful to her.

And he was not going to jeopardize all the good she brought to his family by doing something stupid like putting a move on her.

That Sunday, he picked up Gretchen and brought her over for dinner. She'd baked a chocolate cake for their dessert, and though she was still using a walker to get around, she claimed she felt better every day.

She praised Keely's pot roast and fussed over the kids. "I do miss taking care of them."

"Now that they're both recovered after the mystery bug from hell, I'll bring them to your house this week," Keely promised.

"What day?" Gretchen demanded.

"Tuesday, for lunch—my treat. That means I'm bringing the food along with the children," Keely lectured. "Don't you dare fix a thing." Daniel watched her plump lips moving, admired the shine to those wide green eyes, wondered what it would feel like to press his mouth to the smooth white skin of her throat, to stick out his tongue and learn the taste of her skin.

"Right, Daniel?"

He blinked and stared at his mother-in-law. "Er, what was that?"

Gretchen chuckled. "I swear, you are a thousand miles away. I hope you're not letting work run you ragged."

"Uh, no. I was just, you know, thinking..." *About Keely. Naked.* "But anyway, what was the question?"

"Well, I only said that it wouldn't be right, not to at least have some cookies ready Tuesday when Keely brings the twins over. The babies love my cookies." She aimed a chiding glance at Keely. "*Keely* loves my cookies. I'll send some home for all of you to share."

"Cookies!" Jake pounded his high chair tray and then shoved a hunk of potato into his mouth.

"She needs to stay off that foot," Keely grumbled. "Auntie G, that cake you brought looks fabulous, but cake and cookies are not necessities. For you to take care of yourself, that's what matters."

Gretchen pursed her lips. "I've worked out a way I can sit down to do most of the work."

"Oh, please. Like I believe that one."

"It's true. I'm very careful of my injured foot, and it's healing quite nicely, thank you very much. And part of taking care of myself is doing what makes me happy.

Baking makes me happy, and one way or another, I am bound to bake."

"Bound to bake." Keely pressed her lips together. In the two weeks she'd been living in his house, Daniel had already learned to read her expressions. Right now, she was trying to stay stern, trying *not* to burst out laughing. She glanced toward the ceiling as though calling on a higher power. "What am I going to do with you?"

"Not a thing." Gretchen drew her plump shoulders back. "Just be my sweet girl and stop trying to tell me how to live my life."

Keely glared, but then she gave it up. "All right. Fine. Bake your heart out."

"I intend to."

Keely focused on her dinner. Daniel recognized the move for the ploy that it was. She pretended to let the argument go, but she was only regrouping before trying again. After carefully chewing and swallowing a bite of pot roast, she set down her knife and fork. "I have to ask. What about Mom?"

"What about her?" Gretchen replied way too sweetly.

"She's supposed to be with you, helping you as you recover. Have you heard from her? Have you called her? Do you know when she's coming?"

Daniel considered interrupting, suggesting that Keely leave it alone. Really, Gretchen seemed to be managing pretty well on her own. But then again, siding with his mother-in-law against the woman he needed to take care of his kids… Well, that wouldn't be very smart, now, would it?

If he was going to mess things up with Keely, he might as well just make a pass and take a chance she might say yes—not that he would do that.

Never.

Uh-uh.

Not going to happen.

"Ingrid will come when she comes," declared Gretchen.

"That does it." Keely's eyes had gone flinty. "I'm calling her tonight."

While Daniel drove Gretchen home, Keely straightened up the kitchen and then took the kids upstairs. She watched them in the playroom for a while and then hustled them to the hall bathroom and knelt by the tub to supervise as they splashed and giggled and even allowed her to swipe at them with a washcloth now and then.

"Clean children. My favorite kind," said Daniel from behind her in the doorway. Keely glanced at him over her shoulder. Their eyes met and a hot little shiver slid through her.

Hot little shivers? She'd been having those a lot lately, ever since the day she left the doors open and he saw way more than he should have seen.

It was so crazy, this growing awareness she had of him now, as a man. Like a secret between them, that was how it felt. A secret that created a forbidden intimacy, an intimacy that, really, was only in her mind. She *imagined* he felt it, too.

But she had no real proof of that.

None. Zero. Zip.

As a matter of hard fact, she kept telling herself, this supposed secret intimacy between them didn't even exist. It wasn't real.

So why did it only seem to get stronger, day by day?

"Da-Da!" Jake crowed and waved his favorite rubber duck.

Daniel came and stood over her where she knelt by the tub.

She looked up, over his long, strong legs in dark blue denim, past the part of him she really needed *not* to focus on, to his broad, deep chest, his thick tanned neck, his sculpted jaw. All the way to those eyes staring down into hers.

A weakness swept through her, delicious and hot. She wanted to reach up her arms to him, have him pull her to her feet and tight against his chest. She wanted his mouth on her mouth, hard and deep.

Seriously, what was the matter with her?

Why couldn't she stop imagining what it might be like—if he touched her in a man-woman way. If he kissed her. If he took off all her clothes and took his off, too.

It had to stop.

Nothing was going to happen between them.

She really needed to let this crazy new yen she had for him go.

"Go ahead and call your mother." He dropped to the bath mat beside her. "I'll finish up here."

"Great. Thanks." Did she sound breathless? If she did, she didn't think he noticed. She pushed herself to her feet and turned for the door.

As she went out, Frannie demanded, "Kiss, Da-Da. Kiss," followed by Frannie's usual lip-smacking sound.

Keely stifled a jealous groan. Oh, to be Frannie, to demand kisses of Daniel and have them instantly bestowed.

Not that she would be satisfied with the innocent

kisses he gave his daughter. She would want deep kisses, wet and slow and long.

The kind of kisses she was never going to share with him, the kind of kisses she was not going to think about anymore.

Starting now.

She marched to her bedroom and grabbed her phone, punching up the contact for her mother and hitting the call icon.

It went straight to voice mail. She was leaving a quick, angry message asking Ingrid to call her back the minute she got this when the phone rang in her hand.

After Daniel put the kids to bed, he went looking for Keely.

He didn't have to go far. He found her sitting at her sewing machine in her workroom and tapped on the door frame to get her attention. She turned and gave him a strange little smile.

"You busy?" he asked.

She looked at the length of fabric in her hand as though wondering how it got there. And then she smiled at him—God, that smile of hers. It lit up her face. "Let's get a drink and sit out on the back steps," she said.

Warmth filled him. Even if he wasn't ever having sex with her, it was damn good to have her here in his house with him, someone smart and interesting and pretty to talk to after the kids went to bed. "Deal."

At the wet bar in the family room, he poured himself a scotch and she asked for cranberry juice with ice and a splash of vodka.

Outside, the air was damp and cool, mist creeping in around the thick branches of the evergreens, shimmery and soft-looking in the golden glow of the in-ground lights dotted here and there around the yard. They sat on the deck, with their feet on the steps. Maisey, who'd come out with them, flopped down a few feet away.

Keely shivered, and he almost forgot himself and wrapped an arm around her.

Almost.

But not quite.

Instead, he grabbed a faded afghan off one of the deck chairs and draped it across her shoulders.

"Thanks," she said as he dropped down beside her again. She gathered the afghan close and sipped her drink. "Much better."

He stared off past the playset, along the bluestone path that wound through the clumps of landscaping out to the woodshed and the tree fort his father had built for him and his second and third brothers, Matthias and Connor, back before any of his sisters were born, when he wasn't much older than Frannie and Jake. "Did you talk to your mother?"

"Yeah." She said it on a sigh.

"Is she really coming?"

Keely nodded. "A week from Wednesday, she said. She got hold of a real estate agent, some friend of hers from way back, and bought the Sea Breeze." The landmark pub on Beach Street had been closed for several months now.

"She bought it sight unseen?"

"Yeah. She says the price was right and that it's been her dream for the last decade or so to come home someday and open her own place, that when she pictured that place it was always the Sea Breeze. She's going to settle in with Auntie G and fix up the bar, get it ready for business. She's aiming for a grand opening over the Fourth of July."

"Your mother is something else."

She nudged him with her shoulder. "And you mean that in the best possible sort of way, am I right?"

He was still kind of marveling. "Just like that, she buys a bar."

"She always knew what she wanted and how to get it—not to mention how to manage her money. No, she never got rich, but she's a good businesswoman. She paid for more than half of my college education. And I wouldn't have Sand & Sea or my cottage if she hadn't written me big fat checks when I needed them the most."

"All because of that band of hers?"

"Because of *her*, Daniel." Ingrid not only sang and played lead guitar. She was the owner and manager of Pomegranate Dream.

"I know. But still…"

"When members of the band dropped out, she replaced them and went on. When Pomegranate Dream stopped drawing big crowds, she booked them into county fairs, casinos and smaller clubs. She got her commercial driver's license and started driving the bus herself. She runs everything out of the bus. That keeps the overhead low."

"I thought you hated being raised on that bus."

"It wasn't all bad. Yeah, I always dreamed of a more settled kind of life than my mother ever gave me and sometimes she gets on my last nerve, but she's a dynamo and I admire her." Keely held up her glass and he tapped his against it.

He offered the toast. "Here's to Gretchen and Ingrid making it work."

She laughed. The sweet sound played along his nerve endings, stirring up all that yearning and hunger he kept trying to quell. When she put her glass to her lips, he drank, too.

And then he stood. Maisey got up, as well.

Keely tipped her head back and looked at him. "Going in?" He stared into those moss green eyes that he'd been seeing in his dreams lately.

"A few things I need to catch up on." Actually, those things could wait. But the temptation to touch her would only get stronger the longer he sat there. "I'll be in my study if you need me."

*How about if I need you right now?* Keely thought but didn't say. "Fair enough." She gave him a nod, then turned back to the fog-shrouded yard again. A moment later, she heard the back door open and the tapping of Maisey's claws on the floor. The door clicked shut.

The week went flying by. Keely had that opening at the gallery on Friday night. Daniel called the nanny service and got a woman to watch the kids all day Thursday and Friday, so that Keely could be at the gallery, making sure the group show was ready to go. And he came home from work early Friday to take over kid care from the temporary nanny. Keely was able to work straight through, grabbing a break at six in the evening to run home to her own little house by the beach and change into her favorite vintage teal blue cocktail dress and kitten heels.

By eight that evening, the gallery was packed with artists and their friends, supporters and family. Plenty of paying customers came by, too. The show did brisk business. Keely sipped a nice Oregon Pinot Noir, nibbled great finger foods provided by her favorite local caterer and enjoyed the party.

Aislinn Bravo, one of Daniel's sisters and Keely's longtime BFF, dropped by. Keely was older than Aislinn by four years, but she'd got to know all the Bravos back when Lillie married Daniel. From the first time they met, Keely and Aislinn had hit it off. The age difference hadn't mattered, even way back then. They'd always liked to hang out together. Then when Keely opened Sand & Sea, Aislinn had worked in the gallery for a while and the two of them had grown even closer.

Aislinn had a house not far from the beach. She raised Angora rabbits and made jewelry in her spare time, beautiful pieces that Keely was proud to showcase at Sand & Sea. But jewelry making was only a hobby for Aislinn. She liked variety in her work. She'd done everything, worked on local ranches and at the used-car lot on the south end of town. She'd even worked for Daniel at Valentine Logging, running the office for a while. Now she was essentially a legal secretary.

"So how's the law business?" Keely asked her.

Aislinn wrinkled her nose. "Boring. I think I need a job outside next. Maybe fishing, something on a salmon troller."

"Oh, I can just picture that."

"Hey. I'm a fast learner, and I'm not afraid to get my hands dirty—and how's it going playing nanny for my niece and nephew?"

"I adore them. They have me wrapped around their tiny pinkie fingers."

"Consider this my offer to babysit any weekend day or night that you need me."

"Thanks. I might take you up on that one of these days. So far, though, we're making it work."

"Daniel treating you right?"

"He's been great." *And lately he's driving me wild with unsatisfied lust.*

Aislinn laughed. And then she leaned closer. "You have a funny look on your face. What's going on?"

"Funny how?"

"Evasive much?"

Should she tell Aislinn? Ordinarily, Keely never held back with her best friend. But Daniel *was* Aislinn's brother and, well, it felt somehow awkward. Maybe even wrong.

Because really, wasn't it just a little bit strange for her to suddenly get a wild, burning yen for Daniel Bravo? Not only had he belonged to her beloved Lillie, he was not her type, all stalwart and solid. She went for the artsy guys, the charmers, the fast-talkers, guys like her ex-husband, Roy.

Aislinn watched her, narrow eyed. "That does it. You're hiding something. We need to talk. Lunch, I think. A *long* lunch. Next week's no good. They're running me ragged at the office with a couple of big cases. But the week after that...?"

Why not? By then, she might be totally over this bizarre fixation on Daniel. At the very least, she'd have plenty of time to decide how much to say. "Sure. I can get a sitter from the nanny service. Let's say tentatively Wednesday after next?"

"You're on."

Keely got back to Daniel's at a little after midnight that night. Slipping off her shoes as soon as she got inside, she locked up and turned to find him standing in the open doorway to his study, wearing his usual jeans and a flannel shirt with the sleeves rolled to the elbows, his shoulders a mile wide, muscled arms crossed over his chest, his eyes cast into shadow by the chandelier high above.

Like if Paul Bunyan was a sex god.

Nope. Not her type, no way.

Not her type, but…

More.

So. Much. More.

"How'd it go?" he asked.

"Really well. Good sales. A great crowd. Everyone talking and laughing at once. The kids?"

"We played a lot of peekaboo. I'm worn-out."

She laughed. She'd come to love his dry sense of humor, which she'd never even noticed he had until she'd come to live with him and the twins. "And then, after the peekaboo, the bath that never ends."

"All that splashing." He pretended to grumble.

"Exactly. And then you have to read to them."

"And they just *have* to turn the pages for you."

Maisey's claws tapped the floor behind him. She appeared at his side, plunking down on her haunches right there in the doorway.

Keely wanted to ask him to maybe go out back with her, sit on the deck. It was a clear night. They could count the stars, pick out a few constellations.

She might make a move on him.

Oh, God. She just might.

And where would that take them?

Somewhere wonderful—or straight to disaster?

"Good night, Keely," he said. Did she hear regret in his voice?

Or was that only in her coward's heart?

"Night, Daniel." She flipped her shoes back over her shoulder and headed for the stairs.

Ingrid arrived that Wednesday.

Keely took the kids over to Gretchen's to help out while Ingrid got moved in. Her mom had streaked her graying auburn hair with pink and blue. She looked good, Keely thought, slim and straight and strong as ever, in a giant purple Pomegranate Dream T-shirt with the arms ripped off over a sports bra and tropical print leggings, all that pink-and-blue-striped auburn hair piled in a sloppy updo, red Converses on her feet.

Gretchen started right in, ragging on her about her hair and her clothes. "Honestly, Ingrid. You're fifty years old. Your rock and roller days are over and that outfit is simply not age appropriate."

Keely's mom took her big sister by the shoulders and planted a kiss on her plump cheek. "My rock and roller days will never be over. And don't cramp my style. You know that never goes well—Keely, leave the kids in that playpen and help me carry a few things in from the bus…"

For the next few hours, Keely fetched and carried while Gretchen fed Frannie and Jake too many of the cookies that she never should have been on her feet baking in the first place.

Actually, it wasn't that bad. The kids didn't seem to mind sitting in the playpen while Gretchen fed them and fussed over them. And Ingrid sang as she worked, all the great old songs she and the band used to cover when they toured—"Wanted Dead or Alive" and "Crazy on You" and "Purple Rain." More than once, Keely found herself singing along.

As they made the bed in Ingrid's new bedroom with sky blue sheets and a fuchsia duvet scattered with gold stars, Keely's mom said, "How's it working out, the whole pinch-hit-nanny thing?"

"Really well." *Except for this insane burning lust I've developed for Daniel.*

"The gallery?"

"Runs like clockwork, no problems. I have a great manager, Amanda. And I get by there to check in and help out with whatever needs doing almost every day. I like it. I'm keeping busy."

"You always had a lot of energy."

Keely gazed across the brightly made bed at her mom. "I get that from you."

"As long as you're happy."

"I am."

"But you do seem a little on edge."

No way she was touching that. Keely plumped the hot-pink pillows and grinned like she didn't have a care in the world.

Ingrid let it go. "Well, all right. I'm here whenever you want to talk."

Uh-uh. Not happening.

She followed her mother back out to the bus to haul in more stuff and tried not to think about Daniel and this feeling she had for him that kept getting stronger. Denial wasn't working. Her body seemed to hum with yearning—to touch him. To get close enough to breathe in the scent of his skin.

Every morning she woke up freshly resolved to stop

this silliness. It was all just in her mind, and she'd had enough of it.

But then she'd go downstairs and there he would be at the breakfast table, spooning scrambled eggs onto the kids' high chair trays, answering, "Yeah, Jake," and "Okay, Frannie," at every new imperiously delivered toddler demand. Somehow, the guy who wasn't her type had slowly become the most desirable man in the world.

And her resolution to stop this idiocy?

Out the kitchen window every time.

That night, at eight thirty with the babies tucked in bed, Keely and Daniel sat in the kitchen, drinking coffee that would probably keep them awake way too late. It was raining out. Keely watched the raindrops hit the kitchen window and slide down like tears.

They'd been talking about mundane things—the lumber business, how she would need to have the part-time nanny back a few times this week. She'd got a couple of commissions to make wall hangings. One for a customer's living room and one for a bank in town that liked to support local artists.

And then they were quiet, both staring toward the dark, rainy window.

He said, "Lillie always loved the rain."

Keely nodded. "She said it made her feel cozy and safe, to be inside looking out at the rain coming down."

Another silence. She thought of the wedding portrait that hung in the upstairs hall—Lillie gorgeous in white lace and Daniel so handsome and young in a tux. Two people full of love and hope, with no idea of the ways they would hurt each other.

Keely realized she was holding her breath. With slow care, she let that breath go.

Daniel broke the quiet. "I would have said yes, to the kids, to Lillie getting pregnant. It wasn't…what I wanted. But I did want her to be happy."

Keely sucked in another breath and had to remind herself again to breathe out. It was one thing to talk about Lillie lightly, to remember her fondly—the things she loved, her habits, her quirks.

But what Daniel had just said? Not a light thing. Apparently he'd decided to stumble toward something deeper.

That should feel dangerous, shouldn't it? Or maybe just wrong.

But it didn't.

It felt…honest. Real.

Now Keely longed to reach across the table, to lay her hand over his. "She was *born* to be a mom. I mean, I've always wanted children, but if I never have them, I'll be okay. There's so much to life. I love my gallery, the work I do. My family. Friends. There are a lot of babies to love in the world, even if they aren't my own. But for Lillie, it was an imperative. A yearning in the blood."

"I know."

"Daniel, it was just so wrong that the one thing she wanted above anything was the thing she couldn't have."

A muscle twitched in his square jaw. "Sometimes in life you just don't get what you want. And given that having a child could kill her, I wasn't budging. No kids. We'd already lost my parents and one brother."

The lost brother's name was Finn. He was the fifth born, after Aislinn. He'd vanished on one of those trips that Daniel's parents were always taking. In Siberia, of all places. The family still had investigators searching for him. But a lot of years had gone by, so it didn't look all that likely that Finn would ever be coming home.

Daniel said, "I couldn't do it, couldn't stand to chance losing Lillie, too." He looked across at her, ice-blue eyes piercing. "I've always wondered…" Keely knew what he was about to ask. And then he did ask, "How much did she tell you?"

She couldn't lie about it. Not now. "A lot."

He fisted those big hands on the table between them. "I thought so. I…felt it. In the way you looked at me sometimes. Like you thought I was a real rat bastard, but I was family, so you were going to have to put up with me after all."

She shouldn't have chuckled. But she did. "I was mad at her, too. That she couldn't just accept that her body wouldn't do what her heart wanted so much."

His eyes. They saw inside her. They knew too much and they demanded to know more. "Keely. Tell me what she told you."

"That you were going to have a vasectomy, but she talked you out of it—and looking back, I don't know why that made me mad at you. Except that she also said you didn't want children. It really pissed me off that you didn't want what she wanted more than anything."

He shut his eyes and swore low, with feeling. "'You never know how things will turn out,' she said to me. 'Someday I might not be here.' I said I didn't care. I'd *had* my kids. I'd raised my brothers and sisters as my own. It was enough. I'd done my bit playing dad. I was done. But she kept after me not to do it. It seemed so important to her that I still be able to change my mind in some far, distant future, if something happened to her. So I let it go. I never got around to actually having the procedure." He stared at his own dark reflection in the rainy window. "I should have known what she was up to."

Keely's hands kept trying to reach for him—and then she just gave in. She reached.

And so did he.

They held hands across the table. His were big and rough and warm, and she wanted to feel them, touching her, running over her skin, learning the secrets of her body—and later, afterward, when they were both satisfied, she wanted his arms around her, holding her close.

He said in a low rumble, "I'm still so damn mad at her."

"I know." It came out in a whisper because her throat had clutched.

"I need to forgive her, but I can't forgive her. When we first got married, we used condoms and she used a diaphragm, too. We were so careful. But then her rheumatologist approved her for the low-dose estrogen pill. She was on it for years. I thought it was safe not to use anything else. She didn't tell me she'd stopped taking it until she was already pregnant. I thought the pill had failed and I was furious. I was going to go after her doctor, to sue the guy. That was when she admitted she'd stopped taking the pill. She tricked me. And it killed her."

Keely wanted to hold on to him forever. But if she kept holding on, well, how would she ever make herself let go?

Carefully, she eased her hands away. She wrapped them around her almost-cold coffee and sipped the bitter dregs. "There's no win in not forgiving her. You get that, right?"

"Win? What's any of this got to do with winning?"

"Daniel, what I'm saying is…" Okay, really. What *was* she saying? She tried again. "I mean, you know about forgiveness, right?"

"What about it?" he demanded, gruff. Impatient.

"It's not for the forgiven. It's for the one who forgives. Until you forgive, you're a prisoner of your anger and resentment, at the wrong that's been done to you. But when you forgive, you don't have to be eaten up with anger anymore. When you forgive, you are set free."

"Who told you that?" He sounded almost angry.

She held his gaze. "My mother."

"The crazy rock chick who dragged you all over the country when all you wanted was to come home to Valentine Bay?"

"Ouch."

His expression softened. "Sorry. That was harsh."

"But also true. My mom does what she wants to do, and people get fed up with her. But she really does know stuff. She tells the truth as she sees it. And about forgiveness, well, I think she's got forgiveness right."

He pushed back his chair and carried his empty cup to the sink. "I'm going to bed."

*Let me come with you…*

Ha. Like that would ever happen. *She* might give in, definitely. But Daniel? Even if he really did want her as much as she wanted him, he would see all the ways things could go wrong. He wasn't the kind of man to take dangerous chances.

She gave him a soft good-night and sat alone for a while, thinking of Lillie, who loved the rain.

Lillie, who had betrayed her husband's trust to get what she wanted more than her life.

# Chapter 4

Friday, Keely had the temporary nanny, Jeanine, watch the kids for the whole day. Keely worked all morning on the art-quilt hanging for the bank and gave Jeanine a break for lunch. When the nanny returned to take over with the kids, Keely went to the gallery for a couple of hours.

She stopped by Gretchen's before returning to Daniel's house. Ingrid was at the Sea Breeze, getting a start on the renovations she had planned.

Auntie G brought out the cookies, poured Keely coffee and complained about her housemate. "At least she's finally moved the bus to the bar parking lot. This is a *neighborhood*, Keely. People don't want giant purple vehicles cluttering up the street where they live— especially not when they have half-naked, pot-smoking women painted on the side."

Actually, the half-naked woman was Ingrid herself. More than twenty years ago, she'd talked the famous cartoonist R Crumb into drawing her—in ratty cutoffs and a low-cut tank top, clearly braless underneath, playing her Telecaster and smoking what looked like a big fat cigar, but according to Ingrid was a giant doobie. She'd had the image blown up bigger than life-size and used it to decorate her tour bus.

"I love your mother," added Auntie G, "but she can be so thoughtless sometimes. She plays her guitar at *night*. That's not right. I had to ask her this morning to please just go to that bar she bought when she has to… bang out a riff, or whatever it is she calls it when she beats on that old acoustic guitar of hers and wails at the top of her lungs."

Keely asked gingerly, "What are you telling me?"

Gretchen raised both hands out to the side and glanced toward heaven. "Sweetheart, what do you think I'm telling you? Your mother makes me insane."

"Are you worrying it won't work out, with her living here?"

Her aunt blinked in obvious surprise. "Whatever makes you think that?"

"Well, you do sound pretty annoyed with her."

"Of course I'm annoyed with her. She's very annoying, and she always has been. I knew that when we decided she would be coming home to live. It doesn't mean I don't want her here. She's my sister and I love her and she's going nowhere. We are going to learn to get along and support each other in our waning years."

Keely winced. "'Waning years'? I hope you don't use that term around Mom."

A sly smile curved Gretchen's pale lips. "Oh, but I

do and she hates it, too. She claims it makes her want to scream—"

"Wait." Keely put up a hand. "Let me guess. Because she's *only* fifty and about as far from 'waning' as a vital, brilliant woman can get?"

"Sweetheart." Auntie G's sly smile now had a smug edge. "I do believe that you know your mother almost as well as I do."

"So…no plans to kick her out then?"

"None. Don't you dare tell her I said so, but life is so much more interesting when your mother's around."

Sunday morning, Keely's mom called while she and Daniel and the twins were having breakfast. Keely barely got out a "Hi, Mom," before Ingrid was off and running.

"Gretch has got some potluck thing at her church this afternoon. She asked me to go."

"Well, that sounds—"

"Boring? Stifling? Mind-numbing? Tedious? All of the above?"

"So, then. Let me guess. You're not going?"

"You bet your sweet ass I'm not. I told her that you invited me to dinner up there at Daniel's. And then after I told her that, I realized it was a great idea. So what time are we eating?"

"Hold on." Keely muted the call and turned to Daniel, who was wearing a blue-and-black-plaid button-down, the blue of which made his eyes look like oceans—oceans she could happily drown in.

"What?" he asked.

She shook herself. "My mother wants to come to dinner tonight."

"Sure. Gretchen, too?"

"No, she's got something at church." Keely unmuted the call and said to her mother, "We like to eat with the kids, so it will be early."

"I knew when I decided to move home that nothing in my life would ever be civilized again."

"I'm rubbing my fingers together," Keely teased. It was an old joke between them. As a child, whenever Keely would whine about this or that, Ingrid would rub her thumb and middle finger together to signify the smallest violin in the world playing "My Heart Bleeds for You."

Ingrid released an audible sigh. "I raised you to be wild and free and sophisticated in a boho sort of way, to drink deep from life's bounteous cup. Instead, you live in the same small town where I was born, and you spend your days taking care of your cousin's toddlers."

"Hey. I own an art gallery and my work has been written up in *Oregon Art Monthly*. That's kind of sophisticated."

"I rest my case. What time?"

"Come at four, earlier if you want to. We'll eat at five."

"I'm driving Gretch to the potluck, dropping her off and then picking her up. The church gig is from four to six thirty, so the timing is perfect. I'll bring wine. Two bottles. Red or white?"

"You choose. We're having chicken."

"White then. See you about four."

Ingrid came early, armed with the promised bottles of Oregon Sauvignon Blanc. She joined Keely and the twins in the kitchen.

"It's pouring rain out there." She set the wine on the counter and then smoothed little tendrils of damp pink-

and-blue-streaked hair back from her forehead. "I'll just put these in the fridge, keep them cold for dinner." She grabbed up the two bottles again. "Where's Daniel?"

"He had to run out to the office." Keely slid a beautiful, plump roaster chicken into the oven. "Some minor detail he needed to deal with on a job that starts tomorrow. He'll be back in time for dinner."

Ingrid leaned over the playpen to give kisses to the twins.

Jake held up his arms to her. "Out. Pwease."

And she asked, "Is it okay if I release them from prison?"

Keely opened the cupboard to grab the rice. "As long as you watch them."

Ingrid took the kids out of the playpen and sat on the floor with them while Keely cooked. When they lost interest in the toys Keely had brought downstairs for them, Ingrid turned for the cupboards. She soon had a wide array of pots and pans, lids and utensils out on the floor and she was tapping spoons on the pans and banging pot lids together.

Keely watched her fondly, remembering her own little-girlhood, when Ingrid would use any object she could get her hands on to make music. Keely used to love that, banging things together to make loud sounds.

So did Frannie and Jake. They pounded and banged, laughing and shouting, while Maisey sat in the doorway to the family room, watching through those droopy eyes of hers and occasionally even throwing her head back to howl along with them.

Daniel came in at four thirty. He took over with the kids, and Keely's mom set the breakfast-nook table.

Everything was going so well, her mom chatting easily with Daniel about how his various brothers and sisters were doing. He asked about the bar, and she filled him in on her plans to put a roll-up door in the wall that faced the beach so she could fully open the place up to the outdoors in good weather. Daniel uncorked the wine, and Keely put the kids in their chairs and tied their bibs around their necks. She gave them rice and cut-up chicken and cooked carrots in bowls along with spoons, because sometimes they actually managed to scoop food onto a spoon and get it into their mouths. She handed them their sippy cups of milk.

The adults sat down. Wine was poured and bowls were passed. The kids were focused on their food and acting like little angels. The conversation flowed easily—for a while anyway.

At what point did Ingrid start darting looks back and forth between Keely and Daniel?

Keely wasn't sure.

But when her mother asked, "What *is* this?" tipping her head to the side, eyes narrowed, like she had the scent of something she hadn't quite named yet, Keely got that sinking feeling.

Whatever her mom was thinking, Keely dearly wished that Ingrid might keep it to herself. Her mother often had intuitions and when she had them, they were usually right—and also mostly about the things no one really wanted to talk about.

"Chicken, Mom," she said, going for the obvious, hoping against hope that Ingrid really was only wondering about the food. "It's chicken and mushroom rice. I added a teaspoon of curry to the rice, to change it up a little."

"I don't mean the dinner, which is delicious." Ingrid

gestured grandly at the meal before them and sipped her wine. "But no. This is not about the food." She lifted her glass in a silent toast, first to Daniel and then at Keely. "This is about the two of you…"

"Who two?" Keely demanded, though of course she already knew.

Ingrid sweetly smiled. "Oh, yeah. I'm getting a very strong vibe that you two are having some hot sexy times."

Daniel made a distinct choking sound. Keely sent a frantic glance his way as he coughed into his napkin. "Sorry," he croaked out, looking nothing short of stricken.

Keely longed to jump up and run out into the driving rain, run and run and never come back. Sadly, escape wasn't any kind of option. Besides, she'd done nothing wrong and had nothing to be ashamed of. Her mother was the one who was out of line. She yanked her shoulders back and took a valiant stab at outright denial. "Mom. Come on. Where do you get these crazy ideas?"

"Crazy? I think not. You should see your face. You look like a landed trout…" Ingrid widened her eyes and let her mouth fall open, an apparent imitation of Keely's expression. Then she actually had the nerve to laugh. "And now you are blushing. Oh, yeah. I'm right. I know I am." She reached across and patted Keely's hand. "Baby, come on. Lighten up. I'm on your side. I think this is simply wonderful, really! Daniel deserves a little pleasure in his life, and so do you."

Keely stuck with denial. "You're wrong, so wrong. And you're being ridiculous. Not to mention, you are embarrassing me."

Ingrid sipped more wine and refused to stop smiling. At least she was quiet. For the moment.

Too quiet. The faint sound of the rain coming down

outside seemed to swell to fill the silence. Even the kids just sat there, little fists full of chicken and carrots, staring from one adult face to the other, not sure what was going on, let alone how to react to it.

Daniel spoke up then. "Oh, come on, Ingrid." His eyes still had that freaked-out look, but his voice? Wonderfully calm and assured. "Your imagination is running away with you. Keely's been amazing, taking over with the kids, doing a terrific job with them. We get along great, she and I. But that's it. That's all that's going on here."

Ingrid gave a lazy little one-shoulder shrug. "Well, if you're not having lots of fabulous sex together, you should be."

"Mother," Keely muttered. "Shut. Up."

But Ingrid just went blithely on. "Make hay while the sun shines, I always say. And I mean, whoa!" She pointed at Daniel and then at Keely and then back to Daniel again. Before Keely could remind her how rude pointing was, she let out a loud hissing sound. "Sssssmokin'. You two could burn the house down with the heat you're generating."

Jake chose that moment to crow in delight. He grabbed his spoon, pounded it on his high chair tray and imitated his great-aunt. "*Sssss!* Moke!"

Frannie took her cue from her twin. *"Sssss!"* she hissed, then burst into giggles and pounded her hands on her tray. Rice and pieces of chicken went flying.

Ingrid laughed. "See? Even the kids know."

"You are out of your ever-lovin' mind."

"Oh, baby." Ingrid had the sheer gall to cluck her tongue. "Don't be ashamed."

"Ashamed? I'm not—"

"Sex is natural and right, and far too many of our social norms are nothing more than ways to sap all the joy from life. You know that. I taught you that."

"Can you just drop it? Please?"

But Ingrid was on a roll. Keely purposely refused to even glance at poor Daniel as her mother replied, "No. No, I will not drop it. Not until I remind you both that life is too short *not* to do what comes naturally, and that it's nobody's business but your own if you find a little pleasure along the way—and wait."

Jake clapped his hands. "Wait!" he crowed, and Frannie clapped too.

"Is it Gretchen?" demanded Ingrid. "You're worried about Gretch?"

"Gwet," repeated Frannie experimentally and let out tiny cackle.

Ingrid huffed out a breath. "You think she's going to judge you for somehow 'betraying' Lillie?"

"Ingrid." In a careful, level tone, Daniel tried again to call a halt to this insanity. "Come on. The kids don't need to hear this."

"Oh, please. No harm is being done here. They're too young to understand anyway. As long as we keep the language clean and our attitudes civil, this conversation is totally kid-friendly—and where was I? Right. Gretch. If she's going to judge you for finding what joy you can in this life, well, that is just wrong and she will need to get over it. Lillie was a lovely woman and the world is emptier without her in it. But frankly, she's dead. Gretchen needs to accept that—not that I would ever say a word to my sister about any of this. What you two do in private is none of Gretchen's business anyway. It is nobody's business but your own—and did I already say that? Well. If I did, it bears repeating."

Silence.

Again.

At last.

Keely longed to throw in a snide remark to the effect that if it was their private business, what the hell was Ingrid doing butting in about it? But Keely knew her mother much too well. To challenge her would only set her off again. Thus, Keely settled on a soft-spoken "Tell us you're done, Mom. Please. Just tell us you're done."

Something wonderful happened then. Ingrid nodded. "Yes. I have said what I needed to say. The rest is up to you. Now, lighten up and pass the wine."

Ingrid kept her word. She didn't bring up the subject of Keely and Daniel and their "smokin'" attraction again.

She stayed for dessert, helped clear the table and played with the kids for a few minutes after that. And then it was time to go pick up Gretchen from church. Ingrid kissed the kids, hugged Keely, bade a fond goodbye to Daniel and breezed out the door.

Keely was thinking they would put the kids to bed and then maybe they could talk about her mother's cringe-worthy behavior. She would advise him not to take her mom too seriously, reassure him that it really wasn't a big deal. They could clear the air about the whole thing.

But the minute Ingrid walked out the door, Daniel suddenly remembered he needed to go to the office again—at six twenty on Sunday night.

"Sorry," he said, his gaze skittering away from hers.

"I know it's not right to leave you here to deal with the kids alone on Sunday night. You deserve a little time to yourself, but this is something I really should get handled before—"

"The kids are no problem, honestly. I'll put them to bed."

"I just forgot a couple of important things, and I really ought to get back over there and make sure that—"

"Daniel." She put up a hand. "It's okay. Just go."

And he went—practically at a run. It would have been funny if it wasn't so awkward and depressing.

No, Keely didn't really blame him for fleeing the scene. Of course, he would want to get away after the Sunday dinner from hell that her mother had just put him through. Really, he'd been a prince not to just get up, grab the kids and get out the moment her mother started in on them.

Maybe they would talk about it later. Or maybe they wouldn't. In any case, Ingrid had essentially promised not to bring the subject up again. She'd damn well better keep her word about that.

The kids sat on the kitchen floor gazing up at her expectantly.

"Bath time," she said.

"Baf!" Frannie sang out, and Jake let out a happy cry.

Keely took them upstairs, gave them a long bath and then let them loose in the playroom for a while, getting down on the floor with them, joining in as they played with their toys. As bedtime approached, she led them into her room and cuddled up with them on the bed to read them a few of their favorite stories.

By eight thirty, they were both asleep, one on either side of her. She took Jake across the hall first and tucked him into his crib, then went right back and got Frannie. Neither of them made so much as a peep as she crept from their room and silently shut the door behind her.

Without the kids to keep her busy, the house seemed way too quiet. She stood there in the hall, listening to the distant roar of the rain outside, like a whispered secret in the quiet of the night.

What now?

Thoughts of Daniel came rushing in—the sadness in his eyes the other night when they spoke of Lillie. The freaked-out expression on his face tonight when her mother wouldn't shut up about the hot sex he and Keely ought to be having. The way he wouldn't even look her in the eye before he left tonight.

When would he be home? When he did come back, should she try to talk to him?

Or just let it be?

Until tonight, she'd pretty much convinced herself that he didn't need to know about this crazy crush she had on him, that she could take care of his babies and be his friend for as long as he needed her.

Really, she'd been thinking that this yearning she had for him would eventually fade. Sooner rather than later, she hoped.

Well, it wasn't fading. And tonight had been like that day he saw her naked all over again. She felt stripped in the worst kind of way. Revealed.

And she really didn't know how *he* felt. Sometimes, the way he looked at her, she was absolutely certain he had it bad for her, too.

But that could so easily be wishful thinking. He'd never even hinted that he wanted more than her help with the kids and maybe someone he could talk to.

In fact, tonight at the dinner table, he'd laid it right out there. He'd told her mother that he appreciated her stepping up with the twins, that he enjoyed her companionship...

And nothing more.

She needed to stop obsessing about this.

Maybe she should work.

She wandered into her studio room and sat down at her sewing machine where her current project waited. With her index finger, she traced the shapes of flowers and starbursts she'd sewn into the fabric, flattening her palm on the material, feeling the metallic thread scratch at her skin.

How long had she been the twins' nanny? About a month. So quickly, she'd settled into a life here at Daniel's.

And her original plan to go home most nights? She'd given that up right away when the babies got sick—and then, after they got well, it had just seemed so much easier and more convenient to continue living here.

Convenience wasn't all of it, though. Not by a long shot. She loved it here in the big Bravo house among the tall trees on Rhinehart Hill. She loved taking care of Jake and Frannie, hanging out with Daniel for an hour or two every night, waking up in the morning to find him downstairs fixing breakfast, the twins already in their high chairs, waving their fat little fists full of Cheerios at her, demanding morning kisses.

With a wry smile, she rose and wandered to the window. Through the pouring rain, she stared out at the backyard, lit in smudges of gold by the lights dotted here and there amid the bushes, along the paths—one leading to the side gate and another that wound its way farther back, toward the rear fence. Way back there, a light glowed by the door to the woodshed.

Keely shut her eyes and leaned her forehead against the cool glass. Time to face the truth. The twins were not her children. And Daniel was not her man.

She didn't need to talk with him about the silly things her mom had said. She just needed to tell him he would have to start looking for someone else to watch the kids full-time.

As for working tonight?

Not happening. Her work required a steady hand and concentration. Right now, her mind was a hot stew of yearning and regret, and she felt shaky with emotions she had no business feeling.

No working. No waiting up to talk to Daniel. She'd have a nice long bath and take a good book to bed with her.

And tomorrow, she would tell him it was time for her to go.

With a soft cry, Keely sat up in bed.

The juicy hardcover romance she'd been reading flopped to the mattress and shut with a snap. She'd left the lamp on. She shoved her hair back off her forehead and glared at the clock.

Ten past midnight—and she'd heard something, hadn't she?

A strange sound had jolted her from sleep.

*The kids?*

She sat completely still, willing her racing heart to slow a little, not even daring to breathe, as she listened.

No sound from across the hall—let alone from the baby monitor right there at her bedside by the clock.

Not the kids then.

*Thump-thump.*

There. That. It was coming from the backyard.

Another thump, followed by a clatter.

Distant. Rhythmic.

*Thud-thud.* And then that faint clattering noise, like bowling pins toppling in on each other.

The thudding and clattering continued as she pushed back the covers and went to the window she'd left open a crack to let in the moist night air and the soothing, constant whisper of the falling rain.

She gazed out on essentially the same view she'd had from her workroom—the dark backyard, the bright smears of garden lights through the veil of the rain.

*Thunk-thunk. Clatter...*

Her gaze tracked the path through the trees, seeking the source of the sound.

She saw him then. Daniel. There. Revealed in the light by the woodshed door, shirtless and wielding a splitting maul in the pouring rain.

*Thud. Thud. Clatter.* The log sheared down the center and the two pieces tumbled from the chopping block into the mounds of split wood on either side.

Daniel...

No, she couldn't see him all that clearly, but she knew him by his height, by the breadth of his shoulders, the proud shape of his head.

And who else would be chopping wood in the backyard in the middle of the night?

Those poor logs. He attacked them without pause or mercy.

A tiny stab of guilt pierced her. She shouldn't be watching this. She should leave the man alone, let him work out his obvious frustration in his own way, undisturbed.

But, well, what else could be driving him but her mother's utter tactlessness at dinner?

Maybe something at work?

Yeah. That was more likely. Ingrid's big mouth might have embarrassed him, but shouldn't he be past that by now?

Whatever it was, she just couldn't stand to see him punish himself this way. And maybe, if she went to him, they could actually talk it over, get it out in the open, whatever it was.

Because however he felt or didn't feel about her as a woman, and whatever happened tomorrow when she told him she was leaving, he *had* called her a friend and she truly believed that he'd meant it. What kind of a friend was she if she just left him all alone out at the woodshed in the middle of the night? The least she could do was go to him, ask if he needed someone to talk to and then listen if he said yes.

Decision made, she whirled from the window, yanked an old green zip-up hoodie from the dresser and pulled it on over her pajama top. Barefoot, she opened her door to find Maisey right there, looking up at her expectantly.

"What? You want to go out?" She got a hopeful whine for an answer. "All right," Keely whispered. "Let's check the kids."

She tiptoed into their darkened room and leaned over one crib and then the other. Both slept like little angels—angels who were unlikely to wake up anytime soon. And she would be back within minutes, hopefully dragging the dripping, shirtless Daniel along be-hind her.

Off she flew, along the upper hall, down the stairs, to the kitchen and the mudroom beyond, Maisey trot-ting along behind her. Her red rain boots with the white polka dots were right there by the door. She shoved her feet into them, pulled the green hood up over her head and ran out across the back deck. Maisey trailed her down the wide stairs but stopped to sniff the bushes by the walk.

Keely went on alone, racing down the lighted path to the back fence.

Her boots made splashing sounds, but Daniel didn't seem to hear her coming. He just kept raising and low-ering that maul. He was like a machine, turning to grab a log, plunking it on the block with a thud, cleaving it with a single perfect stroke—and turning for the next one as the pieces fell. Never once did he look up.

Dear sweet Lord, he was a gorgeous man, the beau-tiful, water-slick muscles of his shoulders and arms shifting and bunching beneath his skin as he set and attacked each log.

She stopped not ten feet away from him, her hoodie already soaked through, her pj's clinging wet. Still, he didn't look up.

"Daniel!" she shouted as he turned and bent to grab the next log.

He froze in midreach. And then, slowly, he rose to his height and faced her. Those ice-blue eyes found her, pinned her where she stood.

"Keely." His voice was a low, rough rumble, dredged up from the deepest part of him.

That did it. As he gazed at her, unblinking through the pouring rain, she knew the truth at last.

It was more than just her own wishful thinking and vivid imagination.

She wasn't alone in her need and her yearning.

Daniel wanted her, too.

## Chapter 5

Daniel stood in the rain and stared at the soaking wet woman who'd made his house a home again, the woman he wanted now. Beyond all reason.

Of all the crazy things that could happen in life.

He wanted Keely, Lillie's little cousin, with the wide-set eyes and the soft mouth and the smattering of pale freckles across her pretty nose. He wanted Keely, wanted her so bad he'd cut and run after dinner because of the scary, true things that her mother had said.

Run off like a candy-ass to the office, where he sat for more than three hours, alternately staring at the far wall and playing "Space Invaders" on his phone.

Wanted her so much he'd come straight to the wood-pile when he got home, hoping to chop that want away.

It hadn't worked. Not even a little bit.

And now she stood there in her soggy pj's, drooping hoodie and shiny polka-dot rubber boots, her eyes locked to his—and he wanted her even more now than he had when he ran away from her after dinner.

It was a whole conversation they shared, with not a word spoken, in the space of a few seconds, standing in the pouring rain.

She wanted him, too.

If he'd had any doubts on that score, the look in those big eyes when he glanced up and saw her standing there blew them clean away.

She wanted him. He wanted her.

And now, well, what the hell? Ingrid was right.

Nothing stood in their way. Why shouldn't they have each other?

The maul was heavy in his hand now. He almost dropped it where he stood. But the habits of a lifetime took precedence. A man looked after his tools. Afraid if he broke the hold of her gaze, she might just vanish—disappear like a dream, melt away in the rain— he backed to the woodshed, elbowed the door open a crack and set the maul inside, out of the wet. He pulled the door shut then, until he heard the latch click.

The rain beat down on her, but she didn't move. She had her head tipped up, watching him from under the soggy green hood, but she hadn't spoken except for that one word—his name.

Well, okay. Words were unnecessary at this point, anyway. She'd told him all he needed to know by the simple act of coming for him, of standing right there on the path back to the house, calling his name.

And he was tired. So damn tired of resisting, of coming up with reasons why having her wasn't right.

His shirt was around here somewhere. Where had he thrown it? He had no idea and really didn't care.

Keely. *She* was what mattered. He took a step toward her. She blinked but held her ground.

The rain beat down on him and he welcomed it. His body burned and each cool drop felt so good.

Another step. She swallowed, but she stayed where she was, watching him, unmoving, as though mesmerized by the energy that zapped back and forth between them.

Two more steps and he was there with her, staring down into those wide green eyes of hers. Slowly, in order not to spook her, he lifted his hand.

"Daniel." She said his name for the second time, in a whisper, giving it only her breath, but no real sound.

"Keely." And he touched her, touched the high, wet curve of her cheek. "Like velvet," he said. "I knew it would be."

"I, um, don't know if—"

"Shh." He pressed his finger to that mouth of hers, that mouth he was going to kiss all night long. "You do know."

"Oh, Daniel…" Her breath around his finger, sweet and warm. He wanted his tongue in there, in the heat and the wet. When he kissed her, he would coax her mouth to open for him, take that warm, sweet breath of hers into himself. "I don't know—"

"Yeah, you do. Come on, your mother knew it. We both know and we have known. Since that day you pushed back the shower curtain and stepped out of the tub without a stitch on."

"I shouldn't have left that door open."

"I shouldn't have barged right in. But so what, at this point? We did what we did."

"I was thinking, earlier, that maybe it's time I—"

"No."

"No?" She looked adorably bewildered.

"Forget about earlier." He eased his fingers under the soaked hoodie, along the silky curve of her neck, around to her nape, which he cradled in the palm of his hand.

"Forget?"

He nodded. "Let's just think about right now."

"Um. Okay." A soft, surrendering moan escaped those beautiful lips as she tipped her mouth up for him. "Okay," she repeated as his mouth closed over hers.

It was perfect, that first touch of his mouth to hers, the softness of her cold lips, the warmth inside, slick and welcoming, so good.

She smelled of some faint, tempting perfume and she tasted so damn sweet. Her nose was cold and her hair dry at her nape under the hoodie, like silk against the back of his hand, short little wisps of it curling under his fingertips.

Glad. He was so damn glad.

Glad in the way he hadn't been for years and years. Years of doing what needed doing. The right thing. The careful thing. Looking after everyone else, putting his own selfish desires aside.

Not tonight. Tonight, he would be selfish. He would take what wanted, and he wouldn't feel bad about it.

Because she wanted it, too.

The rain beat down on them, trickling out of his hair and into his face, his mouth. And hers. He could stand here just kissing her forever.

But really, a dry, warm room. A cozy bed.

That would be better.

Reluctantly, he broke the kiss. Pressing his forehead

to hers, he asked her, "Come inside? With me, to my room, into my bed?" He thought his heart might explode as he waited for her answer.

"Yes," she said, and he could breathe again. "Yes, Daniel. Please. Take me inside."

"Done." He put a hand at her back and one under her knees and scooped her right up off the ground.

She let out a little screech of surprise, grabbing for him, wrapping her arms around his neck. And off they went along the winding path and up onto the deck, where Maisey waited under the deck cover, out of the rain. She bumped in ahead of them when he pushed open the mudroom door.

Once inside, he let Keely down so they could both toe off their boots. He took off his socks, too, and she draped her sopping hoodie on a free peg.

When she turned to him, he grabbed her hand and pulled her after him, through the kitchen, along the short hall to the living room, into the front entry and on up the stairs. They paused at the kids' room, just long enough to glance in and see that both of them were sleeping soundly. Maisey had a bed in there. She headed for it.

"Come on," he whispered and pulled Keely along to the big room at the end of the hall, tugging her in there, closing the door and then pressing her up against it to steal another kiss.

She moaned into his mouth, a needy little sound. Everything about her thrilled him, her soft, curvy body, her wet hair, the sweet, sexy sounds she made, the scent of her skin. He kissed his way down over her chin and licked the rain off her throat as she clutched at him, sighing, whispering, "Yes. Oh, yes…"

"I want to see you." He scraped his teeth down her

neck, licked the tight, sweet flesh over her the points of her collarbone. "You taste so good. I can't believe this is happening." He fumbled with the pink buttons on her soggy pajama top. "I really need to get you out of these wet pj's…"

"Let me help you." But instead of getting to work on her own buttons, she went for his belt buckle.

He froze and looked down in total wonder at her soft, pretty fingers as they undid his belt and whipped it away, dropping it to the floor at their feet. When she glanced up, he would have kissed her again.

But then she asked, "Is your monitor on?" They had three receivers—one in her room, one in his and a third downstairs somewhere.

He commanded, "Do not move from this spot."

She laughed and gave him a playful shove. "Go. Do it."

He was back in a flash. "The damn thing is on. Now, about all these buttons…"

"What, these?" She went to work on the row of pink buttons down her front. Quick work it was, too. A moment later, he was sliding the soggy pajama top off her shoulders, revealing more gorgeous expanses of beautiful, smooth skin.

He said, "Beautiful." And he bent his head and took one dusky nipple into his mouth.

"Oh!" She wrapped her arms around him and pulled him close as he drew on the tightened bud, using his teeth just a little, flicking at her with his tongue.

But then she interrupted him, taking his head between her hands and pulling him up so they were face-to-face.

"What?" he complained.

"I forgot." She bit her lower lip and he wanted to take that mouth again, to kiss her right there where her teeth sank into the plump, tempting flesh. "We need condoms."

"I have some—and don't look so surprised."

"You're just so…"

He tried to glare at her but didn't succeed all that well. "Say it. I'm so what?"

"Upright?" she suggested. "Stalwart? Not a guy who has condoms handy, that's for sure."

He groaned, "You're killin' me here. And if you have to know, several months ago, I tried Tinder."

"No. Really?"

"Yeah."

"Daniel." She spoke in a hushed little whisper, like they were sharing a secret too delicious for anyone else ever to know about. "You hooked up with someone?"

"I made a date. As it turned out, the hooking up didn't happen, but I did get the condoms."

She giggled. He loved when she did that. Her whole face lit up. "You have to tell me all about it."

"Later," he growled at her. "Right now, I'm kind of busy." And he swooped down and covered those sweet lips with his.

That kiss went on forever. Her hands stroked his shoulders, gliding upward to wrap around his neck. She threaded those soft fingers into his hair.

And he? He got to go on touching her, first framing her wonderful face in his hands for a long kiss. But he didn't stop there. He needed to touch her. He needed to get intimately acquainted with every perfect, womanly inch of her skin.

He ran his eager hands along her neck, over the damp

velvet flesh of her shoulders, down her arms and back up again. He palmed her waist. And when he pulled her in close and wrapped his arms around her, he got to feel those beautiful breasts against his chest as he traced the delicate bumps of her spine.

Her wet pajama bottoms were in his way. He shoved at them, impatient to be rid of them. The elastic waistband couldn't hold out against him. Down they went.

She was shivering as she stepped out of them.

He lifted his mouth from hers. "Cold?"

"Um," she replied, which could have meant anything. And then she surged up on tiptoe to capture his lips again.

"You're cold," he accused in the middle of that kiss. He clasped her waist and lifted her. Her bare legs went around him. He groaned at the feel of that, her thighs spread wide against his fly, his aching hardness pressing into the heat and wet of her, so close to where he couldn't wait to be.

Were they really doing this?

If this was a dream, please, please let him never wake up.

He kissed her as he carried her to his bathroom, set her down on the rug and groped for a towel.

She allowed him to dry her off, standing there without a stitch on, smiling at him, her eyes moss green and glowing as he used the towel on her hair first and then the rest of her, pausing now and then in order to scatter quick kisses across her skin.

He knelt to dry her thighs, to rub the towel a little longer than necessary along the backs of her knees and down to her slender feet with their purple-painted toes.

When she stopped shivering, he tossed the towel

aside. Sinking back on his bent knees, he looked up her body as she gazed down at him.

How could he resist a long, thorough touch? He trailed a slow hand up her shin, over her knee, along the firm skin of her thigh to the soft white pillow of flesh where her thighs joined. She was just so pretty. With that neat strip of hair, that tempting pink cleft.

He eased a finger into the wet heat of her. She sighed and a low moan escaped her. "More, please," she said, sweet and soft and oh, so tender.

Daniel gave her more, slipping another finger in, using his other hand to grasp her waist, to hold her in place while he touched her at will. And then, wanting even more, he leaned into her and used his mouth, too.

She signaled her approval with a hungry little cry as she widened her stance for him. He took full advantage, kissing her, touching her deeply, moving his fingers within her, trying to pick up every cue her body gave him, trying to show her how much he wanted her through sheer attentiveness to her needs.

It was amazing. It had been such a long time for him, years, since sex had been like this—a glow that got brighter, a hot shiver that kept getting stronger, burning wetter, quivering harder, a feeling of wonder, a pleasure so deep.

His body ached to have her, his hardness painful against the prison of his fly. But he wanted to make it last, take his time with her, to caress every inch of her, drink every drop.

Life could be so cruel sometimes. He might never get this chance again.

She came on his tongue. It was straight-on amazing, her smooth thighs wide, fingers fisted in his hair, her head thrown back, her slim neck straining as she moaned and begged him, "Please, yes. That. Like that…"

He stayed with her, drinking her, until the pulsing within her settled to a faint throb.

And then he commanded her, "Again."

She gasped. "Daniel. I can't."

"Yeah, you can," he insisted. "You are so beautiful, Keely. Like some miracle I never thought to find. And tonight, here you are. And I want to see you. All of you. How you are. What you do. Come for me. Again."

A wild laugh escaped her, followed a few seconds later by a plaintive little cry.

And then she was rising a second time as he played her, as he caught the rhythm she liked with his fingers. Shameless, he used everything he had—his lips and tongue and even his teeth to get her there, to make her go over, lose herself completely to his touch and the wet press of his hungry mouth.

That time, as the pulsing faded, he swept upward, catching her as she started to crumple. He gathered her into his arms and carried her to his bed, setting her on her unsteady feet just long enough to throw back the covers, then scooping her up again and laying her down.

She stared up at him, her damp hair spread out on his white pillow, her mouth soft and vulnerable, eyes full of stars.

Reaching into the bedside drawer, he found the strip of condoms he'd been absolutely certain would be out-of-date before he ever had a chance to use them. He tore one off and set it in easy reach. Then, with a grateful sigh, he ripped his fly wide and pushed down his boxer briefs along with his jeans, letting out a relieved sigh as his erection sprang free.

Stepping out of the tangle of soggy pants collapsed around his ankles, he went down to the bed with her.

"Daniel." She reached for him.

He stretched out beside her and pulled her close. "Kiss me, Keely."

And she did, a perfect kiss. The slow kind, nipping and teasing to start, then going deep and wet.

She touched him, running her hands over him, showing him that she felt as he did, that she couldn't get enough of touching his body. Perfection. There was no other word for this, just lying here with her, touching her as she touched him.

Talk about a dream come true.

Her fingers strayed over his hips and around to his butt. She grabbed on and squeezed so hard. Chuckling, he buried his nose in the velvety curve of her neck.

And then he bit her, right there where her neck met her shoulder. She was so ripe and tender, he needed a taste.

"Ouch!" She slapped him sharply on the shoulder.

"Sorry. I can't control myself. I just want to eat you right up."

"You already did."

They laughed together.

And then she took him by the shoulders and pushed him away enough to meet his eyes. "Daniel. I don't think I've ever heard you laugh before. At least, I haven't for a very long time."

What was he supposed to say to that? He had no idea. So he said nothing, just cradled her head in his two hands to hold her in place for another kiss.

She wrapped her fingers around his aching length

and she stroked him, slow strokes, her grip nice and tight. But he wasn't going to last long if she kept that up.

"Too good," he groaned at her and gently peeled her hand away.

She was the one who reached for the condom. He let her deal with it. She seemed to know what she was doing. Holding him in place, she rolled it down over him.

"Eyes on me," he whispered, taking her shoulders. Pushing her down to the pillows, he rose up over her and settled between her thighs.

This. Now. It was a moment to remember. Those green eyes holding steady on his, shining with heat and pleasure as he came into her.

She felt so good. Tight, giving way to him slowly, so he had to take his time. But slow was fine with him. Slow was just right—no, better than right. Pure perfection, the pleasure rolling over him, through him, threatening to take him down way before he was ready.

He guided a damp curl of hair away from her cheek. "You're so beautiful, Keely."

"Daniel. Is this real?"

He nodded at her slowly, holding her gaze. "I want to make it last forever. But I don't think that's going to happen."

She lifted her hips to him, drawing him deeper.

He groaned at the pleasure as it shimmered all through him, a pleasure that somehow skimmed the sharp, delicious edge of pain.

"Wait," he whispered. "Just for a moment. Just for a little while, I want to be with you. Just for a little while, don't even move."

She licked those sweet lips of hers. And when she

did that, well, he had to kiss her. He lowered his head
and plundered her beautiful mouth.

And the stillness?

It just couldn't last. As he kissed her, she was shifting restlessly under him, raising her legs and wrapping them around him, pushing herself up him as he
pushed into her.

They rolled, and she had the top position. He captured her face in his hands, holding her still so that at
least she had to look at him, *know* him in this intimate
way, feel him in her and with her as she rocked against
him slow and deep, her folded legs pressed tight along
his sides now, her breath all tangled, eyelids drooping.

"Keely. Look at me."

And she did. She looked right at him.

His finish barreled at him much too fast. "I don't
think I can wait for you."

And then she gasped. Her eyes went wide. "Daniel!"
He felt her climax throb around him.

That did it. With a strangled groan, he joined her,
pushing up into her, hard and tight, as his release arrowed down his backbone, undeniable now.

What could he do but give himself up to it?

With a guttural shout, he surrendered, let his finish roll through him, let her sweet, pulsing heat take
him down.

## Chapter 6

Keely loved the tender way Daniel pulled the covers up and settled them around her, as though she was infinitely precious to him.

He made her feel special. Treasured, somehow.

Daniel, of all people.

She'd just...never known.

He kissed the tip of her nose. "I know I'm being selfish, but I want you in this bed with me. I want you to stay here with me. I want to wake up beside you in the morning. And the next morning. And the morning after that. I don't want you to get up and go."

"I don't want to go either." But they were in uncharted territory here. Yes, they were both single and had every right to find comfort and pleasure together. Still. He'd belonged to Lillie for so many years. Keely just didn't know how the family would react. Lillie had died more than a year and a half ago, but for Gretchen, the pain of losing her only child lingered—and always would. How would she take it to see Daniel moving on? And with Keely, of all people? How would his brothers and sisters see it? She really couldn't predict what their reactions would be. With families, well, you just never could tell.

"So you'll stay?" He looked so hopeful. And very sexy, with his bedhead and his beard scruff and that mouth she wanted to kiss again and again.

"I'll stay," she said. "But I really think, at least for the time being, that as for telling the family that we're spending our nights together..." She sought the right words.

He found the words for her. "They don't need to know." And he laughed. For the second time that night. "You should see your face. I've surprised you?"

"Well, yeah. I mean, that was exactly what I was about to say. But I guess I was kind of afraid you would take it wrong."

"No. Uh-uh. This is between us." Now he sounded a little bit grim and a whole lot stalwart, very much the nonsmiling, laughter-averse Daniel she knew best.

She admitted, "It's only, well, I could do without another rant on the wonders of sex from my mother. And I have no idea how Aunt Gretchen will react, but at the moment, I'm not ready to find out. I can't see why we even need to deal with the family about it. Not right now at least. Not while it's all so new."

He smoothed a few errant strands of hair behind her ear. "It's just better..."

"If we keep it between the two of us."

"Da? Da-Da? Da-Da, Da..." It was Jake's voice in a lazy singsong coming from the baby monitor, luring Keely from sleep.

"Da-Da! Keewee!" Frannie joined in more insistently. "Up!"

Keely opened her eyes to find a sleepy Daniel watching her from the other pillow. He reached out, brushed the hair from her eyes and traced the curve of her ear with a lazy finger.

She gave him a slow smile. Wonder of wonders, he smiled back.

And to think, last night she'd been about to tell him it was time for her to go.

Well, forget that. As of this morning, she was going nowhere.

Everything had changed with that first kiss in the rain.

Now she knew that he wanted her, too. Hadn't he proved it in the most spectacular way?

She wasn't giving him up. Not until…

When? She had no idea. And she refused to get all tied in knots about how things would end up.

Right now, it was only beginning and it was glorious.

"What?" he asked gruffly.

"I was thinking that you and I have a thing now. A secret thing, just between the two of us. It's exciting. Also, kind of crazy."

He wrapped his big hot fingers around the back of her neck. "Just as long as you're not trying to tell me you've changed your mind."

A lovely shiver quivered through her. "No way. I'm in."

"Da-Da, now!"

"Coming!" he called, loud enough the kids could probably hear him even through the solid-core bedroom door. And then he spoke low again, just for her.

"I would love to lie around in bed with you for the rest of the day…"

"Me, too. But the kids are hungry and Valentine Logging isn't going to run itself."

That evening after they put the twins to bed, Daniel led her to his room again.

The night before had been spectacular. Keely hardly thought it possible that it could get any better.

But oh, my. It did.

Daniel was the very best kind of lover—attentive and patient. Kind of bossy, too. He could be tender, and he could be just a little bit rough. She loved the way he touched her, the way he said her name as he caressed her and when he was inside her.

As though she was everything.

As though there could never be anyone but her.

He kissed her as though he could never get enough of the taste of her mouth. And he smelled so good, clean and manly, like cedar branches, like the forest right after the rain.

Later, when they settled in with the light off, she stroked her hand down the beautiful muscles of his arm and asked about the woman he'd met on Tinder.

"What can I say, Keely? We both swiped right."

"But you said it didn't happen…" Her hand strayed downward, to his wrist, over the back of his big hand.

He spread his fingers, and she slipped hers between them. "You're sure you want to hear this?"

"Yes, please."

He made a low sound in his throat. "It's not all that interesting."

"Tell me," she demanded.

He muttered a bad word, but he did give in enough to mutter, "So we got on chat together."

She coaxed him. "And then?"

"She seemed nice. I bought condoms, and we met for a drink at the Hotel Elliott in Astoria." A port city near the mouth of the Columbia River, Astoria was about fifteen miles northeast of Valentine Bay. "I liked her," he went on. "She said she liked me, too, and she'd already taken a room. We went upstairs." He buried his face against her neck. "Never mind," he muttered, his breath so warm, his mouth brushing her skin in a way that made her want him desperately all over again. "I'm not telling the rest."

She pushed him away enough to look at him, to hold his gaze. "It can't be that bad."

He rolled onto his back and pulled her down on top of him, guiding her head to rest on the powerful bulge of his shoulder. She felt his lips against her hair. "I went into her room with her and she started to undress and I knew it wasn't happening. I put up both hands. 'Whoa,' I said. 'Hold on a minute.' She stared at me like maybe I'd lost my mind. And I said I was sorry, but this was a bad idea and I had to go."

"And...that's it? You left?"

"Yeah. She called me a few ugly names as I was ducking out the door..."

"Oh, Daniel." She pressed a kiss to his shoulder, and she felt his big hand on her head, gently stroking her hair.

"I should have known better. Because I couldn't, that's all. With a stranger, like that? That's just not me. I've been with Lillie. And now you. I need a woman I can talk to, a woman I can trust. I'm thinking that makes me kind of a dweeb."

She kissed his shoulder again. "Naw."

"Yeah."

Stacking her hands on his chest, she rested her chin on them. "Daniel, no dweeb looks like you."

"I'm a dweeb *inside*, where it counts." He petted her, running his hand down her hair some more, catching a random curl and wrapping it around two of his fingers. "God. You are beautiful."

"You're blinded by lust."

He wrapped her hair around his whole hand and then guided her up so her mouth was an inch from his. "You're beautiful. Don't argue with me."

"You are so bossy."

"And I think you like that."

"It is just possible that I might."

He kissed her. For a man who'd been with only two women, he sure knew what he was doing with that mouth of his.

The kiss led to yet more spectacular lovemaking. They didn't get to sleep until almost two.


"You look tired, honey." Gretchen slid the plate of snickerdoodles closer to Keely's elbow.

Keely took one. "You're a cookie pusher, Auntie G. You know that, right?"

"Enjoy, sweetheart." Gretchen had Frannie on her lap. Jake lay sprawled on the floor, hugging his favorite stuffed rabbit, staring dreamily up at the ceiling. "Your mother said she had a great time at dinner Sunday night."

Keely ate a bite of cookie and tried to judge how much Ingrid might have told her aunt—not a thing, she decided. First, because Ingrid knew nothing. And second, because Ingrid had clearly stated that whatever was or wasn't going on between Keely and Daniel, it was none of Gretchen's business.

"Mom seems happy," she said, "about how things are going with her plans for the bar and about living here with you."

Frannie dropped the rubber frog she'd been chewing on. Gretchen caught it and gave it back to her. Frannie stuck it in her mouth again, leaned back in her grandmother's arms and closed her eyes. "All in all, your mother and I are doing just fine. How about you, honey? You've been juggling kids and work and the gallery for five weeks now."

"It's going really well. I don't get home to my place much, but I've got my workshop set up at Daniel's and we found a dependable woman who fills in for me when I need her. I get in to the gallery several hours a week."

"Are you sure you don't need a break?"

"Absolutely."

"Because I'm getting around without the walker now, and I would be happy to start watching the kids again."

Keely hardly knew what to think. Here she and Daniel had this secret thing going on—and all of a sudden, Gretchen wanted to take over with the kids again? "Just give your foot the full eight weeks to heal," she said gently but firmly. "Then we'll talk."

Frannie was fading off to sleep. She dropped the rubber frog again.

Gretchen caught it and set it on the table. "I have to confess that I'm beginning to feel guilty. I'm afraid we're taking unfair advantage of you."

Keely asked cautiously, "We?"

"Daniel and me. Daniel, because you watch his children. And me, because I'm the one who roped you into this."

"I wasn't 'roped' into anything. You asked me to step in and I was happy to. I'm *still* happy to. I love watching the kids. Daniel pays me well. Honestly, I see no reason to fix what isn't broken."

Gretchen was frowning. "Sweetheart, you've always wanted a family of your own. How are you going to find the right guy if you're living at Daniel's, running yourself ragged taking care of my grandchildren?"

Keely tried not to scowl at the woman who was truly a second mother to her. Seriously, did Gretchen somehow *know* what was going on with her and Daniel?

But that made no sense. If Gretchen knew, she would say so. Wouldn't she?

"How many ways do I have to say it?" Keely pasted on a smile and put real effort into keeping her tone even and low. "I love taking care of your grandchildren. I'm not feeling overworked in the least. And what's this all about anyway?"

Gretchen's blue eyes seemed guileless. "This?"

"Aren't you the one who's always telling me I have plenty of time for marriage and a family?"

"Well, of course you do. It's only, as I said, I'm beginning to feel guilty, that's all."

"Don't. I mean it. There is absolutely nothing for you to feel guilty about."

"But you have your own life, and how can you live it if you're up there at Daniel's all the time? It's not right."

"Auntie G, I'm perfectly happy. I have everything I need up at Daniel's. If things get to be too much for me, I will tell you. I promise."

"Has something got you upset?"

"What? No, of course not." *Except I'm having a totally torrid, amazing love affair with your son-in-law, and I don't know how you'll take it if you find out.*

Gretchen had said she felt guilty. Well, Keely did, too. And there was absolutely no logical reason for her to feel that way.

Her aunt looked at her sideways. "You're sure you're all right?"

"I am. Truly."

"Daniel can be...difficult, I know. He's such a self-contained sort of fellow, so hard to get to know."

"He and I get along great. I mean that." *In more ways than you need to know.*

Careful not to jiggle the sleeping toddler, Gretchen reached across the table and laid a soothing hand on Keely's arm. "You know you can always talk to me about anything that's bothering you."

"Thanks," Keely said, trying really hard to mean it. "I love you, Auntie G, but there's nothing to tell."

The next day, Jeanine came to watch Jake and Frannie from eight to three.

Keely headed straight for her doctor to get a prescription for the pill. From there, she went to her hairdresser for a cut and a color change to strawberry blond. Then at noon, she met Aislinn for lunch at Fisherman's Korner, a cozy diner on Ocean Road.

They both had the fish and chips—the absolute best anywhere—and tall iced teas.

Keely had just swallowed her first incomparable bite of beer-battered Albacore tuna when Aislinn started in on her.

"I love your hair that color. It really sets off your

eyes—and, Keel, why do I have a feeling you've met someone?"

Keely tried her best to look totally unconcerned. "I have no idea what you're talking about."

"You've got one of those faces."

Keely ate a french fry. "One of *what* faces?"

"An honest face. An open face. A face that currently has a definite I-am-getting-it-good sort of glow."

Keely let out a groan. "'Getting it good'? Ew."

"Well, you do. Now. Tell me everything."

Keely had to press her lips together to keep from doing just that. No, she did not want Gretchen to know, but she *did* want to confide in Aislinn. She'd had three true, forever friends in her life so far, the kind of friends to whom she could bare her soul: Lillie, lost to her now. Meg Cartwell, who'd recently moved to Colorado and married the love of her life. And Aislinn.

But Aislinn was not only her BFF, she also happened to be Daniel's sister. Keely had promised Daniel she wouldn't say anything to anyone in the family.

But maybe if she just didn't say *who* the guy was...

Aislinn shook malt vinegar onto her fish. "Come on. You know you're dying to tell me." She set down the vinegar and sipped her tea. "And I'm not leaving this booth until you come clean."

"Okay, fine." Keely leaned closer across the Formica tabletop and confessed gleefully, "There's someone— and that's all I can say."

"Ha! Yes! I knew it. Who?"

Keely picked up another crunchy-crusted, perfect piece of fish. "What did I just say? I can't tell you."

"Omigod!" Aislinn burst out. "No!"

Keely flinched back. "What?"

"I just had a horrible thought."

Keely groaned, "Aislinn. What thought?"

"Is he married? Is that it?"

Keely was still clutching the uneaten piece of fish. Now she dropped it back in the basket without taking a bite and grabbed a napkin from the dispenser at the end of the table. "Married?" She wiped the grease from her fingers. "Please. After what Roy did to me, do you actually think I would turn around and do that to another woman? You know me better than that."

Aislinn slumped against the red pleather seat. "I'm sorry. You're right. Forget I asked. That question was more to do with me than you." A few years back, Aislinn had fallen for a married man. Nothing had happened between them, but she'd been totally nuts for the guy and miserable over it. "Of course, you would never get involved with a married guy."

"Damn right I wouldn't—and you didn't either, so stop beating yourself up about it." Keely picked up the piece of fish again. They ate in silence for a few minutes.

But Aislinn hadn't given up. "Come on. Tell me. Who *is* this guy you're seeing?"

"I *can't* tell you. Not right now."

"Why?"

"It's all new, you know? We just want to be private. That's all. For now." Did that sound lame? Yeah. Maybe. A little.

And Aislinn wasn't buying it. "Okay, I get that you don't want to wander down the street talking about the guy to complete strangers. But you can tell *me*."

"Aislinn, come on. What I will say is that I'm crazy

about him and he's terrific. He's steady and good. And totally hot."

"Steady?"

"Well, yeah."

"But you never go for the steady ones."

"Hey. Give me some credit. I'm thirty years old. About time I grew up and fell for a responsible, trust-worthy human being for once."

Aislinn's eyebrows had scrunched together. "I know him, right? If I didn't know him, why not just tell me who he is?"

"Ais, stop. I told you I can't say—"

"Wait." Aislinn picked up a french fry, studied it as though for clues and then bit it in half. "Really, with the kids and the commissions and the gallery, you don't have *time* for a man." Now she was sounding way too much like Gretchen.

Keely tried to look stern. "I can see I shouldn't have told you anything."

"Get outta town." Aislinn plunked her half-eaten french fry back in the basket, leaned forward and peered hard at Keely as though she couldn't believe what she saw. "No." She sat back again.

"No, what?"

"No, it can't be."

"What are you babbling about? Will you chill?"

Aislinn stared at her piercingly and accused, "It's Daniel, isn't it?"

Keely barely escaped choking on the bite of fish. She swallowed hard and washed it down with a big gulp of cold tea before launching into a stammered denial. "No. Uh-uh. I don't, um… No. Not Daniel. Absolutely not."

Aislinn so wasn't buying it. "Uh-huh. Daniel. Has

to be. Makes total sense. You're around each other all the time. You *live* together. And I can see how you two would be good for each other. You can help him lighten up a little. And for once, you've found a guy with both feet on the ground, a guy you can actually count on. I mean, it was probably bound to happen, if you think about it."

"What? No. Wrong—I mean, not necessarily."

Aislinn laughed. "You are blushing. It's so cute. Cop to it. It has to be Daniel. You're all alone in that big house together every night after the twins are in bed. And you told me at the gallery a week and a half ago how *great* he is." Keely opened her mouth to spout more denials, but Aislinn just shook her head. "Don't lie to me, Keel. It will only hurt my feelings, and I won't believe you anyway."

Keely let her shoulders slump. "I don't *want* to lie to you."

"Hey." Aislinn reached across the table. Keely stared at her outstretched hand. "C'mon." Aislinn wiggled her fingers. "Gimme." With a giant sigh, Keely reached back. They laced their fingers together, palms touching. As they stared at each other, Keely felt acceptance settle over her, that her best friend had figured it out, that it wasn't a *bad* thing, that Aislinn knew her so well—far from it. Keely was grateful to have such a good friend. After a long moment of mutual silence, Aislinn asked softly, "You really like my big brother?"

"I do. I really do."

"Well, all right then." One corner of Aislinn's mouth kicked up in a half smile. "Let's finish our fish." They focused on the food until Aislinn glanced up again. "He *is* a good guy."

Keely nodded. "The best."

"Too bad he's got that poker up his butt."

"Stop!" Keely slapped at her friend with her napkin.

"Hey. It's only the truth. Maybe with you, he can relax, enjoy life a little."

"It's all really new, Ais. We're kind of feeling our way along as we go."

"I just want you to be happy. Both of you."

"Thank you—and I really don't want anyone else to know."

"Keely, I promise you. Nobody's going to hear a thing about it from me."

As soon as the kids were in bed that night, Daniel did what he'd been waiting all day to do. He took Keely's hand and led her down the hall. In his room, he shoved the door shut with his foot and reached for her.

Her happy laughter filled his head as she kissed him. He walked her backward toward the bed. But before they got there, she pushed him into the bedside chair.

He caught her hand. "There is no escaping me." With a tug, he pulled her down across his lap. She laughed again and wrapped her arms around his neck. He couldn't get over how right it felt—the two of them, together. After too many years of just doing what he had to do, he had something really good to come home to at night. He had Keely.

And that was pretty damned amazing.

He nuzzled her neck and breathed in the perfect scent of her skin. She was wearing way too many clothes, though. And she didn't need that big clip holding her hair off her neck. He undid it and set it on the bedside table. Her hair drifted down in soft waves to her shoulders.

"I like this new color," he whispered, combing his fingers through the red-gold strands.

"It's pretty close to my natural color."

"I know. And it suits you." He caught her chin on his finger and guided her closer for a kiss, claiming that mouth he couldn't seem to get enough of. She tasted as good as she smelled.

When the kiss ended, she rested her head on his shoulder. "I had lunch with Aislinn today."

Something off in her tone alerted him. "She okay?"

"She's fine. But she, um, knows about you and me."

*Aislinn knows.*

It wasn't anger he felt, exactly. More like frustration. He wanted this thing with Keely to be just theirs, for the two of them alone and no one else. The family owned him. It was all about them and had been ever since he was eighteen years old.

With Keely, for the first time in forever, he felt free. He didn't want the family butting into that, bringing demands, making judgments, feeling cheated or disapproving that he was crazy for Lillie's little cousin and wanted to spend every moment he could with her.

He just wanted to come in this room with her and have the world disappear. At least for a while, he wanted her all to himself, wanted everyone to leave them the hell alone.

She pressed two soft fingers to the space between his eyebrows. "You're scowling at me."

He took care to keep his voice level when he answered her. "I thought we agreed that, for now, we won't tell the family."

She hunched her shoulders, put her hands between her knees and chewed her lower lip a little. "I didn't tell her. She figured it out." He wasn't sure what to say to that, so he didn't say anything. Keely chided, "Aislinn's not only your sister—she's my best friend, Daniel. She knew there was someone, and she guessed it had to be you. And I just couldn't outright lie to her. So I didn't. She promised to keep our confidence. I believe her."

He really couldn't blame her for breaking their agreement. He *didn't* blame her. She and Aislinn were tight. "Okay, then."

"What does that mean?"

"It means I see your point." He traced the line of her hair where it fell along her cheek. "You can't go telling lies to your best friend. Aislinn *is* someone who keeps her word, so she's not going to say anything. And I'm being completely selfish anyway. I want you all to myself."

She looked at him then, that mouth he couldn't get enough of kissing soft and pliant, eyes so bright. "I kind of feel the same. Like this should be *our* time, just you and me. Most people get a little space to get to know each other when they start something together. The families don't enter into it until things get serious."

*Serious.*

To him, this *was* serious. He didn't really know how to be any other way.

"There's something else," she said.

"You're frowning." He pulled her closer, kissed her cheek, nuzzled the tender corner of her delicious mouth. "Whatever it is, it can't be all that bad."

"It's not. Not really. But I didn't tell you yesterday, and it's been bothering me. I took the kids to see Gretchen."

"You mentioned that."

"Yeah, but what I didn't say was that she got after me to let her take over again with Jake and Frannie. She even said she felt guilty, that she was taking advantage of me."

He had to order his arms not to lock tight around her. No one was taking her away from him, not Gretchen. Not anybody.

But she *had* been taking care of his children for weeks now. It had to be getting old. So really, Gretchen had a point. He made himself ask, "Maybe it's getting to be too much for you?"

That got him an eye roll. "Of course not. I love it here. I love the kids. I'm getting everything done that needs doing, with my work and at the gallery. It's all going great for me."

Suddenly, he could breathe again. But was he being unfair to her? "You're sure?"

She turned a little, caught his face between her hands and kissed him quick and hard. "Yes, I am sure."

"Well, all right then." He caught her hand, opened her fingers and pressed his mouth to the soft center of her palm.

But when he looked up, a frown still crinkled her forehead. "There's more. It wasn't only that Gretchen said she worried about taking advantage of me. She also started talking about how she knew I wanted my own family. She asked how I thought I was going to accomplish that while taking care of your kids and living in your house. I don't know. I couldn't help wondering if she suspects that we're together and she doesn't like it."

"She's pretty outspoken. If she knew, I think she would say so."

"You're right. It was just odd, that's all. Think about it. You and I get together. We decide to keep what we have to ourselves, to have a little time just for us—and suddenly Gretchen, who asked me to take care of the kids in the first place, thinks I should be moving on."

He hated what he knew he had to say next. "Okay. Maybe we're handling this all wrong. Maybe we're just going to have to be up-front about what's going on between us after all. Let anyone who's going to get weird about it go ahead and have at it. Then we can move on from there."

Her gorgeous smile bloomed wide. "I love that you said that. But you know what? I just don't want to do that. Not yet. Do you?"

"Hell, no," he replied with feeling.

"Well, then. It's decided. We'll go on as planned— for a while, at least. And we'll reevaluate as necessary." She snuggled close again.

"Deal." He rested his cheek against her hair and felt way too relieved they weren't immediately inviting the family into the middle of their business.

She fiddled with the top button of his shirt, her head tucked nice and close, over his heart. "This weekend should be interesting…"

It was Easter weekend. Grace would be home Friday. And Sunday, they were planning the kids' first egg hunt, with a big family dinner in the afternoon.

Keely tipped her head back to meet his eyes. "I'm assuming you don't want to tell Grace about us yet?"

"Please no," he answered fervently. "If we tell her,

she's way too likely to blab to everyone. Or get mad at me."

"Why would she get mad at you?"

"As if she needs a reason. One way or another, Grace always ends up pissed off at me."

Her soft mouth twitched. A definite tell. She wanted to lecture him but didn't know how it would go over. "Grace is young and she wants to be free, and to her it seems like you're the one holding her back."

"I *am* holding her back. She doesn't need to be free until she's at least forty—preferably fifty."

Keely gaped. And then she giggled. "Daniel. You actually do have a sense of humor."

He put a finger to his lips. "Do not tell a soul. I have a certain image to uphold."

"You mean the one where they all think you're crabby and uncompromising?"

"And narrow-minded and controlling—oh, and did I mention I never crack a smile?"

That had her grinning. "What in the world do I see in you?"

"I'm handy around the house, good with babies and amazing in bed."

Her cheeks got pinker. He loved to watch her blush. "True." She nodded. "On all counts. And we're agreed that we're not telling Grace yet?"

"We are agreed, yes."

She slipped his top shirt button from its hole. Finally. "You know that means I won't be staying all night with you while she's here? We'll have to be careful or she'll find out, whether we're ready for that or not." She undid the second button.

"That does it." He took her hand and guided it down

to button number three. "I changed my mind. We're telling Grace."

"No, we're not." Button number three gave way, and four and five, as well. "We deserve our privacy for as long as we want to keep what we have just between us. And it's only for Friday and Saturday. She goes back to Portland Sunday." She undid the last button. "At which time we can go back to being secret lovers in a full-time kind of way." She sat up enough to work the shirt off his shoulders.

"I don't know. Waking up without you..." He took her red knit top by the hem and pulled it up. "I don't think I can do that." She raised her arms so he could pull it off over her head. Underneath, she wore a pretty pink bra. He made short work of that, undoing the hooks at the back and tossing it aside. Her breasts were so beautiful. He cradled them, felt her hard little nipples pressing into his palms. She moaned—and jumped off his lap. "Get back here," he commanded.

"So bossy..." But she did come back, swinging one slim thigh across him, straddling him, so his growing hardness pressed right where he most wanted to be— well, except that her jeans and his jeans and two sets of underwear barred the way. He cradled her breasts again. "Oh, Daniel..." She was suddenly breathless. He loved that about her, when she got breathless and wanting, when she looked at him through heavy-lidded eyes the way she was doing now. He rolled those pretty nipples between his thumbs and forefingers, and she let her head drop back, all that glorious red-gold hair tumbling down behind her. "Daniel..."

"Yeah?"

"Um. What were we talking about?"

"Not a clue," he said rough and low, sliding his hands to her waist, lifting her as he stood and setting her on her feet long enough to get rid of her jeans and her panties, her shoes and socks.

He *had* to kiss her. As much of her as possible. Gathering her close again, he pressed his lips in the center of the five freckles on her left shoulder that seemed to him to make the points of a star. He scraped his teeth along her collarbone, licked his way up the center of her throat, over her strong little chin until he reached that plump mouth of hers. She opened for him on a happy sigh.

But only for one too-brief moment. And then she was dropping away from him, folding to her knees in front of him.

She had his jeans undone and down around his ankles in seconds. The woman amazed him. How could he have thought he knew her for all these years and years?

He'd known so little.

And she was so much more.

He put his hands in her shining hair, holding on for dear life as she took him inside that warm, wet mouth of hers. All the way in, right down her smooth throat. How did she do that?

Not that he cared how. What mattered was that she was here, in his room, with him. What mattered was that touching him, kissing him, taking him inside herself, driving him crazy with want and need, seemed to please her every bit as much as it pleased him.

It was too much in a very good way, what she did to him. He didn't last very long. His mind shattered along with his body, into a thousand happy, smiling pieces.

He forgot about everything—all the bits of his life

and his family's lives that he was responsible for. He let it all fade away, the million and one little things he had to keep a constant eye on so that no new disaster could strike those he loved.

With her, he could just let go. With her, at last, he knew what it felt like to be free.

## Chapter 7

Grace arrived on Friday at ten in the morning.

She burst into the kitchen where Keely had the kids in their high chairs for a morning snack.

"Munchkins, I am home!" Cheeks pink and white-blond hair windblown, Grace dropped her giant shoulder bag and overstuffed pack to the floor.

The twins beat on their tray tables in glee at the sight of her. "Gwace! Gwace! Kiss, kiss!"

She went to them for hugs and sticky kisses. Then she turned to Keely. "Oh, look! It's my favorite nanny." She whipped Keely's sketchbook and colored pencil right out of her hands and plunked them on the table.

"Hey!" Keely laughed in protest. But Grace only pulled her out of her chair and waltzed her once around the kitchen, not letting her go until they were back at Keely's chair again.

"God. I'm starved," Grace announced as she knelt to give Maisey a good scratch and a hug.

Keely picked up her sketchbook and pencil and reclaimed her seat at the table. "You want breakfast?"

"Had that, thanks."

"There's tuna salad in the fridge."

"Dave's Killer Bread?"

"Got that, too."

"I love you, Keely. You have all the right answers to the most important questions." Grace got busy gathering what she needed for a fat tuna sandwich, including Tillamook cheddar slices, tomatoes, lettuce and dill pickles. "Old Stone Face at work?"

"Yep."

"How you holding up watching the little darlings day after day?"

"So far, spectacular."

Grace popped a hunk of pickle into her mouth. "I can't believe you're still here, that you've yet to run screaming into the night."

Keely chuckled as she added shading to the mountains in the background of the wide, green field she was sketching, the artist in her hard at work planning how she might create a similar, but more striking effect with fabric and thread. "What can I tell you? I have zero complaints—how's school?"

Grace launched into a monologue about the co-op she lived in, how much she loved studying Shakespeare's relevance to the modern world and how the guy she'd met last Saturday might be driving up to party with her and her friends this weekend.

By the time she finished her sandwich, scooped up her stuff and disappeared into her room, the kids were getting restless in their high chairs. Keely wiped their gooey hands and faces, and took them and Maisey outside for a while.

When she came back in, Grace had emerged from her room. She offered to watch the kids. Keely took her up on it. Promising to return by two, she grabbed her purse and headed out to check in with Amanda at Sand & Sea.

She left the gallery at one and swung by Gretchen's. Keely's aunt was baking like a madwoman in preparation for the family get-together Sunday. Ingrid was nowhere in sight.

Gretchen waved a flour-dusted hand. "She's off at that bar. Have you been by there?"

"No. I keep meaning to stop in."

"Well, go anytime. Your mother will be there. Not that I'm complaining. We get along best, your mom and me, if we're not around each other too much—and have you given any more thought to what we talked about the other day?"

"If you mean my finding someone else to watch the twins—"

"That is exactly what I mean—have a cookie, sweetheart."

Keely took one. They were chocolate with chocolate chips. "Amazing. I think I gained ten pounds just from this first bite."

"You look great. You can afford a cookie or two—and I do still want you to think about letting me fill in with them at least some of the time."

"What did we already decide? You get the go-ahead from your doctor, then yes. I would love a few hours off every once in a while."

Gretchen released a long, drawn-out sigh. "I do worry about you, honey. You deserve a break now and then."

"I have plenty of time to myself."

"Not enough. I'm going to have to talk to Daniel about it."

That did it. Keely knew she had to speak up. "Auntie G, don't you dare."

Gretchen sent her a wounded look, her pink mouth drawn down. "You don't have to snap at me. I have your best interests at heart."

Keely took her aunt by the shoulders and turned her around so she could look her squarely in the eye. "You and I both know how Daniel is."

Gretchen wiped her hands on her apron. "What do you mean?"

"He takes on everybody else's burdens. And that means he has plenty to deal with. He doesn't need you whispering in his ear about how I want him to find someone else for the kids. It isn't true, and it will only worry him. That's just not right."

"I would hardly be whispering," Gretchen muttered. Then she sniffed and lifted her round chin. "I only want what's best for you."

Keely's heart seemed to expand in her chest. It was an ache, but a good kind of ache. "Auntie G…" She wrapped her arms around Gretchen. "I know you do."

Gretchen sniffed again. "You're going to get flour all over that pretty sweater of yours."

"I don't care." She pulled back enough to give her aunt a smile. "And you have to let it be. *I'm* the one who gets to decide what's best for me. And I mean it when I say that I'm enjoying myself with Frannie and Jake. I will have no problem telling you and Daniel when and if I've had enough."

"But…you're happy? You mean that?"

"Yes. I'm very happy with the way things are right now, and I have no plans to make a change."

They made it halfway through dinner that night before Daniel and Grace got into it.

It was the same thing they always fought over. Grace wanted to go out with her friends, and Daniel wanted her to stay in.

"Gracie," he said, and Keely tried to take heart that at least he spoke in a mild tone. "You just got here. We've missed you. It's not going to kill you to stay home tonight."

Grace let out an exaggerated groan. "God. You drive me insane. I've *been* home all day, and I haven't seen Erin or Carrie in weeks. Plus, there's this guy I met in Portland. He and a couple of his friends are driving up, meeting us at Beach Street Brews." The brewpub on Beach Street served local craft beers.

"What guy?" Daniel's voice had gone distinctly growly.

Grace blew out an angry breath through her nose. "His name is Jared Riley. He goes to Reed. I like him, all right? Daniel, come on. He's a great guy and he's driving all the way up here and I'm looking forward to seeing him. And Erin. And Carrie. Okay?"

"I just think—"

"Don't." Grace leaped to her feet. The twins startled in unison at her sudden move. "Just don't. I do not want to hear it." And with that, she shoved back her chair, whirled on her heel and ran across the kitchen, straight to her room, slamming the door good and hard when she got there.

The slammed door scared Frannie. She burst into tears. Jake saw his twin crying and let out a yowl.

Keely and Daniel rose as one. She took Jake. Daniel took Frannie. They both delivered soothing reassurances and comforting hugs until the kids stopped fussing and were ready to go back into their high chairs.

Daniel returned to his seat. Keely stayed right where she was. He didn't notice she'd remained on her feet until he'd picked up his fork again.

"Okay." His fork clattered back to his plate. "What?"

"I've got to say something." She took extra care to make her voice even and drama-free. "You need to give this up, Daniel."

"Give what up?"

As if he didn't know. "This…overprotectiveness with Grace."

"I'm not—"

"Could you just not go straight to denial, please?" Keely waited to make sure he was listening. After he'd glared at her for a solid ten seconds, she continued, "Yes, you *are* overprotective. I get that it's for all the right reasons and you love her and you want her safe. I get that she's the last of your brothers and sisters to strike out on her own and that even if you can't wait for that to happen, you're still going to miss her when she goes."

"I—"

"Uh-uh. Not finished."

He took a long drink of water. "Right. Wrap it up."

"Thank you," she said and tried to mean it. "I get that you want to protect her, that you feel it's your job to keep her safe. But then again, she *is* twenty-one. She sets her own hours and takes care of business just fine while she's in Portland. The first thing she did when she arrived today was offer to watch the kids so I could run errands. It's not right that you still treat her like a child when she comes home."

"I don't..." That time he caught himself in middenial. He drank more water as Jake let out a string of nonsense syllables. Daniel set down his glass—and surrendered in a growl. "All right. I'll talk to her after dinner."

"Wonderful." Keely sank to her chair. As she smoothed her napkin on her lap, she heard a door open. Grace appeared, unsmiling but composed. She returned to the table and sat down again.

"I'm sorry I lost my temper, Daniel," she said. "I promised myself I would stop doing that."

"Ahem," Daniel said stiffly. "I came on pretty strong. Apology accepted."

"Thanks." Grace sat up straighter. "And I *am* going out after dinner."

Daniel scowled. Keely braced for him to start barking orders again. Instead, slowly and carefully, he cut a bite of pork roast. "Just be safe," he muttered, adding with great effort, "and...have a good time."

Grace left at a little after eight. By eight thirty the kids were in bed, and Keely enjoyed a glorious few hours in Daniel's bed.

He caught her arm when she tried to get up to go at a quarter of midnight. "Stay. I don't like it here without you. Grace probably won't come in until after two, and there's no reason she'll come up here when she does."

"Uh-uh. Either we tell her or we don't. Setting ourselves up to get caught is just beyond tacky. She doesn't need that and neither do we."

"Sometimes you're too damn reasonable," he grumbled.

She chuckled and cuddled in close, just for a minute more, nuzzling his broad chest with its perfect light dusting of gold hair and that wonderful happy trail she wished she could stick around and follow to her favorite destination. Again.

He tipped up her chin and kissed her. She savored the moment. And then, with a playful shove, she rolled away from him and out from under the covers.

He braced up an elbow and watched her pull on her jeans and shirt. His eyes, silvery in the lamplight, sent shivers down the backs of her knees.

"Don't look at me like that," she chided.

"Like what?"

"Like you're thinking about all the naughty things you're going to do to my body."

"But I *am* thinking of all the things I want to do to your body. Come on back here. Let me show you."

Somehow, she made her bare feet carry her to the door. "Night," she whispered as she slipped from the room.

Her bed felt huge and empty with just her in it. It took her a long while to get sleep. She wondered if she and Daniel were doing the right thing to make a secret of what they had together. And she marveled that everything about what she had with him felt so good and real and right. As though they were perfectly suited, each to the other. As though this was a love affair that would never wear itself out.

Saturday night Grace went out again. Keely and Daniel stole some precious time alone. She left him at midnight for her too-empty bed, where she lay awake again, missing him, though he was just down the hall—missing him and hoping that this thing between them would never have to end.

Was she being ridiculous? They'd only been lovers for a week.

Didn't matter.

She knew her own heart, knew she was falling. Falling hard.

And scary-deep.

Easter morning, Gretchen and Ingrid arrived at ten thirty with a big basket full of old-school dyed eggs, a cake and a few dozen cookies, plus an array of side dishes to go with the prime rib roast Keely would serve for the main course.

Keely and Daniel helped the sisters bring everything in from the car as Keely tried not to let nerves get the better of her. She dreaded that her mother might start in about the "smokin' hot" chemistry between her and Daniel.

But Ingrid never uttered a single embarrassing word or cast Keely so much as a meaningful smirk. She must have actually meant what she'd said last Sunday night—that what went on between Keely and Daniel was nobody's business but their own.

Gretchen kept the kids entertained while Ingrid, Daniel and Keely hid the eggs out in the foggy backyard.

Aislinn arrived with a salad at eleven, about the same time Grace emerged, sleepy-eyed in pajamas and a giant floppy sweater. Outside, the fog had thinned a little. Grace poured herself a mug of coffee and followed the rest of them out back.

At first, Frannie and Jake seemed unsure of the

whole egg-hunting concept. Ingrid and Gretchen led them around pointing out the bright eggs, many of them in plain sight. And the twins would look up at their grandma and great-aunt, their faces simultaneously curious and confused.

But eventually, they seemed to catch on, laughing and holding up their prizes as they found them. The hunt went on for over an hour, mostly because the twins tended to get distracted. They would plunk down on the grass and put their fingers in their mouths until Gretchen or Ingrid got them up and moving again. By noon, they'd started fussing. Keely took them inside for a little lunch and a nap, leaving Aislinn and Grace to gather the rest of the eggs.

More Bravos arrived. Harper and Hailey, who shared Aislinn's rambling beach cottage with her when they were home, hadn't made the three-hour-drive back to Valentine Bay for the holiday, but Daniel's brothers, Matthias, Connor and Liam, appeared. There was also a great-aunt and uncle, the eccentric brother-and-sister duo, Daffodil and Percy Valentine. The two were the last of the Valentines, the founding family for which Valentine Bay had been named. Neither Aunt Daffy nor Uncle Percy had ever married, and they both still lived in the house where they'd been born. A slightly crumbly Italianate Queen-Anne Victorian, Valentine House sat on a prime piece of real estate at the edge of Valentine City Park. Aunt Daffy kept a beautiful garden, and Uncle Percy considered himself a genealogist as well as something of an amateur detective.

At two, when they all sat down at the long table in the dining room, Keely felt wonderfully relaxed and happy.

All her life, she'd dreamed of a big family around her. This, now, today? It felt a lot like her dream come true.

Gretchen said grace. When the soft *amens* echoed around the table, Keely couldn't help but look to Daniel first. He gave her the most beautiful, private, tender smile. She glanced away quickly, so no one would see.

That evening, Grace returned to Portland and Keely slept again in Daniel's bed.

By Wednesday, Keely had been on the pill for a full week. After they put the kids to bed that night, she and Daniel had the contraceptive talk. He'd only been with Lillie and Keely. And she'd been tested after she broke up with her last boyfriend two years ago. They agreed it would be safe to go without condoms.

But then Daniel shook his head. "I would just feel better if we used both." He looked kind of sad when he said it.

And she understood. After Lillie's betrayal, Daniel was unlikely to trust his partner to take responsibility for contraception. They continued to use condoms, which was totally fine with her.

The next week, at the very end of April, Daniel left for Southern Oregon to meet with timber owners near the California border and to look in on several jobs in progress along the way. It started out as a two-day trip, but there were issues at one of the mills and with a few employees in key positions on two current jobs. Two days stretched to three and then four.

Gretchen insisted she was well enough to help out with the kids, and she did seem to be walking just fine without even a cane. She came every day and stayed for three or four hours, giving Keely a break to work in her studio or stop in at Sand & Sea. On the fourth day,

Ingrid pitched in, too, so that Keely could concentrate on getting everything ready for a new show opening at the gallery on Friday.

With her aunt and mom helping out, Keely had no trouble keeping on track workwise. The nights were lonely, though. She missed the delicious, perfect pleasure of Daniel's big hands on her body, not to mention the addictive wonder of his kiss and the feel of his muscled body, so warm and solid, right there beside her as she slept.

And yes, she spent her solitary nights in his bed. Somehow, it wasn't quite as lonely in his room as in hers down the hall.

Thursday night he called to say he wouldn't be home until Saturday. They talked for two hours—about his work and hers, about Frannie and Jake, about how well it was going for her because she had Gretchen and Ingrid taking up the slack.

"I want to take you out," he said. "Find out what night Jeanine's available, and then I'll make dinner reservations. There's this great place in Astoria…"

*Astoria.* Because as long as they were keeping their true relationship from the family, they'd be safer to take date night somewhere out of town. Same as he had with the woman he'd met on Tinder—and yes, she knew that what she had with him was so much more than a hookup.

They really needed to talk about coming out to the family. The secrecy was starting to wear on her nerves.

"Miss you," he said gruffly as they were ending the call.

*I love you.* The three little words filled up her mind and created a sensation of radiating warmth in the center of her chest. But she didn't say them out loud. A first *I love you* should not be said on the phone.

"Miss you, too," she replied. "See you Saturday…"

She felt the absence on the line as he hung up and she wanted to cry, of all the self-indulgent reactions. He would be home in two days. It was nothing to cry over. She grabbed his pillow from his side of the bed and pressed her face into it. It still smelled faintly of him, kind of piney and fresh.

With a groan, she tipped her head toward the ceiling. "Get ahold of yourself," she commanded out loud, tucking the pillow behind her head and dropping onto her back, feeling mopey and bereft and achy all over.

Hormones? Not likely. She was on the pill now. Her periods on the pill tended to be regular and pretty much mood-swing, bloat-and pain-free.

And it wasn't her placebo week anyway. There were two more weeks to go until her mild, pill-controlled period was even due.

She ordered herself to stop being a big baby and put all thoughts of weird hormone swings from her mind.

Friday, she ran around like a madwoman, handling the hundred and one final details before the new gallery show. It was all worth it, though. The opening went off beautifully.

Saturday, Daniel came home while she and Gretchen were out in the backyard with the twins. Gretchen hung around until dinnertime and then stayed to eat.

Which meant that at seven thirty that night, when Gretchen finally left, Keely still hadn't felt Daniel's big arms around her or enjoyed the taste of his mouth on hers.

They all—Daniel, Keely and the twins—stood at the front door, waving as Gretchen drove away.

The twins loved to wave goodbye. It was, "Bye-bye, Gwamma! Wove you!" from Frannie.

And "Bye-bye, bye-bye!" from Jake.

As Gretchen's enormous silver Escalade sailed off down the driveway, Daniel shut the door. "For a while there I was scared to death she planned to stay the night." Every inch of Keely's skin seemed to spark and flare at the way he looked at her—like she was everything, like he couldn't wait to get her alone and take off all her clothes.

"Baf!" demanded Frannie.

"Baf now!" Jake concurred.

Which was great. Wonderful. The sooner the twins had their baths, the sooner they could all go to bed—Jake and Frannie, to sleep.

Daniel and Keely, to make up for lost time.

They all went upstairs together and straight to the big bathroom. The kids were out of their clothes and into the tub in record time.

"I can't stand it," Daniel muttered.

"What?" Keely sent him a worried glance as he rose from the side of the tub, grabbing Keely's arm and pulling her up with him. "Not having you in my arms."

He hauled her close and kissed her forever, melting her heart and incinerating her lady parts, while Frannie and Jake laughed and splashed and demanded kisses of their own.

A great moment, Keely thought, one that almost made up for not being free to run to his arms that afternoon, when he'd first stepped out on the back deck to tell them he was home.

With obvious reluctance, he let her go. The kids finished in the tub. Daniel and Keely dried them, diapered them and put on their pj's.

The twins were pros at the pulling of heartstrings. As soon as they had their pajamas on, they wiggled and squirmed, demanding, "Dow! Now!"

Once on their feet, they ran to the bookcase, each returning with a stack of favorite kids' stories.

Daniel sat in the rocker, one child on either arm, and read them four stories.

Finally, by the end of *Goodnight, Goodnight, Construction Site*, the twins could hold out no longer. They slept in that endearing way little kids do, heads hanging like wilting flowers on a stem, lower lips sticking out, drooling just a little down their pajama fronts.

"We have to go ahead and tell them, tell the family," Keely said breathlessly ten minutes later.

They were in Daniel's room by then, with the door shut at last. He'd already whipped her shirt up over her head and taken away her bra and was in the process of pushing her denim skirt to the floor, her panties along with it. She kicked off her shoes and she was naked.

"God, I missed you." He grabbed her close.

She wanted to get closer. He helped by picking her right up off the floor so that she could wrap her legs around him. He braced her against the door and kissed her until she feared her lips might fall off. And oh, she could feel him, so hard and ready, pressed against her so intimately, but with his pants and boxer briefs in the way.

She wanted him naked, too.

But she *needed* him to listen to her first. She really did have a point, and she was going to make it.

Fisting her hands in his hair, she yanked that amazing mouth of his away from her. "Listen." She tried to glare at him in a purposeful manner, but she knew her cheeks were flushed and her eyes low and lazy. Even her breathing betrayed her. It came in ragged, hungry little gulps. "I mean it."

"You're so beautiful. I need to kiss you. Kiss you all over. Come back here…"

Somehow, she managed *not* to give in to him. She kept that tight grip on his hair and turned her lips away so he couldn't take them. "When are you going to be ready to tell the family about us?"

"Soon," he said, and a strangled groan escaped him. And well, how could she resist that, when he groaned that way, as though it would kill him stone-dead not to have his hands and mouth all over her?

"Daniel," she moaned. And that did it. He claimed her lips again. And oh, she had missed him, and they had a lot of lovemaking they needed to catch up on. Days' worth, seriously.

She was practically love starved. They needed to get busy making up for lost time.

With another moan, she pressed her mouth to his.

Incendiary, that kiss, a hot tangle of breath and seeking tongues. It went on forever as she unbuttoned his shirt and pushed it off his shoulders. He had a white T-shirt on underneath, darn it. She wanted him closer, needed skin on skin.

Grabbing a fistful of T-shirt on either side of him, she scraped it upward. He let her down to the floor again so she could drag the shirt off over his head.

"There now. Better." She sighed as she pressed her hands to his broad, hot chest, gliding them upward to clasp behind his neck. She dragged that mouth of his down to hers again.

They kissed some more—endlessly, gloriously—as she went to work on his belt and his pants.

Finally they were naked—except for his socks. Luckily, socks had no bearing on what she was after.

He lifted her again. Neither of them could wait. He slid right into her, right there against the door.

Heaven. Paradise. Her arms around him, holding him tight, joined with him at last.

He groaned, broke their never-ending kiss and pressed his forehead to hers. "Forgot…"

She remembered, too, then. "The condom."

"I shouldn't have…" He let that thought trail off. Another low groan escaped him. "Keely. You feel so good." He kissed her chin, the side of her throat. "It should be okay." He kissed the words onto her skin. "Right?"

She was on the pill. Of course, it should be fine.

"Okay?" he asked again—well, more like pleaded, really.

She took him by his square jaw. "Yes." And she kissed him, kissed him so deep as he moved within her. "Missed you," she whispered against his mouth.

"Keely. Me, too. I missed you so much…"

And then all actual words were lost to them. They rocked together, with her wrapped tight around him. They rocked and swayed in perfect rhythm.

Nothing else mattered then. Except that he was holding her, so close, so perfectly.

Her climax came spinning at her, rolling like a river of heat and wonder, down her spine to the core of her where she held him, rocked him, home with her at last.

Alone together, Keely and Daniel.

Right where they belonged.

# Chapter 8

The days went by.

Full days. Happy ones.

Friday night Jeanine came to babysit, and Daniel took Keely to dinner in Astoria. The meal was lovely. He ordered a nice Oregon Pinot Noir. Her stomach had been acting up on and off for the past few days, so she didn't have more than a sip or two. Daniel teased her about being a lightweight and she shrugged and agreed with him.

After dinner, they strolled the Riverwalk, holding hands like lovers do, watching the big boats out on the majestic Columbia, even wandering out onto the East Mooring Basin boat ramp to get a look at the lazy sea lions that had taken over the docks there. It was wonderful.

They didn't get home until after midnight. They thanked Jeanine and sent her on her way, then went upstairs hand in hand, to check on the kids, who slept like little angels, feathery eyelashes fanned across their plump cheeks.

An hour later, tucked up nice and cozy together in his big bed in the dark, Keely said, "I want to tell the family that we're a couple. I know it will probably be awkward. But, Daniel, we really need to do it."

Daniel agreed with her. "We *will* do it. Soon." He went on, "Sometimes it feels like all my life, I've never had anything that was just mine. Everything's about the family, and it has been since I was eighteen. You and me, here, now, in this room with the door closed? It's just us, Keely. You and me and no one else. I'm jealous of that. Protective of that."

She captured his hand under the covers and wove her fingers with his. "It's only that I'm getting tired of lying, you know?"

"We're not lying. We're just…not sharing."

She laughed at that and then she warned, "Before you know it, Grace will be home for the summer and living in this house with us. If we're not telling her, we'll have to start sneaking around again. No more waking up together every morning."

He kissed the tip of her nose. "We've got two weeks till then. Don't rush me, woman." With a low growl, he pulled her closer and bit her lightly on the chin. "Give me a kiss."

She laughed again and kissed him and that led where kissing him usually went—to more kisses and endless caresses and a satisfying ending for both of them.

Later, as she held him close and listened to his breathing even out into sleep, she decided that she would stop pushing him to tell the family about the two of them. He wasn't ready yet, and she needed to give him time. She would leave the subject alone until he brought it up.

She grinned to herself in the darkness. He just needed the proper motivation. Once Grace got home and he got a taste of sleeping alone again, she had a feeling he'd see telling the family in a whole new light.

The following Saturday, they went out again. Jeanine wasn't available that night. But they got someone else from the nanny service instead. Daniel took her to a great seafood place in Cannon Beach. She watched his beloved face across the table from her as they waited for their food. He looked relaxed. Happy.

She was happy, too—except she was in her placebo week on the pill now and her period hadn't come. It didn't mean anything. It would probably come tomorrow or the next day. She felt kind of puffy and crampy and that was a good sign that everything was on schedule.

Except that she'd never got preperiod cramping when on the pill in the past.

She just wanted to tell him about her silly worries. Just open her mouth and say it. *My period's a couple of days late and I'm a little concerned about that...*

He probably wouldn't look all that happy then.

No. Uh-uh. Not doing that.

She would wait. Her period would come. If it didn't come, she would buy a test and take it before she brought it up to him. Then she could joke about it. *Guess what? I had a pregnancy scare! Isn't that hysterical?*

She had a feeling he wouldn't find even a scare all that humorous. He loved his kids, but they hadn't been

his idea. Not by a long shot. He'd wanted a little freedom at last now his brothers and sisters were grown. But
Lillie had got pregnant anyway—and then lost her life
for it. The poor guy had some serious baggage around
having babies.

That she might have to tell him they had another
baby on the way?

Uh-uh. That fell squarely into the category of things
she very much did not want to do.

And why was she fixating on this? She wasn't pregnant. She was a few days late, that was all.

Thursday, her period still hadn't put in an appearance.

At eleven, her mom came over to watch the twins
for her.

Ingrid took one look at her and demanded, "Okay.
What's wrong?"

"Wrong?" There was nothing wrong. Okay, yeah,
she was maybe obsessing over the possibility that she
might be pregnant. Just a little. But how in the world
could her mother sense that? She stared at Ingrid's high
green ponytail and deep purple bangs. "I'm fine. A little tired, I guess."

"You're lying. I can tell. I always could."

"No, I am not lying," she lied.

"Yeah, you are. But you don't want to talk, I get
that. When you do, I'm ready to listen. You know that,
right?"

"I do, Mom. And I'm grateful."

Ingrid fiddled with her bangs. "You like the purple
and green?"

"I do. Purple and green works for you."

"Gretch hates it." Ingrid chuckled.

"And that means you love it even more, right?"

"No, I love it because it looks super bad in a very good way. Gretch hating it is just a little extra bonus that makes me smile."

"I do not understand your relationship with Auntie G."

"And there's absolutely no reason you have to understand, so don't worry about it." Jake toddled over and held up his ragged stuffed bunny. Ingrid scooped him into her arms. "You are the handsomest little man, Jakey."

"Kiss my wabbit." Ingrid kissed the ugly stuffed toy on its matted face.

Keely bent to pet Maisey, who was always following her around. "Okay, I'm outta here." She picked up Frannie, planted a kiss on her cheek and set her back down. "Bye, Frannie-Annie."

"Bye, Keewee. Wove you."

"Back by three," Keely promised.

"No rush," said her mother as she bent to let Jake down.

Keely ran errands, including a quick trip to Safeway, where she bought three pregnancy tests.

No, she did not think she might be pregnant. But if her period didn't come by the weekend, she would take the tests just to prove to herself there was nothing to worry about. She bought three because it never hurt to triple-check, and if the first test came up positive, triple-checking was exactly what she planned to do.

So what if false positives were extremely rare? Negative or positive, she would test and test again, just to be sure.

At lunchtime, Keely sat across from Aislinn at Fisherman's Korner and longed to tell her best friend everything.

But she just couldn't, not about this.

Daniel was Ais's brother after all. Once he knew—*if* it turned out there was anything *to* know—then she could confide in Aislinn. Until then, laying her crazy worries about possibly, *maybe* being pregnant on Daniel's sister felt beyond unacceptable.

Keely had been kind of afraid that Aislinn, like Ingrid, would know she had something on her mind.

But Ais seemed distracted. And Keely was the one who ended up asking, "What's wrong?"

"It's that weird old Martin Durand. Remember, I told you about him?"

"I remember." Durand owned a horse ranch, the Wild River Ranch, inland on the Youngs River. Aislinn had worked there as a stable hand one summer, back when she was still in college.

"He called me—Martin Durand did—this morning, at Deever and Gray." That was the law firm she worked for. "I had no idea the old guy even knew I had a job there. I mean, I've seen him like twice since that summer I worked for Jaxon at the ranch." According to Aislinn, Jaxon Winter, the nephew of Durand's deceased wife, had been responsible for the actual running of the ranch for years. Jaxon also just happened to be the married man Aislinn had fallen so hard for once.

"What did Durand want?"

"He said, 'Hello, Aislinn. This is Martin Durand. Jaxon's divorce is final, in case somehow you didn't know.'"

"Jaxon Winter got divorced?"

"Yeah. Over a year ago."

"You already knew?"

"So?"

"Well, I just thought—"

"Keel. I told you. There was nothing between us. It was all in my mind—now, is it okay with you if I tell you the rest?"

"You don't have to get mad at me."

Aislinn huffed out a breath. "You're right. I'm sorry. I'm just freaked about that call and overreacting is all."

Keely reached across the table of their booth to clasp Aislinn's arm in reassurance. "It's okay. What else did he say?"

"He laughed. Like Jaxon's marriage not working out is funny, somehow. And he said, 'It's been final for a year, Aislinn Bravo. Just in case you might not have heard.' He put this weird emphasis on *Bravo*. 'Aislinn *Bravo*,' he says, like I'm living under an assumed name or something. I mean, that's creepy, right?"

"So Martin Durand knew that you had a thing for Jaxon Winter?"

Ais flinched. "I guess so, but I don't have a clue how he knew. Keely. I swear to you. I mean, it was five years ago. Jax was *married*. Nothing happened."

"Of course it didn't."

"I worked for him for eight weeks one summer. That's it. Once the job was over, Jax never called me. And I never called him. Yeah, I really, um, liked him. I got the feeling maybe he liked me, too, but I think I just wanted to think that, because of how I felt. When I heard he got divorced, it just seemed better to leave it alone— and what business is it of Martin Durand's anyway?"

"It's not his business, not in the least." Keely wiped her greasy fingers on her napkin.

"I hardly knew that old man, never exchanged more than a few words with him. But he always used to look at me funny—kind of like he was keeping an eye on me, you know, waiting for me to sneak in the house and steal the silverware or something? And I swear, he let poor Jax do all the work. Old Mr. Durand would get up at noon and sit on the front porch of the main house in his bathrobe. One of the other hands told me that Jax is his heir because Durand and his wife never had kids of their own and the ranch belonged to Mrs. Durand in the first place and Jax was *her* nephew, so at least Jax gets something eventually."

"I'm happy to hear that. And you know, maybe the old guy was just trying to help out."

"Help out how?" Aislinn demanded, scowling.

"Whoa." Keely patted the air between them. "Back it up. I mean, maybe he was kind of playing cupid a little."

"When he called today, you mean? Ew."

"Hey. I'm just trying to look on the bright side here."

"There is no bright side. That old man is scary." Ais set down her tea glass harder than she needed to. "And I do not feel *helped* by him, let me tell you."

Keely said gently, "You're acting like a guilty person, and you know there is nothing at all for you to feel guilty about."

Aislinn had hold of her straw now. She poked the ice chunks in her glass. "I do feel guilty."

They'd been speaking quietly, but now Keely lowered her voice even more. "I know you didn't do anything, Ais. Stop beating yourself up."

"He was *married*. My heart just didn't care. I felt…

I don't know, like he was meant to be mine. And so I really, really *wanted* to do something."

"But you didn't. That's what counts. And is that—your guilt, I mean—why you've never followed up with him now that he's free?"

"Excuse me, but he's never followed up with me either. And there's no reason that he would. There really was nothing between us. It was all in my mind."

"You do get that you're trying way too hard to convince yourself of that?"

"Look. Like I said, it's just better this way."

"But, Ais, you're not acting like it's better."

Aislinn opened her mouth as if to speak—and then drank more tea instead.

Keely dared to suggest, "Just call him."

"I'll think about it—and can we change the subject? Please?"

They talked about Keely's next show at the gallery, which opened in mid-June. They discussed how Aislinn was really getting tired of Deever and Gray, news that was no surprise to Keely. It always went that way with Aislinn and a new job. She loved it at first, when it was all new and she had lots to learn. Once she'd mastered the work, though, she got bored and started wanting a change.

Aislinn said how happy she was that Keely and Daniel were together and when would that stop being a secret?

"Soon, I hope," said Keely.

"He's holding off, right? He wants you all to himself."

It was pretty much what Daniel had said. "How did you know that?"

"He's my brother and you're my best friend. You think I can't see that you're wild for each other? You're the best thing that's ever happened to him, and he doesn't want anyone else butting in."

Keely didn't know how to feel. There was the unlikely pregnancy she couldn't stop obsessing over. And all the family members Daniel didn't want to tell. But still, Aislinn's joy in what Keely had with Daniel was a definite spirit lifter. "We're that obvious? No one else seems to have figured out what we're up to."

"It's only obvious to me. I mean, I did finally get you to admit he's the one. So when I see you together, I already know what's going on. And it looks to me like what's going on is very, very good."

Keely thought of Lillie, of how much Lillie and Daniel had loved each other once. And now Lillie was gone forever…

Suddenly Keely's spirits weren't so lifted anymore.

"What?" demanded Aislinn. "And on second thought, you don't have to say it. I get it. Lillie, right?"

"How did you know that?"

Aislinn shrugged, as if to say "How could I not?" "He did love her. A lot. But they were so young to have so much piled on their shoulders. They were sort of married by necessity. It's not the same as you and Daniel. You're older now, both of you. You've each been married already, and you can choose each other with your eyes wide-open."

"Are you saying you think Lillie was the wrong choice for him?"

"No. Absolutely not. I'm saying that what you have with him takes nothing away from what he once had with her. It's two different things. You have to see that,

Keel. Accept it. Let yourself be happy with the man that you love."

Keely felt her face go hot. She pressed her hands to her cheeks in a failed attempt to cool them. "I never said the word *love*. You know I didn't."

"Doesn't matter what you said or didn't say. You *are* in love with my brother, and he's in love with you. I think that's terrific, so I do not get why you're all tied in knots about it."

Again, Keely couldn't help longing to tell Aislinn about the might-be baby. But no. Not yet. "You just... never know how things will work out, that's all."

Aislinn scoffed at her. "Is that supposed to be news? Stop worrying about what could just possibly, *maybe* go wrong and enjoy everything that is clearly going so right."

"I'll do that."

"Ha!"

Keely pointed her last french fry at her friend. "As for you, Ms. Bravo. Pick up the phone and give Jaxon Winter a call."

Aislinn glanced away. "I'll think about it."

Keely knew she wouldn't, and that made her sad all over again.

Back at Daniel's an hour later, Keely left the three pregnancy tests in the car until after her mother had gone.

Then she dithered for a while about where to put them. She ended up sticking them in the empty suitcase under the bed in the room where she never slept, ready in case she needed them.

Which, of course, she would not.

Her period did not show up that day, or the next.

On the day after that, Saturday, Grace arrived home for the summer. She put her things away in her room, helped with the twins and pitched in to fix dinner.

When they all sat down to eat, Grace said, "I'm leaving at seven. Carrie's picking both Erin and me up. I can't wait to see them."

Keely caught Daniel's eye and gave him a minuscule shake of her head before he could even think about objecting. He did take the hint about Grace going out—but he just had to ask, "Any luck on the job front yet?"

Grace pushed a string bean around on her plate. "I'm working on it."

"I can put you to work at the front desk, answering the phones—and we can use a clerk in Payables and Receivables."

Grace left the string bean alone and went to work poking at a bite of oven-browned potato. "Thanks, Daniel. I have something I'm working on, though, a job I think would really be fun and interesting."

"What job is that?"

"I'm going to need a few days to see if it pans out, okay?"

"Some reason you don't want to tell me about it?"

"Daniel." Grace set down her fork. "I want to work it out for myself. And *then* I'll tell you about it."

"Summer doesn't last forever," he warned in a ridiculously dire tone. He was close enough that Keely could have given him a good, sharp kick under the table. But she'd interfered enough. He and Grace needed to figure out ways to get along without Keely constantly stepping in to referee.

"Just give me till Monday." Grace ate the bite of potato she'd been torturing.

"Till Monday. And then what?"

"If I can't make it happen by Monday, Valentine Logging, here I come."

Daniel made a point not to say anything critical to Grace through the rest of the meal.

He knew Keely had it right, that he was being overbearing and too protective, and he needed to give his baby sister her freedom as an adult. He had to let her make her own choices. Still, it got him all itchy and pissed off that he couldn't just make the right decisions for her.

The end of her school year had kind of crept up on him. He wasn't ready for it, for Grace to be home all the time. And not only because he worried she would end up wasting her summer sitting around the house and hanging out with her friends.

There was also what he had with Keely. With Grace living in the house, they either needed to tell her that they were together or sneak around.

Sneaking around wasn't something he approved of. It showed a certain lack of integrity. Sneaking around had seemed excusable back at Easter, when he and Keely had just found each other and Grace was only home for three days.

But now?

No. Now, sneaking around was cheap. Unacceptable.

He and Keely hadn't said the words yet. But he meant to say them, and soon. She was *his* in the deepest way. He wanted what they had to continue. Forever, if possible.

And to get forever with her, he was going to have to get honest, not only with Grace, but with the rest of the family, too. Keely was more than ready for that. She'd pushed him repeatedly to come out with the family—though she seemed to have given up on that lately.

He didn't know if he liked that, her giving up. Yeah, he'd felt pressured when she kept after him about it. But her pushing meant she saw them as a couple, as two people with a future together. Her giving up could mean any number of things, some of them not good.

No, he didn't want the family in their business. But the family *was* their business.

So there wasn't a choice in the matter, not really. Telling the family had to be done.

He waited until Grace left and they'd put the kids to bed.

Then he took Keely to his room, shut the door and backed her up against it for a long, sweet kiss. When they came up for air, he caught her hand and led her to the bed. "Okay, I've been thinking." He pulled her down beside him.

She gave him the side-eye. "This sounds ominous."

He might as well just come out with it. "We need to tell the family about us."

"Finally." She laughed. He loved her laugh. It was an open laugh, musical and free. However, he wasn't all that sure he cared for it right at that particular moment.

He turned her hand over, smoothed her fingers open, then curled them shut again. "You do still want to tell them then?"

"You thought I didn't?"

"Well, you stopped pushing for it."

"Daniel." She turned her body toward him so she

was fully facing him. "Pushing wasn't exactly getting me anywhere."

"Hey." He wrapped his arm around her, pulled her close and pressed his lips to the smooth, cool skin of her forehead. "I'm an ass."

She glanced up at him, that mouth he never tired of kissing curling in a hint of a smile. "On occasion, you are most definitely an ass." Before he could act insulted that she'd agreed with him, she went on, "But you're still the best man I know—and you're mine." She whispered that last part, and his heart beat a faster, triumphant rhythm.

"Yeah. As you are mine." It felt so good to say it. He wanted to say more. *I love you, Keely.* The words sounded damn fine in his head. But was it too soon for that?

He lost his chance to go big when she added, "So yeah. We need to get honest with them. It's Gretchen and Grace I'm most concerned about."

"I agree. Aislinn already knows. Your mother made her position on the subject very clear that first Sunday she came to dinner. My brothers and Harper and Hailey have their own lives."

"Exactly." She rested her head on his shoulder. "I think they'll all just be happy for us. And really, Grace should be fine, too, as long as we're up-front with her."

He stroked her hair, rubbed his hand down her arm. Touching her soothed him. Plus, he was reluctant to put it right out there about his mother-in-law. It had to be said, though. "So, it's Gretchen we're talking about really. She's the one who might not be happy to learn we're together."

She nodded against his shoulder. "It's hard to say

how she's going to react. Yeah, Lillie's gone forever and you're single now. But you and me together…"

"There are just too many ways Gretchen could see that as a disloyalty to Lillie's memory," he finished for her. "Too many ways it could stir up all the loss and the grief for her all over again."

Daniel hadn't forgotten how bad it had been for Gretchen when they lost Lillie. His mother-in-law had tried to put on a brave face, but for almost a year, she'd rarely smiled. And she didn't bake a single cookie for thirteen months. That had freaked him out the most. For Gretchen, baking was an act of joy and love. He'd never felt so relieved as the day she showed up at the house to watch the twins with a smile on her face and a big plastic container full of butter pecan sandies.

"We have to tell her, Daniel. We should tell her first of all, privately, just Auntie G and you and me. Then Grace. And then the rest of them, which shouldn't be a big deal. I'll tell my mom, and however you want to tell your other brothers and sisters, that's fine with me."

"Agreed." Still, he dreaded it. He would miss having her all to himself. He knew he was being an idiot. She'd just called him *hers*. No way she was going anywhere. But he felt anxious and jumpy nonetheless. "So, as for telling Gretchen. When?"

"As soon as possible."

"Tomorrow then?"

"No. Tomorrow she'll have all kinds of church stuff going on. Monday night is bingo night at the senior center and Tuesday she plays bridge. How 'bout this? I'll call her, ask her to watch the kids Wednesday, in the afternoon. Then I'll suggest that she can just stay for dinner. We'll tell her then."

"But what about Grace? Chances are, she'll be here for dinner on Wednesday, too."

"We'll work it out, wing it, you know? Get Grace to take the kids upstairs after we eat and tell Gretchen then, maybe. Then once Auntie G knows, we can just tell Grace that night."

He swore under his breath. "Isn't this getting way too complicated?"

"Maybe. But I really think we need to tell Auntie G first. No matter how she reacts, she'll at least know we came to her specifically, that we love and respect her as Lillie's mom and your mother-in-law and the woman who has always treated me as a daughter."

"Okay. Wednesday. We'll try for that."

"In the meantime, we have to be careful. I really don't want Grace to find out by accident, to see me sneaking out of your room or to knock on the door when I'm in here in bed with you. It could upset her, not only because we didn't trust her enough to tell her what's going on, but also because of the problems between the two of you. You're the classic overprotective big brother, and yet you're fooling around with the nanny behind everyone's back."

Okay, that was kind of insulting—to both of them. "I'm not fooling around with the nanny, I'm fooling around with *you*."

She dimpled. How could she be so damned adorable while simultaneously pissing him off? "I think you just made my point for me."

He was getting a headache. "Keely. You can't control everything."

"Says the man who won't let his grown-up baby sister go out on Saturday night."

"I did let her go. I'm working on that. And why would Grace come wandering up here at night out of the blue? We're taking care of the twins, the two of us. She doesn't have the baby monitor in her room anymore. There's no reason for her to come upstairs."

Keely leveled those green eyes on him and chided, "She lives here, Daniel. There's no reason for her *not* to be upstairs whenever she feels like it. I just think it's better if we don't sneak around, period."

Okay, he truly did not like where this was going. "You mean, we're not sleeping together until after we tell Gretchen and Grace that we *are* together?"

Now her eyes widened, kind of pleading with him. But her soft mouth was set. "I really think it's the best thing to do, the *right* thing to do."

He didn't. He thought it was crap. "I get that you won't spend the night with me until all this is settled. But for a few hours after the kids are in bed, we could at least—"

She cut him off with a shake of her shining red-blond head. "It's only until Wednesday. It's not like we'll die from four nights apart."

"Four nights?" He scowled at her. "You mean tonight, too? Come on. Grace won't be home till late. We have hours yet."

She pressed her cool, smooth hand to the side of his face. "I just want to do this the best way, the *right* way…"

"I don't like it." The nights with her were everything. He didn't want to lose a single one. Fate was a real bitch sometimes. You never knew what might happen. A man needed to grab what he wanted and hold on good and tight.

"Oh, Daniel." She kissed him then, a lingering kiss that only served to remind him of all the reasons he needed her here with him—tonight, and every night.

"Don't go."

Gently, she pushed him away. "I think we're doing the right thing."

"But—"

She stopped him with a finger to his lips. "Good night, Daniel." And then she was up and out the door before he could convince her how much he needed her to stay.

Silently, Keely shut the door to the master suite and tiptoed along the upstairs hall to her own room.

Four nights without his big arms around her. She could do that. She'd already done it while he was traveling at the end of last month. *Only* four nights. And then she wouldn't have to leave Daniel in the middle of the night again—not that she *had* to leave him, she reminded herself. She was choosing to leave him in order that Grace would have less chance of finding out they were together until they were ready for her to know.

And really. Did Daniel have it right? Was she making this whole thing way too complicated?

Uh-uh. No. This was the right way to handle it. For everyone—especially Gretchen, who'd already suffered way more than enough. Telling Gretchen first was the right thing to do. And until they told Gretchen, nobody else should know, not even by accident.

In her room, Keely took a long bath to relax. It didn't help much. She ended up lying there alone in the dark, trying not to think about what waited for her in the suitcase under the bed.

The last couple of days, her breasts had felt swollen and sensitive. Her stomach continued to be just a little bit queasy.

The signs were there and her placebo week was over without a period to show for it. But really, she just wasn't ready to know for sure.

And no way was she ready to tell Daniel. She would get through telling Auntie G that she and Daniel were together. After that, she would need to stop being a big fat chicken and pull that suitcase out from under the bed.

# Chapter 9

In the morning, Keely came downstairs to find Daniel at the breakfast table and the kids in their high chairs.

"Sleep well?" he asked, and she felt the knot of tension in her belly unwind. He didn't seem mad or even annoyed at the way she'd left him last night.

"Grace?" she asked, with a glance toward the short hall that led to his sister's room.

"Still sleeping is my guess."

Keely couldn't resist. She needed the contact. She stepped close and bent down to him. They shared a quick kiss. "Missed you," she whispered.

The tender look he gave her made everything right.

She poured herself a scant cup of coffee. For the past week, she'd been allowing herself one small cup a day just on the off chance that she might actually be pregnant. Setting her coffee on the table, she grabbed her phone and autodialed her aunt.

Gretchen answered on the first ring. "Sweetheart. I'm just on my way out the door to catch the early service."

"I won't keep you, but I was hoping maybe you could come over Wednesday around two and watch the kids for a couple of hours."

"Happy to."

"You're a lifesaver. And how about staying for dinner, as long as you're here?"

"I would love it."

They chatted for a couple of minutes more and then said goodbye.

"We're set," Keely said to Daniel as she hung up the phone.

"Good." He caught her hand and pressed his wonderful lips to the back of it as Jake let out a string of nonsense words and Frannie shoved a fistful of Cheerios into her mouth.

Keely bent close to give him one more quick kiss. She'd barely brushed her lips against his when Grace emerged from her bedroom in sleep shorts and a giant Reed College T-shirt.

Her heart lurching into overdrive and her stomach performing a scary pitch and roll, Keely pulled out the nearest empty chair and dropped into it.

Had they just been busted?

Grace went straight to the coffeepot and poured herself a cup. When she turned, she sipped her coffee and announced, "Brace yourselves. It's happened." Her slight grin turned to a full-on smile. "I've found my summer job."

Keely's heart slowed to a more sedate rhythm, and she breathed a careful sigh. Grace hadn't seen a thing.

"Good news," said Daniel, and he even put on one

of his low-key Daniel-style smiles. "Where are you working?"

"At the Sea Breeze." She beamed at Keely. "I had an interview with your mom set for tomorrow, but she was out at Beach Street Brews last night, sitting in with the band they had playing. We started talking between sets, and she said of course I had a job with her if I wanted it. I start tomorrow. Nine to five, Monday through Friday until she opens for business."

"Terrific." Keely got up again and gave her a congratulatory hug.

Grace laughed. "I think it's going be fun. Your mom's the best."

Daniel asked, "What *is* the job, exactly?"

Grace picked up her coffee again. "A little bit of everything. Light construction, helping plan and set up for the grand opening, and playing general all-around gofer for now. Then I'll be a waitress when the place opens in July."

Daniel had that stern look he got when he was about to tell someone something they probably didn't want to hear. Grace's smile fell. But at the last possible second, he must have remembered that he was supposed to be letting her run her own life. All he said was "Sounds good."

Grace's face lit up again. "I think so. Ingrid's paying me twelve an hour to start." She tipped her chin higher, as though still anticipating some sort of criticism. When Daniel only nodded, she went on, "I'll make more when we open. I'll work nights then. Tips should be good."

"Gwace!" Jake made a bid for his favorite aunt's attention. "Hey there!"

"Hey there, Jakey." She went to him and kissed him on his puckered little mouth. "How's my favorite boy?"

"I goo." He offered her a Cheerio.

She took it and popped it in her mouth. "Delicious. Thank you."

Jake jabbered out something that was probably meant to be "You're welcome."

Keely watched the interaction with a giant grin on her face. She wanted to jump up and kiss Daniel for working so hard to let his sister go. Right now, though, she needed to keep a serious lid on the PDAs. She settled for sending him a quick secret glance of love and approval, feeling a little glow inside herself that Grace had a job she wanted for the summer and Daniel had let her go about finding it in her own way.

Daniel felt good about things with Grace—at least he did for the rest of the day.

But their hard-won peace didn't last. After dinner, Keely took the kids upstairs, and he and Grace cleaned up after the meal. Once that was done, his sister vanished into her room. He went to his study off the front hall to check email on his desktop before heading upstairs to help with the baths and the bedtime stories.

He'd left the study door open or he wouldn't have caught Grace on her way out the front door.

Okay, he should have just let her go. Keely would want him to let Grace have her freedom, and Keely was probably right.

But he was out of his chair and calling, "Grace!" before he could remind himself that he had to let his little sister make her own mistakes.

"What now?" She let go of the door handle and turned on him. In a skimpy metallic top, tight jeans and red high-heeled sandals, she had to be headed for another party night. "Erin's waiting out in front for me."

He felt he had to say something. "Doesn't your job start tomorrow?"

Grace flipped her hair back over her shoulder and braced her hands on her hips. "Rhetorical question much? Yes, Daniel. My job starts tomorrow."

"Well, it seems to me that it would be smarter for you to stay home tonight and get a good night's sleep, that's all." He put a lot of effort into sounding more helpful than critical.

Too bad Grace did not seem the least grateful for his wise advice. "I told you. Erin's waiting."

"Don't you want to be rested for your first day of work?"

"God. Listen to yourself. You're like some old mother hen."

"Grace. Come on. I'm just trying to—"

"Stop." She showed him the hand. "I'm going. Please don't worry. I won't stay out late, and I'll be on time for work tomorrow."

"I think this is unwise."

"I know you do. I'm going. Good night, Daniel." She pulled open the door and went through it before he could muster another objection.

Once she was gone, he stood rooted to the spot, listening to the sound of voices out in front, of a car door opening and shutting, and then the engine revving as Erin drove away. He scrubbed his hands down his face, rubbed the tension knots at the back of his neck and returned to his study long enough to shut down his desktop and turn off the light.

Upstairs, Keely had the kids in the tub.

He leaned in the doorway and watched her with them as they splashed her and giggled and played with their tub toys. She was something amazing, all right. With her bright smiles and her easy ways, juggling the kids, her gallery, her mom, her aunt and those quilt things she made. And somehow finding time to fill his nights with magic, too. With her, it was all worth it again, to get up in the morning and go to work every day. To come home to the demands of a whole new family. He could do that, even enjoy that.

As long as she was there, too.

And they were young yet, really, he and Keely. The kids were almost two. Another sixteen years or so and they would head off to college. He and Keely would have the whole house to themselves. They could go where they wanted when they wanted without having to consider who would watch the kids. It was a long time off, but it wasn't forever.

And in the meantime, well, he didn't mind things just as they were—or as they would be, come Wednesday night.

Until then, he'd be miserable sleeping without her. It was his own damn fault, though, and he owned that. He'd been the one who put off telling the family about them.

But as of last night, when she left him to sleep alone, he damn well couldn't wait to break the big news to Gretchen. However that went off, at least once it was over, nobody and nothing could keep him and Keely apart.

"Da-Da!" cried Frannie, holding up a red rubber monkey. She gave it a squeeze and it squeaked at him.

He entered the room, skirted Maisey, who was

stretched out on the floor a few feet from the tub, and knelt beside Keely.

She leaned his way and butted him with her shoulder. "Did I hear you and Grace downstairs just now?"

"Yeah," he confessed.

"Are you trying to avoid admitting that once again, you failed to keep your mouth shut?"

"We got into it. She went out with Erin anyway."

"Da-Da!" Now Jake had the monkey. He squeaked it several times in succession. Daniel stuck out a hand and tickled his round little belly. Crowing in delight, Jake splashed wildly, flinging water at Daniel, getting Keely wet, too.

Keely laughed. "Look at it this way. You made your point with her, right?"

"I spoke my mind, yeah."

"Perfect. You made your point, and she did what she wanted to do. It's a win all the way around."

Screw keeping his hands off her. Nobody here but the four of them anyway—five, counting Maisey. He yanked her close and kissed her while the twins screeched, "Kiss! Da-Da! Keewee!" and splashed water everywhere.

Later, after they'd tucked the kids in, Daniel managed to steal a few more kisses.

But when he tried to coax her into his room, she balked and shook her head. "Tonight and two more nights. Then I am yours—but right now, I'm going to get a little work done in my studio."

Reluctantly, he left her to it.

He went to bed alone and couldn't sleep, missing Keely beside him, hoping Grace was exercising good judgment while staying out way too late.

At 2:46 a.m., he heard her come in. Relieved in spite of his aggravation with her, he turned over and shut his eyes.

In the morning, Grace joined them in the kitchen at a little before eight. She had dark circles under her eyes and a scowl on her pretty face.

He knew that he needed to keep his damn mouth shut. The words got out anyway. "Looking kind of ragged there, sunshine."

She pointed a finger at him. "Just don't start. I'm not in the mood."

Keely said unnecessarily, "Coffee's ready."

With one last dirty look in his direction, Grace headed for the coffeepot.

He had to know. "You still going to work?"

Grace took her time filling her cup. She turned to him slowly, enjoying a long sip before grumbling at him, "Of course I'm going to work. I'm looking forward to this job and I take my responsibilities seriously."

When he left for the office, Grace was still taking her sweet time getting ready in the downstairs bathroom. With his sister occupied behind a shut door, Keely allowed him a quick kiss as he was leaving.

He said, "Call me if she decides to stay home."

For that, she gave his shoulder a playful slap. "Not on your life."

"Nobody does what I tell them to around here."

Keely only smiled sweetly and pushed him out the door.

Keely felt relief when Grace emerged from the bathroom dressed in old jeans, a chambray shirt and a worn pair of black Converse, her hair pinned up out of the way. "Your mom said to wear comfortable clothes, that there might be painting to do today. You think this is all right?"

"As long as you don't mind getting paint on anything, it's perfect."

Grace leaned close. "Has the ogre left the building?"

"Your brother is gone for the day, yes."

"He's such a—"

"Uh-uh." Keely put up a hand. "Don't go there." She pressed her hand to Grace's smooth cheek. "Have a great first day of work." Grace had the strangest look on her face. "What? You okay?"

She seemed to shake herself. "Yeah, sure. I'll take overtime if Ingrid offers it, so don't count on me for dinner."

"No problem. There will be plenty of leftovers to heat up if you have to work late."

"You're the best." Grace gave her a quick hug and headed for the inside door to the garage.

She'd been gone about half a minute when Frannie, on the floor with Jake a few feet away, let out a wail.

Jake had grabbed a stuffed giraffe from her. Keely moderated the dispute, reminding Jake to share and offering him his favorite ratty rabbit in exchange for Frannie's toy. A few minutes later, they were playing as happily as ever together.

Daniel called at ten. Keely reported that, yes, Grace had gone to work on time, and then she said goodbye quickly, annoyed with him for promising to back off his sister and then calling Keely to check up on her.

At eleven, she fed the twins. At one, she put them in their cribs for a nap.

And then, before she could invent more pathetic excuses not to face the truth, she marched into her bedroom and pulled the suitcase out from under the bed.

She took two of the three tests. They both told her what she already knew.

As for when to tell Daniel, she was finished stalling. Tonight, as soon as the kids were in bed, she would break the news that they were having a baby.

She was dropping the second test wand into her bathroom wastebasket when the doorbell rang downstairs.

Quickly, in hopes that whoever it was wouldn't have time to ring again and increase the likelihood of waking the twins, she rushed out into the upper hall and ran down the stairs. Through the etched glass on the top of the door, she could see who it was.

Gretchen. Keely recognized her by the set of her plump shoulders and the halo of carefully arranged blond hair around her head.

But she couldn't see her aunt's expression until she pulled the door wide-open. "Keely. Hello." She looked... irritated, maybe? Her eyebrows were pinched together, her mouth all pursed up.

"Gretchen? Are you all ri—"

Her aunt cut her off. "May I come in?"

"Of course." Keely stepped back. "Come on to the kitchen." She gestured toward the arch that led to the back of the house.

"The babies?"

"Napping at the moment—and it's warm out. How about something cold to drink?"

"No, it's fine. Daniel's at work?"

"Yes."

"It's just us?"

"That's right."

"Good. We need to talk." Gretchen turned and headed for the kitchen. Keely just stood there and stared after her, wondering what in the world was going on. Her aunt paused just past the arch to the living room and aimed an impatient glance over her shoulder. "Well? Are you coming?"

"Sure." Keely hurried to catch up. In the kitchen, she gestured at the table. "Have a seat. I can make some—"

"No. Nothing. Really." Gretchen went and stood by the island. Not sure what to do next, Keely followed her over there. Her aunt stared at her for a long, very uncomfortable string of seconds before announcing, "I just feel I have to say something. It's about Grace."

"Grace?" Keely's stomach lurched. "Is she all right?"

Gretchen wrung her hands, blinked and looked down at them. Shaking her head, she smoothed the ruffles on the front of her shirt and tugged on the side seams of her A-line skirt. "She's making things up. That's what she's doing. Hurtful lies."

Dread crept over Keely, like a cold fog on a dark night. "What lies?"

"Well, I just dropped in at the Sea Breeze to see how things were going. And there was Grace, painting the wood trim on the door to the restroom hallway. She said Ingrid had run out for more paint but would be back soon. I decided to wait and we started chatting, Grace and I. And then, out of nowhere, she asks me if I know about you and Daniel."

Keely blinked. There was a sudden buzzing sound in her ears. She put her hand on her stomach and prayed that everything in there wasn't on the verge of coming up. "What about me and Daniel?"

As if she didn't know.

Dear, sweet Lord, this was the exact wrong way for Gretchen to find out that she and Daniel were a couple. It was supposed to be done on Wednesday, done kindly, with love and respect.

*We never should have kept the secret in the first place*, said an accusatory voice in the back of her head.

But they had. And now came the part where they got to live with their bad choices.

"Grace said she saw you and Daniel kissing, right here in this kitchen, yesterday morning." Her aunt touched her then. She reached out and gently squeezed her shoulder. All Keely could do was stare. "Sweetheart. Don't look so crushed."

"I'm not, I—"

"Because of course, I don't believe a word of it. I just really felt that you should know that Grace is, well, she's spreading tales about you. It's a problem, a big one. She has all these…issues with Daniel, though the good Lord knows why. He's been a saint, we all know that. With Grace, with *all* of his brothers and sisters. He and my Lillie, what they did to keep that family together…"

"Auntie G—"

"No. Wait. I haven't finished. I ask you, where would Grace be if not for Lillie and Daniel? She could have ended up in foster care. Anything might have happened. I just don't understand what has got into her, to speak so disrespectfully about Daniel. About *you*. It's an outrage and—"

"Auntie G." Keely took her arm. "Come on. Please. Sit down." Gretchen allowed Keely to lead her to the table, pull out a chair for her and ease her down into it. "Now, how about some ice water?"

"I—yes. All right. Ice water. Good."

By rote, Keely went through the motions of getting down a glass, adding crushed ice from the dispenser, filling it the rest of the way with water, all the while knowing the moment for exactly what it was.

The moment of truth. All her careful plans to break the news to Gretchen just so, after a nice dinner, in a gentle, reasonable way?

Right out the kitchen window.

It was happening now, like it or not. With Auntie G already upset and saying cruel things about poor Grace. It was happening without Daniel here, with no time to prepare.

"Here you go," she said to her aunt.

"Thank you, honey." Gretchen took the glass and had a long drink. "It's only... I suppose I'm overreacting. But that girl has no right to speak of you and Daniel that way."

Keely pulled out the next chair over and lowered herself into it. Where to start?

The answer was painfully simple.

*Start with the truth.* Nothing would make the news go down easy for Gretchen. And looking at her aunt's red face, Keely doubted that it would have gone much better on Wednesday night.

Better to just say it straight-out. "Auntie G, I'm sorry if this upsets you. But Grace wasn't lying. She did see me kissing Daniel yesterday morning."

Gretchen set down her glass. "What are you...?" She forced out a tight little laugh. "Oh. I understand. An innocent, friendly kiss that Grace has blown all out of proportion then?"

Keely's heart seemed to bounce off the walls of her chest. It was beating so hard. "No. Grace saw what she said she saw. I kissed Daniel. It was a real kiss."

"A real...?" Gretchen scoffed. "Sweetheart, you can't be serious."

"Yes. Yes, I am. Daniel and I have...feelings for each other. We're in a relationship, Auntie G."

Gretchen's flushed face went white. "No."

"Yes. We should have told you sooner. I'm so sorry that you had to find out in this way."

"Sorry." Gretchen spit the word.

"Yes. We...we didn't know how things would work out at first, so we kept our feelings to ourselves. But then, well, we do want to be together. So we were going to tell you Wednesday."

"Sorry," Gretchen repeated, as if she hadn't heard a word of what Keely had just said. "You're *sorry.*" She slapped the table hard enough that her glass bounced. "How could you, Keely? After everything, after all the years, all that I've done for you. All *Lillie* did. We *loved* you. Like a daughter. Like a sister. We took you in, gave you a real home, provided the stability my sister never gave you, the settled family life you always longed for."

Keely's heart no longer felt like it would burst out of her chest with its frantic beating. Now it felt heavy as lead, aching. And out of that ache, she felt fury rising, adrenaline spurting. Hurtful words to match Gretchen's rose to her lips. It took all the will she had to swallow those words down, to try to speak reasonably. "Auntie G—"

"No."

"Please don't—"

"I don't want to hear your ridiculous, unacceptable excuses. I will not accept your apology. You are supposed to be *helping* here, not taking advantage of poor Daniel's loneliness, sneaking around behind everyone's backs. I tried, you know I did, to talk you into letting me take over again. I tried weeks ago, at Easter. But no. You were too *happy* here. You just wouldn't go. And now I know why, don't I? Now I know what you have been up to. It's unacceptable, Keely. Unforgiveable and so cruel."

Keely's carefully banked fury tried to spike again. "You really should hear yourself. You're telling me you *plotted* to keep Daniel and me apart."

Gretchen blinked several times in rapid succession. "Plotted? There was no plotting. How could I plot? I had no idea what you were up to. I was only trying to take the pressure off you—and you wouldn't let me because you were having a secret affair with my son-in-law." Gretchen's eyes had glazed over with tears. "How dare you?" she demanded. "How *could* you?"

Keely said nothing. She let the last of her own defensive fury sputter and die. Now she felt only sadness as she waited to be sure her aunt had finally run out of steam.

"Well?" Gretchen swiped away tears, hitched up her chin and glared.

Keely asked, just to be certain, "Are you finished?"

"I… What? What in the world can you possibly have to say for yourself?"

"Well, first of all, you're wrong."

"Wrong? No. No, I have it right and you know that I do."

"No, you do not. I'm sorry this hurts you, but most of what you just said? All wrong. You say 'secret affair' as though Daniel and I are cheating on Lillie somehow. You haven't accepted yet that Daniel is a single man now. You need to do that. You need to accept in your heart that Lillie is truly gone from this world. We loved her. We lost her. And our lives have to move on."

"Excuses," insisted Gretchen, looking down at the

table, shaking her head. "These are flimsy, cowardly excuses you are giving me."

"No. That's not true. Daniel loved Lillie very much and would never have betrayed her. Neither would I. You know me, Auntie G. And you know very well I never would have done such a thing. But Lillie really is dead, and Daniel and I are both single adults with every right to find a little comfort in each other."

"Comfort," Gretchen uttered the word as though it disgusted her. "That's not what I would call it." She shoved back her chair, her face starting to crumple all over again. "And I… I cannot stay here one minute longer. I can't… I just… I really do have to go." And with that, she was turning, striding out of the kitchen toward the front of the house.

Keely just sat there, staring at Gretchen's half-finished glass of water until she heard the sound of the front door closing hard.

That did it.

Her stomach went beyond merely roiling. It completely rebelled.

Leaping up, she ran for the downstairs half bath, making it just in time to drop to her knees and throw back the toilet seat before everything came up.

# Chapter 10

Once the vomiting had finally stopped, Keely wandered upstairs to brush her teeth and check on the twins. Maisey, who'd been napping in Keely's studio room, wanted to go outside. Keely took her down and let her out into the backyard. Then she went upstairs again and stretched out on her bed. Maybe a nap would help.

But within five minutes, she knew she would only lie there and stew over the absolutely rotten things Gretchen had said. She got up again, went back downstairs and let Maisey in. The dog stretched out on the kitchen floor as Keely put some crackers on a plate and poured herself a ginger ale.

As she was resolutely chewing a saltine, Grace came running in from the garage all spattered in paint, with red-rimmed eyes. "Keely! Are you…okay?"

Maisey looked up with a worried whine. Keely only shrugged and finished her saltine.

Grace darted over and stood at the table, clutching the back of a chair. "She was here, wasn't she—Gretchen?"

"Yeah." Keely took a careful sip of her ginger ale. "She was here."

"Oh, God." Grace burst into tears.

Keely couldn't bear to see her so miserable. "Hey. Come on…" She got up, went around the table and gathered Grace close.

"Oh, Keely…" Grace hugged her hard—for a moment. And then she pulled away. Her nose was red and tears streamed down her face. "Gretchen said she was coming straight over here. I should have stopped her. I should've kept my damn mouth shut."

"Hold on." Keely went to the island, grabbed the tissue box she kept there and brought it back to Grace, who blew her nose and swiped at her eyes. "I'm so sorry. Oh, Keely. I hate myself. I…" She let out a moan. "I should have talked to you or Daniel—well, not Daniel. Every time I talk to Daniel, I just want to scream. But I *can* talk to you. And I *didn't* talk to you…"

"So you did see me kiss him yesterday morning?"

Grace yanked out the chair, collapsed into it and whipped another tissue from the box. "I did. And I pretended I didn't because… Well, I don't really know why. And before that, I kind of figured there might be something going on between you two. It was nothing specific. Just, you know, the way you look at each other. And then there's Daniel. Other than treating me like I'm still in diapers, he's been…different lately. Happier. I know that's because of you. And now, look what I've done. I've ruined *everything*." That brought on a fresh spurt of tears. Keely, still right there beside her, clasped her shoulder and waited for the tears to play themselves out. Finally, Grace grabbed yet more tissues and dabbed at her eyes. "You should probably hate me—yeah. No doubt about it. I deserve your disgust."

Keely moved squarely behind her so she could put both hands on Grace, one on either shoulder. "No way."

Grace let her head drop back. They shared a long look. Then Keely gave Grace's shoulders one more good squeeze and returned to her chair. She ate another cracker and sipped her ginger ale.

Grace drew herself up and said, "I knew what I was doing when I told Gretchen. I was *trying* to cause trouble. I knew it, and I did it anyway. I went straight to the one person who was likely to have issues with Daniel moving on. What is the *matter* with me?"

"Nothing is the matter with you. You're frustrated with your brother, so you did something mean. Now you're doing what you can to make amends."

Grace sniffed. "I told your mom everything."

"Good."

"She sent me here to explain what I did, to tell you I'm so sorry—which I am—and to make sure you're okay."

"I am. I'm okay." Keely almost believed it as she said it. "And yes, it would have been much better if you'd come to me or Daniel about it when you saw us kissing. But, Grace, it's really not the end of the world. You're not the only one who could have behaved better. Gretchen is no saint in this. And Daniel and I shouldn't have kept our relationship a secret from the family. It was one of those things, you know? You start out keeping a secret and then the longer you keep it, the harder it gets to tell the truth."

"But it was awful with Gretchen, wasn't it?" Grace burst out. "Just admit it!"

Keely hated to see Grace so miserable. But she didn't want to lie either. "It was pretty bad."

"I knew it!" Grace wailed. "I'm a complete bitch, and everything's all my fault."

"Gracie, come on," Keely soothed. "Quit beating yourself up. It's all going to work out." Would it? Really? Keely had no idea. But Grace was hurting and Keely couldn't bear to add to her suffering.

Maybe another hug was in order. Keely got up again. With a cry, Grace rose, too. They met midway between their two chairs and wrapped their arms around each other.

Grace grabbed on tight and whispered, "I love you, Keely."

"And I love you."

"Daniel doesn't deserve you." Grace sniffed.

Keely pulled back enough to cradle Gracie's pretty face and smooth her pale hair away from her eyes. "Don't say mean things about your brother."

"Not even if they're true?"

Keely laughed. And then Grace laughed, too, right through her tears.

"Keewee?" called a small, sweet voice from the baby monitor Keely had left on the sideboard by the door to the dining room. That was Frannie.

Jake joined in. "Up, Keewee! Up!"

Keely let go of Grace as the twins babbled to each other over the monitor in the special language only they understood. "Nap time is over, I'm afraid."

Grace nodded. "I need to get back to work anyway."

"Do me a favor?"

"Anything."

"Come home from work right at five?"

"Absolutely."

"If you would watch the kids so that Daniel and I can talk about what to do next...?"

"Of course—he's going to kill me, isn't he?" Grace face-palmed with a drawn-out groan.

"No, he is not." Once Keely told him about the baby, getting mad at Grace would be the last thing on his mind.

A half hour later, Ingrid called. By then, Keely had got the kids up, changed their diapers and turned them loose with their toys in the upstairs playroom.

"Just checking on you," said her mother.

"I'm okay."

Ingrid gave a snort of laughter. "Oh, please. I do know what's going on. And I also know you're about as far from okay as a girl can get."

"Yeah. Well." Keely reached down to Maisey, who lay at her side. She gave the dog a quick rub on the top of her head, followed by a couple of long strokes down her back. At a time like this, having Maisey to pet really did help. "It's been one of those days." Jake wandered over with his ratty rabbit. He held it out. Keely bent and kissed it. The smile he gave her melted her heart to a puddle of mush. She stared after him as he toddled away again.

"I'm so sorry that Gretch has made a damn fool of herself," Ingrid said. "The woman has a dark side. I suppose I should have warned you, but I kind of hoped you'd never have to see it. You always adored her, and now she's let you down. Do you need me to slap her silly?"

"No, Mom. But I appreciate the offer."

"How 'bout some motherly support? I can be there in ten minutes. I'll make you peanut butter and jelly on white bread with the crust cut off."

Keely smiled at that. When she was little and living on the purple tour bus, crust-free PB&J was her go-to comfort food. "Sit tight. Have the peanut butter ready. I'll keep you posted after I talk to Daniel."

"What? You think he's going to get all up in your case about it for some reason? Well, he'd better not or he will be dealing with me."

"Back it down, Super Suzie." "Super Suzie" was a Pomegranate Dream song about a reluctant superheroine named Suzie, who took on all the small-minded bullies in her hometown.

"I'm here," said her mother. "You just need to know that."

Keely shut her eyes and swallowed the sudden lump in her throat. "Love you, Mom."

"Call me."

"You know I will."

Grace got home as promised, at ten past five. Keely had dinner all ready.

She spoke to Grace about how things would go. "If possible, I would like to put off talking about what happened today until after dinner. If you would take the kids upstairs as soon as we're through eating, I'll talk to Daniel privately in his office."

"Works for me. Then if he wants to yell at me, you take over with the kids and he and I can go a few rounds somewhere they can't hear us fighting."

Keely chided, "Don't go planning for trouble."

"I don't need to plan. Trouble between me and Daniel happens naturally, no matter what we do."

Daniel came in at five thirty. Keely had worried that Gretchen would track him down and confront him, too—that she might have called Valentine Logging or shown up at the office unannounced. But if she had, Daniel gave no sign of it. Which was great. Perfect. Keely didn't want to get into it with him until Grace took the kids upstairs.

Grace put the twins in their high chairs while Daniel filled the water glasses and Keely brought the food to the table.

Neither Keely nor Grace felt much like conversation, but the twins kept up a steady chatter, partly in English, partly in twinspeak. Their bright voices filled up what might have been uncomfortable silence.

Daniel asked Grace how she liked working for Ingrid.

Grace put on a bright voice and talked about the job itself. "Already I love working there. Lots of variety. I painted woodwork, ran errands and helped Ingrid rearrange her office in back. We experimented with a couple of possible signature cocktails, and she taught me the POS system she's going to be using."

"I'm glad it's working out." Daniel sounded sincere.

"Yeah," said Grace, both awkward and strangely hopeful at once. "Me, too."

The meal ground on, with Frannie waxing poetic over her love of peas. "Peas! Yummy, yum, yummy, in my tummy!" And Jake chortled maniacally at intervals, beating his spoon on his chair tray, sending food flying.

When it was finally over, Grace wiped up the kids and swept them off upstairs. Daniel cleared the table as Keely loaded the dishwasher.

She'd just set the cycle and pushed the dishwasher door shut, when Daniel said, "Okay. What's going on?"

Her heart kind of stuttered in her chest and then became a warm little ache, that he *had* noticed something was off. That she loved him so and she really had no idea how he would take all that had gone down that day—with Grace, with Gretchen and with two of the tests from under the bed.

"Keely." He moved in closer, smelling of cedar and soap and everything good. Tipping up her chin, he brushed the sweetest, softest kiss across her mouth. "Tell me."

"Let's go into your study?"

He ran a slow finger down her cheek to her chin, stirring up sweet sensations, causing the ache in her heart to deepen. "Sure." His finger trailed along the side of her throat, out to her shoulder and down her arm. He took her hand.

In his study, she eased free of his grip and shut the door.

He went to the sofa against the inside wall, folded his powerful frame down onto the cushions and patted the space beside him. "Come on. Whatever it is, tell me everything."

She approached with caution, hardly knowing where to begin. He reached up a hand to her. She took it but stiffened her knees to stay on her feet when he tried to pull her down next to him.

"Damn, Keely. What?" He searched her face.

She opened her mouth, and the words kind of tumbled out all over each other. "Gretchen, Grace and my mom all know about us. Grace and Mom are fine with it. Gretchen is furious. She came over here today and she—"

"Hold it." He squeezed her hand—and then let go.

Keely wrapped her arms around herself and stepped back. "What?"

"How did they find out?"

She kept her shoulders square and looked down at him steadily. "Yesterday, in the kitchen at breakfast…?"

He knew then. His pale blue eyes went icy. "Grace did see us kissing."

"That's right."

He unfolded to his full height. "I knew it. Grace." He started for the door.

"Daniel," she said forcefully. At least he stopped walking and turned back to her. Good. She wasn't about to let him go after Grace. Not until he'd heard all she had to say. "I'm not finished yet."

A muscle twitched in his jaw. "I'll be back. I want to hear it from Grace, though, okay?"

She clutched her arms tighter around her middle. "No, Daniel. It's not okay. I want you to hear me out, please. Then you and Grace can talk."

"But—"

"No *buts*. I have things to say, and I intend to say them. Grace isn't going anywhere. She'll be here when I'm finished."

A stare down ensued. She didn't feel much relief when he gave in. "Fine, then. Go ahead."

Now it was a face-off between them. She stood by the couch, clutching her middle for dear life. He loomed a few feet from the door. Not the way she'd wanted to begin this difficult discussion.

But no way was she backing out now. "The way it happened, Gretchen stopped by Mom's bar. Mom was out. Grace and Gretchen started talking. Grace told Gretchen that she'd seen us kissing. Gretchen didn't believe her and came running over here to tell me how awful and unappreciative Grace is of all you've done for her. I set Gretchen straight, after which she accused me of betraying Lillie's memory and seducing you in your loneliness and a whole lot of other crappy things that I think I've already blocked from my memory. Then she stormed out."

"I'm sorry," he said. And then he went to his desk, crossed behind it, pulled out his big leather chair and dropped into it. "What a mess."

She stared at his bent head and went on, "Grace came home next. She'd already confessed to my mom what she did. Mom had sent her to me. Grace knows she did wrong, and she feels terrible about it. Your jumping all over her on top of her own disappointment in herself isn't going to help the situation in the least."

His head came up. He cracked his powerful neck, raked his thick hair off his forehead, the beautiful muscles of his arm flexing and bulging as he moved. "Nobody's talked to Gretchen since then?"

"Why should we? I may never talk to her again."

"Keely." His voice was velvety soft, coaxing. He pushed to his feet, but this time he came around the desk to her and reached for her. With a grateful sigh, she let herself sway against him. "You don't mean that." He kissed the words into her hair.

She rested her head on his giant rock of a shoulder. "Right at this moment? Oh, yes, I do."

"Well. We'll work it out." He clasped her arms. When she looked up at him, he bent for a kiss, a slow one. Not deep, but so comforting—and then he ruined it by setting her away from him and announcing, "In the meantime, I'm going to go talk to Grace."

Like hell he was. "I'm still not finished yet."

A frown formed between his thick eyebrows. Apparently he'd noticed she wasn't all that happy with him and his bullheaded insistence on making this disaster all about Grace. "You're kidding." At least he tried to lighten up a little. He made a real effort to speak teasingly. "There's more?"

*Oh, is there ever.* "Listen. I get that you're worried about Auntie G. I am, too. Even though I want to wring her neck right now, I know she's suffering, that she's still not over losing Lillie. I mean, really, who is? Lillie's death isn't something any of us who loved her are ever going to get over. But we do need to learn to go on, to make the most of a world without her in it. So Gretchen's reaction didn't really surprise me. And I do hope she'll get past this. But she *was* in the wrong, Daniel. This is more about her than it is about Grace."

He backed up enough to hitch a leg up on the corner of his desk. "I don't think so. Grace was purposely stirring up trouble and that's what I want to talk to her about."

"She *knows* that. You don't have to tell her. Why don't you try surprising her for once and being a little bit understanding?"

That muscle in his jaw was back, twitching away. He asked in a flat voice, "What else did you want to tell me?"

Her body kind of went crazy on her—throat-clutching, breath-catching, stomach-churning crazy. She worried she would have a choking fit or maybe throw up on him. "I, um…"

"Just say it." He reached for her hand again.

She flinched. She knew if he touched her, she would lose it completely.

"Keely, what in the—"

"I'm pregnant." The words burst from her mouth like a volcanic eruption.

His eyes seemed to tilt back in his head. "What? I don't—"

"It's for sure. I've been feeling strange and bloated and kind of crampy for a while now. My period should have come last week. It didn't. And in the past several days, I've been having... I don't know. All the signs? Breast sensitivity, feeling sick to my stomach. I finally took a test this morning."

"A test," he echoed, as though the word made no sense to him.

She nodded frantically, her head bouncing up and down like a bobblehead doll's. "Two tests, actually. They were both positive. So it's real. It's happening. I'm having a baby."

He'd frozen there, like a statue, one leg on the desk, one arm bent on his thigh. "But we always used condoms except the past few times. You're on the pill."

"It was probably that first time we were together or one of the times right after that. Before I started on the pill or before it started working. Back when we were using just condoms. One of them must have been faulty. Torn, maybe. Or broken." He was still in statue mode, staring straight ahead at her. But also right through her. She threw up both hands. "Daniel. Could you just not look at me like that? We've always used birth control, and I don't know how it happened. I did not plan this, and if you're thinking that I did because of what happened with..." She caught herself. This wasn't about Lillie, and she refused to bring her lost cousin into this. She tried again. "If you're thinking I tricked you somehow, well, I don't know what to say. I would never do that. But I *am* pregnant. It did happen. We're having a baby."

He kept looking right through her.

Something was going wrong with her heart. It seemed to be breaking. A roaring sound filled her ears. Maybe she was drowning.

Drowning in heartbreak.

What kind of silly idiot was she anyway? There was no way to explain herself, no way to get through to him. Not about this. Not when the last thing he'd ever wanted was another child.

"Daniel. I'm sorry, I am. I did not mean for this to happen. But I do want this baby. And I am keeping it. That doesn't mean I expect anything from you. I am fully self-supporting and completely capable of raising a child on my own. And I will, if that's how you want it. You can, you know, think it over. There's plenty of time for you to decide how involved you want to be. My mother raised me on her own, and it worked out just fine." Her throat locked up again, and she swallowed convulsively. "Ahem. So…okay, then. You think about it. Take your time. You don't have to decide anything today."

Daniel watched Keely's mouth move. She looked too pale. The freckles stood out on her adorable nose and twin spots of bright red stained her cheeks.

She thought he was blaming her.

He wasn't, not one bit. He was only struck speechless.

It was way too damn much to take in.

*Straighten up, you idiot. Pull yourself together*, yelled a frantic voice in the back of his mind. He needed to snap out of it, say the comforting, supportive words she had every right to hear from him.

But…

*Another baby.*

More years to add on before he got his empty nest, before he finally knew what it felt like to be free. How many more years? Three, maybe? Four?

"Daniel," she whispered on a bare husk of breath. "You are breaking my heart. I really am sorry, but this is just bad. All wrong, you know? You take the time you need. I'm…well, I'm just as stunned by this thing as you are. I need some time to think, too. I'm guessing Jeanine will fill in where you need her until you can find somebody permanent. If she can't, you'll just have to work it out, because, really, I've gotta go."

"Go?" He blinked, shook his head, brought himself back into the moment. "What are you saying to me?"

"Daniel. I'm saying I'm going to pack a few things and go."

"No."

She stood up straighter. "Yeah."

"You're leaving?"

"Yes, I am."

"Just like that? You can't leave." He got up from the desk. "We have to work this out, damn it. We have to decide what to do next." He reached for her.

But she only jerked back another step. "No, we do not. We don't have to decide a thing right now. For me, this has been one never-ending train wreck of a day, and I'm in no condition to decide anything. Right now, I need a break. I need to get away."

"Get away?" he echoed numbly.

"Yeah." Now her chin hitched up. She'd set her mouth in defiance.

"Get away where?"

"I haven't decided yet. I'll...call you. Let you know."

Could this actually be real? "This isn't happening."

"Yes, Daniel. It is. I don't like it. I'm not happy." She darted around him and went to the door. "But right now, I just need to go."

What could he say to make her reconsider? "If you walk out that door, I'm not going to follow you."

"Terrific. Please don't." She pulled the door open, went through and shut it behind her.

Keely called her mother as she paced back and forth, grabbing stuff she thought she might need and tossing it into her suitcase.

Ingrid skipped the hellos and went straight to "Are you okay?"

"I need a break, Mom."

"And I'm just the one to make sure you get it."

"Meet me at my house?"

"I'm on my way."

Keely ended the call, stuck the phone in a pocket and finished packing. She zipped the suitcase, grabbed her big shoulder bag and headed for the door. From down the hall, she could hear Grace in the bathroom with Frannie and Jake. Grace said something, and Jake laughed.

Frannie giggled. "Mine!" she announced.

Keely's heart just seized up at those sounds.

Maybe they weren't her babies, but her silly heart had somehow claimed them. She left her purse and suitcase in her room and went down the hall and through the open bathroom door.

Jakey called, "Keewee!" and splashed with both hands.

Grace turned from the tub. She knew instantly that something had gone very wrong. "Bad?" was all she asked.

Keely nodded. "I'm taking off for a while. Sorry to leave you on the hook, but I can't stay here right now."

"It's okay." Grace levered back on her heels and came for her, grabbing her, pulling her close.

Keely hugged her back, hard. "If he makes you too crazy, come stay at my house. And if I'm not there, I'll text you where I put the key."

"Oh, Keely. What do you mean, if you're not there? Where are you going?"

"Hell if I know."

"Keewee!" called Frannie.

Grace released her and she went to them. She knelt to kiss their wet cheeks and whisper, "Bye-bye. Love you."

"Wove you!"

"Bye-bye!"

Their beautiful, wet faces almost changed her mind, made her stay.

But then she thought of Daniel, of the words he didn't say and the bleak, distant look in those cold blue eyes. She pulled herself to her feet.

With a last nod at Grace, she marched back to her room, grabbed her suitcase and her purse and dragged them down the curving staircase and out the front door.

# Chapter 11

Ingrid was already there, as promised, sitting on Keely's porch, her hair a red never seen in nature— candy apple, fire-engine red. It perfectly matched the paint on Keely's front door.

Keely pulled into the pebbled driveway, jumped out and ran to her mother's waiting arms. Grabbing on tight, she sobbed, "I love your hair," as she burst into tears.

"Come on. It's all right." Ingrid held her tighter. She smelled of sandalwood and a hint of weed. The silver bangles on her wrists jingled against each other as her hands moved, soothing and stroking, over Keely's shoulders and down her arms. "Let's go inside." She didn't wait for Keely's answer, just turned her gently and guided her to the red door.

In the kitchen, Keely sat at the table as her mother made tea. Outside, dark was falling, fog creeping in.

When she sat very still, she could hear the sigh of the ocean, down the hill and across the rolling dunes from her back porch. She'd always loved that sound, like the great Pacific shared a secret just with her. It was the main reason she'd chosen the cottage, snared on a short sale for a ridiculously low price. Ingrid put the steaming cup in front of her, and Keely sipped it slowly.

Her mother took the chair across from her. "Tell me."

And Keely did, starting with the pregnancy tests she'd taken that afternoon, moving on to all the bad stuff Auntie G had said and ending with the awfulness that had happened in Daniel's study. When she was finished, her mom poured them more tea.

Keely stared into the steaming cup. "I don't believe how Daniel reacted. When I told him about Auntie G, he blamed Grace. And then, when I said there would be a baby, he looked at me like I'd hauled off and punched him in the face."

"He's a good man. He'll recover. You'll work things out."

Would they? She just wasn't sure. She wrapped her arms around her middle and the new life growing there. "I left most of my stuff up there at the house, my Berninas included. I dread going back for everything."

"Stop. Your sewing machines will be there when you need them. Don't get ahead of yourself."

"Oh, Mom. I still don't really believe it, you know? A baby…"

"It's fabulous," declared Ingrid. "You're going to be an amazing mom. And babies bring good luck. You're living proof of that. Best thing I ever did, having you."

Keely answered her mom's broad smile with a wobbly one of her own. But then she thought, *Daniel*, and that brought the misery crowding in on her again.

Ingrid said, "Have you told him you're in love with him?"

How did her mother know these things? "It seemed too early, you know? Too soon."

"Forget that. You're having a baby. You two will get nowhere until you face how much you mean to each other."

"Until today, I kind of thought we *had* faced it. No, we hadn't said the words. But I *believed* in us, that we were really together, you know? That we had what I've been looking for all my life. Now, though, I'm not so sure."

"Give it till tomorrow. You'll feel better. You'll be ready to talk to him again."

Keely let her head drop back and groaned at the ceiling. "Mom. I don't want to think about tomorrow, about what will happen next. And right now, I'd just as soon never talk to Daniel again."

"You don't mean that."

"I just want to get away, okay? I want to take off, like we used to when I was little, get on the road in the Pomegranate Dream bus. I want to drive up to Seattle, see Dweezle." Dweezle Nitweiler had been the band's first bass player—or maybe the second? Keely wasn't absolutely sure. "And then we could maybe head on to Boise, see what Wiley Ray and Sammy are up to." Wiley Ray was a drummer. His wife, Sammy, had sung backup and played the marimba. Last Keely had heard, Wiley Ray and Sammy had five kids. She sent Ingrid a sharp glance. "Don't you dare say I'm running away."

"Wouldn't dream of it."

"So…?"

"You want to go, baby girl? We are outta here."

Her spirits didn't lift exactly. But the awful pressure in her chest seemed to ease just a little. "You mean it? Really?"

"I'll call Grace, put her in charge at the bar while we're gone."

"That's a lot to ask of her. She just started today."

"I'm my own boss. If nothing gets done until we get back, I'll reschedule the opening. Not a big deal, but you'll need to get in touch with Amanda about the gallery."

"And Aislinn. I'll call her, too. She'll help out wherever she can." Keely leaned across the table and held her mother's gaze. "I mean it, Mom. I don't want to dither around about this. We're leaving tomorrow."

"You got it." Ingrid pulled her phone from her pocket. "We'd better start making calls."

Twenty minutes later, Amanda had said she could handle the gallery no problem. Aislinn, Keely learned, had just quit Deever and Gray. She would be picking up the slack wherever Amanda needed her.

Grace had instantly agreed to take over at the bar. She said that, yes, she could meet Ingrid there in half an hour to get emergency instructions on being the boss.

When Keely took the phone to see how she was holding up, Grace reported that the kids were in bed and Daniel had been surprisingly civil. "I'd just put the kids in their cribs, about half an hour ago. He came upstairs as I was going down, just said good-night and went on up to his room."

The ache in Keely's chest intensified as she pictured him, alone in the room that had become both of theirs.

To reclaim her resolve, she closed her eyes, sucked in a slow breath and focused on the goal, which was to get out of town. "Mom has a key to my house. She'll give it to you, just in case you need a place to get away."

"Thanks, Keely. Be safe."

They said goodbye. Keely handed her mom back her phone, and Ingrid left to meet Grace and stop in at Gretchen's to pack a bag for the trip.

"Don't even talk to her," Keely advised with a sneer as Ingrid was leaving. "She'll only say rotten things you don't need to hear."

Her mom just chuckled. "Sweetie, don't worry. I've been dealing with your aunt a lot longer than you have."

It was after ten, and Keely had just finished repacking her suitcase for their open-ended tour of the Great Northwest and beyond, when Ingrid returned.

Keely ran out to the living room when she heard the front door open. "How'd it go?"

Ingrid rolled her Frida Kahlo Skull Art spinner suitcase in the door and then shut it behind her. "Grace is up to speed. As for Gretchen, I told her everything."

Keely felt slightly breathless suddenly. "What do you mean, everything?"

"That you and Daniel had words and you need a getaway, so we're going on the road, you and me, up to Seattle, probably over to Boise and after that, wherever the wanderlust takes us. She was outraged, she said, that I could even think about taking you on the road at a difficult time like this."

"That sounds just like her."

"My sister is remarkably consistent in her opinion of a nice road trip. So I said that a time like this is exactly the right time to go on the road, after which I asked her what was *wrong* with her to begrudge you and Daniel a chance at happiness?"

"What did she say to that?"

"I didn't give her time to say anything to that. I just told her where she could stuff her self-righteous attitude, after which I broke the big news that you and Daniel are having a baby."

"Omigod, Mother." Strangely, Keely felt nothing but relief that Gretchen knew about the baby. "What did she say?"

"Not a word. I have to admit I found her silence supremely satisfying."

Keely sank to the couch. "All of a sudden, I'm hoping she's okay. I mean, I wanted to strangle her this afternoon, but I do love her and I don't want her to be suffering or worrying about us."

Ingrid came and sat beside her. "It's all going to work out."

"You keep saying that."

She hooked an arm around Keely and pulled her close. "I'm your mother. That's what mothers say."

Keely surrendered to her mom's embrace. She let her head rest on Ingrid's shoulder. "I'm so tired, Mom."

Ingrid stroked a hand down her hair. "We don't *have* to go anywhere, you know."

A weakness stole through her, to give in to her own misery, to go to her room and cry for a while. And then maybe tomorrow, to head up Rhinehart Hill to try to work things out with Daniel...

But then her belly knotted, and she ground her teeth at just the thought.

No way.

She wasn't working anything out with him if he

couldn't accept the baby. She hadn't meant to get pregnant, but now that she was, well, she *wanted* her baby. If he didn't, that was his loss. She couldn't be with a man who refused to love and welcome his own child. "I need this trip and I am going. Don't you dare back out on me now."

"Baby doll, I'm in if you're in."

"Good."

Rising, Ingrid took Keely's hand and pulled her to her feet. "Come on then. Let's get some sleep. I want to get an early start in the morning."

Daniel went to bed at a little before eleven, an exercise in futility if ever there was one. He spent the night staring into the darkness, afraid he'd lost Keely forever.

No, he argued with himself. That could never happen. The words had not been said, but they lived inside him.

He loved her.

And he knew she loved him—or at least, she had until she'd witnessed his reaction when she told him about the baby. Was it actually possible that he'd killed her love stone-dead?

He didn't know what to do, how to make it up to her. Somehow, he had to figure out what to say to her, how to tell her, how to prove to her that she was everything while also convincing her that he was happy about the baby...

*The baby.*

Every time he thought about the baby, he went numb. He needed to cope with that, with the reality of that. If he didn't, he had a sneaking suspicion he would only blow it all over again when he tried to make it up with her.

\* \* \*

The kids woke up at six thirty as usual. The monitor by the bed came to life as they called to him. "Da-Da, Da-Da!"

"Keewee!"

"Up! Now."

As Daniel dragged himself out of bed and reached for his jeans, Jake's said, "Gwace! Up."

And Grace answered, "Hey, sweet monkeys. Good morning to you." She must have taken a monitor to her room last night so she could go to them if they needed her—and so she could give him a break this morning.

Daniel sank to the side of the bed, his chest gone tight, his jeans still in his hands.

Grace. Keely had it right about her. Grace was a good kid. She helped a lot. And she deserved to be treated as an adult.

He'd been way too hard on her. That had to change. He pulled on his pants along with yesterday's wrinkled shirt and headed for the playroom.

"Grace," he said, when he stood in the doorway to the playroom.

"Morning." She handed him Jake and picked up Frannie. "Let's get some breakfast."

"B'eafus. Yum!" Jake decalred and stuck his fingers in Daniel's mouth.

Daniel pretended to chew on them, which made Jake chortle in glee.

Downstairs, Grace poured kibble and fresh water for Maisey and got the kids their fruit and dry cereal. Daniel scrambled eggs and fixed toast for all four of them.

When they sat down to eat, Grace revealed that

Keely and Ingrid had gone on a road trip. "I'm temporarily promoted to manager of everything that needs doing at the bar, which unfortunately means there's no way I can watch the kids today."

*Where did they go and when will they be back?* he longed to demand. Instead, he said, "Congratulations on the promotion. As for the kids, you've been a lifesaver, always helping out with them. Don't worry about today, I'll figure something out." Aislinn probably had to work. Harper and Hailey were still at U of O until the second week of June. He would try the nanny service. If they couldn't help him, he would take a damn day off from the office. Gretchen would most likely come running if he asked her to watch them, but over the past sleepless night he'd realized he was seriously pissed off at his mother-in-law. He wouldn't be reaching out to her until his anger had cooled a little.

Grace set down her fork with a bite of scrambled egg still on it. "Did you just say I'm a lifesaver?"

"I did. And you are. And I'm going to do my best to respect your, er, adulting skills and be a better big brother to you."

She just looked at him for several seconds, her blue eyes suspiciously moist. "Thanks," she said in a husky little whisper. At his nod, she added, "They went to Seattle first. And she does have a phone, you know. You need to just call her."

"Yeah," he said with a half shrug.

Grace shook her head at him. "You're not going to call her, are you?"

He didn't answer her. She made one of those my-brother-is-an-idiot faces and let it go at that.

* * *

Aislinn had to work at Keely's gallery that day. The nanny service had no one to send on the spur of the moment, so Daniel stayed home.

The sun came out early. He took the kids for a walk, letting them lurch along beside him until they got cranky and then tucking them both into the double stroller to push them back home. He took them up to the playroom, changed their diapers and then stretched out on the playroom floor to keep an eye on them as they played with their toys.

The twins alternated between using Maisey as a pillow and decorating Daniel with various toys, placing them on his chest and stomach, then grabbing them up and wandering away, only to return with some other toy to set on him.

Frannie bent over him and asked, "Keewee?" causing his heart to pound like it wanted to burst from his chest and go searching for the woman he didn't want to live without.

He replied, "She went on a little trip."

"Back soo'?" demanded Frannie.

He didn't know how to answer that and settled for the painful truth. "I don't know."

With a snort and a sigh, Frannie dropped to her butt beside him. She reached out and patted his shoulder with her fat little hand. He stared at her, loving her, as Jake plunked down on his other side.

"Da-Da," Jake said and lay down next to him.

They weren't close enough. He gathered Frannie in with one arm and Jake with the other. They settled, tucked right where he needed them, on either side of his heart.

For a minute, maybe two, he knew the sweetest sort of peace.

He thought of Lillie, and for the first time, the anger didn't come. He felt only gratitude and tenderness, that if she had to go, she hadn't left him alone. She'd given him these two little ones, not as an eighteen-year sentence to struggle through.

But as a gift. The greatest gift.

What was freedom, really? He'd never had much of it, and he'd believed that he hungered for it.

But freedom was nothing. Not compared to his children, not stacked up against Frannie and Jake.

And the new baby, his and Keely's baby?

What a jackass he'd been.

He wanted the new baby, too. He truly did.

That guy who wanted freedom? He, Daniel Bravo, wasn't that guy and he would never be. He was a dad and a damned good one. He wanted his woman back, so he could be a husband, too. He wanted it all with her—the two of them together openly, with the family around them, raising Jake and Frannie and the new baby, as well.

Downstairs, he heard the front door open.

*Keely?*

His heart raced with hope. Maisey perked up her floppy ears as the kids wriggled free of his hold and sat up. Footsteps mounted the stairs.

Gretchen appeared in the open doorway to the upstairs hall.

"Gwamma!" Frannie got up and went for her.

Gretchen scooped the little girl into her arms, kissed her once on her forehead, then propped her on her hip. "My sister and Keely have gone to Seattle."

"I know. Grace told me."

"What is the matter with you, Daniel? I can't believe you let Keely go." She scowled down at him.

"What are you doing here?" Toys dropping off him and clattering to the rug, he rose. "I thought you were furious with her—and with me."

"I was." Frannie squirmed, so she let her down. Both kids headed for the toy box as Gretchen continued, "And I was wrong—don't look at me like that, Daniel Bravo. I'm capable of admitting when I'm in the wrong. I love you. And I love her. She's the only daughter I have left. And she took off with Ingrid in that embarrassing purple bus, took off to Seattle to visit someone named Dweezle. I know it's your fault, Daniel. I behaved very badly, and I realize that now. But she wouldn't leave just because of me. What did you do to her? What did you say?"

Shame rolled through him. He confessed, "All the wrong things."

"I knew it." Gretchen sagged in the doorway. But then she seemed to catch herself. She drew herself up. "I've been trying to call them. Both of them. My calls go straight to voice mail."

"Maybe they don't want to talk to you."

She made one of those faces women were always making at men, as though they can't help wondering how one-half of the species could be so thoroughly aggravating and hopelessly dense. "No kidding. Have *you* tried calling them?" When he didn't answer, her expression turned smug. "Coward."

He couldn't let that remark stand—even if it did happen to be true. He grabbed his phone from where he'd left it on the kids' dresser and autodialed Keely.

And got voice mail.

As he waited through her recorded greeting, he tried to decide what the hell to say.

He had nothing. Whatever he managed to sputter out would be hopelessly inadequate.

And what good would leaving her a message do anyway? He needed to be there. He needed to see her beautiful face when he told her all the ways he'd been a thickheaded jerk and begged her to please, please forgive him.

When he ended the call without leaving a message, Gretchen rattled off Ingrid's number. He tried that, too.

"Voice mail," he admitted, as he hung up.

"We need to stop wasting time and go get them," Gretchen cried. "We have to apologize and mean it and beg them to come home."

He completely agreed with her—in theory anyway. "Go get them how, exactly?"

"I know what route they took."

"How do you know that?"

"Ingrid told me. The Coast Highway to I-5."

"Why would she tell you that?"

"Why does my crazy sister do anything?" A determined gleam lit her eyes. "You think we can catch up with them?"

*We?* "How 'bout this. If you'll stay here and look after Frannie and Jake, I'll—"

"You can stop right there," she cut in before he could finish. "I have apologies to make, too, you know. I'm going with you. And I'll thank you not to argue with me. Arguing will only waste valuable time."

They took Lillie's minivan. It had plenty of room. Gretchen sat in the first row of back seats between the kids' car seats, armed with snacks and toys to keep them happy through the drive. Maisey went, too. She claimed the front passenger seat. Daniel rolled down her window so she could let her ears flop in the wind.

"I know we're going to find them," Gretchen kept saying as the miles rolled by. Daniel didn't share her certainty. They crossed the bridge at Astoria and entered Washington State, heading north along the coast, at first with the mouth of the mighty Columbia on one side of them and then, as they aimed true north, other, smaller rivers and then Willapa Bay. Once past the bay, they headed slightly inland again, where the trees grew thick and the banks at roadside were covered in moss and sword ferns, sometimes with green meadows stretching toward the mountains to the east.

The longer they rode, the more certain he became that Gretchen was kidding herself. That damn purple bus with the giant cartoon of Ingrid playing her Telecaster emblazoned on each side was probably miles and miles ahead of them. Depending on when the two women had set out, they could have reached Seattle by now—or changed their route or got off the highway for a bathroom break just long enough for the minivan to roll right on past.

They were approaching South Bend, and he was about to tell Gretchen they needed to give it up and go home when they rounded the next curve of the highway and he saw it—the butt end of the giant metallic-purple vehicle rolling along at a majestic pace about a hundred yards ahead.

Gretchen made a low noise in her throat, a sound both self-satisfied and triumphant. "What'd I tell you? There they are."

* * *

Ingrid was up to something. Keely had no doubt about that.

So far, they'd pulled over to the side of the road a total of six times since they left home. It had not escaped Keely's notice that her mother only thought she had engine trouble when there was enough of a shoulder that to stop wouldn't be illegal or dangerous. Only then would she start complaining that the engine was knocking or maybe it was one of the tires going flat as she eased the giant vehicle to the generous space at the side of the road.

Then she would get out and check the tires and go around to the back of the bus to look in on the engine. Each time, she took forever about it. When she came back, she would shake her head and say how everything seemed okay after all. She would start the bus up again, and they would get back on the road.

After the most recent of her pointless inspections, she'd insisted that before they moved on, they might as well have some of the tea and muffins she'd brought along.

Keely didn't want tea or muffins. She sat on the bench seat next to the door, holding her phone, hoping Daniel would call.

And he did call. Once, at a little after ten, causing her pulse to race, her whole body to catch on fire and her tummy to heave alarmingly. She almost answered that call. But she let it go to voice mail. Better to just hear what he had to say before she decided whether to talk to him or not.

He hung up without bothering to leave her a message.

And they drove on. And stopped. And drove on. And stopped.

After four hours on the road, they were just now approaching South Bend, Washington. The shoulder was wide and clear on one side. Any minute, her mother would start in about the engine knocking and when she did, Keely was going to throw back her head and scream.

Behind them on the road, someone honked. People did that all the time. The bus was big and purple, after all. And there was also the famous R Crumb cartoon of her mother playing guitar and smoking suggestively plastered on both sides. Keely craned her head to check the road behind them in the giant side mirror just as whoever it was honked again.

"A white minivan," she murmured to herself. Her heart started racing again. "That's Lillie's van! Mom, it must be Daniel."

"About freaking time," muttered her mother, as she smoothly turned the big wheel and eased the bus to side of the road.

"You planned this, didn't you?" Keely accused.

The hydraulic brakes hissed as they stopped. "Let's just say I planted the seeds. I told your aunt what route we were taking. Gretch did the rest—and she took her own sweet time about it, too."

"I'll go first," proclaimed Gretchen as Daniel pulled in and stopped behind the bus. "You stay here with the babies. Once I've made my apologies, it will be your turn. I'll bring Ingrid back here, and we'll watch the babies while you and Keely have some time alone in the bus."

He wanted to argue with her. Unfortunately, her plan made a scary kind of sense.

"Wish me luck," she said briskly and eased out between the two car seats with surprising flexibility. She slid the door shut and walked quickly to the door on the right front side of the bus. Her gait was even and steady, without a trace of a limp left over from the injury that had broken four bones in her right foot and given him the chance to get to know Keely. To learn to love everything about her, to find what he hadn't realized he needed most: the right woman to stand beside him, the truest kind of freedom, the kind he found in her arms.

He had both front windows down and heard the bus door open. Gretchen disappeared inside.

Keely watched in the side mirror as her aunt got out of the minivan.

From behind the wheel, her mother was watching, too. "Gretchen's coming this way."

"I know. I can see her."

"She looks determined."

"Oh, yes, she does."

"Shall I let her in?"

"Yes." Keely rose and went through to the galley area. She couldn't make herself sit down for this, so she just stood by the table. "I'll talk to her in here."

The door opened with a wheezing sound. Keely heard her aunt's footsteps on the stairs.

"I would like to speak with Keely," Gretchen said stiffly.

"Through there," her mother replied.

And then Gretchen came and hovered in the doorway, her head high and her plump shoulders back. "I'm sorry," she said. It came out in a whisper as her shoulders drooped and her blue eyes filled with tears. "I had it all wrong. I said terrible things, and I have no excuse for them. I really thought I had made my peace with losing Lillie, but now I see I still have a ways to go on that. But I didn't want to let you leave without saying that I love you so much, sweetheart. And I am sorry for the rotten things I said to you. They were born of my own pain, untrue and completely unfair to you, to Grace and to Daniel, too. You and Daniel have every right to find happiness with each other. I hope that you do. I hope you can get past all the trouble I've caused and somehow find your way back to each other. I...well, I..." A tear escaped and trickled down her cheek. She sniffed, swiped the tear away and held her head high again. "I guess that's all. I'm sorry. I love you. Someday, I hope, you'll find a way to forgive me."

Keely's heart ached so bad. But it felt a little lighter, too. And there was only one thing to do now. "Of course I forgive you. I love you, Auntie G." She held out her arms.

With a soft cry, Gretchen came to her and grabbed her close.

In the back seat, as Daniel waited, the twins babbled to each other, amazingly content even after more than two hours in the car. Maisey, beside him, gave a little whine. He got out, went around to her side, let her out to do her business and then gave her a boost back in.

He'd just settled in behind the wheel again when Gretchen emerged from the bus. Ingrid, her hair a blinding cherry red, stepped out right behind her. They marched toward him.

Ingrid went to the driver's door, Gretchen to the passenger side. The sisters leaned in the windows.

Ingrid said, "You're up. Make it good."

His heart went wild inside his chest. But somehow he spoke calmly. "I'll give it my best shot." He turned to his mother-in-law. She'd clearly been crying. Her eyes and nose were red. "Did she accept your apology?"

Gretchen gave him a brave little smile. "She did. And I'm grateful."

"I'm glad for that," he said.

She nodded. "I do love that girl."

The next move was his. He got out. Ingrid took the seat behind the wheel. Gretchen put Maisey in the back and then came and sat next to her sister.

"This may take a while," he warned.

"Not a problem," replied Ingrid.

"We've got water and snacks and toys for the babies," said Gretchen. "Take as long as you need to show her how much you love her. We'll be waiting right here."

Ingrid had left the bus door open.

His heart in his throat and his pulse roaring in his ears, Daniel mounted the steps and went inside.

"Keely?"

"In here."

He found her sitting in the galley, on the long seat across from the table, wearing a little white T-shirt, faded bib overalls and white Keds. She rose as he went to her.

Tired. She looked tired, those green eyes sad, her bright hair gathered in a messy bun on the top of her head. His arms ached to hold her. He kept them tight at his sides.

"I did everything wrong," he said.

"No." Her lush mouth curved in the saddest little

smile. "You did so much right. Almost everything. But, Daniel, I can't be with you."

"Because of the baby?" When she bit her lip and nodded, he clarified, "You think I don't want our baby."

For that, he got another nod, a tiny one, the barest dip of her pretty chin, as her face flushed deep red and her eyes shone with tears. It gutted him to see those tears, to know he was the cause of them.

"Keely. Don't you cry." His hands lifted of their own accord—but he lowered them when she fell back a step. He went on with his confession, "I found out today that I'm not who I thought I was." She frowned, like he'd spouted some nonsensical riddle. He said, "I've been bitter. I've believed that my freedom had been stolen from me."

"You *believed*?" She seemed to ponder the word. "Are you saying it isn't true?"

"That's right. I had it all wrong, what I want. What I need. And what you saw when you told me we were having a baby—that was the man I *thought* I was coming up against who I really am. In my bitterness, I'd convinced myself that what I wanted, what I *needed*, was freedom. I couldn't wait for Frannie and Jake to be grown, to get my so-called freedom at last. It took your leaving me to make me see that I'm not that guy. I'm a family man and I will always be. Everything I really need, I already have. Or I did, until yesterday, when I chased you away."

She searched his face. "Are you telling me, then, that you're okay with the baby?"

"More than okay. I've been stupid and blind. But the truth is I *want* our baby. I love you, Keely. I want us to be a family—all of us—you, me, Frannie, Jake, the little one that's coming—and more babies, if that happens, if you want them. I want to marry you. With you, I have everything. The family I need and the right person to talk to, the one I want beside me when things are good *and* when times get tough, the one who makes me free in all the ways that matter."

She stared up at him—hopeful and yet cautious, too. Proud and beautiful and true. "Daniel, I do love you, so very much."

*She loves me.* His heart beat at the wall of his chest, urging him closer. "Keely…" Again, he would have reached for her.

But she put her hand up between them. "You really mean this? I need to know. I need the brutal truth from you. If your heart isn't open, if you still have doubts about taking on another child, I need you to tell me."

He captured her raised hand, brought it to his chest and pressed it close, at the spot where his heart beat so hard for her. "No doubts. No regrets, not a one. Not anymore. I hate that you left, Keely. But I understand why. You were right to leave. It put the fear of God in me, let me tell you. It showed me the hard truth, that I've been a complete ass in a whole bunch of ways. It showed me that I could actually lose you.

"I couldn't stand that," he said. "I want you and I want our baby. I want us all to be together. I love you, and I want to spend the rest of my life with you." He lifted her hand higher, bringing it to his lips so he could kiss the tips of her fingers, one by one. "Just think about it, okay? Go ahead with your mom, up to Seattle and wherever else you need to go. Just, while you're away from me, know that I will be waiting, hoping that when you come back, you'll be coming home to me, that someday you'll say yes and be my wife."

She lifted her other hand and pressed it to his cheek. So cool and soft, that hand, soothing him, easing the painful pounding of his heart, a balm to the ache of longing in his soul. "Daniel." She said his name in a breath as she lifted her sweet mouth to him.

A kiss, so slow and tender, growing wet and deep. It ended far too soon.

She sank back to her heels again. "I love you, Daniel. And yes, I will marry you. As for the road trip, I don't need it anymore. I'm ready to go home."

Eight weeks later, on the last Saturday in July, Keely married Daniel in the backyard of their house on Rhinehart Hill. The whole family attended, all the Bravo brothers and sisters, Great-aunt Daffy and Great-uncle Percy, and Ingrid and Gretchen, of course. There were a lot of family friends as well, including several of the musicians who used to play with Pomegranate Dream—Dweezle, Sammy and Wiley Ray among them. Meg Cartwell McKenna, Keely and Aislinn's mutual BFF, came too. She and her husband, Ryan, had driven in from Colorado.

Keely wore a vintage fifties' white lace dress that came to midcalf with a short veil. She was already showing, her stomach noticeably rounded, as she walked the petal-strewed grass between the rows of white folding chairs, her eyes on the man waiting in front of an arbor covered in roses.

When Daniel smoothed back her veil and took her hands in his, Jakey shouted from the front row, "Da-Da! Keewee!" and everybody laughed.

Keely said her vows, strong and proud. Daniel's voice was rougher, lower, the words meant for her ears alone.

And when he took her in his arms for the kiss that sealed their bond, each to the other, she knew she had found the love and trust that mattered most between a man and a woman. She felt such joy and gratitude, that he would be hers and she would belong only to him.

From this day forward.

They held the reception right there in the backyard, including dinner and champagne toasts and, later, a four-tier cake. Ingrid and her former bandmates played music on the grass.

And after dark, when Keely stood on the upper deck outside the master bedroom to throw her bouquet in the glow of endless strands of party lights, she took careful aim before she flung the lush bunch of sunflowers, orange dahlias, baby's breath and daisies into the waiting crowd below.

The flowers sailed out, bright and hopeful, full of the promise of love-to-be. They landed right where she wanted them.

In Aislinn's outstretched hands.

* * * * *

*After escaping her abusive ex, Cassie Zetticci is
thankful for a job and a safe place to stay at the
Gallant Lake Resort. Nick West makes her nervous
with his restless energy, but when he starts teaching her
self-defense, Cassie begins to see a future that involves
roots and community. But can Nick let go of his own
difficult past to give Cassie the freedom she needs?*

*Read on for a sneak preview of
A Man You Can Trust,
the first book—and Harlequin Special Edition debut!—
in Jo McNally's new miniseries, Gallant Lake Stories.*

"Why are you armed with pepper spray? Did something
happen to you?"

She didn't look up.

"Yes. Something happened."

"Here?"

She shook her head, her body trembling so badly
she didn't trust her voice. The only sound was Nick's
wheezing breath. He finally cleared his throat.

"Okay. Something happened." His voice was gravelly
from the pepper spray, but it was calmer than it had been
a few minutes ago. "And you wanted to protect yourself.
That's smart. But you need to do it right. I'll teach you."

Her head snapped up. He was doing his best to look at her, even though his left eye was still closed.

"What are you talking about?"

"I'll teach you self-defense, Cassie. The kind that actually works."

"Are you talking karate or something? I thought the pepper spray…"

"It's a tool, but you need more than that. If some guy's amped up on drugs, he'll just be temporarily blinded and really ticked off." He picked up the pepper spray canister from the grass at her side. "This stuff will spray up to ten feet away. You never should have let me get so close before using it."

"I didn't know that."

"Exactly." He grimaced and swore again. "I need to get home and dunk my face in a bowl full of ice water." He stood and reached a hand down to help her up. She hesitated, then took it.

*Don't miss*
A Man You Can Trust *by Jo McNally,*
*available September 2019 wherever*
*Harlequin® Special Edition books and ebooks are sold.*

www.Harlequin.com

HSEEXP0819

"There won't be another bus going that way until the day after tomorrow."

"Are you sure?" Gemma Lapp stared at the agent behind the counter in stunned disbelief.

"Of course I'm sure. I work for the bus company."

She clasped her hands together tightly, praying the tears that pricked the backs of her eyes wouldn't start flowing. She couldn't afford a motel room for two nights.

She wheeled her suitcase over to the bench. Sitting down with a sigh, she moved her suitcase in front of her so she could prop up her swollen feet. After two solid days on a bus she was ready to lie down. Anywhere.

She bit her lower lip to stop it from quivering. She could place a call to the phone shack her parents shared with their Amish neighbors to let them know she was returning and ask her father to send a car for her, but she would have to leave a message.

Any message she left would be overheard. If she gave the real reason, even Jesse Crump would know before she reached home. She couldn't bear that, although she didn't understand why his opinion mattered so much. His stoic face wouldn't reveal his thoughts, but he was sure to gloat when he learned he'd been right about her reckless ways. He had said she was looking for trouble and that she would find it sooner or later. Well, she had found it all right.

No, she wouldn't call. What she had to say was better said face-to-face. She was cowardly enough to delay as long as possible.

She didn't know how she was going to find the courage to tell her mother and father that she was six months pregnant, and Robert Troyer, the man who'd promised to marry her, was long gone.

*Don't miss*
Shelter from the Storm *by* USA TODAY
*bestselling author Patricia Davids,*
*available September 2019 wherever*
*Love Inspired® books and ebooks are sold.*

www.LoveInspired.com